NO PRINCE

STEVIE J. COLE
LP LOVELL

Copyright © 2020 by Lovell and Cole publishing

All rights reserved.

No part of this book may be reproduced in any form or by any electronic or mechanical means, including information storage and retrieval systems, without written permission from the author, except for the use of brief quotations in a book review.

Cover Design: Lori Jackson Designs

Cover Model: Andrew England

Edits: Wallflower Edits

❀ Created with Vellum

Love is the same for a poor man and a king.
   unknown

1

ZEPP

Velma's was the only hole-in-the-wall bar in Dayton where there wasn't a cover and naked girls working poles. Christmas lights framed the windows year-round, and tonight they blinked on and off, almost in time with the twang of country music that seeped through the open windows.

Wolf parked his pickup at the back of the lot, cutting the headlights while he left the engine running. "I'll just wait for you to give me the signal," he said when Bellamy and I piled out.

The place was full of rundown beaters, cars with busted windows and rusted out roofs. But even pieces of shit could be sold for a good chunk of money.

Bellamy dropped his dad's police bag beside the wheel of a rusted Hurst Old, kneeling to rummage through for the file. "This thing's a piece of shit."

The car was a wreck, but any idiot knew these things could go for an easy fifty-grand with some new interior and a paint job—which made us selling it for four a steal. "We'll each get a grand a piece for it."

"Yeah." Bellamy worked to jimmy the lock, while I watched the entrance of the bar. The seconds ticked by without the pop of the lock. "Dammit," Bellamy huffed. "It won't catch. It's jammed or something."

I tugged at the door while he crammed the file farther under the rubber seal. "What the..."

The bang of a screen door broke up the rhythm of banjos and guitars. I popped up, staring over the dented roof of the Hurst, then gave Bellamy a shove. "Hurry up, man."

My gaze narrowed on the silhouette slinking through the parked cars. Something about the sway of her hips seemed familiar. The curvy redhead stepped underneath the fluorescent glow of Velma's sign, and I groaned. Monroe James went to my school. She lived two trailers down from my best friend, and the last thing we needed was a possible witness who knew our names when the guy reported his car stolen.

"Shit, man. Keep going. I've gotta go distract this chick." I moved away from the car, striding over the gravel toward Monroe.

Her pace slowed. Through the dark, I could barely make out her narrowed gaze aimed at me.

I made a blatant show of looking over her long legs. And damn, that skirt was short. "Nice skirt," I said.

"Eat shit." She stepped around me without missing a beat.

I faltered. That was not how this shit went. *Ever.* I complimented a girl—she swooned. I spun around. I wanted to call her a bitch, but she was headed straight toward Bellamy. So I swallowed my pride for a second and started after her. "You should learn to take a compliment, you know?"

"You should learn to fuck off."

My jaw clenched. She was a row over from the damned Hurst. God, I did not need to be dealing with this right now.

"You don't have to play hard to get. I've heard you're easy, Monroe."

"I've heard you have herpes. I'm busy, so again, fuck off."

I didn't have time for this. I brushed past her. She could turn us in if she wanted. We'd sell the Hurst before the cops ever showed up at my house anyway. Lack of proof was a bitch. "Bell!" I shouted across the parked cars. "Hurry the hell up."

Her steps over the gravel quickened, and she popped up right beside me. "Are you stealing that car?"

"What if I am?" I stopped a few feet in front of the Hurst.

And I knew that look, the way her gaze swept over me while she bit at her lip. Before tonight, I hadn't said a word to Monroe, but that didn't mean I hadn't noticed the girl. Curves. Big tits. Tiny waist. Red hair. She was hot in that look-at-me-and-I'll-kill-you kind of way, which made her hard *not* to notice. This wasn't the first time I had thought about sinking my dick into her.

"Well, that might change things." Her finger trailed down my chest. "I do like a bad boy." Most girls did. It was their kryptonite.

"Yeah?" I grabbed her, pinning her against the car. "You wanna be tainted by the bad boy, Monroe. That it?"

"You gotta be kidding me," Bellamy grumbled. "Seriously, Zepp?"

She threaded her fingers through my belt loops and snapped my body tight to hers. I imagined grabbing her by the waist and throwing her face down onto the hood of the car, going at her until my dick was raw.

Her lips brushed my jaw. "Do you wanna fuck me, Zepp?"

"I wanna ruin you."

Bellamy groaned in the background. "Great. I'm going to the truck. Let me know when you're ready to work, dickhead."

And now I was totally going to screw her against this car. "Are you a screamer, Monroe?"

Her fingers raked the back of my neck, and she pulled me close. I waited for her to go for my fly and pull me out, but instead, she rammed her knee into my groin. I doubled over, grabbing myself while I fought for a breath, but the pain only got worse. It felt like my nuts were in my throat. My legs buckled, and my knees hit the gravel.

I heard the jingle of keys before the car door opened and slammed shut. Not even two seconds later, the engine growled to life, shaking the ground.

"What the hell, man?" Bellamy shouted, running up behind me when the reverse lights came on. The tires spun, kicking gravel everywhere before she shot off, leaving nothing but a cloud of dust in the glow of the taillights.

"Did she just take the car?" Bellamy snatched the bag from the patch of grass.

Still clutching my nuts, I staggered to my feet. "What does it look like?"

"That was four grand!" Bellamy paced behind an old Cadillac, the flash of Velma's neon sign bouncing off the back window. "Your dick just cost us four grand."

Not only had Monroe stolen a car out from under me, but she had also just taken a blowtorch to my ego.

"Shut up, Bellamy." I started toward Wolf's pickup.

Wolf's brow wrinkled when I opened the passenger door. He glanced back at Bellamy settling into the extended cab. "Am I high, or did Monroe James just steal that car?" He snorted. "I mean, tell me I smoked too much weed and I'm hallucinating."

I swiped a hard hand over my face, then slumped down in the seat. "Just drive, would you, Wolf?"

"Holy shit." He put the truck in reverse, while I stared through the dirty windshield. "She stole the car?"

"Because Zepp was trying to fuck her."

I turned in my seat to glare at Bellamy. "Like you wouldn't."

"I would," Wolf offered. "Always wondered if the whole red in the head, fire in the hole thing was true." The neon lights bounced over the dashboard before the truck sputtered onto the highway.

We made it to the four-way stop before Bellamy exhaled in the back seat. "She cost us four grand. Four grand."

Wolf shot a sadistic smile my way. "Wanna go set fire to her trailer?"

The guys gave me grief about Monroe getting one up on me the whole way back to Wolf's. By the time he pulled up to his double-wide, I was fuming. I climbed out before the other guys did, slamming the door hard enough to rock the truck. I was almost to my motorcycle before I noticed the tarp-covered car parked in Monroe's drive.

"Oh, you have to be kiddin' me." Halfway across the road, a smile spread over my face. I couldn't believe the girl was that stupid.

2

MONROE

Shit, what did I do? I had kneed Zeppelin Hunt in the balls. People said that Zepp was the king of Dayton High, but I didn't think so. No, Hunt wasn't anything so shiny. He was simply at the top of the food chain—a thug. The bad guy without morals. And in a place like Dayton, that was saying a lot. He was not a guy you kneed in the balls and stole a car from. But if it were a toss-up between him and Jerry, my mom's shithead boyfriend, I'd take my chances with Zepp.

I gripped the leather steering wheel in my hands, flooring the accelerator as I drove down the deserted county highway. The car fishtailed when I turned onto the dirt road that led to the trailer park. Like the rest of Dayton, it was a shit hole. Park homes littered the place like garbage spilled from a bag. My stomach knotted when I sped past Wolf Brooke's trailer, hoping Zepp had never noticed I lived by one of his friends. I cut the engine outside my mom's, hurrying to cover the stolen car with a tarp before I went inside.

My mom had passed out on one of the ratty floral

couches, a fresh track mark in her arm. She didn't budge when the trailer door slammed closed behind me or when a thud came from the back. Jerry stumbled out of the bathroom, the ash falling from the cigarette between his lips when he fastened his belt.

He swiped a hand over his greasy hair. "You get the car?"

I dropped the keys into his waiting palm and held my breath as I shouldered past his huge frame, hoping he'd just let me go. My mom's boyfriend could be unpredictable at the best of times. I breathed a sigh of relief when I closed the flimsy door to my bedroom and slid the lock in place.

I'd almost fallen asleep when I heard the smash of glass outside somewhere. It wasn't unusual in Dayton. People were forever fighting, breaking shit, stealing things... The sound of an engine coughing to life made me sit up, though. A horn blared right outside the trailer. Headlights poured through the threadbare curtains, bouncing over the walls of my bedroom as I headed to the door.

Jerry stood at the living room window, the curtain yanked back just as a car gunned it away. I knew—I just knew it was the Hurst. And I knew exactly who had stolen it right off my drive.

Jerry's angry glare swung to me, his fists already balled. "You get followed, Monroe?" he said through gritted teeth.

"No."

He moved closer, each step an angry stomp that set my nerves on edge. "Then, you ran your mouth."

"No, I didn't."

I could have told him what happened, but it wouldn't have changed a damn thing. It would have still been my fault. "It got stolen off the drive. That's not my—"

His hand collided with my cheek, and I hit the floor with a thud. The metallic tinge of blood coated my tongue, and my fists balled. Despite the fear that wound around my throat like a vice, adrenaline fired through my veins, and the urge to fight back kicked in.

"This is your problem, you little cunt." He jabbed a finger at me. "I suggest you fix it before I take payment in other ways."

His gaze dragged over me, forcing bile to rise in my throat. Jerry was handsy and threw a mean punch when he was pissed, but the one thing he had never done was try to fuck me. That was more than I could say for every other boyfriend my mother had brought around. I'd learned how to run and hide at an early age. Then how to fight back. That didn't mean Jerry never would, though, and it didn't make me any less scared of him. Jerry took joy in my suffering. He liked my pain, my fear. More than anything, though, I think he enjoyed the fight—the fact that I never just took it.

"I'll get you another car!" My voice broke under the strain of panic.

His eye twitched before he grabbed my throat and hauled me to my feet. He threw his head back on a laugh when my nails raked his arm. Then he slammed me to the wall, the entire trailer rattling from the force. When he smashed his nose against my cheek, I wanted to recoil, but I couldn't move. "I want *that* car!" He tossed me onto the floor like trash. "You have two days, Monroe."

I hated Jerry with a passion; I really did. He wasn't around all that much, but he made my life hard, just like every other deadbeat boyfriend my mom had dragged through here. It was the way of things in Dayton. A part of life that I hated myself for accepting, though I had no choice. No out. Some kids my age dreamed of a nice life in a big house with a flashy car. I had a single dream: to get away from Dayton. This town was a cesspool, pulling people under, drowning them in its filth. I just had to graduate with good grades. Then I was gone.

DAYTON HIGH. I could practically smell the poverty and teenage pregnancy from the parking lot. My best friend Jade crossed the lot and fell in step beside me.

"You look like shit."

"Gee, thanks." I'd barely had any sleep last night, thanks to a particular asshole.

We stepped through the double-door entrance and into the narrow hallways filled with students. Even through the regular morning chaos, I could spot Zeppelin Hunt a mile away. All six foot plus of tattoos, and arrogance, as always, surrounded by his boys: Hendrix, Wolf, and Bellamy. They leaned against the lockers while a group of girls hovered nearby.

A spark of anger ignited in me. I could not believe he'd come to my house and stolen that car off my damn driveway. I needed it back, or Jerry was going to kill me. And that meant talking to the asshole. As a whole, I didn't fear Zepp's bad-boy reputation like most people, but I'd kneed him in the balls—after I had tried to seduce him. He was going to be pissed.

I took a breath and stalked toward him with my fists balled. Just... I was going to be assertive. I'd just tell him. I walked up behind him, the scent of leather and car oil falling over me. Raising my hand, I hesitated before I squared my shoulders and flicked his shoulder. "Hey."

A hush fell over the hallway when he turned around, leaving me staring at his chest and the black material of his

T-shirt plastered over hard muscle. I could feel the gaze of what felt like half the school on me, the minions watching the big, bad wolf huff and puff.

When I tipped back my head, I met dark eyes that were every bit as hard and angry as I had expected. This close, in the daylight, Zepp was the kind of good looking that was impossible to ignore: angular cheekbones, full lips, a permanently tensed jaw. And eyes that promised he'd ruin me in all the worst ways.

"You took my fucking car."

His nose ring glinted under the harsh, fluorescent bulbs as he cocked his head to the side like a cat toying with a mouse. One side of his mouth quirked slightly, but it was the only crack in an otherwise impenetrable mask. "And?"

"I need it back."

"And I need my dick sucked." His gaze flicked over me before he walked off, enormous shoulders parting the sea of people.

My pulse ticked up, both panic and anger fighting for dominance. Zepp was an ass, and being a bitch to him would get me nowhere, so I swallowed down the urge.

I jogged after him. "I'll give you a thousand bucks for it." It was most of the money I had, but it was worth it not to have to deal with Jerry.

He stopped mid-stride, turning to glare down at me. There was a pause, a flicker of curiosity that flashed through his eyes, like he could sense my desperation. "Would it make your life easier if I sold it to you?" There was a mocking tone to his voice that made me want to punch him.

"Obviously."

"Then, no." Arrogant bastard. He went to move on, but I grabbed onto his arm.

"Really? Easy cash. And you won't sell it."

"Maybe you should be more careful where that knee of yours goes." He closed in, shoving me against the nearest locker with a bang. He loomed over me, all coiled muscle and raging temper. "You want that car?"

I didn't like him, but that dangerous energy in such close proximity did something to me that I couldn't deny. His gaze dropped to my mouth.

"Get down on your knees and suck my dick, then maybe I'll think about selling it to you."

My temper went sky-high in an instant. "No car is worth touching your dick."

"Your loss." He shoved back from me with a glare before heading down the hall, his boys followed him, people scrambling to get out of their way.

Jade stepped beside me, brows raised.

Then Chase popped over my shoulder, letterman jacket in place. "What was *that* about?"

People were staring, cupping their hands and whispering.

I sighed, then shook my head and started down the hall. "Nothing."

"Bullshit," he said. "What the hell are you doing talking to Hunt?" Chase was the only guy who would ever get away with questioning me, and only because it came from a good place. Like every other guy in Dayton, he knew Zepp was a complete asshole.

"He has something I need, that's all."

Jade shot me a confused glare. "Since when does buying weed include getting shoved against a locker and practically humped?"

"I was not practically humped!" Heat spread over my cheeks, and Jade's eyes skirted away like she would agree to disagree. "And I'm not buying weed."

"Moe." That had been Chase's nickname for me since we were kids, and I hated it. He clamped a hand on my shoulder, halting my steps. "Please tell me you aren't messing around with that dickhead."

"Of course not. Look, just—leave it." I walked away from both of them, dropping into my English class.

I had until tomorrow night to get that car back, and I didn't want to find out what would happen if I failed.

3

ZEPP

Our house was a constant revolving door of people. Most buying, some selling. And girls... Friday night meant the bass pumping through the speakers was heavier than usual.

Hendrix dropped to the couch beside me, cracking open a beer. "Slut alert." He cackled into his Miller Lite before Leah Anderson, one of the rich girls from Barrington, slipped onto the couch, then onto me.

Knees straddled my hips while her arms came around my neck. "Hey, Zepp." She tucked blond hair behind her ear, shoving her tits closer to my face while I stared through her. She was a cheerleader who possessed a level of depth equivalent to a puddle of dog piss. But she was nice to look at, plus, it gave the pricks at Barrington a rise when their girls came over to the trash side of town to be tainted by the bad boys.

"Hey, Zepp?" Wolf's voice rose over the crowd in my living room. He pushed through a few girls blocking his way. "Got something for you."

Monroe was right behind him, her cleavage on full display.

I glanced over her ripped fishnets and tight leather skirt, imagining her on her knees. "Decided to take me up on my offer?

"In your dreams. We need to talk."

I shoved Leah out of my lap, telling her to go up to my room. She hesitated and glanced at Monroe with a well-practiced, prissy-bitch, condescending glare. "He has much better offers than you," she said, then stood up, and, for a second, I thought Monroe was going to punch her.

"Well, you look like you suck dick like a champ. So yeah."

People walked between us, laughing on their way into the kitchen. By the time they had moved on, Leah had left, and now it was just Monroe and me.

"Let me guess." I swiped a cigarette from the table and lit it. "You want the car?"

There was a pause, one where she looked completely put out to be here. "I need it."

"We've already been over this."

The girl had shown up to have the same conversation we'd had earlier in the hallway. Unless she was getting on her knees and pulling out my dick, I wasn't giving her shit.

"I'm not sucking your dick. You don't want money." Monroe folded her arms over her chest on a sharp exhale. "So, what do you want?" Relentless *and* desperate enough to offer herself up like a fishnet-clad sacrificial lamb, which meant endless possibilities for me. "I'll swap it," she said. "For a more valuable one."

I didn't need her help to steal cars. Between my boys and me, we had that covered. And a hot girl like Monroe could do a lot more for me than lift vehicles.

"I don't want a more valuable one. But…" I took a puff from my cigarette, staring at her long enough that I caught her swallow. "I would take three months of your unfailing service."

"Service?" Her eyes narrowed. "Again, I'm not screwing you."

"I'm not talking about sex. Think of it as a personal assistant."

The bump of speakers filled the silence, the hum of conversation. Monroe's nostrils flared. I could almost see her weighing her options, and I couldn't help but wonder why the hell she wanted that piece of shit car so bad. I dropped my cigarette into a beer can, then shrugged. "Don't want it bad enough? No problem."

On a groan, Monroe dropped her arms from her chest. "I need the car now," she said. "I can't wait—"

"You can have it tonight."

That snapped her mouth shut. A slight furrow appeared in her brow. Making a deal with me—especially one this vague—Monroe had no way to know what kind of shit she may end up involved in. "If I agree to this… it needs to stay quiet."

"So it's a deal then?"

"Fine." The hint of a smile pulled at her lips. "Where's the car?"

If I had to guess, she thought she'd get the car and bail on this deal, and I couldn't blame her. Nothing held her to it —except me.

I rose from the couch, towering over her as I forced her back a few feet. "And don't be stupid. You know what I'm capable of." I twisted a tendril of her red hair around my finger and tugged it. "Don't you, *Roe*?"

Her jaw ticced, hate radiating from her like stink off shit

before I turned away. I was already through the front door when her angry footfalls chased me down the steps. "Where's the car, Zepp?"

"Oh. That car? I sold it," I threw over my shoulder.

"What! I'm not doing shit for you without it."

"Shut up with your whining already. I'm taking you to get it." I had sold the thing the day we stole it. But even if that car sat parked in my backyard, I would have sold it before I "gave" it to Monroe. No way in hell I would take a cut off my earnings.

Thirty minutes later, she had the car. And I had her—for three months.

4

MONROE

Monday morning, I stood outside the doors of the high school, watching students hurry through the congested halls while anger still pulsed through my veins. Zepp had dropped me at the gate of Karl's Carmart on Friday night with a pair of bolt cutters. I made a deal with him for a car *I* had to steal. Again! To make matters worse, I had to hotwire it, which meant Bubba knocked a hundred bucks off. And of course, Jerry made me pay for that out of my pocket. Like I didn't make him enough money. Now I was indebted to Zeppelin Hunt, of all people. He was into stealing, dealing, and illegal shit that I didn't need to be more involved in than I was already.

I wove between kids with backpacks and hurried through the combination on my locker, thinking that maybe I could fly under the radar and not draw Zepp's attention.

Jade popped up beside me, fiddling with her lock before yanking it open and cramming her backpack inside. "Good news. Mom ungrounded me."

"How did you get out of that?"

She glared at me with a frown. "I went to church."

"So Jesus has forgiven you for smoking weed in your bedroom?"

"Probably not. But Mom thinks He has so..."

I laughed. "Well, I'm working tonight, or I'd come and hang out with you."

She slammed her locker door, then leaned against it. "How that place is still open is beyond me. They should have been busted by now."

"Because Dayton cops don't give a shit about a few seventeen-year-olds getting their tits out."

"True."

I hated my job. I really did, but it was good money, and it was nearly impossible to find work in Dayton. I had three choices: stripping, drugs, or prostitution. And stripping was the lesser of those evils.

We moved away from the lockers and started through the corridor. Jade was rambling about some girl in her calculus class when she stopped mid-sentence. "Oh shit, Monroe." She nudged me with her elbow, her gaze aimed at the end of the hall where Zepp was walking straight toward me. "He's so scary and hot, and God, I would so fuck him."

"He's an asshole, Jade."

Zepp sauntered toward me, parting the sea of students before him.

Near-black eyes roamed over me, and I wanted to slap myself for the way my pulse ticked up. He shoved his phone into my hands. "Number." He said it loud enough that a couple of the girls walking past stopped and stared. There was only one reason Zepp asked a girl for her number.

"Why would I give you my number?"

"Because I told you to." Our eyes met, battle lines drawn. An unamused laugh slipped past his lips, and I hated that I found it sexy. "Phone number, Monroe."

I reluctantly keyed in my number, then shoved the phone against his chest and stormed off, Jade in tow.

Jade leaned in, clutching her books to her chest. "You totally just gave Zepp Hunt your number. And everyone saw," she whispered.

Yes, they did. One request: keep it quiet—and he couldn't even stick to it. He pissed me off so much that it was all I could think about for the rest of the school day and into the evening.

I had to work that night, and that anger festered as I worked the pole and lap danced for sleazy men until two in the morning. When my shift was over, I went back to the dressing room and got changed, then checked my phone. There was a string of missed texts from an unknown number.

Unknown Caller: I need a favor.
Unknown Caller: Don't ignore me, Monroe.
Unknown Caller: WTF are U doing?

It had to be Zepp. My fingers were typing out a response when that same number flashed across the screen. I answered it, pressing it to my ear while I shouldered my bag. "Yeah?"

"You asleep or some shit?" Zepp's deep voice came down the line. Rap music thumped in the background.

"What do you want?"

"You. At my house. Now."

"No."

Silence crossed the line. I could imagine that sharp jawline of his ticing with frustration. "Don't be stupid, Monroe."

One of the girls pranced into the room, counting

through her cash as she made her way around me.

"I had one request, Zepp. Discretion."

"What the fuck are you talking about?"

"You asked for my number. In the middle of the damn hall. That is not discrete."

A deep laugh rumbled through the speaker. "I ask for girls' numbers all the time."

"Well, great." And now I looked like one of his sluts. One of the girls giggled at her changing table, and I went into the hall. "I don't want to be associated with you in any way. Got it?"

"Jesus Christ... You have twenty minutes to get to my house with two cases of beer," he said, then the line clicked.

He had hung up. I stared at the blank screen, anger bubbling away like a boiling pot. Zepp couldn't hold up his end of the deal, so neither would I.

5

ZEPP

Twenty minutes had passed. Thirty. The party had started to thin out, and I still didn't have any beer. I moved through the drunk girls leaned against the wall, and Wolf glanced over at me, one brow raised and a slight pull on his lips.

"She's got some balls, dude. Some major balls." He snagged a joint from one of the girls and took a puff. "What are you gonna do, Zepp?"

And that, I wasn't sure of. She was a girl—one who wasn't eager to fuck me—which meant I had limited options. I wasn't going to hurt her, but I sure as shit could embarrass her. "I'll figure it out." I shouldered through the living room, then took the stairs to my room. That girl was unbelievable.

There was a soft knock at my door before it cracked open. I looked up from the bed as Leah slipped inside. I was not in the mood for her bullshit tonight. The problem with girls like Leah, they thought they would come to the shit side of town, bang one of the broken bad boys, then clean him up and make him into something close to shiny. Tying one of us down would have been like hanging a lion's head on a wall. A trophy. Something any Barrington girl could brag about.

She flopped down onto the bed, stretching her arms out in a piss-poor attempt to look sexy. "You wanna have sex?"

I jerked my chin toward the door. "I'm sure my brother would be more than willing."

She sat up, her cheeks tinging red. "Come on, Zepp." She rubbed over my crotch. "I know you want me."

"Jesus Christ! I just told you to go fuck my brother." I shoved her hand away. "Get out."

Leah shoved to her feet with a huff, stomping across my bedroom like a spoiled brat before she slammed the door on her way out. The most pathetic thing about it was: Leah would text me later that night. She'd show back up next weekend because she didn't care that I didn't respect her. The way I saw it, respect wasn't nearly as important to her as image. And that was pretty damn sad.

Monroe, on the other hand... She wouldn't even buy me beer. Something told me that if I talked to her that way, she'd draw blood. I dragged a hand down my face. I was livid at her, but still, those legs and that attitude... I hated her almost as much as I wanted to fuck her. Maybe that was why, later that night, I found myself beating one out to the idea of having Monroe James' thighs wrapped around my hips while I showed her what being a bad girl was really about.

THE NEXT MORNING, Hendrix dragged some kid who had

been selling weed into the bathroom to beat his ass while I leaned against the tiled wall, a smoke pinched between my lips.

Hendrix pulled back to smack him again, but the bell rang. I chucked my cigarette into the sink, then blew smoke in the guy's bloodied face before we ducked out into the halls and parted ways.

Half of the students in my English class already had their heads down. A handful of the go-getters had binders open on their desks, looking over their notes, like earning valedictorian would make a difference in a place like this. It wouldn't.

I snagged one of the papers off the edge of Mrs. Smith's desk, then headed to my seat to erase Bobby Graham's name and pencil in mine.

A string of catcalls rang out, and I looked up from the paper just as Monroe strutted between the desks. A little plume of anger rose in my chest, but when she turned around to take her seat, my gaze dropped to the short, plaid skirt that stopped just a couple of inches below her ass. Had she been a guy, that little stunt last night would have resulted in a physical altercation. But she wasn't a guy. She was a shit-hot girl with an ass I wanted to leave a handprint on. Bellamy was right. My dick did get me in trouble.

Monroe had barely settled into her seat before one of the football players crossed the room, then perched his meaty ass on the edge of her desk. He said something to her.

She rolled her eyes. "Like I told you last time, fuck off." She went back to her book, and a collective snicker followed by a "burn" erupted from the class while dickweed stalked back to his seat, cheeks crimson.

That girl was like a feral animal that would gnaw off

someone's arm before she'd let them pet her. Lucky for me, I had a shock collar for her in the form of a debt. One that she would repay whether she liked it or not. I rose from my chair, placed the stolen essay onto the teacher's desk, then dropped into the empty seat beside Monroe.

"Is it that you're brave or stupid?" I offered the most son-of-a-bitch smile I could muster while I twisted a tendril of her hair around my finger.

Her nostrils flared, and she tugged the strand free from my hold. "The fact that self-respect doesn't cross your mind says a lot about the company you keep."

"Stupid it is." Frowning, I grabbed her desk and yanked. A hush fell over the classroom when the chair's metal legs screeched across the tile floor, bringing us nose to nose. We glared at each other like lions preparing to either fight or screw. Or both. "You fucked up, Roe." I leaned over to grab her, and the chair tipped to its side. "Didn't want anyone to know about us, huh?" Then I shoved my hand under her skirt. Before I could get far, her warm thighs clamped shut, but that didn't keep me from moving my hand back and forth under her skirt, giving the rest of the class a very dirty illusion. One that garnered a rush of whispers while Monroe shifted in her seat, cheeks flushing.

The classroom door clicked open, but I didn't budge. Her fingers wrapped around my wrist, tugging my hand. But I refused to move it on pure principle. "Bet you wish you had just gotten my beer now, huh, Roe?"

"Get off her, Mr. Hunt." Mrs. Smith swore under her breath. "Mr. Hunt. Miss James!" A loud clap sounded. "Save it for after class!"

"After class it is," I said, squeezing Monroe's thigh before I rose to my feet. "My house, Roe. Tonight. Eight." Then I brought my fingers to my lips, pretending to suck the taste of her off on my way across the class, leaving the whole room staring at Monroe.

The girl who didn't want to be associated with me was now—for all intents and purposes, as far as gossip would be concerned—fucking me.

6

MONROE

I headed for Barrington, my mind still a storm of emotions. My hatred for Zeppelin Hunt was growing by the second, but I was more annoyed at myself. I should have just gotten the damn beer, but my temper had risen like an angry rattlesnake, refusing to back down. And now, he'd made sure everyone thought I was another one of his skanks.

Some girls saw Zepp in all his brooding, shithead glory, and they wanted to either be used by him or save him. He might have been hot, but I would never degrade myself with that asshole. And I didn't give a damn about saving him. My biggest error was allowing him to see just how much I didn't want to be seen with him because now he was going to make my life hell. My resistance was so pointless it was almost laughable.

By the time I pulled up to Max Harford's iron gates, I'd had enough time to stew over everything, and my chest was tight. I slammed the door to my heap of a Pinto and stormed up to the white brick house. Before I had even rung the bell,

Max opened the door, flashing a wide smile that screamed all-American good boy.

"You're early."

"Yeah, that okay?" I stepped inside the marble foyer and, as always, felt like dirt that the maid would want to sweep up.

"Of course. Only an idiot would mind a little more time with you." His gaze dropped to my legs for a fleeting moment. "You look nice today. Like the skirt."

I tried not to scowl. Compliments were not welcome, but I had to remind myself that with him, there was no backhanded dig. Even though Max was Barrington's golden-boy quarterback and should have been the biggest of all dicks, he was actually okay.

"Thanks," I mumbled.

I followed him through to the massive kitchen, all sparkling and white. He disappeared behind the door of his stainless-steel refrigerator, then popped back with a can of Grapico. I eyed the purple can when he handed it to me.

"I know it's your favorite." He shrugged a shoulder on his way into the sitting room.

I couldn't remember telling him that Grapico was my favorite. "That's nice of you." I tapped a finger over the ring pull, fidgeting as I followed him over to the couch.

"Just a quick stop at the store. It's fine." He patted the spot beside him. "My dad's working late tonight."

"Okay." I put my books on the coffee table, then checked my watch, barely paying attention to anything else. I had three hours before I had to be at Zepp's, and that thought had a nervous churning settling in my gut.

THE ENGINE to my piece of shit car sputtered when I pulled up outside the Hunt house. Anxious energy crept through my veins on my way up the overgrown sidewalk and onto the rotting porch. I debated leaving a few times before I finally knocked on the door. Voices shouted inside. Heavy footfalls came toward the entrance, and a series of locks clicked before the door swung open to Hendrix. He took one look at me, and that was enough to have disgust crawling over my skin. He was almost as good looking as his brother, but he was even more of a whore than Zepp.

"Who you gonna bang first, Red?" He bit his lip on a grin. "Me or my brother? You want us at the same time, that's extra."

"Gross. I'm here for Zepp."

"Final answer?" He opened the door wider, then stepped to the side. "'Cause, my dick's bigger."

"Congratulations." I shouldered past him, cutting through the entranceway while he laughed. I headed toward the kitchen, and seconds later, the pop of fake gunfire came from the living room.

Zepp sat at a small breakfast table; his brows pulled together while he studied the screen of the laptop in front of him. His hand rested on the worn tabletop, tattooed fingers clenched in a fist. He always looked so angry. And dangerous.

I stood in the doorway and cleared my throat.

His response: Sliding his phone across the tabletop. "Order me some pizza."

I wanted to strangle him, but instead, I mumbled "dick" under my breath before dialing the number to Pizza Barn and placing an order for two pepperoni pizzas. When the delivery guy asked for the address, I looked at Zepp. "You know the shit hole house at the end of Victory Lane?

There." Then I hung up and chucked Zepp's phone back at him.

"Will that be all?" I asked, acid dripping from my voice.

He didn't even look up from his laptop, let alone respond. He was such an asshole.

"Fine." I headed for the hall. I hated being Zepp's bitch, but trying to get out of it had backfired. So this was what I had to deal with—beer runs and pizza orders.

"I didn't tell you, you could leave, Monroe."

I stopped in the doorway of the kitchen, staring at the peeling wallpaper before I turned to face him. "Really, Zepp? Can we just not?"

The condescending glare he directed at me had my temper spiking. He was such an arrogant prick with his stupid nose ring and muscles. "Screw you and your small-dick power trip."

A cackle came from the living room. "Told you mine was bigger," Hendrix shouted, but Zepp's gaze remained fixed on me like a hunter staring down the sites of a rifle.

He took a chair from the table and shoved it toward me. "We made a deal. Which means you should shut the fuck up and sit down."

My jaw clenched when I took the seat, forcing myself to swallow my pride.

I hated his too-perfect face and the way he looked at me like a cat toying with a mouse. "Keep being a dick just because you can, but I can make these three months real hard for you, too."

He pushed up from his seat, patting my head when he rounded the table. "That's cute."

My teeth ground over each other so hard it's a wonder they didn't crack. I closed my eyes and counted to ten in my head so I wouldn't pick up this chair and toss it at his head. "God, you're a prick," I mumbled so he wouldn't hear.

And that was that. We didn't say a word to each other for the next half hour.

Bellamy and Wolf showed up, and once the guys had scarfed down their greasy pizza, we piled into Wolf's rundown pickup and headed across town, eventually rolling through the winding roads of Barrington.

Wolf cut the lights before pulling to a stop outside one of the large brick houses. "Why are we here?" I asked, my gaze fixed through the cracked window.

Zepp climbed out, and the guys followed. On a resigned sigh, I opened the door, and the warm, night air wrapped around me. The second my feet hit the sidewalk, Zepp moved toward me, a burning cigarette hanging from his lips. The smirk on his face made me take an uneasy step back. I didn't trust any of them for shit.

"Now, what I need you to do..." His gaze dropped to my chest before he grabbed onto my shirt, yanking the material until it ripped. "Damn, nice tits."

Hendrix snickered behind him while Wolf and Bellamy lingered in the shadows.

I swatted his hand away, glancing down at my exposed bra. "What the hell, Zepp? I love this shirt."

His gaze lifted from my torn shirt to my face. "Cry for me." Smoke crawled through his lips with each word, that cold gaze cutting right through me.

"What?" A shiver of awareness trickled through me. They could do whatever they wanted to me right now, and no one would know. Swallowing my unease, I folded my arms over my chest. "Tell me what I'm doing here."

The burning ember of his cigarette reflected in his near-pitch-black eyes. He thumbed behind him to the glossy, red door illuminated by a lone porch light. "You're going to go bang on that door until that rich bitch opens up. Then you're going to tell her some dickhead boyfriend of yours is after you while you keep her in the kitchen."

"Why?"

He leaned in close, his thumb stroking over my cheek in a way that made my breath catch. "You're the distraction. Now, cry." The rasp of his voice burrowed beneath my skin in ways that I hated.

I closed my eyes, inhaling the scent of smoke while the warmth of his breath fanned over my face. It wasn't hard to make myself cry; I just had to allow a glimmer of life's hard reality to creep through the walls I had constructed to keep it out. For a moment, I let myself drown in the hopelessness that I fought so hard.

When I opened my eyes again, tears broke free. Yet, even through the blur of life's shitstorm that welled in my eyes, I zeroed in on Zepp's ski mask-covered face. Despite being covered, I could still see the crinkle of a pleased smile in the corner of his eyes.

"Good girl," he said before slinking into the shadows, the others following behind like loyal subjects. Dickhead.

Within seconds, they'd disappeared around the back of the house. And I took that as my cue. I ran up the drive, then pounded my fist fast against the door, over and over. The fact that I was the only one at risk here bubbled to the surface. It was my face that would be seen. The second that reality set in, I went to turn from the door, but the porch light came to life, and the door opened without the slightest of creaks. A willowy woman in a silk robe with a strand of pearls at the base of her throat stood at the entrance, a bewildered look on her face. "Can I—"

I was screwed now. Better make this believable. "Please.

Help me," I choked, glancing over my shoulder. "He's after me."

Her gaze stopped on my ripped shirt, then she grabbed onto my elbow and yanked me inside. "Come in, dear. Hurry." The large door closed behind us with a thud, and she guided me along the shiny, hardwood floors. She led me into the living room, but I didn't sit. He said to keep her in the kitchen.

"Please, could I have a glass of water?" I clutched my throat—"parched" from "running."

"Of course." She motioned for me to follow her.

We passed through the hallway, and I noticed the perfect family portrait centered on the wall. That was when I realized just how messed up Zepp was. In the ornate, golden frame, Leah stood between the woman leading me through the hall, and a guy I guessed was her dad, all of them smiling at the camera. This was Leah's house. I shook my head while I followed Leah's mom into a kitchen that was bigger than my entire trailer. It made me hate the woman in front of me while wishing I could be like her.

"Here." She placed a glass onto the marble, kitchen island. I gulped half of it, thinking that even their water tasted better.

Her thin brows pulled into an expression of concern. "What happened, dear?"

"My ex-boyfriend. He— Wouldn't take no for an answer." My voice broke a little, and I forced tears to pour down my cheeks, before swiping at them. I had no idea what I was supposed to do here.

"Oh, my." She gasped, her hand moving to her chest in horror, as though shit like that didn't happen every day. "Did he..." she trailed off, unable to say the word rape.

Jesus, Leah sure as hell hadn't inherited her mom's innocence.

"No. I got away." I wiped away more tears. "Can I use your phone?"

With a nod, the woman fetched the phone. My gaze drifted across the hall while I pretended to call someone who would give a shit about me. That was when I noticed Zepp in the hallway, like an ominous shadow. His dark eyes burned through the slit in his ski mask like smoldering coal before he disappeared down the hall.

Nervous energy wound through my veins as I sat and waited for the guys to finish. I almost jumped out of my skin when the knock finally came at the front door. Leah's mother moved ahead of me to answer it. Bellamy stood on the Welcome mat. His gaze met mine before moving to the woman. "Thanks for helping my sister."

"That's no problem." She placed a hand on my shoulder. "You really should involve the police, dear. It's just not right."

Bellamy wrapped an arm around my shoulder; I guessed to really sell it. "Thank you for your help."

As soon as the door clicked shut behind us, we both sprinted across the manicured lawn for the truck. One of the guys opened the door to the back cab. I threw myself in, and Bellamy tumbled in behind me. The door was still open when Wolf pulled away from the curb, tires screeching.

We hadn't made it out of Barrington before guilt settled in my gut. That woman had tried to help me, even if she was rich and raising bitches like Leah Anderson. And we had robbed her. Although I knew it was all things she could afford to lose, it felt wrong.

"Looks like you can follow directions," Zepp said from the front seat.

"You robbed your girlfriend?"

He barked out a laugh. "I don't date girls, Monroe. I fuck them."

"Spreading her legs should surely buy her some loyalty. Damn." That was cold.

Hendrix snorted beside me. "Nothing about Leah deserves loyalty. Not even her pussy."

I couldn't imagine sleeping with someone and finding out that I meant absolutely nothing to them. I wondered if Leah had any clue how disposable she was. For a second, I pitied the bitch. It was fleeting, though, because she'd have to be stupid to see Zepp as anything more than the asshole he was. Not like he tried to hide it.

My phone vibrated, and I took it out, reading over a message from Max. Hendrix leaned over my shoulder, and I glared at him, locking my phone.

"Harford?" Disgust laced his voice.

If I had to guess, Hendrix didn't know anything more about Max than the fact that he attended Barrington, but as far as most people in Dayton were concerned, that was enough. There was always beef between our schools, and Max was public enemy number one because he was the quarterback. The golden boy with a perfect life handed to him on a silver platter. He was all that, but he was also okay for a Barrington guy.

"You're talking to Harford?" Hendrix kicked at one of the bags filled with stolen stuff that sat on the floorboard. "Why the hell are you talking to that asshole?"

"None of your business."

My gaze caught the rearview mirror just in time to see Zepp glare into the backseat.

"Fucking the golden dick quarterback, huh?" He laughed, lighting a cigarette. "There's your self-respect."

It was right on the tip of my tongue to deny it. "Says the guy fucking and robbing the cheerleader."

"Cheerleade*rs*. Plural." He cracked the window, and a stream of smoke billowed out.

"Congratulations."

Guys like Zepp and Hendrix could bang all the rich girls they liked. But the second a Dayton girl picked a Barrington guy over them, especially the quarterback, the guy had hell to pay and she was a slut—then again, weren't girls always the sluts, while the guys were studs?

It was late when I got home. My mother laid, passed out on one couch, another track mark in her arm. Jerry was on the other couch, several beer bottles scattered around his feet and a bottle of whiskey dangling from his hand.

Great. Jerry was a horrible drunk.

"Where you been?" he slurred.

At the very least, I knew I should try to appease his drunk ass, but I couldn't help the indignation that rose in me. Despite knowing it would piss him off, I said, "Out." One word I knew I shouldn't have, but I was still fighting.

No matter how much power he had over me, I'd never stop; because the moment I did, I would become just like my mom. A tragedy. Screwing dirty men to pay for a habit, all so I could escape the very existence I'd created. She was weak, but I refused to be.

That drunk, angry glaze in his eyes was all too familiar to me, and the second he took a step toward me, I knew what was coming, so I braced myself.

7

ZEPP

LEAH: They took my cat's rhinestone collar. Like WTAF is wrong with people?

Hendrix was the one who took that. Surprisingly, the guy at the pawnshop had given us seven bucks for it. Leah had been texting me non-stop. Like I gave a shit about her problems. Hell, I was the reason for half of them, she just didn't know it. Sure, we may have taken her grandmother's pearl necklace, but in the grand scheme of things, her family wasn't hurting. They were out a few heirlooms and diamond necklaces that probably hadn't seen the light of day in the better half of a decade, and Hendrix and I got to keep a roof over our heads.

Me: Why are you bitching to me about this stuff? Don't you have a boyfriend?
LEAH: Me and Max aren't dating!!!!!

They never were dating when Leah wanted dick worth a damn...

I closed the texts without responding and shoved my phone to the side of the desk when Mr. Weaver passed out exams. I read over the first question and bubbled in C. Halfway through the test, my name crackled over the intercom system.

"Zeppelin Hunt. You're needed in the principal's office."

Tossing my pencil down, I glared around the room. The other student's eyes shifted away when I pushed up from my chair. If one of those pricks had the balls to snitch on me for selling weed, I was going to kill them.

I stopped outside Principal Brown's office, and Monroe's muffled voice drifted from the other side of the door.

"Some rich lady says a redhead robbed her, and you figured, 'it must be some trash kid from Dayton High. I'll go looking for a redhead there.'"

I waited to see what would follow, but all that came was silence. I pushed down on the handle. Monroe didn't bother to look up when the lock clicked, and I stepped into Brown's office.

As expected, Brown's disapproving gaze met mine. What wasn't expected was Officer Jacobs standing in the corner, sleeves tight-rolled over his half-muscled arms in all his dipshit glory. The guy had had it out for us ever since Hendrix popped his daughter's cherry in the back seat of his patrol car. I was sure this just made his day.

I leaned a shoulder against the wall and shot Monroe a stern glare while I played out how this was about to go down. If I had my guess, she had probably said I made her do it. Told them she hadn't stolen a thing—which would be true. The only problem was that it was her word against mine. There would be no proof. I had been in every room in Leah's house, on purpose, so any fingerprints of mine, Leah would have to answer for that. There weren't any security cameras, so the police would be hard-pressed to find evidence outside of Mrs. Anderson's identifying Monroe in a lineup.

"Ask him." Monroe jerked her chin toward me.

"Miss James," Jacobs sighed. "Using that shithead as an alibi doesn't make you look any less guilty."

Forget that Jacobs called me a shithead. Monroe had used me as an alibi? I had to stop myself from looking at her. Because an alibi was the last thing I had expected since getting me locked up in juvie would have bought her freedom.

Monroe drummed her fingers over the arm of the stiff chair. "But *looking* guilty doesn't stand up in court, does it?" A smug smile flashed across her face like she'd won. "And unless you're arresting me, I'm pretty sure you aren't allowed to interrogate me on school grounds."

Jacob's nostrils flared. "That can be arr—"

"Mr. Hunt," Brown interjected, his attention swinging over the stack of student records on his desk to me. "Miss James said she was with you Monday night. Is that true?"

I raked my teeth over my lip, then dragged my gaze over Monroe's legs. "Yeah. She was."

Officer Jacob's pulled out his dipshit notepad, pen in hand like he was some amateur detective. "Between what times?"

"Well, let's see." I moved behind her chair, placing my hands on the wooden back. "I had my *cock* in her from about ten until midnight. But she was at my house until Tuesday morning when she gave me a blowjob in the shower."

Brown coughed before loosening his tie like it was a noose ready to hang him, while Monroe reached behind her, looping her fingers through mine. "Baby," her hold tightened until her nails sliced into the back of my hand, "why don't you stop talking now?"

Jacobs rolled his eyes on a huff. "You expect me to believe that?"

"Feel free to swab her for my DNA," I offered with a shrug.

He glanced at Brown. "The lady said a redhead who looked on the poor side was picked up by a dark-headed guy."

Brown frowned, tapping a pen over his desk. "I understand, but that isn't exactly evidence, Dan."

"My come would be, though, right?"

Brown let out another choked cough, grabbing at his already loose tie as he leafed through papers, his cheeks gradually growing to nuclear reactor red. "Miss James. Mr. Hunt, you may leave."

Kicking back from her chair, I made a sweeping motion toward the door with my arm. Monroe shoved up, going through the doorway first. I watched her ass then shot a stern glare at Jacobs before I stepped into the empty secretary's office. The second I was outside Brown's office, Monroe punched me in the gut, eyes flaming. "Feel free to swab her?"

"Just trying to sell it." I brushed past her, then the latch to Brown's door clicked.

"...not a word of it," Jacobs said. "Thank you for your time anyway, Ed." A shiny loafer crossed the threshold. Jacobs had enough experience with me to know I was a liar, which sent a spark of panic through me.

I took Monroe by the waist, shoving her against a filing cabinet, aiming to make the idea that we were fuck buddies more solid in Jacobs's mind. She grabbed at my shoulders, ready to push me off, but I squeezed her waist hard enough to make her breath catch. "You better moan and act like you want this," I buried my face against her neck, kissing and biting.

Her tense body relaxed a little, her hands snaked down my back, and she let out a very convincing groan. It didn't matter that she was acting, my dick still went rock hard at the breathy sound, begging for five minutes in a locked room with her. And that was problematic. I hated the idea of her but loved it at the same time.

Another muted groan made its way up her throat. It took every ounce of restraint I possessed not to pick her up and wrap her thighs around my waist and give Brown and Jacobs a show they'd beat one out to for days. Not to mention, give Monroe something to take home and think about.

I could feel someone standing beside us. When I pulled away from Monroe's throat, I locked eyes with Jacobs. "Gotta problem?" I asked, my hands still on Monroe.

With a tic of his jaw, he walked into the hall. But I caught the bastard stopped at the office window. Monroe went to pull away, but I held onto her tight, planting my lips back on her throat. "He's still watching." The coconut, girly scent of her shampoo made my hormones drunk, and I couldn't help but press my hips against hers a little, just for the pressure.

Her fingers fisted at my shirt. "Is he gone yet?"

I took a quick glance over her shoulder. Jacobs had started down the hall, but I was enjoying myself too much. "No." I sank my teeth into her neck and sucked, imagining what a deep, purple hickey would look like on her throat, her tits. Her breath caught again, fingers flattening over my chest.

Oh, she was into it. Definitely into it.

The change-of-class bell rang. I debated slipping my

hand over the curve of her ass. She would slap me for it, but it would be worth it. The bang of lockers and scuff of shoes crept in from the cracked doorway. But Monroe was still right there, pressed against me. Breath all ragged, her palms still on my chest. It wasn't until a few students pounded fists against the office window that she shoved me away, and the look of absolute mortification on her face was damn near priceless. Maybe she had the same problem as me: she wanted me just as much as she hated me.

I adjusted my dick in my jeans while giving her a long once over. "Wouldn't take much. Would it?"

"That's a big leap." She patted my cheek. "I'll grind on you if it keeps me out of juvie. Beyond that, I'd rather take a run and jump at a wasp's nest." She turned on her heel, red hair flying behind her when she went to make her grand exit from the office, pretending like she wasn't the least bit fazed.

But she knew it, and I knew it. I was absolutely going to fuck that girl.

HENDRIX JUMPED UP, slapping his hand over the top of the cafeteria doorway. "Jacobs is a dick." Hendrix stopped beside Wolf and Bellamy in the line, taking a tray before he thumbed back at me. "He got called to Brown's office."

"What for?" Wolf watched one of the freshmen girls strut past, blowing a kiss to her. "Blowjob in the girls' restroom?" he asked me over the clang of silverware and plastic trays.

"No. Jacobs had Monroe in there."

"Jacobs? What the..."

Bellamy shook his head. "We should have known better than to use a redhead."

"What's wrong with a redhead?" Hendrix piled rolls onto his plate then swiped two cartons of chocolate milk.

Bellamy grabbed utensils from the wall caddy. "How many redheads do you see, dumbass?"

"Oh. Right." Hendrix glared over his shoulder at me. "That's your fault, man."

"She's not the only redhead in Dayton and Barrington," I said.

"Nah, but she's the only hot one," Wolf chuckled, taking a plate of cheese fries that smelled like dirty dishwater. When he looked over at me, the smile faded from his face. "Chill out, dude. I'm not trying to hit on your chick."

"Fuck off, Wolf."

Hendrix cackled, then launched a fry at my forehead. "Zepp and Monroe sittin' in a tree, F-U-C-K-I-N-G," he sang.

I shoved him hard enough that he stumbled, sending a few of his rolls tumbling to the floor. I loaded my tray down with greasy food, then paid the cashier and headed into the crowded lunchroom. Most of the tables were full. Students sat shoulder to shoulder, laughing and talking. We passed our usual spot, and my brother groaned.

"Sarah Fletcher was giving me the eyes, man. Why do we have to go sit with the angry ginger and the weirdo?"

Ignoring him, I dropped my tray to the table beside Monroe. "Miss me?" I sank to the stool, and the rest of the guys fell into empty seats around the two girls.

"If only I got the chance."

"Ah, come on, Roe." I rubbed a finger along the high collar of her shirt, and she shoved me away. "We're practically a couple now. Haven't you heard?"

"I have a boyfriend. So no, we're not."

A boyfriend? She wasn't dating anyone from Dayton, which left Barrington. And pissing off one of those pricks was always welcomed.

"Who? Harford?" Hendrix snorted before cramming a roll into his mouth.

I didn't believe for one second that she was dating Harford. Monroe was hot, but Max *dated* girls like Leah. Girls his uppity parents would approve of because social status mattered in places like Barrington. Monroe wasn't dating him. Fucking him? Sure, and the thought of it made a spark of jealousy ignite inside me.

"Gonna be a shame when the rich boy breaks up with you for bumping uglies with my brother," Hendrix said.

Monroe dropped her napkin to her plate with a roll of her eyes. "I'd rather screw a cactus, so unlikely." Like the idea of her and me together, in a bed, was that farfetched.

"Not what the rumors are saying, *bae*."

"I don't want anyone thinking I'm sleeping with you," she said.

"People are going to think what they think, and I don't really give a shit." I tossed a fry into my mouth.

"You're a dick." Grabbing her tray, she pushed to her feet and headed to the garbage, her friend following suit. "Maybe I'll have the quarterback pick me up. Make a show of choosing a Barrington prick over you."

Or just make the Barrington prick look like a dumbass for thinking he had a loyal girl when she was, from the looks of it, screwing me. No matter how Monroe tried to spin it, it would be her and the quarterback who looked like idiots—not me. Monroe chucked her food—tray included—into the garbage can, then left the cafeteria.

Hendrix watched, shaking his head before stuffing

another roll in his mouth. "Harford? What a waste of some good tits."

It was past eleven that night when Wolf left my house to go home. Hendrix and I sat on the couch playing *Call of Duty*. After I kicked his ass three times, he chucked the controller to the carpet and went to bed, sulking like a toddler who had shit himself. I fell back onto the lumpy sofa, staring at the ceiling and listening to the constant hum of traffic that happened late at night in a neighborhood full of drug dealers and pimps. My phone flashed with a text.

LEAH: Can I come over?

Before I had typed out No, the little response bubbles danced over the screen.

LEAH: Max saw texts from you.
LEAH: He got mad and lost it.

If he had lost his shit over texts, it wasn't my texts, but hers. Half of the time, I didn't respond to her. The other half, I was a condescending asshole.

LEAH: Please let me come stay at yours.
ME: Have you ever slept in my bed?

The answer to that was no. Girls didn't sleep in my bed.

ME: That's not changing tonight
LEAH: I thought he was going to hit me.

I stared at that text. Max was a rich bastard. An entitled prick who was most likely raised by a set of entitled pricks. My mom had messed around with a few of the men from Barrington when I was little, and they had treated her like shit. Yelling and cussing, calling her names. Because as far as they were concerned, she was beneath them. I could see Max being just like those assholes, but then again, Leah was spoiled and manipulative. I wouldn't put it past her to lie about Max almost hitting her to try to gain some pity.

ME: Sounds like you have shit taste in guys
LEAH: Your an asshole.
ME: *you are

Then I sent a thumbs up and settled back, scrolling through my phone. I ran across the text to Monroe from the night when she didn't get my beer. And down the rabbit hole, I went.

I searched her name on social media. Nothing came up, but I found the weirdo's page. Amongst the Jack Skellington images and the Edgar Allen Poe quotes were a few pictures of her and Monroe. And they were both actually smiling, and damn, Monroe wasn't just hot when she smiled, she was downright beautiful.

I followed the tag in Jade's images, and the only photos on Monroe's account: a picture of a sunset over an interstate, and one of some mangy-looking orange tabby cat. The girl had two Instagram pictures that weren't even selfies. No way in hell she would fall for Max Harford, she seemed too good for that bullshit. Or maybe I just wanted to believe she was.

THE MORNING SUN streamed through the windows of Frank's Famous Chicken, the hole-in-the-wall fast food place that straddled the city limits of Dayton and Barrington. The place reeked of grease and Clorox, but their chicken biscuits were only a buck apiece.

Bellamy plucked a hash brown off of Wolf's trey. "Did you study for Weaver's test?" The asshole was looking at me, like I studied for anything.

"Is that a serious question?" I didn't bother to look up from my food.

"How the hell have you not failed yet?"

Because I had a good memory, and as long as I halfway listened when I pretended to sleep in class, I could do well enough to pass. "Hell if I know."

The bell over the door dinged. Hendrix let out a howl. "You gotta be kidding me." He nudged my side, jerking his chin in the direction of the group that had just walked in: Harford and a few of the other letterman-jacketed rich kids. "What the hell are they doing on this side of the tracks?"

From the way Harford and his dipshit friends glared across the restaurant at our table while they waited to order, I assumed it was to stir up a fight. If those Barrington dicks wanted to start one, I'd be more than happy to oblige.

Hendrix rubbed his palms together with a wide, sadistic grin reminiscent of The Joker's. "I bet one quick pop to his mouth," Hendrix threw a fast jab at the air, "and Richie Rich would be crying like a little bitch."

They gathered their trays and filed into a booth on the opposite side of Frank's. Two seconds later, three of the four were over at our table, staring down at us.

Max squared his shoulders, the guys surrounding him, puffing out their scrawny chests. "Hear you're trying to talk to my girl, Hunt?"

It wasn't just that he still wanted Leah when he knew she'd been jonesing for my dick that made me laugh, but top that with the fact that he thought he stood a chance against me in a fight—that was ridiculous.

I pushed to my feet, towering over him, and waiting for the chance to tackle him to the ground. "Leah doesn't do much talking when my dick's in her mouth."

His nostrils flared, a splotchy-red flooding his face. "Not Leah, dumbass. Monroe."

A shred of shock rippled through me, muscles going rigid. And Max must have seen it because his lips quirked. I balled my fist, ready to land a punch on his face, but froze when Jacobs and two other police officers strolled in. Jacobs stopped a few feet away, and Harford acknowledged the shithead with a wave.

The second Jacobs stepped out of earshot, Harford inched closer. I couldn't throw a punch with Jacobs' in here, and Harford knew it.

"Oh, what? Hurt your feelings that your white-trash slut wants a little taste of money?"

Anger rattled through me like a volcanic eruption, my fists begging to collide with the side of his face.

"The thing is, Hunt. She was completely worthless to me, just a way to get off. At least until I realized she was supposed to be yours. Now, every time you kiss her, you're sucking on my dick."

The word worthless played on a loop until my chest grew tight enough that I struggled for a decent breath.

"Don't do it, Zepp," Bellamy's voice broke through the enraged trance I was spiraling down. "Jacobs' will haul your ass outta here."

"I swear to God, Harford." Jaw tensed, I moved closer,

bringing our face centimeters apart. "Let me see you out in public, and I will kill you."

I caught the way he flinched, the flicker of worry that flashed through his eyes before he quickly masked it.

"Zepp..." There was a warning in Bellamy's tone. I took a step back, and Jacobs was watching.

Harford glanced around the table, snagging a hash brown from Hendrix's tray. "Fuck you, Hunt. And your trashy whore." Harford started off, and Hendrix kicked at his shin. Max tumbled forward, then face planted the grimy floor. On a growl, he shoved to his feet, dusting bits of food from his jeans.

Jacobs stepped between us. "There a problem here?" He looked at Max and the Barrington guys, ignoring us.

"No, sir. Just talking about the game in a few weeks."

Jacobs patted Max on the back. "With you playing, you guys have got the championship in the bag."

Max flashed us a fake-ass smile. "See you guys around." Then he and his crew went back to their table like the privileged little shits they were.

Jacobs shuffled a little closer to our booth, looping his thumbs through the belt loops on his uniform. "One screw-up from you kids, and I swear, I'll have you in juvie faster than you can wipe your poor ass." He gave a final glare to my brother before moving back to the counter and grabbing his order.

Wolf grabbed a piece of chicken and chucked it at Hendrix's forehead. "Just had to go stick your dick in the police officer's daughter, didn't you? You dick. Like we need any more heat on us."

Hendrix lobbed some ice back across the table. "Shut up, man. She had big titties."

They kept arguing, and my blood pressure continued to

spike. I had never wanted to throw my fist into someone's face as bad as I did Harford's, and the longer I sat in the same restaurant as him, the harder that urge was to ignore.

I was still pissed when we got to school. I didn't think I could let that little encounter with Harford slide. By the time I got into my first class, I was agitated enough that I needed a cigarette. I made it fifteen minutes into some dumb lecture about the Industrial Revolution before I got up to take a piss—and have a cigarette.

I rounded the corner to the bathroom, wading through the thick cloud of smoke filling the small room. Whatever cheap weed that guy was smoking smelled like shit. I unfastened my fly and stood at the urinal, shaking it off when the guy behind the closed stall door said, "Nice panties."

Smoking weed and fucking? Not a bad combination. I moved to the sink, then heard Monroe tell the guy to stop looking.

An unsettled feeling took root in my gut. Harford. Now some other dickhead at Dayton? Without thought, I kicked the door off its hinges, sending it crashing against the metal divider.

Monroe screamed, and I expected her to be bent over with some guy behind her, but she wasn't. Instead, she sat perched on the edge of the toilet seat, one leg crossed over the other, while she clutched her chest.

One of the football players stood, plastered against the other divider, joint in hand, his wide eyes glazed. "What the hell, Hunt?" He made a small step forward, and I tilted my head, inviting whatever he wanted to bring.

After that morning, I was ready for a brawl. But then, he froze, his bravery evidently short-lived.

"It's fine, Chase." Monroe stood, giving a dismissive wave toward the door. "Just go."

His gaze pinged between Monroe and me.

"He won't hurt me," Monroe assured him.

He stubbed out the joint on the divider wall, eyes locked on mine when he shifted past me.

"If you were hoping for a quickie, I'm good," she said.

The restroom door shut behind Chase, and I pressed Monroe against the divider until the metal corners creaked. Anger morphed to lust. A magic trick only her warm body against mine could pull off. "Seemed pretty into it yesterday."

"I'm a good performer."

As hard as her fake moans had me, I could only imagine what the real ones would do. "Oh, I bet you are." I traced my finger over the collar of the turtleneck she wore, moving my mouth closer to her neck. "You know what else I bet? That you're gonna look so good when I make you come."

She went tense.

"Three months," I said. I inched the neck of her sweater down. "Try not to give in to me." An ugly, green bruise peeked out from the collar of her shirt, and my stomach bottomed out. I yanked the fabric down farther, and she fought to tug it back up.

"Take your shirt off."

"No." Her jaw tightened. "I'm not screwing you."

But we both knew that wasn't why I wanted her shirt off. If I had to bet, there were more bruises on her. Leah's text popped to mind, followed by Max's smartass grin. I grabbed her sweater, so focused on her that I didn't catch her hand rear back until I felt the sting on my cheek. Gritting my teeth, I fisted the material and pressed my nose to hers. "Take. It. Off."

Her arms came over her chest. A hateful glare danced in

her eyes, but I could see something else underneath it she was fighting.

My blood boiled, sizzled, and popped through my veins like an angry hit of heroin. "Take off the goddamn shirt. Before I tear it off of you."

"Just leave it, Zepp." Her shoulders fell, like a little of the fight had left her.

Part of me knew I should leave it alone, that there were some parts of our lives meant to stay in the darkness, but I wanted to prove myself wrong. I wanted to find nothing underneath that shirt but pale skin. Balling the material in my fist, I slowly lifted it past her navel to her ribs, revealing a smattering of ugly, fading bruises. For a moment, all I could see was my mother. All I could hear were the lies she told to cover up the abuse. As shit as our lives were, this was the part of it I refused to accept.

"Who?" I said through gritted teeth. "The fucking Barrington quarterback?"

She tugged the sweater from my hand, hiding the marks from my view. "No. Just let it go." Her gaze met mine, hard and unreadable. "You know how this shit works. We're just surviving, right?" An undercurrent of defeat hid within her sarcastic tone. And the shittiest thing about that statement —she was right.

All of us here, we were only surviving, just trying to make it to the next day and possibly find a little bit of enjoyment from a quick high or a good fuck. Because a few seconds of bliss was honestly as good as it got for us.

With one breath, all trace of vulnerability disappeared, and in its place materialized something untouchable. A wry smile pulled at Monroe's lips, and she patted my cheek. "Don't go soft on me, Hunt," she said before slipping out of the stall.

For the rest of the afternoon, the image of her bruised body stayed at the forefront of my mind, the word survival playing on a loop. I sat in the back of Weaver's class, head down like always, but instead of sleeping, I was thinking. About her. About Max, and how I wanted to smash in his face.

By the time I had finished up with detention, I had pretty much plotted Harford's death. Wolf was in the parking lot, throwing his football gear into the bed of his truck when I came out of the school.

"What'd you have detention for?"

I pulled a cigarette from my pocket and lit it before fastening my backpack to my bike. "Smoking on campus."

"Lame." An engine revved on the highway, rock music blaring. I glanced over the deserted parking lot as an electric-blue, vintage Corvette Stingray barreled around the school's entrance. It fishtailed when it took a turn into the lot, then raced around to the side of the school.

"Who the hell has a car like that in Dayton?" Wolf asked.

"Nobody."

Monroe jogged out of the building to the passenger door of the Vette then climbed inside. The car sped past, slowing in front of us long enough for me to catch sight of Max Harford with his shit-eating grin before he peeled out onto the highway.

That was when I decided I would let that stupid rumor about Monroe and me spread; that I'd dump gasoline on it and set fire to it because if people thought she was mine, he wouldn't be able to touch her.

8

MONROE

Balancing my coffee in one hand, I dialed the combination for my locker and tugged it open. I was running on three hours of sleep after working last night, and I'd debated ditching this morning, but that wasn't going to get me out of that strip club or this shit town. I grabbed my books and rounded the corner, stepping straight into the path of a fight. A jock shoved some guy right into me, knocking me over and sending my books and coffee flying across the hall.

Glaring at him, I rolled to my feet. "Thanks, dickhead."

Zepp was like a predator; all the little birds stopped tittering when he was near. Maybe that was why I felt him before the guy's gaze slid past me, and the color drained from his face.

"Give her, her fucking books." The low growl came over my shoulder.

The guy nearly dropped to his knees to scoop up my belongings, dusting off the covers before handing them to me. I didn't need Zepp's help. I could fight my own battles.

When I turned around to shout at Zepp, he was halfway down the hall with Hendrix and Wolf.

Ever since I'd made that deal with him, my life had been nothing but upheaval. I didn't like his attention, and I definitely didn't enjoy the way my body threatened to betray me anytime he got a little too close. I couldn't deal with going to the cafeteria and playing our twisted little game. So instead, I marched outside to the parking lot, sat on the hood of my crappy car, and texted Jade.

A few minutes later, she snuck around the side of the building, then sprinted across the parking lot and hopped up beside me. "You okay?"

A cloud rolled across the sun, stealing the warmth for a moment. "Yeah, I just needed to get away from all... *that*." I waved a hand toward the school.

"You mean Zepp and Hendrix?" She laughed when I narrowed my eyes.

A few of the football players made their way out of the gymnasium, heading toward the football field, Chase in the middle. He glanced across the parking lot and shot me one of his charming smiles, then waved.

Jade leaned back against the windshield, a dreamy glaze to her eyes that almost made me embarrassed for her. "Chase is hot. Why haven't you ever dated him?"

I laughed. The idea of Chase and I being anything aside from strictly platonic was amusing. He might have been the popular guy now, but that boy had always been too nice for his own good. Football was the only thing that saved his ass from getting beaten.

"Chase isn't my type," I said.

"No one's your type."

That wasn't true. Zepp was exactly my type, and I

evidently had horrible taste in men because Chase was far less of an asshole.

"You sure you aren't lesbian?" she asked on a snort.

I rolled my eyes. "If I turn, you'll be the first one to know."

The breeze kicked up, and the clouds rolled away, allowing sunlight back through.

"Look, you're hot, but I don't want you." Jade exhaled on a laugh. "I also don't want to get beaten up by Zepp."

That cut all humor. "I hate him."

"He looks at you like he wants to bend you over something and go to town."

My cheeks heated when I glared at her, and she had the nerve to smile.

Jade pushed off the hood of my car. "And you look at him like you'd let him."

"I do not! You're supposed to be on my side."

"I am. Which is why I think you should bang him."

The girl was unbelievable. "You're insane, Jade." I slid off the car and started after her.

"Just saying. It wouldn't be the worst experience in the world."

"I am not fucking Zepp!"

She threw me a look that said she absolutely did not believe me, then thankfully changed the topic of conversation to gossip about one of the teachers who was screwing around with a student.

We walked around the track until the bell rang to change class, then we went back inside before parting ways. I hooked a right down one of the corridors, my steps faltering when I saw Zepp in the middle of the hallway, forcing students to pour around him. Tattooed arms folded over his chest as his gaze zeroed in on me like he'd been waiting for my arrival. The way he looked at me as he approached made my cheeks heat and my pulse hiccup. He threw his arm around my shoulders, the distinct smell of male that oozed from him almost suffocating me.

"I'll pick you up tonight at eight." Zepp threaded a tendril of my hair around his finger, smirking like the bastard he was. "Wear that red-plaid skirt of yours. And a white crop top."

The words grated over my nerves like sandpaper. "Do I look like your personal Barbie?"

"And a red-lace bra," he continued, his eyes on my chest. "If you don't have one, I'm sure I could find one somewhere around the house." A sly grin spread across his lip. "What are you? 34D?"

I folded my arms in front of me. "You should probably ask Leah. She'd appreciate dressing up like a fuck doll."

That didn't even get a reaction. Talking to Zepp was like talking to a brick wall. "And, of course, the boots." He glanced at my feet and raked his teeth over his lip on a subtle groan.

I left him there. I wouldn't wear any of that shit on pure principle.

"Eight o'clock, Roe," he called after me.

HEADLIGHTS OF CARS raced by on the highway, stirring the long grass that flanked the trailer-park entrance. The cool breeze whipped around me, making me shiver. The short shorts I had on were no better than the tiny skirt he'd demanded I wear, but for one, I wasn't bending to Zepp's whims, and two, at least my crotch was covered—and that could only be a good thing around him. I didn't trust him, but worse, I didn't know that I could fully trust myself.

A lone headlight appeared at the end of the road, barreling toward me before turning into the entrance. The bike rumbled to a stop beside me like an angry cat. Zepp glared through the visor of his helmet, making a blatant show of dragging his gaze over my bare legs when he pulled it off and handed it to me. "Forgot to wear the skirt?"

"Forgot. Sure. If that's what you need to tell yourself." I pulled on the helmet, then mounted the bike. The second my arms came around his waist, a disturbing sense of familiarity settled over me. He throttled the engine, and the bike shot off down the highway. My hold on his waist tightened, the hard muscle beneath my palm impossible to ignore. The heat of his body seeped through his jacket and into my chest. The smell that was all Zepp wrapping around me when he kicked up the speed.

We passed the abandoned oil factory and several blocks of project houses. Then he took a sharp left onto a dirt bike trail that led up the hill, through the trees, and over the rough ground. The trees gave way to a clearing at the edge of the dump. At least twenty pickup trucks had backed up in a loose circle around a large bonfire, their tailgates open with people sprawled out on them. Zepp parked his bike underneath one of the trees, and I hopped off when he killed the engine.

I removed the helmet and hung it on the handlebar of the bike, taking a quick survey of the shithole excuse of a party. "Why exactly are we here?"

He shoved a Ziploc bag in my hand. "Come back when that's gone."

I stared down at the bag of weed. Dealing drugs? That was why he'd brought me here? It wasn't like this was a bunch of goody-goodies, selling a little dope shouldn't be hard. So why did he need me? Headlights came through the tree line, busted subwoofers rattling before Wolf's truck sputtered to a stop beside us.

Hendrix climbed out, thumbing at his nose while Wolf and Bellamy rounded the back of the truck. "Showing your tits to get a sale is cheating."

God, he was an idiot.

"How much?" I asked Zepp.

"Ten a bag."

When I turned around, the kids closest to us were staring. Great, I officially looked like one of Zepp Hunt's minions.

It took less than an hour to get rid of the weed, and I managed to score a beer while doing it. I chucked the empty can into the fire, then headed through the crowd of Dayton outcasts. I rounded one of the pickups, stopping for a fleeting moment when I noticed Zepp on the rusted tailgate of a Chevy, a brunette in a short skirt straddling his lap. Her fingers combed through his dark, unruly hair while she rubbed her boobs against his chest. Something nasty jabbed at my gut, and I told myself I didn't give a shit.

God, he was so predictable. Here I was, earmarked like a leper because he had decided to stake a stupid claim on me. Yet there he was, carrying on like the whore he was.

Cutting back through the party, I beelined for the truck with the beer keg in the bed. A group of football players lingered at the back. Chase sat on one of the lawn chairs beside it, talking to a girl.

Dale Davison put a beer bottle to his lips and slowly took a swig before speaking. "You finally gonna suck my dick, Monroe?" A few of his friends laughed.

Comments like that were a daily occurrence, and I'd

have thought, with the number of times I'd told Dale to fuck off, he would have given up trying.

Chase rose to his feet and gave Dale a hard shove. "Shut up, Davison." He grabbed a cup from beside the keg and glanced over his shoulder at me. "You want a beer, Moe?"

"Sure. Thanks."

The girl Chase had been talking to looked me up and down with a glare. Like I was competition. "Aren't you dating Zeppelin Hunt?" she asked, a bitter tone to her voice. She glanced from me to Chase, then back, a cunning smile to her lips, like she thought slipping that snippet of information would be enough to make him shun me.

"No, I'm not."

"Moe wouldn't date that prick." Chase came to my defense.

The girl turned and walked off in a huff.

"Sorry," I said.

Chase poured a beer, foam spilling over the top as he handed a cup to me. "Don't worry about it. Not my type."

We moved closer to the fire. Chase and I weren't super close these days, but we'd been friends since forever, and he was the only person I wanted to hang out with here.

"I never see you at these things," he said, nudging my shoulder with his.

"I never come to these things." Socializing wasn't on the top of my priority list, especially not with these people.

A small frown set on his face. "I let you braid my hair when we were six, and you won't come to a party with me. But Zepp Hunt..."

"It's not like that."

"So what? You're dealing weed for him now?"

I didn't like the accusation in his voice, but I chose not to answer. I couldn't exactly deny it, but I wasn't about to explain the deal I'd made either.

"*Are* you dating him?" His narrowed gaze drifted beyond the flames of the fire, and I followed it to where Zepp was still on the tailgate, a beer bottle in hand, and the same girl now shamelessly grinding on him. But his attention wasn't on her or her short skirt. It was pinging between Chase and me.

I sucked in an annoyed breath, my fingers tightening around the plastic cup in my hand. "I already said I'm not."

"Seemed like it in the bathroom the other day. And he's looking at you like you are."

"Well. I'm not," I said, shooting an angry middle finger at Zepp.

Chase's face said he didn't believe me, and it pissed me off. If one of the few people who actually knew me didn't realize that I had higher standards than to date that prick, I was pretty much screwed. I tipped back my beer, downing it in several gulps.

"Sorry I left you with him the other day. I wasn't sure..." Chase drifted off, guilt washing his features.

"It's fine, Chase. I told you to go. It's not like he's gonna hurt me." There wasn't much I was sure of, but I, at least, knew that.

"You should be careful with them, Moe." He rubbed a hand over the back of his neck. "They don't play."

"I know. It's fine." I glanced down into my empty cup, and Chase took it from my hand. He strode to the keg, fiddling with the pump.

A loud pop erupted from the bonfire, and I moved closer, loving the red-hot heat on my face. That's when I spotted Zepp walking toward me like a rolling storm. Each step angry and deliberate. A bottle of liquor swung at his side.

Tension wound through my gut, my muscles tensing. Chase appeared next to me, handing me my drink, seemingly unaware of the disaster heading our direction. I instantly downed the beer because Zepp was only a few steps away.

He looked at me like I was a running back that he was about to tackle to the ground.

"Don't you dare—"

Thick arms came around my waist, and Zepp tossed me over his shoulder. I dropped the cup and pounded my fists against his back, but it didn't make him stop. He continued across the dump to the tree line.

He set me down, pinning me against the rough trunk of a pine. His nose was inches from mine. "You're not here to flirt." He took a hefty swig from the bottle, his gaze laser-focused on me.

Rolling my eyes, I fished two hundred dollars out of my bra and slapped it in his hand. "There's your damn drug money."

He crammed it into his back pocket while invading every inch of my space. "You didn't wear what I told you to."

I thought we had already been over that. I leaned in until my lips were almost against his when I whispered, "I don't belong to you, Zepp. I'll wear whatever the hell I want."

The subsequent laugh that came from him pissed me off. Everything about him pissed me off—including the girl who was just in his lap. And the fact that it bothered me irritated me more than he ever could directly.

I pressed closer to him, my anger ready to bubble over. "And I'll tell you one thing," I said. "Keep this shit up, and

I'm going to make your life really hard." I patted his cheek a little harder than necessary. "Baby." Before I could take another breath, he had me caged against the tree. His proximity made me weak in ways I would never admit.

The leather of his jacket creaked as he inched toward me. "You already do." With one swift movement, he grabbed my wrist and placed my hand against his hard crotch, then offered a full-on, bad-boy smirk. "*Baby.*"

Like an eclipsed sun, he blocked out everything that wasn't him until even my cold heart beat a little faster, pining for the very thing I hated. And that hate was always a tentative, fine line. The more he annoyed me, the more this thing between us crackled to life, whispering sordid promises into my ear.

In the dark, his eyes seemed like a bottomless abyss, one that I found myself tiptoeing the edge of.

"I'm trying to decide where I'll fuck you first." His whiskey-laced breath fanned across my lips, causing heat to unravel in my stomach. "On the hood of your boyfriend's shiny car or one I steal."

His words trickled over my senses like warm liquid. I should have pushed him off or walked away. Anything —*anything* but played his game. Yet, I craved this dangerous dance between us. And alcohol made me brave.

"You gonna steal something pretty just for me?" I snaked my hand over his hard chest, then lower. The whiskey in his hand dropped to the leaves with a muffled thud. When I tilted my chin back, Zepp looked at me like he was about to snap. "Because that Vette really does it for me," I whispered.

He fisted my hair, dragging my head to the side and placing his lips by my ear. "I bet he doesn't even make you come." The deep rasp of his voice pulled at something in me.

"What if he's better than you?"

An arrogant smirk crept across his face, before his hand skimmed up the back of my thigh, fingertips teasing the hem of my shorts. My breath caught as heat shot across my skin. Part of me wanted to know what it felt like to be desecrated by Zeppelin Hunt. But the bigger part refused to be another notch on his metaphorical bedpost—no matter how hot he was, or how much beer I'd drunk.

"I'm not Leah Anderson." I grabbed his wrist and tugged his hand away. "You'll have to work a little harder than that to get into my pants."

"I really don't think I will." His nose skimmed along the side of my throat, warm breath heating me in places I wish it didn't. The arrogant dick. "And I would be willing to bet, you go home tonight and play with yourself, thinking about my lips on your pussy."

I was fast being pushed out of my depth here. Zepp was well-practiced at this, and my body hadn't gotten the memo that I didn't like him.

Someone staggered to the tree line a few feet from us, choking and coughing before the scent of vomit reached me, causing me to gag. I was grateful for the interruption, though.

Zepp snatched the bottle from the ground, twisting off the top and taking a sip before he passed it to me. I didn't even like whiskey, but he had me so wound up, I didn't give it a second thought. I pressed the bottle to my lips and took a hefty swig while I let Zepp Hunt lead me from the shadows and back to the party like he owned me.

Fighting him was pointless. He always won because I'd sold my soul.

For three whole months.

For a shitty car.

9

ZEPP

Never in my life had I met the challenge I had in Monroe. I glanced around the party, unable to ignore the stares of several girls. It would be easy enough for me to bang my frustrations out with someone else. But unless it was Monroe in my bed, at this point, my ego wouldn't like it.

For the last half hour, I had sat on Wolf's tailgate with her, neither of us saying a word.

She snagged the bottle from my hand, draining it of the last drop before it hit the ground with a thud.

"I swear, Roe. If you throw up..."

Flipping me off, she hopped down from the tailgate and headed toward the bonfire. A shitty pop song blasted through the speakers, and she tossed her hands up and moved in beat with the bass. God, she had to be shitfaced if she was dancing. She lasted all of two minutes before some guy moved behind her, eyes on her ass.

Like hell I was letting him dance with her.

I jumped off the tailgate and shouldered my way through the people dancing, slipping right between him and Monroe. One stern look from me and the pussy retreated, his tail tucked like a stray dog.

I gripped her waist, leaning down beside her ear and inhaling the scent of the bonfire mixed with her sweat. "If your clothes were off, this would be a hundred times better."

Her nails raked across the back of my neck as she pulled me closer. "Right here?" Her ass pressed against me when she circled her hips. "In the middle of a party?"

"Why not?" My fingers tightened on her sides, my dick drawn to her like a magnet. "I would make it worth your while, Roe." I pressed my lips to her throat in a kiss. "I really would."

"I don't doubt it." She pushed against me again, the friction enough to force a little bit of pre-come to the tip of my dick. I was so into dry humping her that I didn't notice Bellamy skirt by me until he slapped my shoulder. "We sold out," he said. "Let's roll."

Reluctantly, I let go of Monroe and started toward the truck. I made it to the pickup, only noticing Monroe wasn't with us when I opened the door. I grabbed Bellamy's arm when he went to climb in the back and nodded toward the fire. "Go get her."

His brow wrinkled. "You go get her; she's your girl."

"The hell she is."

A small smile pulled at his lips. "So, she's fair game?"

My fist balled.

"Yeah," he laughed. "What I thought."

I shoved him. "Go get her before we leave your ass."

"Yeah, dude," Wolf shouted from the front, cranking the engine then laying on the horn.

With a laugh, Bellamy started across the field. The best thing that could happen right now was for us to drop her at home and me to spend a few minutes with a bottle of lotion, jerking her out of my system. I stood by the truck, watching Bellamy try to wrangle Monroe. She swatted at him, flipped him off, then staggered a few steps. When he tried to help her, she punched him in the arm. I almost laughed when I jumped over the side of the truck. She was feral, that was for sure. When they headed toward the truck, I climbed into the passenger seat.

"Where's my brother?" I asked Wolf.

"Said he had a ride." He checked the rearview mirror and chuckled. "She's like an angry chihuahua."

"She's a pain in the ass." Or a pain in the cock. Whatever worked.

The back door opened, and Monroe shouted at Bellamy before he shoved her into the cramped extended cab. "Jesus Christ. Do you ever stop talking?" Bellamy exhaled before climbing in behind her and slamming the door. And... Drunk Monroe kept bitching.

Wolf glanced at me, and I jerked my chin toward the back seat.

"Just drop her at the entrance of the park, Wolf."

"No." Her hand landed on my shoulder. Tangled hair covered her face when she leaned between the front seats. "I can't go home drunk. Take me to Jade's."

Wolf shot a glance at me as he put the gear in reverse. "How 'bout we leave her here?"

I shrugged. "Where's the weirdo's house?"

"By the cemetery?" Wolf chuckled.

Jade did look like the kind of kid who would hang out by tombstones, lighting candles, and call a séance or some crap. Wolf threw it into drive. Leaves crunched under the tires, and the car bounced over ruts.

"It's near...here." Monroe huffed.

I glanced at her in the rearview. "You don't know where she lives. Do you?"

"Of course I do."

"Well, figure it out, or we're dropping you at the trailer park." I wasn't taking her back to my house, and we weren't going to drive around for an eternity trying to find her friend's house.

The headlights moved over the trees. Wolf slammed on the brakes and pointed through the dirty windshield on a cackle. "Look at your brother, dude." The lights were shining right on Hendrix going at some girl he had bent over in the woods. Wolf lowered his window, then leaned out and shouted, "Get it, dude. Get angry at that pussy!" He tapped his horn a few times before pressing the gas.

Hendrix swung a victorious arm in the air, then smacked the girl's ass. No dignity whatsoever. Everyone in the truck laughed—except, of course, Monroe.

When Wolf finally pulled over in front of the trailer park, Monroe was snoring. The truck idled on the shoulder of the road.

Wolf glanced from Monroe's passed-out ass to me. "You gonna carry her?" I knew nothing about Monroe. For all I knew, I could cart her drunk ass up to her trailer and some beer-bellied man would stagger out onto the makeshift porch, toting a shotgun.

"Hell no." I glanced back at her, head resting against the window. "Just take her to my house."

Wolf kicked the car around, and we headed back down the deserted stretch of highway. "How about we drop her at Harford's?" Bellamy said from the back, and my jaw ticced a little. "Bet he'd love that shit."

"I'm not a pussy delivery service." A small flare of anger

ignited inside me. Sure, it would be a slap in the face to the prick if I dropped her on his stoop. Most likely give me the chance to give him the beating of his life for laying his hands on her. But I sure as shit wouldn't put her in that situation.

The truck sputtered through the slums, weaving between the beat-up cars parked along the side of the street until the headlights landed on my sagging front porch, and we all climbed out—except Monroe.

I banged my fist over the back-passenger window. "Wake the hell up, Monroe. I'm not carrying you."

She pushed up, swiping hair from her face with a confused look. She stumbled onto the driveway; her expression scrunched when she glanced at my rundown house. "Why are we here?"

"You said you wanted to sleep with Zepp." Wolf shrugged a shoulder, and Monroe shot him a death glare.

"Bullshit."

I didn't have the patience to listen to her crap, so I started up the path and unlocked the door while she argued with Wolf. Man, did he have her wound up by the time she staggered inside the house.

"I would rather screw...Hendrix," she slurred. "Wait, no. He's disgusting. You, Wolf." Her shoulder banged into the doorway, and then she stopped to glare at me like I had something to do with it. "You're a dick."

She headed toward the living room, but I caught her by the elbow and redirected her toward the stairs. God knew what state Hendrix would be in when he got home, and I could only imagine the fight that would break out if he attempted to harass her. And he would. On top of that, I wanted to see the look on her face in the morning when she woke up. In my bed. Most likely with little recollection of how she got there. Cruel? Of course it was, but *that* would be priceless.

Monroe missed a few steps, nearly eating the carpet several times before we made it to the top. "Wait." She stopped outside my bedroom, face scrunched and arms crossed in typical Monroe eat-shit-fashion. "Where are you taking me?"

"To bed."

Her brows hitched. "I'm not getting in your bed."

"What? Don't want to tell the quarterback prince you slept with me?"

She opened her mouth to argue, but the ratty thread of patience I had left snapped. I tossed her over my shoulder and carted her into my room, throwing her onto the bed like a ragdoll. She boomeranged right back up, glaring at me while I stripped down to my boxers.

"I'm not having—" Her gaze dropped to my chest, then lower—"sex with you."

"I don't have sex, Monroe." I leaned over, gripping the edge of the mattress while I inched close to her reddening face. "I fuck."

The springs creaked when she pushed to her feet and brushed past me. I dropped to the bed when her shirt came off, and I thought, finally we were getting somewhere. My gaze skirted over her back, stopping on the thin strap of her red lace bra, and I knew we were getting somewhere. Of all the things I'd asked her to wear, she had chosen that. "Red lace bra, huh?"

"Red lace bra," she said in a mocking tone, then gave the clasp a swift flick. Her bra was on the floor. She was nothing but bare back and fishnets and a pair of tiny shorts. My dick hardened while I tried to decide where I would start with her, rough or soft. One glance at those combat boots, and I settled on rough. But then, she put her shirt back on and kicked off her boots.

My brain short-circuited, sparking for a few seconds until she slipped between the sheets on a huff, then flipped onto her side to face me. This was not how these things went...

She aimed her probing gaze at me like she thought, maybe, if she studied me hard enough, she would find something. Monroe could stare as long as she wanted; there was nothing to peel back. Nothing inside. What she saw was what she got.

"You know," she finally slurred, patting my cheek. "You'd be pretty if you weren't such an ass."

I snorted. That was her grand revelation. Like looks had anything to do with personality.

Seconds ticked by before she rolled onto her back, body all stiff like a corpse. "This was your plan all along. Get me into your bed." She waved her hand around for a second. "I like your light."

I glanced at the faded, hula girl lampshade, remembering when I had begged my mom to buy it for me from the thrift store when I was eight. Three bucks she didn't have but bought it for me anyway. Total kill switch to the mood.

"Your house is nice," she said.

"My house is shit."

Monroe lifted a finger, jabbing the air. "But it *is* a house." She sounded like Jack Sparrow, Jesus Christ.

"Yeah."

I tried to ignore the fact that she was beside me. This entire thing was weird. She was shitfaced. And not naked. And in my bed. I just wanted to go to sleep and pretend that I didn't have a girl in my bed that I wasn't going to screw.

But she flopped over toward me, then poked me. "Can I ask you something?"

"No."

"Why are you such a dick? Or do you just want people to think that? Because you know, it's a whole lot of dick...ness."

I grabbed the pillow, curling it around my head. I should have left her ass downstairs. I could not deal with drunk girl ramblings. "Don't you need to throw up or something by now?"

"Nope. Just laying here. With your dickness."

The noise from Hendrix's TV drifted beneath the door, filling the silence. For a second, I thought she'd passed out, but then the mattress bounced. Springs creaked when she sat up abruptly and scooted to the edge of the bed. She wriggled out of her shorts, then the fishnets. Thanks to the streetlight's electric haze coming in through my window, I could just make out how great her ass looked in a thong before she fell back beside me.

Switch flipped back to game on.

"Don't even think about it," she said, like she could read the thoughts running amuck in my mind. "I'm hot."

The number of times I had heard shit like that from girls. Ten seconds later, they were touching me, teasing me. Grabbing my dick. I was screwing Monroe tonight, she knew it. And now, I knew it. Like those little shorts made a difference in how hot she was. Yeah, right.

Fighting the smirk, I rubbed a hand down my stomach, over my hardening dick. Any second now...

"I'm *not* fucking you." She poked two fingers against my chest, then shoved at me.

I felt my brow furrow. This was not how this shit usually went. It was the "I'm hot". I'm not like this. Followed by a kiss and them getting naked, shoving my dick down their throats while repeating how unlike "this" they were.

"Oh my God. You really thought I would, didn't you?" She laughed.

I fisted my cock, then turned on the pillow to glare at her through the dark. "You're the one half-naked in my bed."

"Oh, yeah. Please. Zepp." The condescending, monotone pitch to her voice grated at my nerves. "Screw my brains out." She rolled away, laughing. "I don't understand how you ever get laid."

It shouldn't have bothered me. She was one girl out of a million—and I guessed, maybe that was why it did bother me. She was the girl who had managed to catch my attention and the only one who didn't want it. "I think you do," I said.

"What? They don't care that you're a dick?"

"They aren't exactly here for my personality." I shifted closer, my dick pressing against her thigh when I went to nip at her ear, and I didn't miss the way her breath hitched a little. "Are they, Roe?"

Her palm met my chest, her brows tugging together. "That's kinda sad," she whispered, then shoved me back.

My jaw tensed. That was a dose of reality I hadn't asked for. Especially from her drunk ass, but I refused to give her the satisfaction. "Says the girl hung up on a Barrington piece of shit." I held her gaze, waiting for something to break. But it never did.

"Do you just want him to be a piece of shit? Because he's rich?"

She thought I was jealous of the little shit? "Fuck you, Monroe." I shoved away, settling onto my pillow and staring at the wall.

Maybe she was into the materialistic bullshit, the idol

worship of Barrington and their money. Their money didn't make them any different than the assholes in Dayton; it just gave them different problems. Maybe she didn't have any depth after all.

The silence of the ghetto filled the room. "He's actually not bad," she said.

I waited. Jaw tensed, blood pressure ticking up second by second. She thought he was a good guy, and he thought she was a worthless whore. One he could hit.

"Are you really going to do that, Monroe? You really going to defend him?" My mom always defended those assholes because of what their money could do for us if she could only tie one down. I wanted Monroe to be better than that.

"You don't know him." She huffed and rolled over. And that was often the excuse my mother gave: *You don't know him.*

Silence engulfed us, but it did little to settle the anger rumbling underneath my skin. I'd seen the damn bruises. I didn't need to know him.

I WOKE to someone banging a fist on my door.

"If that's the quarterback, give him my regards." I swatted an arm out, but my hand met empty sheets. Another series of loud bangs rattled up the stairwell. "Wake up, assholes!" Bellamy's voice came through the window beside my bed. "We've got a problem!"

"Shit." I threw the covers off, grabbing my jeans, and stepping into them on my way to the stairs.

Bellamy continued to beat on the door. I was ready to punch him by the time I opened it.

"You don't know how to answer a phone?" He paced the entranceway, elbows out, hands cupped behind his head before he shot off to the kitchen. "We gotta get the weed outta here."

"What the hell are you talking about?"

"Jacobs and the rest of the task force are heading this way. Heard it on Dad's scanner."

I shouted for Hendrix, and nearly busted my ass getting into the kitchen. I opened cabinets, raking out baggies of weed. Bellamy grabbed a garbage bag and yanked out drawers, dumping the contents inside. With each gram I tossed, my pulse ticked up. In a city riddled with meth and heroin dealers, kids peddling weed at parties should have been the least of Dayton's task force's concern. "They don't have any reason to raid us," I said, slamming one cabinet door and going to the next.

"Some Barrington kid got pulled over last night." Bellamy chucked a pipe into the trash. "Said the weed he had on him came from us."

"They can't prove that!"

He made a knot in the garbage bag, scowling. "They can if they come raid your house."

After a frenzied ten minutes, we had the house cleaned out. Not a trace of weed. Not a single pipe. Not even a roach. Bellamy took the Hefty bag of weed and paraphernalia with him when he left. And then Hendrix and I waited for the raid.

Red and blue lights flashed through the window. Brakes screeched. Doors slammed. "

Here we go," I said, heading to the door just before a hard knock came from the other side. "Police. Open up."

I knew there wasn't anything in the house, but still, the idea had a cold shot of panic rushing through my veins. I opened the door, locking eyes with Jacobs. "What do you want?"

His lips set in a hard line. When he moved past me, his shoulder knocked against mine hard enough to push me back a step. Other officers filed in, their boots clomping over the floor while they spread out. They tore off the couch cushions. Ripped up heating vents. Pots and pans clattered in the kitchen, followed by the sound of glasses shattering. They tore apart the house. An hour later, all they had found was a crumpled beer can behind the stove.

The cops moved out, all except Jacobs. He stopped by the door, his gaze shifting between my brother and me. I shot him a smug grin. Dick, thinking he could arrest me.

"I know you're both little shits," he said, hand on the open door. "And that redhead of yours," a sick grin set on his face "they'll cut her pretty face up with razor blades in juvie."

"Get the fuck outta my house." I raised my hands to shove him, and Hendrix's hand clamped onto my shoulder.

That beer can he found wouldn't send me to jail, but assaulting a police officer definitely could. And that's all Jacobs wanted. He moved onto the porch, and I slammed the door.

That was the initial stirrings of a shitstorm. I could feel it.

"Where did Monroe go?" Hendrix asked.

"Hell if I know."

Wolf grabbed a book from his locker, then slammed the door shut. "Do we know who the snitch is?"

"Not yet," I said. The temptation to drive over to

Barrington and douse half the yards in gasoline, setting fire to the lots had definitely been there. But that would have been stupid as hell.

Hendrix started down the hallway beside me. "I swear to God, that snitch is getting stitches when I find out who he is."

Wolf chuckled before him and Hendrix ducked into class. I was almost to the gymnasium when I spotted Monroe. Her steps quickened when I approached her. She tried to dart past me, but I hooked my arm around her shoulders. "I need you to come over Thursday."

"I can't. I'm busy." She tried to slip out of my hold, and I tugged her a little closer to me.

"Cancel it."

"Can we not do this now?" She turned her face away.

Something was off with her. I took her chin, forcing her to look at me. The scabbed-over split on her bottom lip was impossible to ignore. That son of a bitch had smacked her for staying over at my house. Evidently, the quarterback had a death wish. One I'd be happy to grant. My temper spiked, the pressure building like flammable vapors in a tank. The tardy bell rang, followed by the bang of lockers and a flurry of students rushing to class.

For once, I didn't want a scene, so I dragged her into an alcove by the water fountain. "Your little piece of shit boyfriend..." I imagined him hitting her, calling her worthless, the same way those rich bastards had done to my mom, and my vision went out of focus. "I'm going to break his legs, and he can kiss his scholarship goodbye."

"It's not Max." Panic laced her voice.

I leaned in close to Monroe's ear. "I will kill him, Roe." And with that, I shoved away, slamming my fist against the wall on my way around the corner.

10

MONROE

My week was going just great. Jerry and I had gotten into a fight on Saturday, which earned me a split lip. My shit box car wouldn't start. Again. Which meant Jade had to drop me at Max's house. And then there was Zepp...

I will kill him, Roe. The words rang around my head for what felt like the hundredth time as I sat in Max's huge kitchen. I'd screwed up. I never said I was dating Max, but I had let Zepp assume.

Well, assumption was the mother of all screw ups, because now Zepp wanted Max dead.

I could have just told him the truth, but the last thing I needed was Zepp thinking he could take Jerry because the simple fact was, he probably couldn't. High school kids were one thing. A dirty meth dealer was another entirely. Truthfully, I didn't want Jerry to hurt Zepp, and that was why I'd kept my mouth shut, inadvertently creating a different problem. At the root of it, I knew Zepp only gave a crap because Max was from Barrington.

"So, I just need to divide it again?" Max asked, snapping

my attention across the marble breakfast bar. His brows pulled together as he stared at the textbook in front of him.

"Yeah." I moved around the counter and turned the page.

"Why does anyone need to know about algebra?"

"Who knows? But you need to for that A." The little pep in my voice made me cringe. Max was paying me. I felt like I owed it to him to try to be nice, like a normal person.

"I just want to play football."

I envied the fact that his life was so easy, that he had room to have passion for something so trivial. After we had finished going over quadratic equations, I shoved my books into my ragged backpack. "Just keep practicing. You'll get it."

"Doubtful," he said on a snort. Max led me into the hotel-standard foyer, then opened the door. Light from inside cut across the manicured lawn. "Hey." He grabbed my wrist before I reached the first step, but quickly dropped it when I gave him a sharp look. "I know I already asked, but you really should come to my party this weekend."

I could not imagine anything worse than a Barrington party. "Uh, thanks. But I'm busy."

"I get it. Hunt wouldn't like it." A small smirk pulled at his lips. "Huh?"

"I'm not dating Zepp." I felt like I had to defend myself.

"Good. He's scum."

I didn't know what to say to that.

"Come on; it'll be fun." He swept a tendril of hair from my face, making me uncomfortable. "Bring a friend if you want."

I was annoyed at the mention of Zepp, and I wanted off Max's porch. "Maybe." I backed toward the step. "I'll let you know."

With a smug smile, he closed the door. I stared at my

phone on my way down the stairs, typing out a text to Jade to let her know I was ready to be picked up. It was only when I reached the end of the long drive that I looked up, and my steps faltered. The lights on either side of the Harford's gates reflected off the shiny, black paint of a motorcycle. A figure separated from the shadows. He took a puff from his cigarette, the bright end glowing before he dropped it. Embers skittered over the pavement.

I froze. A list of questions flipped through my mind: How did he know I was here? How did he know where Max lived? Why was he here?

"I told you I was gonna kill him." A wild flicker of rage burned in his eyes when he started across the lawn.

I ran after him, placing myself in his path, then slamming both palms against his chest. Like that did any good.

"Get outta the way, Monroe."

"Zepp. Stop!"

For a split second, he stilled. But then his gaze shot over my shoulder to Max's house. He jabbed an angry finger in the air, mumbling, "you motherfucker." I turned. Max was at the window, his judgmental stare fixed on us.

That was enough.

Zepp took determined strides toward the front, like a total psycho. I guessed this was what everyone was so scared of, the side of him that had earned him his reputation.

I ran past him, taking the first two steps and blocking his path. "It's not him."

"Move," he grunted.

I grabbed his face and forced him to look at me.

His eyes were a churning pit of chaos, demons dancing around a fire within their black depths. "I swear to God, Monroe..."

"I'm not dating Max!"

He glanced back to the window, his face boiling red. "You think it's funny, you little bitch? I will take your guts and hang them over the freeway." He rounded me and pounded his fist over the wooden door.

"You really think Max Harford could hit me?"

The only guy who had ever managed to lay a hand on me more than once was Jerry because he was built like a linebacker, and he was a piece of work.

Zepp slowly faced me, veins bulging in his neck. "It's not whether he could, it's whether you would let him."

"Oh, fuck you, Zepp!" I descended the steps.

He could bang on Max's door the rest of the night for all I cared and get himself arrested.

"He's not my boyfriend. I just let you think that." I started down the sidewalk. "And he definitely hasn't hit me."

"So what? You're just fucking him?"

My jaw clenched, teeth grinding over each other. I could have just told Zepp the truth, but pride reared its ugly head. And that little thing inside me that refused to back down stamped its feet like an angry toddler. "What if I am?" I said, turning and walking backward. "Pissed off that it's him and not you?"

That got him. Good. Zepp stormed down the steps, nostrils flaring. He latched onto my jaw, and his hot, angry breaths rushed across my face. His temper should have scared me—that would have been rational. But for reasons I couldn't explain, I felt safe with Zepp, and I might have been the only person in this town who could say that.

"I don't give a shit about anything but who hits you."

Something twisted in my chest. "Then why ask if I'm screwing him?"

His hand dropped to his side, then swept through his hair as he took a step back. There were seconds, minutes, eternities before he spoke. "Because a guy like that doesn't deserve your fucking time."

The tension fizzled between us like one of the fireworks that never quite exploded as he walked down the drive. My anger petered out, and on a sigh, I followed him to his bike.

"I'm offended you think I'd screw a private school quarterback. And just so you know, I've never *let* anyone hit me in my life," I said. I hated the way his expression morphed from rage to pity. "Don't you dare look at me like that." I jabbed a finger at him.

We stared at each other. The distant whine of cop sirens trickled through the night. The Harfords had probably called the police—I wouldn't blame them. Something foreign passed between us, making my chest tighten.

"And just so *you* know, Roe," he tossed the helmet to me, and I caught it against my stomach. "I won't *let* anyone hit you, either." There was no missing the threat in his voice.

His display should have pissed me off, but the sad fact was, no one had ever cared enough about me to get so angry. No one in my life had ever been willing to fight for me. And the look in Zepp's eyes when he thought Max was hurting me—he was willing to kill.

The motorcycle rumbled to life, and I slipped on the helmet, then straddled the back of his bike, wrapping my arms around his waist. I absorbed the warmth that I shouldn't have craved so suddenly, but Zepp gave a shit. And that complicated things.

HE PULLED up outside Wolf's place then cut the engine.

"Thanks," I said, getting off the bike and handing him the helmet. I headed toward my trailer.

"Want a beer?"

When I turned around, he was already on Wolf's deck, propping a rickety ladder against the side of the doublewide. I could have gone home and probably should have, but I couldn't deny the little pull I felt toward him at that moment. A beer couldn't hurt. Right? He scaled the rungs like a nimble cat, disappearing over the roof. With a groan, I climbed up after him.

There were two ratty, nylon deck chairs secured to the shingles, along with a wooden cubby that housed a mini-fridge. From up here, I could see most of the trailer park, and the lights of the passing cars and big rigs on the highway. To see it all like this was kind of depressing. This was all there was.

He took two beers from the fridge, tossing one to me before he folded his massive frame into one of the chairs. "If you're not sucking Harford's dick, what were you doing at his house?"

"I tutor him," I confessed, sinking down beside him.

"You?" He snorted. "Tutor?" He threw his head back against the lawn chair on a hard laugh.

Asshole. People made quick-fire judgments about me all the time. They saw me as white trash in a short skirt. No prospects. Certainly, no brains. I was used to it, hell, I encouraged it, so why did it bother me that he saw me the same way?

"Is that so hard to believe? You thought I was dating him!"

His gaze dragged over me, slow. The subtle rake of teeth over his lip drew my attention, triggering the hazy memory of this mouth on my neck Friday night. A flash of heat stung my cheeks.

"Tell anyone, and I'll kill you."

He snorted. "Okay."

The silence stretched between us, the distant hum of the highway permeated only by the buzz of cicadas. I had to wonder why he cared enough that he'd turn up at Max's house. He was so desperate for Max to be the bad guy.

"Why do you hate Max so much?"

He stared across the trailer park. In the distance, I could just make out the twinkling lights of Barrington. "Those assholes get every opportunity."

I shrugged. "That's just the way the world works."

"They think they're better, but meanwhile their moms are popping Vicodin, chasing it with champagne, and their daddies are jerking their dicks at the strip clubs." He chugged his beer. "They're no better than us."

His comment hit a little too close to home. How many times had I danced for those kinds of guys?

"Preaching to the choir," I mumbled, before tipping up my beer. Zepp was right, we had zero opportunities, and that made a hard life even harder.

Silence fell over us like a comfortable blanket for a few minutes. I took in the strong set of Zepp's jaw, his lips, a brow that seemed permanently crumpled with the weight of the world, and my heart tripped a little. There was a savagery to him that most feared, down to the way he looked. Zepp Hunt was an animal because he had to be. But I wasn't so sure he was as awful as everyone thought.

One of the neighbors started yelling, breaking me from my thoughts.

"How did you know where Max lives?"

He took a sip of beer. "Until you decide to tell me who hits you, I'm not telling you."

My temper prickled beneath my skin.

"I'm *working* for you for three months, Zepp. That's it.

You don't get to dictate my life." I glared at him. "I can handle myself." I didn't need a white knight or a savior. This was not a fairytale. I was no damsel, and Zeppelin Hunt was certainly no prince.

He leaned over his lawn chair and grabbed the arm of mine, invading my space. The scent of beer danced on his breath, caressing my face. "For the next three months, I *can* dictate it," he said. "And I will."

Back and forth we went, and every time I thought he might just be okay, he made me hate him again. Carved from stone, Zepp was hard, implacable. An asshole most of the time, but he had fought for me when he thought Max was hurting me. And that meant something because no one had ever cared before. Under the weight of that sad realization, my temper snuffed out.

"Thank you," I said before I pushed to my feet and descended the ladder.

I still didn't like him, and he was still a dick, but perhaps he was less of a dick than I had thought.

11

ZEPP

I sat in calculus, drawing a picture, trying to take my mind off her. I didn't know jack shit about Monroe, and yet, the idea of her cost me sleep and my sanity. By the time the bell rang, the page was covered with a half-finished sketch of a forest filled with demons. A girl from the back of class stopped beside my desk. "That's good," she said.

I slammed the notebook closed, got out of my seat, and headed to the cafeteria to meet up with the guys.

Spaghetti splattered up from the tray when I dropped it to the table beside Monroe. She tensed, stopping mid-sentence as the rest of the guys took seats around her and Jade.

"Come on, Monroe." Jade stabbed at the carrot on her plate. "I even have a dress for tomorrow. It'll be fun to go to a party."

Hendrix cocked a brow. "What kind of dress? Like one of those sacrificial gowns people wear to slaughter goats and shit?"

My gaze fixed on Monroe, but she wouldn't look at me.

"Whose party, Roe?" I twirled the watery noodles around the prongs of my fork before cramming it into my mouth.

"No one's."

I looked at Jade, and she froze like I was a T-rex that wouldn't notice her if she didn't move.

"Whose party?"

She frowned at me. "I'm not telling you."

Hendrix sidled up to Jade, placing his nose inches from her cheek. "Whose party?"

Jade put her hands on Hendrix's shoulder, lip curled like he was a dirty rag before she shoved him away. "Oh, my God. Max Harford's."

Monroe tossed a bread roll at Hendrix, then a piece of celery at me. "You're a pair of pricks."

God, Monroe just didn't know when to quit. Tutoring them. Going to their parties.

Monroe turned on me. "Don't you even think about it, Zepp! I'm not going."

"Maybe you aren't, but *we* are." Showing up, uninvited to one of Barrington's parties, was like taking a shit on their face. Plus, by the end of the night, we could probably coerce some girl into telling us which little rich prick had ratted on us.

A fissure of concern crossed Monroe's face before it hardened like setting concrete. "The Harfords called the cops on you, Zepp. You cannot show up at their house."

I felt the guys' stares all lock on me. Wolf lobbed a carrot at me. "Why the hell was Max Harford calling the cops on you?"

My jaw tightened. I told the guys most things, but that shitshow was none of their business.

"Oh, he didn't tell you?" A smug smile touched Monroe's

lips. "Zepp turned up at Max's house last night, threatening him. He thought I was dating Max."

I glared at her.

"You kick his ass?" Hendrix asked.

She crumpled her napkin in her palm, then dropped it to the table with a smartass grin. "No, he did not."

"Should have crammed his balls up his asshole," Hendrix said around a mouthful of noodles. "You have shit taste in dick, Red."

"Oh my God." She slapped her palms on the table, glaring at my brother. "I tutor him."

He choked on his spaghetti, spitting half-chewed noodles all over Wolf's tray. "You. Tutor?" Hendrix doubled over with laughter. "What do you tutor? Sex Ed?"

Bellamy and Wolf joined in, barking out laughs.

She pushed to her feet and started across the cafeteria, her tray still at the table. "You're *all* pricks," she called over her shoulder like that was some magnificent revelation.

"It's just a couple of rich kids playing with their dicks after you leave."

She flipped me off before shoving through the lunchroom doors.

Max Harford was going to hate the day he invited her to that party.

―――

Regardless of the current situation with these dickheads, anytime Dayton kids got wind of a Barrington party, we always showed up to piss on their fun—just like they did with us. But this was the first time we'd crashed a party at one of their houses.

Wolf parked at the end of the cul-de-sac, and we filed

out. A group of Barrington girls strutted up in tight jeans and high heels. Hendrix grabbed at his crotch. "My dick is already hard with the possibilities."

Offensive pop music poured out into the night when Wolf opened the front door, joint pinched between his lips.

A spiral staircase wound its way to the upper level. Massive oil paintings decorated the walls, and a stuffed zebra head hung by one of the arched doorways. This was what rich people spent their money on. Things that didn't matter. Shit that made them feel important, that they thought would impress their party guests. It was the first time my pity overtook my envy. These assholes were just as lost as I was but on the flip side of the coin.

Hendrix's face lit up like a thirteen-year-old seeing tits for the first time. "Do you know how much shit we could steal?"

"Dude," Wolf blew out a cloud of smoke. His gaze lifted to the ridiculous crystal chandelier hanging over our heads. "I'll take the chandelier."

I popped them both on the back of the head. "Don't steal anything."

"Yeah." Bellamy shouldered between us. "Barrington cops don't fuck around."

A group of jocks with their Crest-white smiles stopped talking the second we walked in. A glare was all it took for them to turn away. They may have been the kings of their precious private school, but in the real world, they didn't amount to shit.

Hendrix clapped his hands, rubbing them together while his attention strayed toward the living room. "How about stealing some cherries?" I followed his gaze to the group of girls by the fireplace, smiling and twirling hair around their fingers.

"Keep your dick in your pants, for once," I said.

Hendrix mumbled "whatever" under his breath, and we took a collective step as a group. People shifted away like our poverty would rub off on them. My steps faltered when I noticed Monroe in the kitchen. I had never seen her in anything that didn't threaten to show her ass if she bent the wrong way, and the skirt she was wearing didn't come close to showing anything. Jade stood beside her, laughing and chugging beer. Jesus. They were actually trying to impress rich assholes who didn't deserve a second glance from them.

Max shifted behind Monroe and handed her a beer. She tipped back her drink. Then her gaze slowly turned—like she could feel my eyes burning through the back of her red-fucking-head. Her face washed white before she touched a hand to Max's arm, then made a beeline for me. I thought about shouldering through the crowd of preppy dickheads and grabbing their star-quarterback, snapping his neck, and spitting on his face, showing that dick what a bully actually was. But then the smell of cheap perfume wrapped around me.

"Oh, great. You came." Sighing, Monroe latched onto my arm and tugged me to the side of the room.

"Thought you weren't coming." I looked back at Harford, my blood heating. His beady eyes locked on me like I was a challenge. "Change your mind, Roe?" I asked.

"Jade wanted to come." Her eyes rolled to the back of her head. "And I knew you guys wouldn't be able to help yourselves. Call it a feeble attempt at damage control."

Damage control. For these pricks? What the hell ever. I tugged at the hem of her skirt. "What's up with this shit? Trying not to look like poor, white trash?" Because that's exactly how Max and his friends thought of us.

"Fuck you, Zepp." She went to move away, but Max

shouldered his way behind her. Two other dickwads in letterman jackets flanked him.

"You aren't welcome here, Hunt." He folded his gym-rat arms over his chest.

All I could do was toss my head back on a laugh. Where this kid came from, a pussy punch to the face was considered a fight. He had no idea what a few broken ribs and a fractured skull was like.

Hendrix lurched forward, but I caught the back of his hoodie and yanked him back, like a Pitbull on a leash. My brother loved a fight a little too much. "Let me get the pretty blond one, Zepp."

Monroe moved between us. "Jesus Christ." She glared at me like I was the one being a dick. "You're really going to start a fight, Zepp?"

"Hey," I shrugged. "All I did was show up."

She faced Max. Adrenaline fired through me when she told him we would go.

Max flashed her a smile. One full of intention. *"You're invited, Monroe."* It pissed me off that she couldn't see through his fake bullshit. I cracked my neck to the side, knuckles aching to smack against his face.

"You hitting on *my* girl, Harford?" I took a step toward him, shoulders back, fists clenched.

Max Harford was a poster boy that needed a goddamn throat punch. I would gut him before he ever touched Monroe.

Wolf and Bellamy did a vulture circle around the two guys flanking Max's side. And still, the brave bastard took a half-step forward. It took everything in me not to pop him in his mouth.

"You sure she's your girl?" he said.

She wasn't, but that didn't stop me from grabbing her

like she was. I yanked her close, placing one certain hand on her ass before I claimed her mouth with mine. She stilled in my hold before her fingers bunched in my shirt. Her lips parted. If I ever got her in bed, she wouldn't sit down for a week without feeling me. "Tell him you're mine, Roe." I bit at her lip before she shoved me back a step.

"God, will you stop this macho shit? He wasn't hitting on me." She took my hand, her silent show unexpected—the way she squeezed until I felt my knuckles pop, not so much. "We're friends, aren't we, Max?"

When a guy wanted to screw a girl, nothing would bruise his ego more than being called a friend, which was why I shot a shit-eating grin at him.

"Yeah. Of course." His lips twitched into a we'll-agree-to-disagree smile before his gaze swung from her to me. "Friends."

I skimmed my fingers beneath the hem of Monroe's shirt, and I stared that fucker down.

Backing into me, her grip on my hand tightened. "We should go."

"Like I said," Max's eyes locked with mine, "you're invited, Monroe. Always." One sentence that served as a nuclear explosion, a toe over the line already drawn. My muscles tensed.

"Can we just beat their asses already?" Hendrix groaned from behind me.

Before I could answer, Monroe grabbed a handful of my shirt. "Zepp..." she said, a warning tone in her voice. She knew I'd beat the shit out of him given a chance, and the thought that she wanted to protect him made me even more eager to slam his face through a window. Or a piano. Or both. "Let's go find a bathroom," she said, gliding a hand over my chest, but I didn't budge. She tugged on my hand in an attempt to lead me away.

I had never backed down from a fight in my life. But even as pissed as I was, I knew kicking his ass with that many witnesses wouldn't end well. The only reason I was able to move from the spot was the fact that Monroe was, at least, trying to make the exit insulting to that prick.

The partygoers parted when Monroe led me into the hallway.

Hendrix fell in line beside me. "Should have beat his ass, Zepp." He eyed Monroe when she stopped in the bathroom doorway. "You're making him soft."

With a shake of her head, she pulled me over the threshold, then slammed the door in my brother's face. He was right. I should have sucker-punched Max right in his rich-boy face. I shouldn't have cared. She wasn't mine, but the idea that Harford *thought* he could have her was like having a metric ton of dynamite in my head, fuse lit, and on the verge of explosion. And that last comment of his: *"You're welcome, Monroe. Always,"* was a fuck you if there ever was one. And I had let him get away with it. All because she was afraid I would hurt him.

I turned on her, jaw clenched. "Worried about your little boyfriend out there?"

"God, you're an idiot." She pinched the bridge of her nose. "If you get into a fight, who is going to come off worse?"

I stopped pacing to glare at her, my eye twitching. No way in hell she thought Harford could take me. "Who the fuck do you think?" My voice boomed around the ritzy bathroom.

She leaned against the marble sink with a frown. "You. It

will always be you. Because they will call the cops, and they aren't hauling Daddy's boy to jail, are they?"

I paced again, all too aware Monroe was right. These Barrington dick's bankrolled fathers always knew the right people. They always got off on the "but he's from a good family" excuse. They were always the heroes, and we were always the villains. I glanced at my reflection in the mirror. Damn, did we both look out of place in this pristine bathroom with all its expensive soaps and folded hand towels. Maybe they were better...

"God, I hate them," I said through gritted teeth.

We stood in silence. If I had to guess, both hating the Barrington kids for the sheer fact that they had things we never would. Like folded fucking hand towels.

Monroe dropped her head on a sigh. "I don't know why the hell I agreed to come to this."

Someone banged on the door. Hendrix faked a high-pitched moan from the other side. "Right there, Zepp. Get my G-spot." A loud chuckle followed before the door rattled again. "Come on, man. I gotta whizz."

Monroe shoved away from the sink and looked at me. "Can we just leave?"

The petty side of me wanted to stay until the last person left, but she wanted to go. My petty bullshit wasn't worth it. "Whatever. We'll go." I opened the door and stepped into the narrow hall.

Hendrix had one of the Barrington cheerleaders cornered, one hand trailing down her arm while the other swatted at one of the family portraits on the wall. He whispered something into her ear, and she blushed. Dumbass.

"Hey, dickface?" I said. "Where are the other guys?"

Hendrix glanced over the girl's shoulder. "Wolf went up

to a room with some girl. And Bellamy..." His attention went back to the girl. He was like a squirrel chasing nuts.

I walked over and whacked his head. "I'm ready to go."

"Man." He scowled, stepping away from the girl. "I'm about to take whatever this chick's name is into the bathroom and pound her brains out."

Like a typical Barrington girl, she stood there, pretending she didn't hear it. Another one of those, *I'm not like this, let me choke on your balls girls*.

"Can you give a man a minute to get his nut?" Hendrix shook his head like I'd just pissed in his Cheerios.

"God, you're awful," Monroe said.

"Don't hate the player, Red." He patted her shoulder. "Hate the motherfucking game."

My brother was an absolute idiot. I gave him a shove. "Ten minutes and we're out."

I led Monroe into the living room and pulled her into my lap on one of the leather sofas. She went rigid and folded her arms over her chest. Max stood at the far side of the room, chugging beer. I placed my hand on Monroe's leg, and she tensed even more. I didn't miss the subtle hitch of her breath as I trailed my finger a little higher. There was the curiosity to go farther until my hand sank between her thighs and I had her moaning.

My gaze dropped to her mouth, and I thought about how good her lips felt. "Tell me you didn't like it."

"Didn't like what?"

"That kiss."

She hesitated. "Do you care if I liked it or not?"

"What if I do?"

"Then that would make you less of an asshole."

I swept a finger over her bottom lip. "What if I wanted to do it again?"

Her cheeks stained pink as she focused on my mouth. "I—"

"Zepp!" Leah's annoying high-pitched voice nearly split my ears.

"Great." Monroe rolled her eyes and pushed to her feet, swaying a little. "I need to find Jade."

The second Monroe had left, Leah crossed her arms over her chest and shot daggers at me. "You'd rather screw that trash than me? I can't believe you, Zepp!"

Shouldn't have been hard for her to believe. Monroe was prettier. Smarter. Why wouldn't I pick her over Leah's shallow, fake ass?

"I actually like her." I shoved up from the couch. "You were just a hole to stick my dick in, which technically makes you the trash, Leah."

I didn't wait for a reaction; I got my ass out of there. I was halfway down the hall when Hendrix shouted, "cocksucker" from somewhere upstairs. A naked guy flew over the railing, landing on the hardwoods below with a thud. Hendrix launched himself from the first-floor landing with a war cry, landed in a crouch, then leaped onto the guy, whaling on his face.

Several Barrington's guys shouldered through the crowd. One grabbed Hendrix by the shoulders, and Hendrix busted his nose. The other guys latched onto my brother, and I latched onto them.

Fists swung. Heads butted. Blood splattered. Shit around us broke. Eventually, I was ripped off by Bellamy, while the group of rich guys wallowed on the floor.

"Get outta here, Hunt," one of the letterman-jacketed pricks shouted, keeping his distance. "We'll call the cops."

"Just say the word, Zepp." Hendrix swiped at the blood on his shirt. "I'll fuck the little rich boys up."

The group of guys hid behind their threat like pansy-ass pussies.

These little bitches *would* call the cops. And we'd end up in jail. Which meant we needed to get the rest of the group and get the hell out of there. I spit a mouthful of blood to the floor. "Where's my girl?"

One of the guys that had been with Max at Frank's chicken grinned. "Oh. She decided to stay."

Bellamy came out of nowhere and gripped my shoulder before I could nail the guy in the face. "Not worth it, dude. Barrington cops..."

I tore away, glancing between Bellamy and Hendrix. "Handle this shit while I go find Monroe."

I went from the kitchen to the basement to the study, and I didn't find her—or Harford.

I made my way up the curved stairwell and pushed open the first door I came to. Wolf had a girl perched on the bathroom counter, skirt balled around her waist and thong around her ankles. She screamed, but he kept pumping into her while grinning at me.

"We gotta go," I said. "Help me find Monroe."

He picked up his pace. "Give me ten seconds."

"Now, Wolf!" I shouted, turning away and heading to the closed door at the end of the hallway.

I could barely make out Monroe's voice telling someone to get off. And my foot went through the door. It swung open on busted hinges, light from the hallway spilling into the dark room.

Harford jumped up from the bed, eyes wide as he backed away from Monroe.

"Don't touch me," she slurred. Then did a piss-poor job of sitting up.

Adrenaline zapped through me like a livewire. There

were no thoughts, just a roaring in my ears like a freight train.

"You motherfucker!" I rounded the bed and busted Harford right in the temple, and he collapsed to the floor in a heap. The urge to beat that bastard within an inch of his life ate away at me, but I needed to get Monroe out of there.

"Zepp?" She frowned, her eyes half-closed. "Iwannago." Her words ran together.

I scooped her dead weight into my arms. Pissed that I had let her out of my sight. "We're going," I said, heading out of the room with my chest in a vice grip. Knowing there was no way she could have drunk enough to be that messed up.

Wolf was on his way down the steps, face bloodied, and Jade unconscious in his arms. He glanced back at me. "This is fucked up, man. Fucked up." When we hit the bottom of the stairs, we walked into absolute chaos.

Groups of people were fighting. Beer bottles smashed the walls, girls cried, and Hendrix screamed at the top of his lungs while Bellamy cracked a vase over some guy's head.

Someone yelled, "Five-O is coming. Five-O."

"Let's go," I shouted to the guys, following Wolf to the door.

Outside, people dashed across the lawn, dropping beer cans and plastic cups. Engines roared, and headlights flashed before cars peeled off in a cloud of dust. The street in front of Harford's house looked like something out of the *Fast and the Furious*.

We piled into Wolf's car. Cop sirens wailed in the distance, and we quickly pulled off amidst the BMWs and Mercedes.

By the time we got back to the house, Monroe was out of it. And Jade was one-hundred percent unconscious. I tucked

Monroe into my bed, guilt gnawing away at me. If I hadn't messed with her about going to that stupid party or hadn't let her walk away from me...

The image of Harford on top of her played on a loop through my head, and that was when I decided that I was going to fuck up Harford. He would have raped Monroe and gotten away with it. Tomorrow, had she remembered what happened, it would be his word against hers. I couldn't change what had happened to Monroe, but I sure as shit was going to make sure Harford paid.

That next afternoon, I grabbed my baseball bat, rode back to Barrington, and did exactly that.

12

MONROE

I only awoke because someone clicked on the lamp beside me. The first thing I saw when I opened my eyes was the hula girl lampshade. I struggled through the foggy haze of my mind, trying to remember how I had gotten in Zepp's room. But a black void of nothingness consumed my memory.

On a groan, I sat up, head pounding like a marching band. I stilled when my gaze landed on Zepp, leaning against the far wall. The torn material of his white shirt covered with blood splatter.

"Uh. Hi?" My gaze drifted from his clothes to the murderous look in his eyes.

The sky beyond Zepp's bedroom window was nearly black, which left me disoriented. I couldn't recall when I had gotten here. "What time is it?"

"Almost nine," he said, moving across the room.

Nine? I shoved the covers back, then staggered to my feet and swayed. "What day is it?"

"Saturday. Lay down."

"What happened last night?" My gaze swept over his shirt once more.

The seconds ticked by before he finally exhaled a heavy breath. "You're so damn lucky." Anger radiated from each punctuated word.

My pulse ticked up as he started to pace, panic breaking through my foggy mind. "Zepp! What happened?" I took in the bloodied shirt once more. "What did you do?"

"I took care of the assholes that roofied you and your friend."

Roofied? I got drugged. *Jade* got drugged. Closing my eyes, I lowered myself to the bed as guilt plowed into me. "Is Jade okay?" I whispered.

"I guess. Wolf took her home."

I stared at the comforter, trying to force some memory to light of who it was or what he had done. "Did they...?" I couldn't even finish the sentence. Disgust crawled over my skin like insects. His next words could break me.

"I don't know what he did, Monroe." He dragged a hand down his face. "You still had your clothes on. He did too."

I nodded, staring at his worn carpet while fighting the tears that threatened to rise. There was a moment where I felt so soiled, so degraded. And then like everything else in my life, I forced it down into a box that I locked away. "Who was it?"

Zepp's gaze met mine, full of fire and hate. "Harford."

My stomach dropped. Max? I thought... God, I was so stupid. Max tried to rape me. How did I not see his intention? How did I misjudge him so badly?

My eyes moved to the blood-stained baseball bat in the corner of the room. "Is he alive?"

"Why the fuck do you care?"

I shoved to my feet. My hand landed on Zepp's chest,

tentative and unsure. I didn't know how to face him without my armor in place, and right now, I was stripped bare. "Because I don't want you going to jail for me."

Max deserved jail, Zepp didn't.

Rough fingers brushed my waist before he pulled me close, resting his chin on my head. I closed my eyes and basked in the warm safety of his embrace.

"I'm gonna go to jail for something, Roe. Might as well be you." And then he moved away, walking out of the room.

Something in me shifted beneath the weight of his words. Zepp was a thug, but I could no longer convince myself that he was bad. And in a world of pure shit, not bad was practically angelic.

The pipes underneath the floorboard knocked before I heard water cut on in the bathroom. I grabbed my phone from the nightstand, starting a text to Jade before the room tilted and my head span. I fell back onto the bed, inhaling the subtle scent of Zepp that lingered on the sheets.

Me: You okay?

It was a stupid question, but I didn't know what else to say.

Jade: I'm fine.

Guilt niggled away at me. I couldn't deal with all my other emotions right now, so I focused on that. On her.

Me: You sure?
Jade: Yeah, I'll call you tomorrow.

I stared at the ceiling, hoping that Zepp had hurt Max

while worrying about the repercussions if he had. I'd only seen a glimmer of Zepp's temper, but from the look of his shirt, his wrath had been wicked. My stomach was in knots by the time Zepp stepped back into his room, covered only by a towel. When he went to his dresser, he dropped it, and I looked away.

The springs of the old mattress creaked under his weight when he got into bed. The smell of soap and a hint of citrus floated around me.

In the space of twenty-four hours, something vital had changed between us; the ground had shifted. He'd saved me from what was undoubtedly the worst thing anyone could have done to me. And without me even consciously giving it to him, Zepp had earned my trust.

"You came for me," I finally said.

"Yeah." No explanation, just a simple affirmation.

I reached out, hesitating before my fingers met the hot skin of his chest. Zepp surprised me by grabbing my wrist and holding me against him. The strong beat of his heart thrummed against my palm as the silence stretched between us.

He rolled to his side. "I'm sorry." A rare vulnerability crept through his ironclad exterior, and he looked at me like he was searching for something. For the first time, I noticed the air of sadness that Zepp wore like an old coat, broken and hopeless, battered, yet, dependable.

"Why?"

He shrugged a shoulder, twirling a piece of my hair around his finger while I stroked tiny circles on his chest.

"Thank you," I whispered.

His fingers brushed my cheek before he rolled to his back, holding my hand captive.

"I really thought he was okay." I rested my forehead

against his broad shoulder, and his hold on my hand tightened.

"No, he's fucking scum."

Max was, and the fact I had ever thought otherwise made me stupid. Lesson learned. Again. Trust no one. Except maybe Zeppelin Hunt of all people.

13

ZEPP

The next morning, I dropped Monroe at the entrance of the trailer park because she asked me not to take her at her house. She got off the bike and dragged the toe of her boot over the ground, leaving a line in the dirt.

"Thanks. For." Another swipe of her foot. "You know."

"Yeah."

Her gaze met mine for a moment before she turned and started walking away.

I waited until she made it halfway down the dirt path before I took off on my bike, speeding past her, then swinging into Wolf's drive. His dad was on the porch, pouring out food for the stray cats in the neighborhood.

"Hey, son." He straightened, taking his *Bible* from the porch railing and tucking it underneath his arm.

"Hey, Mr. Brookes."

"How's your brother?"

"Good."

One of the cats jumped up through the porch spindles,

slinking around Mr. Brookes' ankle. He bent down to stroke its back. "About to leave for church. If you wanna go?"

Any time I showed up on a Sunday, he'd ask me, and every time I would say, "Maybe next time."

"A'ight then." He patted my back before he started down the steps to his car, then I slipped inside Wolf's trailer.

Out of all of us, Wolf had the closest to what I would call a home. Frilly curtains framed the windows, and a floral area rug spread out in front of the sofa. Knick knacks covered the shelves of the entertainment center. His dad hadn't changed a thing since Wolf's mom had died from cancer a year ago. And I got it. I hadn't even opened the door to my mom's room.

"Where you at, Wolf?" I shouted across the trailer.

"Getting food." A cabinet door closed. Wolf shuffled into the living room with a half-gallon of milk and a box of Fruity Pebbles. He sank onto the couch, cradling the milk while he shoved his hand inside the cereal box. "You took Monroe home?"

That would be the only reason I was on this side of town so early. "Yeah."

He tossed the plastic milk cap to the table, then lifted the container to his lips and chugged. "Shit's fucked up, dude."

And it was. It really fucking was. I expected a lot out of Barrington kids, but what happened Friday night took them from being rich pricks to absolutely worthless pieces of shit. I fell back onto the recliner in the corner of the room, swiping a hand down my face.

"You worried you're gonna get arrested?"

"No." Honestly, I didn't care if I did.

Monroe wouldn't have stood a chance at getting that

son-of-a-bitch arrested, and if my beating the shit out of him was all she got, well, it was better than nothing.

"Too bad you didn't kill him." Wolf shoved another fistful of cereal into his mouth before grabbing the remote and turning on the TV, flipping to the NFL previews. And I sat there, zoned out, half paying attention because all I could think about was Monroe.

I stayed at Wolf's until dinner. His dad heated up some Hungry Mans and made me say the blessing. After we'd eaten, I went by my house, grabbed my baseball bat, headed to the junkyard on the south side, and scaled the fence.

It had been months since I had come here, months since I had needed an outlet. For a while, after my mom had died, I'd made this a nightly stop, beating and bashing up old cars, taking out my anger with each swing of my bat. And while I had tried to get every ounce of rage out of my system when I took this bat to Harford, it hadn't been enough.

I made my way through the heaps of scrap metal and rusted appliances. The distant whoosh of cars on the interstate sounded like some inner-city crash of waves, but it did little to soothe the tension coiled in my muscles. With each step over the littered ground, my grip on the bat tightened. Over the past few days, guilt had mixed with the constant stream of anger that hummed through my veins. Guilt because I felt I unintentionally had a part to play in everything that had happened to Monroe. I couldn't help but think I'd set in motion a chain reaction, some screwed up domino effect that ended with Harford slipping that drug into her drink. I pulled the bat back over my shoulder and swung at the fender of an old Ford truck. The wood cracked against the metal, the impact vibrating up my arms. I aimed, then took another swing. How much of what happened was about Harford hating me, hating that Leah had a fling with me? I had no doubts that his selfishness and wanting to piss me off was a driving force.

The windshield shattered underneath the bat, cubes of glass scattering the ground. With each whack, I swung harder and blamed myself more until sweat covered my brow and my damp shirt clung to my skin like cellophane. I thought laying claim to her would protect her, and in turn, I had set things in motion that ruined her.

I was just as toxic as the city of Dayton. And I didn't know how to fix it.

———

My shoulder ached the next morning from swinging that damn bat, which made it a pain in the ass to turn my bike around the sharp corner that led to the school.

Wolf stood outside the front doors, smirking at the phone in his hand. "Dude," he turned his device around. I skimmed the headline about the Barrington Star Football Player, Victim of Gang Violence. "Gang violence?" Wolf cackled before cramming his phone in his back pocket. "That's hilarious. You're a gang now, Zepp."

He gave me a congratulatory whack to the back when we started through the entrance. I had threatened Max within an inch of his life if he so much as hinted to the cops it was me. And for once, the dipshit must have listened.

Wolf and I parted ways, and I went straight to Monroe's locker, waiting against the metal door while the guy on the other side of her door shuffled through his books. I searched the crowded hallways for Monroe's red hair until the tardy bell rang. Locker doors clanged shut, and the lull of conversation fell silent when kids shot off to their first classes. I sent a text to Monroe: U not coming to school?

The whoosh of the toilet in the girls' bathroom echoed through the empty hall. "I heard the entire thing all started over her sleeping with their quarterback," a girl's voice drifted from the restroom.

I moved away from Monroe's locker, shifting closer to the open doorway. "She's dating Zepp..." another girl's voice floated into the hall.

"Please, Courtney. Zepp Hunt doesn't date girls."

"I heard those Barrington guys do some pretty shitty things to Dayton girls—" The roar of the hand dryer cut into their conversation.

My jaw tensed while a helpless, sinking feeling crept through my chest. There was nothing I could have done to change this. The rumble of the dryer cut off.

"Come on. Like you said, she's screwing around with Zepp Hunt. She has to be a whore."

It was like someone had doused my body in gasoline and threw a match. By the time they rounded the divider that kept people from seeing into the restroom, I could feel the veins in my forehead pulsing.

"Who would drug a slut?" The girl froze, her mouth still open when both girls stepped into the hallway. The shorter of the two clutched at her friend, eyes wide and cheeks stark white. "I uh..."

"Need to learn when to shut your fucking mouth!"

They both jumped when I slammed my fist against the locker, leaving a dent in the metal before I turned and headed to my class.

Monroe: No

And God, was I glad she wasn't coming. At least it would give me a day to get the dumbasses in this school straightened out.

14

MONROE

My chemistry textbook was open to the section about covalent bonds, my scribbled notes scattered over my bedspread. The rock music blasting through my earphones made it hard to focus, but I would rather strain through the rift of guitars and drums than my mom's theatrical moans.

Studying was the only way to keep my mind from tripping over the what-ifs, the only way to keep me from thinking about things I didn't want to acknowledge. I didn't realize the time until I got up to use the bathroom and noticed the sky outside my bedroom window was dark.

I had just settled back onto my bed with my calculus book when my phone dinged.

Jade: U around?

Guilt pressed down on me like a lead weight. I hadn't checked on her, too wrapped up in my own self-pity. God, I was a crap friend.

Me: Yeah. Are you okay?

I felt horrible about what had happened to her. And responsible. Jade was still naïve, and I wasn't supposed to be, and yet...

Jade: I'll come get U?
Me: Sure

I shoved my books to the side and grabbed my jacket before leaving. When I passed Wolf's trailer, I found myself checking the drive for Zepp's bike, disappointed by its absence. I continued down the dirt path to the entrance of the trailer park, kicking myself for caring where Zepp was.

A lone headlight cut through the dark, followed by the chug of Jade's run-down Jeep pulling onto the shoulder. I yanked the dented passenger door open and slid onto the tattered seat. An oversized hoody—that I was pretty sure belonged to Wolf—practically swallowed Jade's tiny frame.

"Are you okay?" I asked.

"No." She grabbed the stick shift, then floored the accelerator.

The wind whipped through the cracked windows, sending the smell of cigarettes and gasoline swirling around me. At the end of the road, she slammed on the brakes. The seatbelt dug into my shoulder, and everything in the backseat flew into the floorboard.

"Okay..." I wasn't good with things like this. I had no idea what had happened that night to either of us, and I was still trying to grapple with my own feelings. But I was worried about her. "Did Zepp and Hendrix tell you what happened?"

The jeep lurched forward. "I want to kill those Barrington guys."

"Pretty sure Zepp might have done that already," I mumbled.

"I went to the police."

I sighed. The cops in Dayton wouldn't do anything. Those guys were Barrington—their parents were police officers, doctors, and lawyers. And we were no one to them. "Jade..."

"And you know what they said?" She took a deep breath, then another. "They said there wouldn't be enough proof." She floored it around a turn, tires squealing. "Said they came from good families. And let's not forget, they're star football players for Barrington."

I dropped my chin to my chest. "It's just the way it is." I hated it. More than anything, I hated that I accepted that. That I encouraged my friend to accept it. I was a fighter, but this life was hard, and you had to pick your battles.

"Sometimes, you just have to take these things into your own hands." By own hands, I meant Zepp's. "I'm pretty sure Zepp and Hendrix would break a few more bones if you want. They're probably not above murder."

She shook her head, then cranked up the volume to the radio. Angry rock bled through the speakers, and we kept driving across town until we wound through the well-lit, manicured suburb of Barrington.

Jade turned down a service road that led behind Barrington High's football field. She parked by the chain-link fence surrounding the stadium, then cut the engine before she got out. She already had the tailgate of the Jeep open when I rounded the back, and two rusted canisters of gasoline sat in the grass.

"We burning this shit down?" I asked.

With teary eyes, Jade lugged the canisters in the air, dropping them on the other side of the fence with a thud before she hopped over, then marched to the fifty-yard line.

I climbed over the fence and started toward her through the darkness. She walked backward, tilting the can. The strong smell of gas caught on the breeze. A slow heat built inside my chest as I thought of Max and the other Barrington guys—of Jade and me. Of what would have happened had the "bad boys" not stopped the "good guys." A bit of burned grass wasn't going to cut it. "Got some matches?"

She tossed a match card from Velma's at me, and I shoved it into my bra, then snagged the second can and crossed the field. Jade could burn grass all she liked; I wanted something more far-reaching. There was a row of narrow windows at the back of the locker room, set low due to the sloping hill in which the building sat. I lifted the metal canister and swung it, the single pane glass smashing. I then opened the lid and tipped it through the window, shattered the next window, poured a little more.

Nothing was more satisfying than tossing that match and watching the instant whoosh of fire, the orange glow permeating the entire building in a matter of seconds.

The field was burning, and the locker room was an inferno by the time we got back to the car. Smoke billowed through the broken windows, and flames visibly licked at the door. It wasn't any sort of justice really. But if this is what Jade needed to feel just a tiny bit better about the wrongness of it all, then I would happily set some shit on fire.

THE UNCONSCIOUS MIND. A place I liked to remain as long as

possible, far away from the reality of Dayton. Something pulled me back into my bedroom with threadbare curtains. My phone vibrated across the nightstand with a series of beeps, and I groaned before snatching it to stare at the screen.

Asshole: R
Asshole: O
Asshole: E
Asshole: U coming to school or what?

Of course it would be Zepp.

Me: No. Thanks for waking me up at 7am, though.

He didn't need to know that sleep had evaded me for the last two hours.

Asshole: Want me to show up at your house?

That was all I needed. Him. At my house. If my mom were sober she'd probably try to sell him a blowjob for twenty bucks. Then there was the possibility of a John showing up. Or Jerry. I didn't want him to see anything of my life because I was ashamed of it.

Me: Definitely not

I settled back onto my pillow, closing my eyes, fully expecting another text any second. My phone remained silent, and a small tremor of anxiety tore through me. What if he was already on his way here? I typed out another message.

Me: `Seriously, do not come here.`

Seconds seemed like minutes.

Me: `Zepp!`

On a groan, I tossed my phone onto the bed, then threw back the covers. Pissed. All I wanted was to be left alone for a while. To not have to deal with people. And Zeppelin Hunt, of all people, was evidently the one trying to drag me out of my wallowing.

DAYTON'S HALLWAYS seemed even more cramped than usual. The gossip about the fight at Max's house and Barrington's newly torched field still floated through the corridors like a bad smell, passing from one student to the next. I shouldered my way through the press of bodies, past the jealous glares of girls, and when I got to my locker, Zepp was waiting for me. One broad shoulder rested against the locker beside mine, and the look on his face said everything. He thought I was fragile. Fuck. I didn't need this at eight in the morning because I *was* fragile, in a way I despised and could barely admit to myself. And I hated the idea that he saw it. I forced it down, putting on a front that I hoped would hold.

"Hey." I twisted my combination lock, then opened the door, trying my hardest to ignore him as I wrestled my chemistry book free.

"Have fun setting fire to Barrington's field?"

"That was Jade." I slammed the door. "The locker room was me."

"Little bit of a pyro, huh?" A smug grin spread across his face when he took a piece of my hair and twirled it around his fingers.

A touch of relief wound its way through me. His annoying little habit of touching my hair felt normal. Like maybe he would just let it go, and I could pretend none of this had ever happened.

"Maybe." I forced a smile and started to class.

I made it three steps before I realized he was following me. He fell in line beside me, barely an inch separating us. Surely, he was not walking me to class? Zepp Hunt was not chivalrous. "Um... hi?" I said.

Instead of acknowledging me, he ripped the decorations off Chase's locker when we passed by, tossing them to the floor. He remained beside me the entire way down the hall, walking off without a word when I ducked into history.

I took a seat at the back of the class, opening my book and keeping my head down. It felt like everyone was staring at me, whispering, but I told myself it was my imagination, that I was paranoid. I focused on the words on the page until Chase dropped to the seat beside me.

"Careful. That might be social suicide," I said, tracing my pen over the word slut someone had scribbled in Sharpie over the corner of the desk.

I expected Chase to say something that would make me feel better, but instead, he greeted me with silence. When I lifted my gaze from my desk, I met an angry glare. Chase's jaw tensed, his stare hardened.

"What the hell is up your ass?"

His palm landed on my desk, covering the word slut when he leaned in close. "Did you fuck Harford?"

My stomach dropped. Of course, there were rumors. I wouldn't have expected any less of the kids at Dayton, but Chase? I expected him, of all people, to defend me, not believe it.

"You did, didn't you?" He shook his head, disgust evident in his tone. "Damn, Monroe."

Shame quickly shifted to anger, forming a tight knot in my chest. Chase had no idea what had happened that night, and the fact he believed it so easily hurt. "Fuck you, Chase."

"I thought you were better than the Barrington quarterback." He pushed to his feet, his disgusted gaze holding mine.

"What did you just say to her?" A shadow loomed over my desk, and when I glanced up, Bellamy was squaring up to Chase.

"It's fine, Bellamy," I said.

"Wow. Harford. Hunt. Even got Hunt's little minions running around after you."

Bellamy smiled right before he nailed Chase in the gut. I might have felt bad for him if he hadn't deserved it so much. Chase doubled over on a cough, and Bellamy grabbed the back of his neck, mumbling something in his ear before he sent Chase stumbling down the aisle.

Bellamy fell into the vacated seat, and we didn't speak for the entire class.

I had expected gossip to be floating around—about the fight, possibly about Max getting beat up. What I hadn't anticipated were the rumors defending Max and making me out to be a whore. Stupid me.

It was always the girl's fault.

15

ZEPP

The sun sank below the jagged TV antennas jutting up from the trailers. Wolf slumped down in the lawn chair, scrolling through his phone. "Ah, shit, dude. That Barrington chick I was banging the other night said she knows who ratted on us."

With everything else going on, I'd almost forgotten about that, and for a second, I wanted to pat Wolf on the back. "Who?"

"She said she doesn't wanna text it. Said she'd tell me on our date."

I slowly turned to face him, one brow lifted in question. We didn't do dates. We had girls over and screwed them, without the entire "I'll pay for your dinner and a movie" bullshit.

"A date?" I said.

Thumbing over his nose, he leaned over his knees and snatched up a twig from the roof, tossing it over the gutter. "Yeah. I know. But two hours at a movie to know which little prick snitched on us..."

"Taking one for the team." I slapped a hand over his shoulder.

"Oh, naw, dude." He grinned like a fool. "You're coming too. The girl's friend wants a date with you."

"I swear to God, Wolf. If you promised some chick that I would go to the damn movies."

He clasped a hand to my shoulder. "Come on; she's hot. Blonde. Big tits. A gymnast. You're guaranteed a piece of that pussy."

Like that made a difference. No way in hell I would endure two hours plus of some shit movie with a Barrington girl for a possible orgasm. Or some Barrington snitch's name. No damn way.

"I already told her you would do it. Suck it up, dude."

The door to Monroe's trailer creaked open, catching my attention before it banged shut. She rounded the corner, dragging a garbage bag behind her. The words Wolf was saying were nothing but a hum in my ears.

"Whatever, man," I stood and halfway waved him off as I crossed the slanted roof. I grabbed the top of the ladder and started down, pausing when Wolf asked me where I was going.

His gaze shifted over my shoulder in the direction of Monroe's trailer.

"I gotta ask Monroe about some shit," I said before continuing down to the porch.

"Yeah." He snorted from the roof. "Right."

The streetlights came on when I started across the dirt road, the one over Monroe's lot flickering. She hoisted the bag up, and the garbage can tumbled over with a clang. She swore, dropping the bag and kicking at the dented aluminum before setting it upright. She crammed the trash inside, so focused on giving the can one last kick, that she didn't notice me. Dusting off her hands, she spun around, then froze. "Uh, hi." She glanced at Wolf's trailer, then back at me. A wrinkle creased her brow. "You okay?"

"Yeah." I brushed past, turning around to face her while I backed toward her porch steps. "Gonna invite me in?"

"My mom's in there." Her gaze drifted to the trailer behind me, a hint of panic reaching her eyes. "And she's cracked out."

With that comment, I froze. I remembered what having a cracked-out mom was like—not wanting people to come over because I didn't want them to see my mom messed up. Despite all her faults, she was a good mom. She had tried. And I loved her. I couldn't stand the thought of people not understanding there was more to her than they saw.

Like me.

Like Monroe.

She stared at the trailer for another second, an unreadable expression settling on her face before she jerked her chin to the opposite side of the road. "Come on."

We crossed through one of the lots, past an El Camino on cinder blocks and a yappy dog crammed in a kennel.

"Sorry. My mom isn't good in the evenings. Or ever. Really."

I thumbed over my nose. That was personal shit—I didn't do well with personal shit. It made people real, and it was best to keep people outside of the guys at a distance.

"I don't know why I'm telling you this." She stepped over the downed chain-link fence that separated the row of manufactured homes from an overgrown field that ran underneath the interstate, and I followed, the awkwardness growing thicker than the humid air around me.

"What do you do out here? Bury bodies?"

A small smile curled the corner of her lips. "How did you know?"

"You put off that psychotic, redhead vibe."

She snorted. "Look who's talking."

Dusk settled in just as we cut into the woods, the temperature dropping from the thick shield of leaves overhead. The noise of cars backfiring and dogs barking gave way to the chirp of birds and the distant babble of a brook. Monroe carved a path through the pines until we reached a small clearing in the middle of the woods where a fallen tree laid across the creek's path. I stood by the water, watching it move over the rocks, not sure exactly why the hell I was back here with her.

"Did you want to talk or something?" she asked.

I turned around. Monroe had plopped down on the moss-covered trunk, one leg kicked up.

"What?" Taking a seat beside her, I pulled a cigarette from my pocket and lit it. Instead of focusing on her, I focused on the smoke billowing over the creek, my leg bouncing.

"You came over to my trailer..."

"Yeah. And?" I was good with girls. Great at talking their panties off. This shit...I glanced at Monroe out of the corner of my eye. Yeah, I was shit at whatever the hell this was.

"We can go back." She dropped her boot to the ground.

I didn't want to go back. But I had no idea how to keep her here. I honestly had no idea who she really was. "When's your birthday?" I said, then took another drag.

"August twentieth. Why?"

Another pull from the cigarette. A shrug of my shoulder, my gaze still aimed at the water. I had never felt so stupid in my life.

She snorted. "I thought you were supposed to be good at this."

I chucked the half-smoked cigarette into the water, watching it careen over the rocks. "I don't talk to girls, Roe. What the hell am I supposed to ask you?"

"How do you not talk to girls? There's a different one crying in the bathroom over you each week."

I had never promised a single girl a thing, never given a hint that I cared. And it wasn't like I didn't have a reputation; why would a girl waste her time crying over me? "What the hell is wrong with girls?"

"I know, right? You practically have asshole stamped on your forehead. The truth might ruin your chances." A small laugh bubbled past her lips. "Don't worry. Your secret's safe with me."

That comment made me turn to look at her. A slight smile played at her lips, and I couldn't help but think about kissing her, but I wasn't sure how to do that if I wasn't trying to fuck her. Monroe thought I wasn't an asshole, and while that was cute, it was dangerous for both her and me. "I'm not a nice guy, Roe."

"A bad guy wouldn't bother with the warning."

"And a good guy wouldn't have girls crying over him, would he?"

She traced her finger over a groove in the log. "They wanted a bad boy..." Her gaze met mine. "You gave them exactly what they asked for."

And that was where she was wrong. Those girls wanted a bad boy they could fix. They wanted a guy that would be good *for* them. And that wasn't me. I would never be good for anyone.

The wind kicked up for a second, blowing through the tree limbs and letting the last rays of dimming sunlight through. A sliver of golden light touched her face, and damn, if it didn't make her look beautiful.

"You should know, Monroe. Girls don't really want a bad guy." I grabbed a pebble from the ground and pushed to my feet, skipping the rock across the creek. "They only want one they can fix."

"I didn't realize you were broken." Monroe stepped beside me, studying me like she wanted to pick apart my layers, one at a time, and that made me uneasy. "You're really not bad, Zepp."

Her gaze fell to my mouth, and fingers brushed my jaw. Then she pressed her lips to my cheek—To. My. Cheek— before she turned away, heading back down the path to the trailer park.

I felt like a deer in headlights, confused as fuck and ready for the damn car to just run me over.

NEVER IN MY life would I have thought I would be standing at a movie theatre concession stand on a Thursday night while Wolf bought a tub of buttered popcorn and a soda for some chick he'd already banged.

Yet here we were. The aroma of burned popcorn and rich-girl perfume wafted around me.

The cookie-cutter, private school girl I'd been forced to accompany shifted closer, brushing her arm against mine. "I want some popcorn."

I waved toward the counter. "Well, go fucking get some. No one's stopping you." I may have been forced into this shit nightmare, but I wasn't dropping a penny on anything but my stupid movie ticket.

A deep pout shaped her lips. That look may have

worked on her rich daddy. Too bad, Samantha, that crap didn't work on me.

"You gonna get some popcorn or what?"

Wolf turned away from the counter, cramming a handful of popcorn into his mouth while he laughed.

Samantha didn't get popcorn, but she did whine to her friend about it on the way into the theatre.

Wolf made his way up the dimly lit stairs, settling into a seat on the back row and kicking his sneakers up onto the chair in front of him. His date sat beside him, all smiles. I went down one of the aisles a few rows in front of them, then flopped into a seat, hoping Samantha would keep going. But she didn't.

Previews for the new Marvel movie rolled across the screen. She sat right beside me, making a dramatic show of crossing one leg over the other, then adjusting the hem of her skirt. Of course she had worn a skirt. Girls wore crap like that to the movies for one reason and one reason only. And I had no interest in fingering her—even if she was halfway-decent looking.

That was when I realized just how much Monroe had fucked me up—I wouldn't even finger a half-way decent girl.

As if the movie and Samantha's clear desperation weren't torture enough, Wolf dragged me to the Waffle Hut afterward. His date must have been a damn good negotiator because she was making absolute dicks out of us both. Dinner and a movie. Such bullshit.

After everyone had placed their drink order, the girls disappeared to the restroom. I leaned my forearms over the table, staring across at Wolf. "I swear to God, Wolf. I'm going to kill you."

"What?" He grabbed one of the grease-covered menus and popped it open. "You didn't get any head?"

"Fuck you."

He laughed. "Never thought I would see the day Zepp Hunt was pussy whipped."

I chucked the saltshaker at him. If there was anything I was not, it was pussy whipped, especially when the girl in question hadn't even gotten hers out around me.

"Shame too." On an exhale, he tossed the menu down. "I got some killer head in the theatre."

Giggles drowned out the crappy music playing over Waffle Hut's sound system, and our "dates" came back to the table, smiling as they slipped into the booth beside us.

Samantha twirled a piece of hair around her finger, glancing around the hole-in-the-wall restaurant filled with bikers and the local prostitute propped against the jukebox smoking a cigarette. I was one hundred percent certain she had never been to a place like this in her life.

"This place is..." She cleared her throat. "Um. Cute."

Wolf must have seen the last thread of patience I had with this girl leave. That was the only reasonable explanation as to why he decided to stoke the fire. "Zepp." His hand slapped the table. "You gonna see if Samantha wants to come hang out at the house sometime?"

"Oh, I would love to." She nodded like one of those stupid bobbleheads assholes have stuck to their dashboards.

"Wolf, you gonna get that fucking name before I take this steak knife and stab you?" I took the knife and fisted it, my gaze aimed right at him.

The bell over the door dinged. The whoosh of the highway swooped inside, followed by Jade, then Monroe.

"Oh shit," Wolf snickered. "And the plot thickens. Dum. Dum. Dum!"

I took the pepper shaker and nailed him in the forehead.

I wasn't sure what was going on between Monroe and me. But whatever it was, I liked it. Enough that I couldn't even enjoy the spoils of some Barrington bimbo. And even I knew that a girl like Monroe wouldn't toy with the idea of me for long.

"Move." I shoved Samantha, but she didn't budge.

"Excuse me?" she whined.

God, I didn't have time for this crap. I stood in the booth, placed my boot onto the table—knocking Samantha's soda in her lap—then hopped to the floor. The shriek Samantha let out was enough to make the entire Waffle Hut fall silent. Definitely enough to warrant the daggers Monroe shot at me before a slight frown slipped over her face.

I flopped down in her booth, slid right up next to her, and flung my arm around her shoulder.

She shrugged out of my hold, focusing her attention on the laminated menu. "Are you on a date?"

"Do you care?"

"That I'm your scapegoat for a shitty date with a Barrington girl? Yes." There was a level of hostility to that statement that I thoroughly enjoyed.

"It wasn't a date," I said.

Jade folded her arms over her chest with more attitude than I had ever seen her give. "Sure looks like a date."

"It's not." I rested my forearms over the table. "I don't date girls. I don't take them out. I don't invite them over to my house for extended periods." I glanced at Monroe, hoping she picked up on that last bit; she sure as shit had been at my house more than any other girl.

"Great. Well, then maybe you should go back to your 'not date,'" Monroe said, flipping the menu over to the dinner selection. No one ever ordered dinner from Waffle Hut... "She looks like she misses you."

I brushed a piece of hair behind Monroe's shoulder, focusing on her lips. "You're hot when you're angry, you know it?"

"You're full of shit, you know it?"

"You should learn to take a compliment." I snatched the menu out of her hands, and she took it right back.

"Oh, Zeppelin Hunt wants in my pants." She pressed her hand to her chest, fluttering her eyelashes before a sour expression settled on her face. "What a compliment." She waved a hand toward Wolf and the Barrington girls. "It obviously doesn't take much."

"You know what?" I pushed up from the table. "Fuck you." Then I headed to the door, glancing back at Wolf. "I'm out, man."

"Dude, you rode with me."

"I can fucking walk."

She pissed me off, and I wasn't even sure why. She hadn't done anything, but...God. Women! I made my way through the group of middle-aged bikers loitering in the parking lot, then heard Monroe calling my name. But I kept going. I was almost to the road when she latched onto my arm.

"Zepp!"

"What!" I spun around to face her. My heart pounded in my chest, a form of self-hatred for giving a shit about what she thought of me. "What, Monroe?"

Her hands landed on her hips, her boot tapped the ground, and finally, she blew out a sharp breath. "Sorry. You don't owe me an explanation. We're..." Her brow tightened. "Friends. I guess."

No the hell she was not trying to pull that friend bullshit with me. Whatever *this* was between us, it sure as hell wasn't friends. I snorted. "Sure, Monroe. Friends."

Her gaze lingered on me like she wanted to say more,

but then she turned back toward the Waffle Hut. "Jade's ordering you a milkshake."

So she had felt guilty before she even came out to chase me down... I started after her, catching up and walking close enough that our arms touched. "Do I look like a guy who drinks milkshakes, Monroe?"

"Who doesn't drink milkshakes? You really are a psychopath."

"And you really are hot."

16

MONROE

The dismissal bell for fifth period rang. Students crammed their books into their lockers, then filed out the back doors for the pep rally. Yeah, screw that. There were many things I'd rather do—gouge my own eyes out being one. The mass of students went left, and I hooked a right toward the parking lot.

I made it to the edge of the breezeway, then paused at the sound of Mr. Brown calling my name. When I spun around to face him, he frowned at me. The way his arms folded over his chest made his oversized suit jacket puff out at the shoulders. "Skipping school, are we?"

"I'm just getting something from my car," I lied, plastering a fake smile to my lips.

"You aren't allowed to go back to your car during school hours. You know the rules." Jesus, this wasn't Barrington. Any given lunchtime, you could find kids sitting in their cars smoking weed. He was just a dick. He thumbed behind him to the field. "May I suggest you don't allow Zeppelin Hunt to taint your otherwise spotless record."

Of course, this was Zepp's fault. Because I couldn't just

not want to go to the stupid "team spirit" bullshit. I started down the sidewalk and spotted Zepp ahead of me, walking backward with a smug grin on his face. He waited for me, throwing an arm around my shoulders when I caught up to him. The scent of smoke and leather greeted me, familiar and somehow comforting now.

"Brown bust your ass?" He laughed like the smartass he was.

"I'd rather shit in my hand and clap than watch this bullshit."

We followed the herd of students through the fence surrounding the football field, then into the bleachers. I followed Zepp up the rusted steps to where Hendrix and Bellamy sat with Jade. I eyed her, wondering if she had willingly chosen to sit with them or not.

I leaned forward to glare at Hendrix. "If your brother tries to screw Jade..." I whispered to Zepp, and he placed a finger to my forehead, pushing me back.

"He's not fucking your friend. Calm your tits."

"He'd stick his dick in a cinnamon roll if it got him off."

Feedback crackled through the speakers, followed by upbeat dance music. The head cheerleader bounced onto the field, ponytail swinging, smile beaming before she stopped center field in front of the microphone. "Are you guys ready to beat Barrington this weekend?"

Every fiber of my being cringed. "Kill me now."

Zepp plucked a joint from his pocket, placing it to his lips and lighting it. Right there in the middle of the pep rally.

Other cheerleaders ran onto the field, doing flips and shouting while the football players strutted out, led by Chase. Wolf meandered along at the back of the herd, looking lost because he was probably stoned.

Zepp's gaze dropped to my legs, thick smoke crawling through his lips. "Those skirts would look killer on you."

"Well, we all know you have a thing for cheerleaders, Zepp." I wouldn't be seen dead in a cheerleader's uniform.

"Not cheerleaders, babe. I just have a thing for pussy."

"Good to know." I hated that I cared because it wasn't like I didn't know he was a whore.

A slow smirk worked over his lips. "Jealous, Roe?"

Our eyes locked. "You want me to be?"

The pungent aroma of marijuana wafted in front of my face. Zepp folded his arms, resting them on his knees before he leaned into me. "I wouldn't hate it if you were."

I looked out over the field, hating this pull that took root inside me. I didn't know when I had stopped hating him. Probably around the time he saved me from being raped. Or maybe when he tried to kill a guy he thought had hit me. I didn't want to be that girl, but he made it so hard.

I glanced across the stands, really paying attention for the first time. Half of the girls' gazes lingered on Zepp like they'd give up every shred of dignity they had for a moment of his attention. And they looked at me like the bitch who was stealing their thunder. "I don't get jealous over things that aren't mine," I said.

He snorted. Wolf busted through one of the stupid banners the cheerleaders had painted with little hearts and stars, completely lacking the enthusiasm of the other players. I glanced at Zepp, at the hard set of his jaw, the way the sun glinted off the silver loop in his nose. The lines between us were shifting. We'd been enemies, but we weren't that now. I had told him we were friends, but we weren't that, either, and I wanted something from him. I just didn't know what.

"What are you doing later?" he asked, still not looking at me.

"Not sure. Why?"

"You should come over."

"Are you asking me to do a job, or...?"

"Does it matter?"

Our eyes met, and something passed between us. For a moment, we were simply circling each other, neither of us willing to concede.

The cheerleaders started a chant about kicking Barrington's ass, and I managed to pull my gaze away from Zepp's. I glanced over at Jade. Tears were in her eyes, her arms hugging her chest.

"Shit. I gotta go take care of Jade."

Zepp's hand landed on my thigh before he stood up. I shifted behind the guys to sit beside Jade.

"You okay?" I asked, but she just shook her head.

"What's he doing?" Bellamy said.

I followed his gaze to the field just as Zepp hopped the chain-link fence surrounding it. He strutted up to the cheerleader and snatched the microphone. "Fuck Barrington!" His deep voice rumbled through the speakers, and the student body cheered.

"Fuck them and their rich-dick daddies and their slutty girls." He grabbed his crotch and thrust like a well-rehearsed rockstar. "They can all suck my dick, just like Brown."

The roar of the crowd grew louder, and Hendrix stood up, fist-pumping the air and thrusting his hips. "Yeah. Fuck Brown and his little bitch ass."

Zepp was insane, but I couldn't help the smile or the little flutter in my chest as I watched Zepp Hunt do exactly what he did best: Be bad. For me.

Brown stormed across the field, followed by a few of the teachers. I stood and took Jade's hand, tugging her down the steps.

"Oh, look," Zepp's voice echoed across the field. "Here he comes now to get on his knees and suck my shit."

Another loud boom of laughter erupted around us. Brown snatched the microphone. Ear-splitting feedback rang out when he cut the sound off.

I grabbed Jade's arm, tugging her down the bleachers before darting into the parking lot. Despite the tears spilling down her cheeks, she laughed when we stopped beside her Jeep. "He's going to be in so much trouble."

"Nothing he's not used to," I said, climbing into Jade's car before she cranked it and we pulled away.

We spent the afternoon driving around, listening to music and talking about anything but Barrington. We pulled out of the 7-11 on the edge of Dayton, Slushies in hand. Jade was pushing sixty when a red light caught us and she came to a screeching halt.

The word "slut" drifted through Jade's cracked window. When I glared at the guys in the shiny SUV beside us, they laughed.

"We hear you Dayton girls climb dick like champs." They all cackled again, and Jade shrunk down in her seat.

Heat bled through my entire body. If I could have gotten out of the car and spit on them, I would have. But the best I could do at the busy intersection was flip them off. "You couldn't pay me enough of your daddy's money to make me touch your shriveled dick."

The driver hurled a Big Gulp at Jade's Jeep. Soda and ice splattered the windshield. The traffic signal turned green, and they sped away, their laughter rising above the hum of the engine.

It took Jade a moment to press the gas. And all the while, my temper grew into a raging inferno, churning and spitting.

"Assholes," I said on a growl.

Her tear-filled eyes fixed on the road. "How are you okay, Monroe?"

"I'm not," I admitted. "I'm just good at hiding it." I would never tell anyone else that.

She swiped at her tears, but more kept coming, and I didn't know what to say or do. I was a shit friend. I hadn't cried since I was eight years old when my mom overdosed for the first time. A horrible feeling settled in my gut, and the acceptance I'd forced upon both Jade and myself suddenly felt like chains shackling me. I wanted to be okay, but deep down, I wasn't. Because Max and his friends wouldn't feel a drop of remorse for what they did to us. I wanted them all to pay, but nothing felt like enough, not even Zepp's beating. They'd heal, but I wasn't sure Jade would. I wanted to take something from Max the same way he'd taken something from me. There was only one thing I could think of that meant something to him, no matter how inconsequential it might be by comparison.

"Take me to Barrington," I said.

17

ZEPP

I stared at Monroe's name on my phone, at the message typed out on the screen: you ok?

Hendrix came through the front door, followed by Wolf, and I deleted the text. They dropped their backpacks onto the floor and went straight to the beanbags in front of the TV, switching on the PlayStation. "How long did you get suspended for?" Hendrix asked, tossing a controller to Wolf.

"Three days."

Wolf narrowed his eyes. "That's it? Dude, Brown's going soft."

Even Brown hated those Barrington kids and their parents. Had I not thrown in the offer for him to suck my dick, I would bet all I would have ended up with nothing more than a week's worth of detention.

The guys had barely gotten into their game when an engine revved outside, setting off the alarm on a neighbor's car. Hendrix looked over his shoulder, ears practically perking up. "Is that a V8?"

Another roar rattled the aluminum windows, and I headed across the room, twisting the plastic blinds open.

Harford's electric-blue, 1970 Stingray Corvette idled in my drive, door open, and Monroe's long, fishnet-covered legs swinging out from behind the wheel. "God-fucking-damn."

I stepped onto the porch just as she perched on the hood like some *Sports Illustrated* swimsuit model, crossing one leg over the other.

"Brought you something," she said, trailing a fingernail over the checkered-flag emblem, and as hot as she looked on the hood of that car, that wasn't some piece of shit, rusted out heap. That was a fifty-grand classic car, belonging to the guy I had beat to within an inch of his life. With the passenger window busted out and, if I had to guess, she had hotwired it. That was a connection I did not need.

"What the hell, Roe? Why do you have Harford's car?" I hurried down the porch steps, stopping beside the shiny car. "In my motherfucking driveway!"

The smile on her face crumpled, a bitter expression replacing it as she pushed to her feet. "Because it means *he* doesn't have it."

Cop sirens wailed in the background. That noise was a constant on this side of Dayton, but I had a good feeling, this time, they were after her.

"Get in the damn car," I said, jogging to the open driver's side door.

"Hell no." She shoved me, then sank behind the wheel, glaring at me. "I stole it, I drive."

Biting back an aggravated groan, I went to the passenger side and climbed in. The thing practically sat on the ground. A twinge of jealousy rose inside me when I noticed the completely restored original interior. Spoiled dick.

The motor growled, rumbling through the leather seats. Monroe shoved it in gear, and the car flew onto the street, tires screaming. Monroe literally drove it like she stole it, flying over potholes and careening sideways around the corners. When the call of police sirens rose over the engine, she gunned it harder, winding through the slums until we hit the entrance ramp to the freeway and the speedometer pressed one-fifty.

I swiped a hand over my jaw, staring at the interstate in front of us. I got it. She had lost it, but dammit, stealing his car and bringing it to my house? She could have just set it on fire...

Some shitty rock song blared through the speakers when Monroe cranked up the radio. A laugh fell from her lips. "I love this car."

The fact that she was acting like this was some kind of joyride snapped the thin thread of patience I had been clinging to. I cut off the music. "What the hell were you thinking, Monroe?"

Her arms went rigid against the steering wheel. "He deserves it."

Max deserved a lot worse. Worse than what I had already done to him, but the thing was, this all would be a blip on the radar. His cuts and bruises and broken bones would heal, and insurance would give his parents money for the stolen car. As much as we wanted to believe we'd stuck it to Harford, it wasn't anything he couldn't dust off his preppy, designer shoes. "And what the hell are you going to do with it?" I asked.

"You can sell it."

"Are you insane? I can't sell this!"

"It's got to be worth at least thirty grand. Yes, you can!"

I didn't take Monroe for stupid, but this was stupid. "This isn't some old drunk's piece of scrap metal! It's a 1970 Stingray Corvette. In mint condition." I glanced at the busted window. "Almost. Flags would go up everywhere if I tried to sell this thing, and then my ass would end up in jail."

Her knuckles washed white from how hard she held onto the steering wheel. There it was. I had sucked the moment of fun out of it—taken a dump on her pinch of bliss.

"Well," she said, jaw clenched. "I can't return it!"

I tossed my head back against the seat, then pointed to the exit ramp the Vette was barreling up on. "Just—Get off the interstate."

With a groan, she jerked the wheel, skidding across the lanes to make the ramp. I couldn't sell the thing, and part of me wanted just to ditch it on the side of some backwoods road, but then, Harford would get it back. There had to be a compromise. We wound our way through county roads until we came to a dead-end by Marvin Lake. Monroe glanced from me to the lake and back again.

"Put it in neutral," I said, and she stared straight ahead, fingers curling around the leather steering wheel. "You stole it." I opened the door and stepped out. "You sink it."

"No..." She gave an adamant shake of her head. "No, Zepp." There was a touch of heartache in her tone. And, I got it. Ruining a vintage car like this was damn near sacrilege—but I'd go to hell before I went to jail or let Harford have it back.

I rested an arm on the roof and leaned down to look at her through the busted window. "Either it goes into the lake, or we go to juvie."

"Shit. Fine." On a sigh, she got out and slammed the door so hard the entire thing rocked. She rounded the back, placing her hands on the shiny paint and throwing her weight into it. It didn't budge. "Help me then!"

I slapped my palms over the trunk, forcing the vehicle

forward. Leaves crunched, and twigs snapped underneath the wheels. Halfway to the bank, she stepped back.

"Oh, you done?" I mumbled.

Sweat beaded my brows by the time the front wheels dropped off the embankment. One, final shove and the streamlined nose made a splash. Water poured through the windows before the vehicle sank below the murky surface of the lake.

"Thanks for the help," I said, glaring at Monroe, who stood at the bank's edge, picking at her nails.

Her gaze swept over me. "Good to know the muscles aren't for show."

I fished my phone from my pocket to call Hendrix, but, of course, there was no service. We were in the middle of nowhere, a good thirty miles from Dayton. Without a car. And I had shit to do. A small spark of anger ignited inside me. Maybe this had been some type of therapy for her, but it was pointless. The Corvette was in the lake, we were stranded, and Max would end up with a new car anyway.

"You do realize his parents will probably buy him a new car before he can even miss that one." I tossed my hands in the air. "But as long as you feel better."

"Fuck you." Her hands went to her hips. "It's all I'm going to get because he's not going to jail for trying to rape the local white trash." She started through the tall grass toward the water.

She was right. I had beaten his ass, and I had found a little bit of justice with each swing of the bat, each crack of bone. I had done my damnedest to take away the scholarship he didn't deserve, just like he would have gladly taken something from Monroe. But it didn't make me feel any less guilty that I hadn't found her two minutes sooner; it didn't change anything about that night. And neither would her stealing his precious car.

I grabbed a cigarette from my pocket and lit it, watching Monroe come to an abrupt halt at the lake's edge. She dragged a restless hand through her hair, shoulders hunched before she wrapped her arms around herself. I wasn't a shrink, but any idiot knew: no matter how hard Monroe seemed, she was just a girl. One who had been put in a shit situation by shit people—the same people who looked at us like we were worthless scum, all because we didn't have money. And there was the irony; morals didn't mean shit. They didn't mean shit to people who had money because money could buy a person's way out. And they didn't mean shit to us poor fuckers because we had to ignore them in order to survive.

I tossed the cigarette down, stomping it out before I crossed the long grass and stopped a few feet behind her, no idea how to handle this.

"Hey," I placed a hand on her shoulder, then rubbed over her back. "You're not about to freak out on me, are you?"

"I'm fine." But the slight crack to her voice told me she wasn't.

"We just sunk a fifty-thousand-dollar car in the lake, Roe..."

"At least he doesn't have it, though, right?" A half-hearted laugh slipped through her lips. "Should have torched it on his driveway."

That would have been better, but again, nothing either of us did would change what had happened. She knew that. I knew that...

"I'm just angry." She turned to face me, cheeks red and tears welling in her eyes. "I know better than to trust anyone. Guess I was due a reminder." She took a heavy breath. "Everyone wants something, right?"

I had no idea what to say or do, so I stood there for a second, watching her fight emotions until something in my chest went tight, and I couldn't take it anymore.

That had always been my motto: Don't believe in anything or anyone. Not to get my hopes up, because, given a chance, people let you down. Every time. I stared at the angry colors of the setting sun reflecting from the lake. "If they say they don't, they're liars."

"I know."

I could almost see her thinking, most likely wondering what it was I wanted from her. And had she asked me that a week ago, there would have been an easy answer to that question. But now, it was way more complicated. Sure, I could kiss her—fist her hair and give her a quick fuck, but outside of that, I had nothing to offer a girl like Monroe. Feelings tried to creep up in my chest, and I quickly snuffed them out, turning away from her and starting toward the gravel road. "We're gonna have to walk."

We passed lake houses and a string of RVs without a word. I zoned out to the crunch of gravel beneath my feet, thinking about how shit this must have been for Monroe, knowing that those guy's family names meant more than a girl's dignity.

"God, this place is a shit hole." She kicked a crumpled beer can into the overgrown brush. "I can't wait until the day I leave."

There was her hopeless hope, and I hated it for her. Dayton was like a spiderweb, and the harder someone fought to get free of it, the more tangled up they got in its invisible, sticky threads. I scrubbed a hand over my jaw.

"You ever think about leaving?" she asked.

I snorted. "No." We waited for a string of cars to pass before we jogged to the other side of the road. "No one gets out of Dayton, Monroe."

"No one fights to get out. There's a difference."

My mom did. And look where that got her. An uncomfortable feeling settled in my chest, like rats stirring in a nest. We crossed into an abandoned Piggly Wiggly parking lot, and I checked my phone again for service, dialing Hendrix's number when I saw I had a single bar and telling him to come get us. I sat on the curb, and Monroe dropped down beside me, pulling her knees to her chest and resting her forehead on them. "Did you get in trouble at the pep rally?"

"Suspended for a few days." I placed a cigarette to my lips, staring at an ant crawling across the pavement.

"If it's any consolation, it was a very committed performance."

I snorted a laugh. "I meant it. Brown can suck my dick."

"I'm sure you have better offers."

I focused on her, inhaling a puff of smoke. "Not the one I want."

"Well, thank you." She snatched a weed growing from a crack in the concrete, tying it in knots. "Tell me something about you, Zepp."

Way to change the subject, I thought, and I took another pull of smoke. "You gonna tell me who hits you yet?"

She dropped the twisted weed from her fingers. "No. Because it's not a big deal. And that look"—she pointed at me—"tells me you'll make it one."

No matter what she wanted to think, it was already a big deal. "Don't want to tell me? Fine." I chucked the cigarette across the vacant parking lot, and it rolled to a stop by an abandoned crate. "Think I won't find out, though?"

"It's Dayton. My mom's an addict and a whore. I live in the roughest trailer park in town." She shrugged. "Why do you care?"

Because I knew what could happen. I had watched it happen to my mom, and I didn't want anything to happen to Monroe. "Doesn't matter." I pushed up from the curb, walking to the side of the road while I fought the emotions screaming to surface. Of course, she followed me.

"You know you're cryptic as fuck, right?"

"And you're stubborn as fuck."

"I didn't ask you to get involved in my life."

I spun around, pissed that she wouldn't tell me. Pissed about everything to do with our shitty lives in this shitty town. "But you sure as hell showed up in my drive. With a stolen car." I stepped toward her, my voice rising. "That belonged to the guy I nearly killed!"

"Oh my God. Yes, I stole the car. Let it go already."

My jaw cracked. I was pretty sure my eye was twitching. This girl was un-fucking-believable. "Let it go?" I exhaled, shaking my head. "Let it fucking *go*? Sure, I'll let the fact that you almost cost me a lifetime in prison go, Roe." I tossed my hands in the air. "No problem."

"Oh, sorry for thinking you might want to make some money!" She stomped a few feet away. Then whirled around with her finger pointed at me. "You know, you're an asshole."

"Tell me something I don't know, Jesus Christ." I pulled another cigarette from the pack, thinking this girl was going to give me black lungs before the end of the year.

She stormed over and snatched the cigarette from my hand. Chucking it to the concrete, she stomped on it, then headed toward the road, her hips swaying with each heavy step.

God, she made me livid. She headed across the deserted parking lot, fuming.

I grabbed another cigarette, placed it to my lips, and lit it. "Now, who's the asshole?"

"I'm not riding with you!" She started down the shoulder of the highway.

I blew out a cloud of smoke, guessing she thought she was going to walk the thirty miles back to Dayton. And I was going to let her. She made it to a graffitied telephone booth, then stopped.

"Change your mind?" I shouted.

Her back was to me, but I could still see the movement when she crossed her arms over her chest. I could only imagine she was huffing and puffing, pissed as hell because she knew she had no choice but to ride back with me.

The low rumble of an engine came from the distance. An old pickup barreled down the road toward us, and Monroe hitched out a thumb. My jaw tensed. The girl had no self-preservation. At all. At this rate, she was going to give me black lung *and* an aneurysm. The truck slowed. Just great.

I tossed my smoke and stormed after her. "Are you insane?"

The Chevy sputtered to a stop right as I reached her. The window lowered, and a middle-aged man wearing a baseball hat leaned out. "Need a lift?" His gaze dragged over her like he was starving and she was a rare T-bone steak.

I grabbed her arm to yank her back a step. "What the hell do you think you're doing?"

"What does it look like I'm doing?" Monroe's nostrils flared as she wrangled free of my hold.

"You okay, sugar?" the man asked.

I shot a pronounced look at him. "She's fine." My blood pressure spiked when he didn't pull off. "I said, she's fine."

Her defiant glare met mine. If she tried to get into that car... "I'm good," she practically growled. "Thanks."

Gravel crunched under the tires when the truck moved off the shoulder, back onto the highway. A sick feeling settled in my gut. She was going to get in the car with that guy. "Seriously." I pointed to the taillights disappearing over the small hill in the distance. "That was stupid."

"I don't want to ride with you! And I do it all the time." She gave a wave full of attitude down her body. "I'm still alive."

Jesus Christ. I dragged both hands down my face, frustrated. God, I needed something to punch.

"You don't think I can take care of myself? Is that it?"

"Don't start this shit." I jabbed a finger toward her and took a step. "You're a girl. You don't stand a chance against a guy, Monroe. No matter how tough you think you are."

Her eyes went wide, her hands balled into fists, and then she threw a punch to my stomach. That was probably the hardest blow she could land, and I didn't even flinch.

"Case in fucking point." I flicked her forehead. "You're a. *Girl!*"

Her face glowed nuclear red. An actual growl rumbled through her clench teeth when she shoved at my chest. "I don't need you!"

That was an unexpected blow dart to the chest. I thought we both needed each other on some level. Or maybe I just wanted her to need me because there was a part of me already too entwined with Monroe to let her go.

I gripped her jaw and drove her against the cracked glass of the phone booth. "Say it again."

She moved closer. Her heated breath washed over my

face, bending my frustration into want, and my grip on her tightened.

"I don't need you," she whispered.

"You're a goddamn liar!" I covered her mouth with an angry kiss, full of teeth and tongue. The feel of her lips and her tiny frame pressed against me was something I had desperately needed. Her kiss, the drug that granted me the fix I had been craving. Her fingers raked through my hair, pulling me closer, and the kiss grew deeper, more brutal. I would have kissed that girl forever, and that was enough of a realization to terrify me, which was why I shoved away from her.

To protect me.

To protect her.

"Fucking liar," I said, turning back to the Piggly Wiggly parking lot.

18

MONROE

The country roads rushed by the window as I sat in the back of the old sedan, refusing to look in Zepp's direction. He'd pissed me off. And then he'd kissed me—when I was pissed. I hated the way my heart beat a little faster, the way that kiss made me feel—weak.

"You two bang on the hood on Harford's ride or something?"

I glared at Hendrix in the rearview, and a grin stretched over his lips.

"It's tenser than my dick in here," he said.

"Speaking of stolen cars." I eyed the twisted ignition cables dangling from the steering column. "Why are you riding around in one?" Stealing cars to sell was one thing, but cruising around in them, that was just asking for a pair of cuffs.

"It was Old Man Otis'." Hendrix bowed his head then crossed himself, swerving across the lane. "God rest his perverted old bones."

Zepp grabbed the steering wheel, redirecting the car back onto the highway. "Eyes on the road, dick."

"You grave robbed?" I asked.

"He doesn't need it anymore." Hendrix cackled like a hyena. "Besides, that man was a dick. And I robbed his front yard. Not his grave." He turned up the radio, and twangy country music crackled through the speakers. He glanced at Zepp. "What happened to Harford's corvette?"

Before Zepp could answer, I did: "He pushed it into a lake."

"What the hell did you do that for, you idiot?" Hendrix did a full turn around to look at me, the car veering to the shoulder. "Why'd you let him do that?"

I whacked him the back of his head. "Look at the road! Jesus Christ. Who taught you to drive?"

He looked forward again. "Old Man Otis." The car turned onto the highway by the high school, and I leaned between the front seats. "Can you drop me at school? My car's there."

Hendrix looked at Zepp like he was God and needed his approval.

"Don't look at him." I clipped him around the head again.

"Ow! Call your girl off."

Zepp said, "She's not my girl" at the same time that I said, "I'm not his girl."

Hendrix barked out a laugh. "You two are so bumping uglies." He did a little dance in his seat while singing: "Bow-chica-wow-wow."

"Take me to my damn car, Hendrix!" I needed out of this car with these two.

"Please, God. Yes!" Zepp groaned. "Take her to her fucking car."

I glared at the back of his head. The second Hendrix pulled up at the school gate, I got out, slamming the door behind me. The sedan backfired when they sped off.

I had no idea what had happened. How Zepp and I had gone from shouting at each other to him pinning me against that phone booth. I hated that I liked it. That kiss was rough and angry and unexpected. I stopped in the middle of the abandoned parking lot, staring at my car. I had told him I didn't need him, but some part of me already did. I was screwed. For once, my car decided to start, and I had never been so grateful for the shit box's co-operation.

On Saturday night, I called in sick at The White Rabbit. I couldn't stomach stripping and having men leer all over me. It had only been a week since Max had drugged me, but things like that happened all the time. The situation sucked, but sitting in the trailer did nothing but give me time to think. Which was the only reason I went to the mall with Jade.

Jade thumbed through the discount rack while I watched, already bored and regretting my decision to come here.

The distinct click of heels stopped right beside me. The girl huffed, and I glanced over, having to stop from rolling my eyes. Of course, it would be Leah in her sweater and plaid skirt, even a damn headband. She couldn't be any more Barrington if she tried. Two of her friends were with her, like little clones in matching outfits. She flicked through the clothes with a curl of disgust to her lip before her gaze drifted to me.

"Oh, look. It's Dayton's trashiest white trash." She lifted a brow, crossing her arms over her chest with way too much attitude.

"God, fuck off, Leah." I matched her stance. "You're Barrington's biggest bitch. We get it."

She dug a fist into her hip, striking a classic cheerleader pose. "Just so you know, *my* boyfriend wouldn't want you." She stepped closer—both hands on her hips now. "So that little lie you're spreading around about him trying to sleep with you, you may as well give that up. It's pathetic."

Me trying to sleep with *him*? Zepp was the one who had started that damn rumor.

Despite that, heat crawled through me, a twinge of jealousy tightening my chest. It shouldn't have bothered me that Leah thought she had a claim on Zepp, but it did. I'd never show her that, though. "Zepp's all yours. Whatever you've heard is bullshit."

Her nose wrinkled like she'd sniffed dog shit. "That scumrat? Eww." The girls beside her giggled, and it pissed me off. She was all over him only last week. "I'm talking about Max Harford. You know, the quarterback for Barrington."

My stomach dropped at the mention of his name. I knew she'd dated Max before, but I figured she'd moved onto Zepp.

Jade was beside me in an instant. "Good luck with that. Guess he doesn't have to drug you."

"Like he would even have to try with that slut." Her eyes cut over at me.

"You can keep your rapey boyfriend to yourself." I shifted closer, and she took a noticeable step back. "Not sure he'll get it up now, though. I hear someone messed him up real bad."

Her eyes narrowed to slits, cheeks reddening. "And that thug should be in jail for it!"

I took a step, backing her into a rack of clothes. "He's not the one who should be in jail."

She sank back into the sweaters a little more. "Honestly, with the way you dress," her poisonous gaze flicked over me, "you deserved it."

Before I registered the movement, my fist drove into her perfect nose. She toppled back into the rack, screaming while she clutched her face. Then, of course, the tears started. Her friends looked at me like I was some kind of monster.

"Oh shit." Jade grabbed my hand and dragged me out of the shop in a hurry.

The churning in my stomach grew by the second. Leah may have been a bitch, but that fact didn't stop the words looping through my mind: *You deserved it.* A guy strolled out from a shoe store, his eyes lingering on my legs like I was a passing meat platter. For the first time in my life, it bothered me. For the first time ever, I wanted to hide. Everything built up into a frenzy, a cyclone swirling through my head at max speed.

I ducked into the next clothing store, and my eyes strayed to the rack of jeans. I snatched two pairs and paid for them, not even worried about the unnecessary money I was spending. Right now, I didn't care. Jeans suddenly seemed like a safe haven, and I hadn't owned a pair since I was twelve.

Jade watched me take the bag from the cashier, a little line sinking between her brows. "Are you okay?"

"I'm fine, Jade." I wasn't.

We left the store, and I went straight to the mall restroom to change. I didn't recognize the girl staring back at me in the full-length mirror. Sadness smoldered in her eyes like the ashes of something that had once burned so bright. I instantly hated her.

Jade took one quick glance at the jeans, and a small smile touched her lips.

Jade was the one person I knew I wouldn't have to explain this to. "Lunch?" she asked.

I wasn't hungry, but I nodded anyway. "Yeah."

We went to the burger place in the mall and took a seat at one of the bistro-style tables. The food court always made me edgy. It was in the very center of the mall, surrounded by the mezzanine walkways of the second and third floors. There had been several shootings here. I mean, it was a mall near Dayton. And that was just one of the reasons I didn't like coming.

A child screamed a couple of tables over, and I nearly jumped out of my skin.

Jade eyed me like I was losing it. "Seriously, Monroe, are you okay?"

"I'm fine!" I shouted, earning me a glare from the Mother's Day Out group at the table beside us.

Jade's eyes went wide for a second.

I dropped my chin to my chest, sweeping a finger over the table. "Sorry."

"It's fine." She stood up. "I'm gonna go order a burger, want one?"

"Sure. Thanks."

Jade crossed the busy food court, standing in line at the Burger Barn. I hated that I had snapped at her like that, but I just... My phone buzzed. When I pulled it from my bag and glanced at the screen, I felt a small smile tug at my lips, but then I scowled.

Asshole: What R U doing?

I was still mad at him for whatever that was yesterday. I typed a reply, deleted it, retyped.

Asshole: I keep thinking about kissing U.

My cheeks heated. That kiss was everything I had expected from Zepp. Hot and angry. Rough. But I wasn't about to give him any inclination that I liked it.

Me: I keep thinking about what an asshole you are
Asshole: Don't make me call U a liar again Monroe
Asshole: Come over
Me: I'm busy
Asshole: I doubt that.

So arrogant. A few seconds passed before my phone buzzed again.

Asshole: What if I tell U I'm sorry?
Me: *You.
Me: What for? Kissing me or being an asshole?
Asshole: Neither
Me: Then what are you sorry for?
Asshole: Things

He clearly didn't know how an apology worked.

Me: Things? If this is a bid to get in my pants, you're failing

Honestly, I knew we were long past that, but if that wasn't the aim here, it left us in a gray zone that I didn't know how to navigate. Lust, I knew what to do with that. I'd been fending it off since I grew a pair of tits. But Zepp didn't treat me like everyone else. He didn't disrespect me, and he didn't look at me like a piece of meat. I didn't know how to deal with that.

Asshole: Am I? Really?
Asshole: What if I miss yoU?

Dickhead.

Me: You saw me two days ago
Asshole: And?
Asshole: Still miss yoU

I hesitated.

Me: Must be my charming personality

Asshole: Nope. Totally yoUR tits.

Me: Obviously
Asshole: yoU coming over or what?
Me: I don't know
Asshole: See yoU in a few, Roe.

Evasive prick.
On a sigh, I tossed my phone onto the table. Somewhere

along the line, hate had become want, and I knew, just *knew* how stupid that was. Zepp fucked and chucked girls regularly, each one thinking she was going to be the idiot to change him. But I didn't think for a second that I could change him, and I wasn't about to be his next heartbreak. Every fiber of me knew he was a bad idea, but he also felt like the only safety in a world of chaos. Dangerous. So very dangerous.

AFTER DROPPING OFF JADE, I went home to my mom's dilapidated little trailer. I sat in my tiny room, studying, trying to purge my mind of thoughts. As I stared at the pages of my history book, this feeling crept up on me, burrowing into my chest and hollowing out a void that felt all-encompassing. It was the deep ache of loneliness—something I rarely allowed myself to feel because I was always alone. When I was younger, my mom used to have lucid moments between the highs. For a few minutes, it was like I actually had a mom, and God, how I craved that sense of just... having someone. Anyone. A lump clogged my throat. As if he could sense my weakness, my phone vibrated with a text from Zepp.

Asshole: Where R U?
Me: Home
Asshole: UR supposed to say: on my way to UR house

I inhaled a deep breath, resenting this pointless flicker of hope that I felt. Zepp Hunt wasn't a guy to pin any kind of hope on. My head knew that, but my lonely heart...

Me: Don't you have better things to be doing?

It was a Sunday night, but I was sure *he* could be doing other things.

Asshole: No. Come over.

Seconds passed before the next text came through.

Asshole: Please

I was sure Zepp rarely said please to anyone.

My indecision meant it was late by the time I pulled up outside his house. Fundamentally, I knew I should ride this shit out alone, the same way I always did. But a horrible little voice whispered that I didn't need to.

I knocked on the front door, then leaned against the frame, listening to the crickets chirp in the grass. The door creaked open, spilling light onto the porch. Zepp filled the entrance, a T-shirt and loose sweatpants looking better on him than they had any right to.

"Hey," I said, hating how awkward I sounded. But this was the first time I had come to Zepp's because I wanted to. Because he had invited me.

His gaze roamed over me, stopping on my jeans for a beat too long. "Jeans, huh?" He stepped to the side, inviting me in before he closed the door, locking the deadbolt and the series of chains commonplace in Dayton.

"Yeah." I moved down the hall and into the living room, Zepp right behind me.

He fell onto the tattered couch, grabbing a game controller from the table. "Why jeans?"

"Where are the guys?" I wasn't going down this road with him.

His lips pressed into a hard line. "Gone."

I swiped the other game controller from the table and settled onto the sofa beside him. "Show me how to play."

"Show you how to play?" He laughed, before scooting to the edge of the couch and brushing his knee against mine. "You played anything before?"

"My mom didn't exactly deck out the trailer with a game console. But I can bowl with a rock and beer bottles."

He smiled—the first genuine smile I had ever seen on Zepp Hunt's face. And it made my heart do a stupid flip-flop. Just great.

"Right." He took my thumb, then mashed it against one of the buttons. "This is what you press when you want to jump." He moved my finger to the red dot. "This one shoots. And this one—" My thumb bumped the toggle. "It's how you run and shit. You know, move your guy."

"Okay. I got it."

I pressed against the switch, and my army man darted across the screen. Bullets zoomed past, and I ducked behind a bush. Zepp shot me down in less than a minute.

When the next game started, he shifted a little closer on the couch. The pop of rapid gunfire came through the speakers, loud enough to wake anyone in the house. I glanced over my shoulder to the entranceway, wondering if Zepp's parents were around. I'd never seen them, but that wasn't uncommon in Dayton. Half of us had a hooker mom, a deadbeat dad, or a parent working three jobs just to survive.

"Is your mom here?"

His finger jabbed harder over the controller. "No."

Zepp killed my avatar, the screen turned red, and I flopped back on the sofa. "Why do you have to kill me? Why can't we just be friends?"

He glanced at me with a brow raised. "It's a game. We fight each other."

"You know how they say video games promote violence..." I sat up when the sound came back through the speakers. "Hendrix."

Zepp chuckled. "He was fucked up way before we ever bought a game console." His tongue peeked between his lips while his fingers went wild over the buttons. "He tied up some kid with a cable lock in third grade, then put him in a wheelbarrow, and dumped him on the train tracks. All because the kid kissed the girl Hendrix had a crush on."

"Oh my God. He's probably a shrink's wet dream."

We kept playing, and I kept dying—until several games in, where I finally shot him. I gave Zepp a smug smile. Then the game restarted.

"So, since you're smart enough to tutor..." He stared at the screen, moving his player across the desert. "I guess you're gonna go to college or some shit, huh?"

"Yeah. I'm good with numbers. Figure I can probably get a scholarship for accounting."

He snorted. "An accountant?"

"It's good money."

Seconds ticked by. Zepp kept shifting in his seat, his fingers pressing harder at the buttons like he was frustrated.

"What about you?" I asked. "Are you applying to college?"

"No."

I could sense his tension. I wanted to ask why not, but

Zepp was an ever-shifting labyrinth of walls coming up before sliding down for the briefest of moments.

We sat and played, and for a couple of hours, I thought about nothing else but trying to kill Zepp's character. After the first ten games, I couldn't work out if I had gotten good, or if he just let me kill him.

The GAME OVER message flashed across the screen when I shot his avatar. Zepp took the controller out of my hand and tossed it onto the table. "Tired?"

I wasn't, even though it must have been the early hours of the morning by then. "Trying to get me into your bed?" I said. Not that I hadn't already been in it, but drunk and drugged didn't count.

"Does it matter?" He pushed up from the sofa, grabbed my hand, then pulled me to my feet.

"Yes." I snorted. "I'm going to go. I didn't come over here to jump in your bed, Zepp. I just needed..." Him. I had needed him.

"And I didn't invite you over for a fuck." He yanked me closer. "I just want you to stay. Al-fucking-right?"

Clutching his shirt, I rested my forehead to his chest, inhaling his intoxicating scent. I wanted to stay, which was the exact reason I should have left. But instead, I whispered, "Okay."

He led me up the creaking staircase to his room. The door shut behind us.

One quick glance at my jean-clad legs, and he thumbed at his nose ring. Then he fell onto the chair in front of his small desk. "Come here."

With each step closer, nervousness wound through me. A stifling beat of silence stretched between us before Zepp's fingers brushed the bare skin of my waist. "What's with the jeans, Roe?"

"I uh..." I scrambled for something—anything but the truth. "I wanted a change?"

"Bullshit." He pushed to his feet. His entire frame bristled with the aggressive energy that was as natural to him as breathing. My palm pressed to his stomach, meeting the rock-hard muscle beneath his worn shirt.

"What? I'm not allowed to wear jeans now?"

"I've never seen you cover those legs." Rough fingers skirted underneath the hem of my shirt, leaving heat in their wake. "Not even in the middle of last year's snowstorm."

My gaze fell to the floor. Zepp and I had never spoken until I jacked that car from him. The idea that he had noticed anything about me a year ago shouldn't have caused that stupid flutter in my chest. But it did.

I had no explanation for him, though, because the truth was, the clothing I'd always worn like armor now made me feel stripped and vulnerable. Leah's words had cut a wound far deeper than I ever should have allowed. I was festering from the inside out, and for the first time in my life, I didn't feel comfortable in my own skin. But I wouldn't tell him any of that.

He pressed a finger under my chin, forcing me to look at him. "I liked the damn skirts and fishnets."

"Well, that's okay then. Zeppelin Hunt likes it."

We were so close, and I gravitated toward the heat of his body—the warmth of his touch. Zepp had become a safe haven; an unlikely protector I didn't want but at that moment, needed.

But I didn't know how to do this with him. Awkwardness crept up on me, and I took a small step back. He looked at me like he didn't know what to do. Like he was absolutely lost, and for some reason, I couldn't imagine

Zepp Hunt had ever been lost when it came to a girl in his bedroom.

He rubbed a hand over the back of his neck on his way to his dresser, grabbing a T-shirt from the bottom drawer. He tossed the balled-up shirt to me.

I glanced down at the worn material in my hand. "Thanks."

"I can give you boxers if you want."

"I'm good."

I avoided making eye contact with him before going to the bathroom to change. I slipped into the band T-shirt that smelled of everything Zepp. My reflection caught in the toothpaste smeared mirror, and I judged the girl staring back at me because she was weak for a hopeless boy.

I stopped in the doorway when I noticed Zepp sprawled on top of the sheets in nothing but his boxers. All inked, tanned skin, and chiseled lines on display. He brought a joint to his lips, his gaze trailing over me in a way that made my heart skitter in my chest.

"That shirt looks good on you, Roe." He held out the joint to me when I crawled onto the bed. "You should keep it."

I didn't often smoke, but my nerves were on edge. So I took it, inhaling a deep breath. "Thanks," I said, a pungent cloud drifting in front of my face. I took another drag, then passed it back to him. Seconds later, my muscles relaxed. All tension evaporated, and I didn't give a shit about anything but Zepp. I wanted parts of him that girls like Leah Andrews could never hope to see.

"Tell me something about you."

He absentmindedly twirled a piece of my hair around his finger. "I'm fucking high..."

So was I, but if anything, it made that wall I usually

surrounded myself with crack and crumble. "Tell me something no one else knows about Zeppelin Hunt."

"I just told you I was high, right? Like no one else knows that right now. For sure." He dropped my hair on a laugh.

"So am I. But you don't see me avoiding shit."

"The first time I noticed you was two summers ago when you were washing some shit car in your drive. I told the guys you were off-limits." He nudged me. "You're welcome. Hendrix would have tried to screw you."

That was almost sweet. For Zepp. "But you never even spoke to me."

"I told you, I never talked to girls I don't sleep with."

"Should I be offended that you never tried that, either?"

"Are you kidding me?" He rolled to his side, trailing a warm finger across my lips. "Do you have any idea how bad I want you?"

And how many girls had he said that to? How many had fallen at his feet for that line? I wanted something from him, but it wasn't that.

Something crackled to life when my palm slid over the hard plane of his chest. Like static electricity igniting each particle of air between our bodies. Everything I knew about Zepp told me he was a bad idea, I knew it, but in that moment, he was simply a boy who made me feel.

"What if I just want to kiss you?" I whispered.

"I wouldn't stop you."

Strong fingers dug into my hips, and there was a pause, a precipice we both seemed to linger on. Zepp's lips met mine, stealing every trace of breath from my lungs. He made me want to break for him because that kiss said he'd catch my scattered pieces and rearrange them into something hard and indestructible.

His gentleness only lasted a few moments before he

snapped, pulling me into his lap. The kiss grew every bit as brutal as he was, and heat blazed across every inch of my skin when Zepp pressed up between my legs, solid arms banded around me.

"You feel so good, Roe," he mumbled against my lips. His hands went to my ass, and I moved them back to my waist.

"Fuck." He pressed against me again, agitated, like a wild animal pacing the bars of a cage.

I could sense him ready to snap.

"Tell me you don't want to?" He groped at my chest, and I guided his hand back to my waist again.

"I'm not fucking you," I said on a staggered breath, though I couldn't deny that I liked the way he felt pressed between my thighs.

"Other things." He fisted my hair, teeth sinking into my bottom lip as he pushed up against me. Heat shot through me like a drug. "We can do other things."

Gripping his jaw, I forced him back an inch. "Just a kiss," I breathed. But I was pretty sure that Zeppelin Hunt had never had "just a kiss" in his life, and this...well, this was so much more than just a kiss. I knew that.

"Bullshit."

"I don't want to fuck you, Zepp."

He froze, hands on my hips. "Then why are you kissing me?" He sounded so confused, and I almost smiled.

"Do you hate it?"

His mouth covered mine. His hands fisted my shirt. "No." Then he groaned and tore away, resting his forehead against my throat. "I'm too high for this shit." He gave me one last, hard kiss, then shifted me out of his lap, and rose to his feet.

He disappeared into the bathroom, leaving the door

slightly cracked. A few minutes passed before a guttural groan came from the doorway. Zepp Hunt was in his bathroom, jerking off because I'd driven him to it. He could have pushed me for more, tried to fuck me, but he hadn't. From him, it was almost sweet.

A few moments later, the bathroom light went off and Zepp came back to bed. "Just a fucking kiss my ass," he said, crawling under the sheets and flipping onto his side before he switched off the lamp.

That night, I fell asleep to the sound of Zepp's aggravated breaths.

19

ZEPP

Monroe had left before I woke up. The girl was making a habit of sleeping in my bed, not fucking me, then bouncing the next morning. And now, I couldn't get her out of my damned mind.

I swept the red tip of the pencil across the page in a focused attempt. I had spent half an hour trying to mix the colors to match the highlights in her hair. Another fifteen on the ripped fishnets...

My phone vibrated on the table beside me.

WOLF: Found the snitch. We'll come get you after school.

An hour later, we were hightailing it out of Barrington down the backroads that led to Dayton while the sun set behind the horizon.

"Those snitches are getting stitches." Hendrix cackled from the backseat, then grabbed my headrest and shook it. "That guy pissed himself right before you nailed him. All over the place like a little bitch."

Wolf and Bellamy chuckled.

My brother enjoyed fighting. I fought because it was necessary. Dayton wasn't like Barrington. Money didn't give you power. Violence did. And the second someone was viewed as weak, they were fucked.

I wiped at the blood splatter on the knee of my jeans, whatever bullshit the guys were carrying on about fading into the background. Had Bellamy not caught wind of that raid, both my brother and I would be in juvie. That piece of shit Barrington kid deserved every punch he had received.

Wolf turned onto the highway. "And then the kid offered us a hundred bucks to leave him alone." Another round of laughter filled the cabin. "Dumbass." He leaned over the wheel a little, squinting through the windshield. "Is that...Monroe?"

Halfway down the stretch of road, a bright-orange Pinto sat on the shoulder. Steam billowed from the hood. A redhead leaned against the side, her jean-clad legs crossed over one another and her thumb stuck out. Hitchhiking. She was hitchhiking. Again.

"Goddamn it. Pull over."

The truck veered off the highway, stopping behind her car. I slammed the passenger door, then started down the patch of litter-strewn grass. Monroe waved at me. Waved *and* smiled. Oh, she knew I was pissed.

I threw both hands in the air before I got to her, blood pulsing behind my eyes. "Seriously?"

She eyed me up and down. "Did you kill someone?"

"Don't ignore me. What the hell are you doing?"

"My car broke down. I need to get back to Dayton."

"So you hitchhiked? Instead of calling me?"

Her eyes rolled to the back of her head. "It's not like I don't know Wolf's truck."

I had to squint to make out her car. Her bright-orange, eyesore Pinto. No way she knew it was Wolf's truck. "Really?" I snatched her wrist, yanking her thumb up. "This was out when we were at the end of the road." I tossed her hand down, and she immediately folded her arms over her chest.

"Well. You're clearly busy." She swept a hand down my frame. "Killing someone, apparently. You know, you really should be less conspicuous."

She was unbelievable. And stubborn. I stuck a hand into her pocket, and she jerked away, but not before I grabbed her phone. "This," I shook it in her face. "Use the damn thing, Roe." Then I shoved it against her chest before striding to the front of the car.

The second I lifted it, steam enveloped me. Leaves covered the engine full of rusted parts and duct-taped hoses. "Holy shit..." The battery was bungeed down with a wire coat hanger. I understood not having the money for the upkeep, but this was beyond ridiculous.

"What?" She glanced over my shoulder. "Is it dead?"

"It should be." I knocked off a pile of leaves. "What are you trying to do, set the thing on fire? Girls." Shaking my head, I slammed the hood. "Get your shit outta the car."

"I can't leave it here. It'll get stolen."

I brushed past her, starting toward Wolf's truck. "No one wants that piece of shit."

"Like you wouldn't steal it."

Stopping, I thumbed back at the smoking hood. "That is where I draw the line. And I'll get one of the guys to come to get it." I continued to the truck, waiting for her to grab her things.

She grumbled when she climbed into the back beside my brother.

"Hey, Red. Like the jeans," Hendrix said before I closed the door.

Monroe argued with my brother the entire way home. When we got inside, he stomped over to the couch and snatched up the game controller, flipping Monroe the bird. "Wanna let me whoop your ass in *Call of Duty*, Zepp?" He grabbed the remote, and the TV flickered to life.

"You're just gonna sit there covered in someone else's blood?" Monroe said.

"It's dried." Hendrix scowled, glancing back at me. "Who is she? Mary Poppins?"

"Well, that's fine then. Dried hepatitis." She looked at me, pulled her phone from her pocket, then pressed it to her ear. "God, he's gross." Then she let out a groan. "Dammit, Jade. Answer your phone." She jabbed her finger over the screen before tucking it away.

"Don't wanna hang out?" I asked, starting up the stairs.

"Not like I can go anywhere," she said, following me. "And I'm definitely not sitting with American psycho there."

"It's not *that* much blood."

"Well, that's all right then," she said, her voice dripping in sarcasm as she brushed past me and into my room.

Into. My. Room.

With any other girl, that would have meant game on. But with Monroe...I had started to think if I could get in a session of dry humping, I would be doing good. Stopping at the doorway, I pulled off my shirt and tossed it at her. She swatted it away before her eyes landed on my chest, then dropped lower.

"Welcome to come take a shower with me," I suggested.

"Trying to get me naked?"

I smirked. "Always." I headed to the bathroom, leaving it cracked just in case...

By the time I stepped into the shower, my dick was at full mast. Every creak of the floorboard caused it to twitch in anticipation. There was that small hope that I would walk back into that room and Monroe would be naked and spread-eagle on my bed, waiting. But I'd been fantasizing about fucking her for so long, I would probably come in less than a minute. Which was why I jerked one out real quick before I washed off.

When I got back to my room, Monroe wasn't naked. She wasn't spread-eagle. She wasn't even on my bed. She was beside my desk, staring down at the sketchbook I had left wide open. On the picture I had drawn of her. I went to my dresser to grab clothes, pretending I didn't care; that she had not seen some vulnerable part of me when it absolutely was.

"You drew this?" she asked.

"Yeah."

"You're really talented, Zepp."

Ignoring her, I grabbed a pair of boxers from my drawer. Her seeing that sketch had exposed more of me than I wanted her to see and that compliment made me feel like some wounded wolf, limping through the woods.

"Thanks for giving me a lift," she said quietly.

"Yeah. Sure." I dropped the towel, watching her watch me in the mirror before I stepped into my boxers.

"What are you doing tonight?" She sat on the edge of the bed, tracing a finger over the bedspread. She was cute when she was awkward.

I snorted. "Not shit. You?"

"Sitting at your house and waiting for Jade to pick up her phone." She paused for a second. "She's probably bored of rescuing me every time the shit box breaks."

There was a part of me that hated she had called Jade

instead of me. God, I was so screwed. "Just call me from now on."

She chewed at her lip. "You realize this is a weekly thing..."

"Don't care." I sank to the bed beside her.

She fidgeted, knotting her fingers in her lap. "See if you're still saying that at the end of our three months." She snorted.

I drew a circle over the knee of her jeans. "I think we're a little past that. Don't you?" Seconds passed, my chest growing tight.

"I think..." Her gaze dropping to my mouth as she hesitated.

Fuck this. I gripped her hair, then pressed my lips against hers hard before I pulled back. "You think what?"

"We aren't friends," she breathed.

"No shit." Then I pinned her to the mattress, settling between her thighs. Her hands trailed over my back, and I leaned down to kiss her again.

"Cockface!" Hendrix shouted.

Before my bedroom door smacked against the wall, Monroe shoved me off and sat up.

"I knew it!" Hendrix pointed at me with a perverted grin before he threw himself onto the bed.

God, I wanted to strangle him.

"Bumping uglies." He cackled.

"Get out!" I smacked him in the forehead. "Dick."

"Look, this fuckfest is gonna have to wait." He waggled his eyebrows at Monroe before looking back at me. "The guy they stole the Trans Am from has already reported it. Bell said it's on the police scanner."

"Fuck off, Hendrix." I shoved my foot into his side and pushed him onto the floor with a thud. He was screwing with me because he thought I was about to get laid. No way the guys caught.

"Seriously, man." He popped up from the floor, the smile completely gone. "They're on their way here. We gotta get this shit moved."

The screech of tires sounded through the bedroom window, and Hendrix headed to the door. "Come on, man. Seriously. Bros before hoes and all that shit."

By the time I had thrown clothes on and made it into the overgrown backyard, Hendrix was filing down the VIN.

"It has a tow bar. With balls on it." Monroe eyed the rusted-out Trans Am before dropping onto the porch step. "What the hell are you gonna tow with that?"

"Jesus Christ..." The only thing that car was towing was a cooler full of Bud Light. "What the hell? That is not the Trans Am Tony wanted."

Wolf stopped screwing on the new license plate to glance over his shoulder. "Some guy had OD'd in that one. So we improvised."

I covered my face with my hands. This was the stupidest shit they had ever done. And that was saying a lot. "You improvised?" I kicked gravel at the car, then glared at my brother, because I was certain he was behind this. "You did this, didn't you?"

"I mean..." He waved a hand at the car. "It's a Trans Am."

"Whose?" I asked. Hendrix wasn't even with them.

"The guy from the Dollar Store."

I had to close my eyes and count to twenty. Then thirty. As much as I wanted to nail him in the face, he was my brother. "You're an idiot."

Bellamy popped up from under the hood. "The damn thing won't crank." He chucked a ratchet across the yard, smacking against the concrete birdbath. "It's junk. Don't even know why the guy bothered to report it."

Wouldn't start? I headed around the front of the car. "How does a hotwired car just die?" I pushed him out of the way and leaned over the engine. One look at it and I cussed. It died because it was a literal piece of shit. One with a pair of balls hanging from a tow bar. That the cops were after. "It's the alternator."

A stolen car. With balls. And a broken alternator. This had to go. Now.

"Wolf!" I shouted. "Go run down to the Dollar Store and get some pantyhose."

"What? No." He glanced around the back of the car, jerking his head toward Monroe. "Make the girl do it. I'm not letting Paul start rumors about me crossdressing and shit."

Monroe glared at him like she would kill him. "I'm less likely to wear pantyhose than you are."

Wolf frowned before chucking his keys at her. "You're a girl. I have balls."

"Debatable. You are a football player."

"Roe," I said. "Please?"

With a roll of her eyes, she snatched the keys from the ground and walked over to where we stood in front of the car. "Who's paying?"

Wolf slapped twenty bucks into her hand, then pointed at her. "I want change. And those Nacho Cheese Doritos."

"No chance." She strolled around the side of the house. Seconds later, an engine roared.

Wolf glanced at me with brows pulled together. "She's gonna bring back my truck, right?"

I went to work, wiping down every inch of the inside to make sure there weren't any prints. I barely ran the cloth over the glove box, and it fell open. A matte Glock sat tucked away amidst crumpled napkins. It was usually old mail, a box of condoms, maybe a syringe. But this... I took the cold metal in my hand, knowing I could get at least two-hundred bucks for it down at Tony's Pawn Shop. I tucked the gun under the waist of my jeans and finished wiping down the surfaces.

"Doritos. Pantyhose." Monroe tossed a bag at Wolf, and seconds later, he had the makeshift belt in place.

The engine roared to life, and Bellamy and Wolf peeled out of the backyard, leaving track marks through the tall grass.

I pulled the gun from my jeans, holding it up. "Found this in the glove compartment."

"Oh, shit." Hendrix's eyes lit up.

"You should probably toss that." Leave it to Monroe to shit on my parade. "Could belong to a serial killer for all you know."

I shoved it back into the waistband of my jeans. "I can get a couple hundred bucks for this thing."

"Oh, well. *That's* worth jail." She delivered a condescending shake of her head, then started back to the house.

"Hey." Hendrix shuffled up beside me, nodding toward Monroe as she made it to the steps. "We don't have any slots left at Tony's this month. You think..."

For once, my brother made sense. We each were allowed to trade stuff at Tony's Pawn once a month. And I didn't want to hang onto this thing for three more weeks.

"Roe?" I shouted, and she stopped, turning around with her hands on her hips. "Wanna do me a favor?"

"Depends. Does it involve the serial killer gun?"

"Of course it does."

"Then, no." She turned back to the house.

"What? Too chicken shit to go sell a gun?" That got her. All I had to do was question her a little.

She gave the gun a flippant glance. "I want half."

It was either give her half or chuck it in the woods and get nothing. Thumbing over my nose, I started to the house. "Fine."

"And you're coming with me."

I slipped a hand around her waist. "Of course."

We rounded the house and climbed onto my bike. "You're tainting trailer trash, Zepp," she teased before the engine roared to life. "And that's quite a feat."

Oh, I was only getting started...

Fifteen minutes later, we pulled past the prostitutes by the phone booth and into Tony's Pawn Shop's parking lot. The pink fluorescent light blinked on and off. Monroe hopped down from the bike. The second she removed her helmet, she shot a sketchy gaze around the parking lot, lingering on a group of hookers.

"You know all the best places to take a girl, Zepp," she said.

"Try to hold off on fucking me until I get you home. Okay?" I tucked the gun into the back of her jeans. Something about the way it peeked out made my dick hard. All *Tomb Raider* looking and shit... "I'm not gonna lie. That's fucking hot."

She rolled her eyes. "Wait." A frown settled on her face like some terrible realization had just overcome her. "Why do I have to sell this? Why can't you?"

"Tony's made a deal with us. We can each come in once a month. No questions asked. And our allotment is already up."

"Tell me the truth, am I gonna get arrested for this?"

Like I would let her go to jail. "Tell me that's not a serious question?"

She shifted closer, glancing over her shoulder. "It might have killed people!" she whispered.

"Tony doesn't give a shit." I pointed toward the barred doors. "And he writes down fake names."

On a sigh, she turned and crossed the lot.

A couple of minutes later, she stomped out. "He won't take it." She shoved the Glock against my stomach. "Says he needs paperwork."

"What the..." I tucked it into my jeans.

Tony always took anything we brought in. Jewelry, knives, guns—without the paperwork. Then again, he knew us. He didn't know Monroe.

"Fine," I said.

We drove back to the house. When she climbed off the bike, I took the helmet from her, putting it on.

Monroe glared at me with suspicion. "Where are you going?"

"To sell the gun." And then I pulled away.

I drove over to the Northside—a place I wouldn't dare take Monroe. Dayton was bad, but this place... The things I would do for a few hundred bucks. I was glad to get the hell out of there, speeding around corners and running red lights. As soon as I got back to my side of town, I pulled into the Jet Pepp to buy a pack of smokes and condoms. Just in case. And when I came back out to the pumps, some cracked out man was walking off with my bike.

"What the hell, man?" I sprinted over. The second I went to deck him, something tore across my skin. Fire radiated from my arm; then, I noticed the blade in the man's hand. "Stupid crackhead!" I punched him in the face, knocking him back before I grabbed my bike. I cranked the engine and pulled off, not noticing the blood on my arm until I reached a red light.

By the time I got back to my house, blood drenched my sleeve.

Bellamy glanced away from the game when the door slammed shut behind me. His gaze landed on my arm. "What the hell, man?"

Monroe tossed her controller onto the sofa.

Wolf paused the game, plucking the joint from his lips as he turned around. "Are you bleeding?"

"No shit, dumbass," I said, going to the kitchen to grab a beer, popping it open and chugging it with the door still open.

I took another beer and shut the fridge.

"What happened?" Monroe leaned against the doorway, arms folded over her chest.

"Got cut by some hobo."

She pushed away from the doorframe and stopped in front of me, grabbing my wrist and inspecting the cut. "That needs stitches."

"I'm not going to pay three hundred bucks to get someone to sew me up at the hospital."

"I know." She shoved me toward one of the kitchen chairs. "Sit down."

"I'm not letting you sew me up, either." I cocked a brow, but she ignored me, moving to the cabinets to rummage through them.

She filled a pot with water, then placed it on the stove before dumping half a container of salt into it.

"It didn't nick anything important, or I'd have bled out..."

She came back and gripped my arm, poking around the slice. "I know. But I'm guessing it wasn't a squeaky-clean blade. You can't close it unless it's clean, Zepp."

"Who said anything about closing it?" Like hell I was letting that girl anywhere near me with a needle.

"You can't leave it like that. You got any superglue?"

I laughed. "You're kidding me, right?"

"My mom went through a self-harm phase on a bad batch of crack." She grabbed the pot of water and some paper towels, then came back to the table and started cleaning the cut. "Couldn't exactly take her to the ER because she'd end up in the nuthouse. So, superglue." She shrugged. "It works. Where's the glue?"

I pointed to the drawer beside the stove. Roe grabbed the crinkled tube, then came back and pinched the skin around the wound together while unscrewing the green cap with her teeth. The second that shit hit my skin, I winced, gritting my teeth at the obnoxious sting.

She smirked. "Don't be a baby."

I couldn't remember the last time anyone had taken care of me like that. And it wasn't until that moment I realized how much I wanted—needed something like this. Monroe blew on it before she let go. I glanced down at the disgusting, wrinkled skin held together by dried globs of glue.

"I should go home," she said, pushing to her feet. Her car wasn't here, and it was late.

"Is Jade coming to get you?"

"She didn't answer. Her mom must have taken her phone again."

I watched her for a second, shifting on her feet and staring at the floor. "You could just stay."

She chewed at her lip. "Or, you could just take me."

"I could." But I didn't want to. I passed through the doorway into the living room.

"What if I don't want to stay?"

I stopped beside the couch. "Do you not want to stay?" I

waited, knowing this—*us*—was becoming a habit. That we were both probably out of our element. We were loners when it came to relationships, but the more time I spent around her, I was finding it hard to believe that anyone would really want to be alone. Even her.

Monroe tugged at a loose thread on her sleeve. "I don't know."

"Well," I grabbed onto the railing and started up the steps to my room. "Until you do know..."

I was halfway up the stairwell before her footsteps followed behind me and down the hall. She stopped in the doorway.

"Change your mind?"

"Not sure yet." She moved to my desk and took a seat, running her hand over the open sketchbook. "Can I see your other drawings?"

I didn't share those with anyone. Ever. Not since my mom had died. That book was full of nightmares and regrets, worst of all, hopes.

"You don't have to," she added.

I stepped up behind her, staring over her shoulder at the sketch I had made of her. Part of me wanted to show her, and that scared the shit out of me. "Why do you want to see them?"

"I don't know." She traced a finger over the outlines. "Maybe I just want to know more about you."

On a snort, I took the sketchpad in my hand. "And you think drawings are gonna tell you something?"

"This tells me more than you've ever said." Her finger tapped the page. "Cryptic, remember?"

I thumbed through the edge of the pages. "And when are you going to let me know something about you?" I didn't miss the way her shoulders tensed, like she was getting ready for a fight.

"What do you want to know?"

A thousand things. I moved to my bed and took a seat, flipping to the first page. A ghastly green face stared back at me, the word CRACK in yellow letters instead of teeth. It was my mom, the way I saw her when she wasn't sober. "For every picture I show you, I get a question. Okay?" I held out the notebook. When she grabbed it, I didn't let go for a second. "Because I don't let anyone see these—*ever*." The moment her gaze dropped to the page, I focused on the bedspread. I didn't want to see her reaction.

"Ask me."

I had no idea where to start because I wasn't sure how many pictures I was okay with her seeing. With each page, those pictures got darker and darker. Which meant I should start with the question that ate away at me. Get that one out of the way. "Who hits you?"

Her gaze snapped to mine, and she closed the book. "This was a bad idea."

"You don't want to keep going? Fine. But you already saw the picture. And that's my question." My jaw tightened. "Answer it, Roe."

She inhaled a hard breath, her gaze falling to the bed. "It's not that bad. He only gets fisty if he's drunk. Or I piss him off."

Not that bad. I fisted the sheet, trying to temper the anger coursing through me.

"You have to promise you won't do anything," she said.

As much as I wanted to be the one to deliver some justice, at this point, I would be just as happy to pay someone else to do it. "*I* won't do anything."

"Fine. It's Jerry. My mom's boyfriend. Pimp. Dealer."

And Jerry was going to get his ass beat. I handed the book back to her.

"That's it. No death threats? No chest-beating?" She hesitated before opening the sketchbook.

"What's the worst memory you have?"

She stilled, though her gaze never lifted from the paper in front of her. "My eighth birthday, my mom overdosed the first time. Next."

Something about how fast she answered—like it was almost rehearsed—bothered me. She went to turn the page, but I put my hand over it. "I can't lie to you with these. Don't lie to me."

She closed her eyes and dragged a hand through her hair. Her mouth opened, then closed, then opened again. "Fine. My worst memory is the first time one of my mom's boyfriends tried to rape me," she said in a rush, and I swallowed. "I was twelve."

My pulse kicked up, and there was a moment where I wasn't sure I wanted to know everything about her.

When she opened her eyes, they were hard and unreadable. "Still want to know about me?" There was a bite to her tone, anger, fear...I wasn't sure.

I stared at my sketchbook, thinking. There were pictures and lines, short sentences, and thoughts that told more than my lips ever would. "Depends on how much you want us to know about each other." I tapped the book in her hands. "It's not pretty."

"The truth never is. Anything pretty is always a lie." She went to my bed and settled against the headboard before she flipped to the next page.

"Do you like yourself?"

"I'm not sure," she said, confusion wrinkling her brow.

I fell onto the mattress beside her, looking over her

shoulder at the drawing of gnarled up trees and wolves, then flipped the page for her, sweeping a hand over the picture of gallows, a handful of pills, and a gun. She touched her fingers to the paper as if the objects were real. "Do you wish you were like them?" I asked.

"Who?"

"Barrington." As much as we hated them, we'd be stupid not to wish we had semi-functional families and money. I just hoped that had we been that lucky, we would have appreciated it instead of being entitled pricks.

"Don't we all at some point? I hate them, but I have to ask myself if I'm not really just bitter that they got a better hand. I think that if I had their money, it wouldn't make me an asshole. The same way they probably don't think they're assholes."

Next page. Next question.

"Why do you want to come off like the bad girl?"

Her gaze lifted from the paper on a half-smile. "Are you telling me I'm doing a bad job?"

"Pretty much."

"I don't like people."

"No shit," I said. "But you still didn't answer the question."

"I don't like needing people. And I'm not someone for anyone to rely on."

"Why?"

She turned the page. Demons and devils crawled through a ribcage filled with spiders' webs.

"Because people always let you down." She hesitated for a second. "Human connection is a lie we tell ourselves we need. We don't need anyone but ourselves, and it's best that way."

Even for me, that was fucking sad. "You want to be alone then?"

The papers rustled when she flipped them. "I just want something real."

"And how will you know when something is real?"

Another flip of the page to a pencil drawing of a screaming head inside a screaming head inside a screaming head, until there was nothing but a black void.

"Do you draw what you feel?" she asked.

"Avoiding my question?" I touched a hand to the page. "It's the only way I can draw. Otherwise, it's just shit."

Her eyes narrowed as she stared at a spot on the wall. "I don't know. I guess...it's real when you trust someone."

I moved my hand, and she went to the next drawing. And before I even realized that I had verbalized it, I asked her, "Do you trust me?"

"Yes." Another flipped page.

"Why?"

Her fingers gripped the edge of the book, and this time she hesitated before her gaze met mine. "Because you gave a shit. And no one else ever has."

I could sense how exposed she was. My pulse pounded a little harder, words on the tip of my tongue I wasn't sure I wanted to spit out. I took the notebook out of Monroe's hand and placed it on the nightstand. "You're the only girl I've ever given a shit about." I grabbed her hips and pulled her on top of me.

Her hands went to my face. "Good." And then she kissed me.

20

MONROE

The morning sun crept over the top of Frank's Famous Chicken. I could not deal with the thick smell of fried food this early.

Despite my telling him I didn't want anything, Zepp shoved a tray of food in front of me when he fell into the booth. I glanced at the chicken peeking out from the biscuit, the breading shiny with grease.

I did, however, take the paper cup of coffee, clutching it in my hands as I watched him. This was weird in the sense that it felt so normal. I had seen something of him last night that no one else had; something in those pictures made me long for the kind of connection I had always shunned so easily. Maybe pain just seeks company, and people like us needed someone just as broken to help us feel whole.

Zepp scarfed down half the container of hash browns. "Eat the biscuit, Roe."

"I don't really eat breakfast." I sipped my coffee. "And I sure as hell don't wake up half an hour early just to get some Frank's Famous Chicken. Who does that?"

"This shit is good. You're crazy."

I rolled my eyes and picked at a piece of biscuit. It seemed to appease him enough.

The door to the restaurant banged open. I glanced over Zepp's shoulder just as Max and Leah walked in. Max's eyes locked with mine for the briefest of moments; a sick smirk slipped over his lips. My stomach bottomed out, and it felt like insects were crawling over my skin. I dropped my gaze to the table.

"What's wrong?" Zepp asked before the click of crutches moved past our booth.

"I'm fine."

Zepp's gaze followed Max across the restaurant, anger churning from him like Niagara Falls. He looked like he was ready to blow.

The tension was like a lead weight on my shoulders. All I wanted to do was run so I didn't have to be in a room with that entitled asshole, but I forced myself to remain seated. Max Harford wasn't going to chase me out of anywhere. Not even Frank's Famous Chicken.

Shoving to his feet, Zepp snatched up his tray. His angry stare fixed on Max like he'd kill him if he even looked my way. I dumped my untouched food and walked to the door, trying to calm my racing pulse. I hadn't seen Max since that night, and I had tried my best not to think about it. Now, though, everything was fighting to the surface, trying to break out of that box it had been shoved in. I didn't want to be this weak.

―――――

WE STOPPED off at the trailer so I could shower and change, and by the time we pulled up in front of the school, I was regretting my choice of outfit. A skirt. The same skirt I'd worn for years, that now made me feel naked and exposed.

I had let Max and Leah change me, and I hated that. The way I dressed had nothing to do with what had happened to me, and everything to do with the shitty person Max was. That's what I kept reminding myself as I climbed off Zepp's bike.

Zepp snagged my wrist and yanked me close. His lips landed on mine for a brief moment before he sped away, leaving me bewildered in a cloud of exhaust fumes. Zepp had just kissed me. At school. And I wasn't ignorant enough to think that didn't mean something.

I kept my head down as I cut through the packed hallway. A horrible, little knot of self-consciousness pulled at my gut, and I tugged at the hem of my skirt. For the first time since I met him, I wished Zepp were here. I hated that awful sense of need.

I was on my way to the cafeteria at lunch when I heard Dale Davison.

"Hey, Monroe." He broke away from the group of football players huddled against the lockers. "Hear you locked down Zepp Hunt. Your pussy must be pure gold." A boom of laughter filled the hallway.

"And you must be really stupid," I said on a sigh.

His gaze moved over me in a way that I'd usually brush off. But today, it set me on edge.

"You know—" He stepped forward, and his fingers brushed the material of my skirt.

Something hot and volatile tore through me like a freight train. And I snapped. Why did these guys think they could touch me without permission? That they could say whatever they wanted and expect me to brush it off. Why? Because I wore a skirt? Because I "asked for it"...

My vision went red, my fist balled, and before I knew what I had even done, I punched him in the throat. He coughed, eyes going wide as he stumbled back. It felt good to hurt him. I hit him again. When he fell to the floor, I was on him, punching him over and over. A hot and feral rage coursed through my veins, driving me like a demon on my shoulder. Dale. Max. All of them. They all deserved this. Even though Dale never fought back. Not once.

I didn't stop until a thick arm wrapped around my waist, hauling me away. Adrenaline fired through my veins, and I kicked and shouted at whoever had a hold on me.

"Chill out, Moe. What the hell?" Chase threw open the fire door and dragged me outside the school before the door banged shut behind us.

He held up his hands. "Damn, Moe."

I drew in labored breaths, and my hands started to shake. I pressed my forehead to the cool brick wall, trying to calm my racing heart.

"What did he do to you?" Chase asked. Like he cared.

I was just some slut in his eyes, apparently. "Fuck you, Chase." I yanked open the door and stormed back inside toward the girls' restroom.

Jade spotted me in the hallway and silently followed me inside and locked the stall door behind us. I slid down the wall to the floor.

"Are you okay?" she asked, leaning against the divider

In a strange way, hitting Dale had been cathartic. "Yeah, I am."

"You literally just broke Dale's nose..."

"Yeah, well. He's a dick." It wasn't an excuse. I knew I had come unhinged.

"Of course he's a dick." She glanced at my shirt. "Gross. His blood's on you."

I stared at the spots on my shirt. "Great." The intercom system squeaked. "Can Dale Davison and Monroe James please report to the principal's office."

"Shit." I pushed to my feet, heading to the door. "Probably going to get suspended."

As I turned into the corridor that led to the office, I saw Dale approaching from the other end. His face looked bad. Really bad. His nose was crammed with tampons and his lip split. I couldn't believe I'd done that.

Dale didn't say a word to the principal, other than he had walked into a locker. I knew that had nothing to with me and everything to do with Zepp and the fear he instilled. It felt like those little threads that pulled me to Zepp had just grown tighter. I was starting to feel like one of them, and while I knew that wasn't a good thing, deep down, I longed for that sense of belonging.

21

ZEPP

Green buds scattered the table. Wolf puffed on a joint while he stuffed a Ziploc bag with weed.

"Hey. You still hang out with Dizzy?" I asked.

Dizzy was the guy who first got us into selling weed—until he ended up in jail for an assault charge.

"Off and on. Why?"

I snatched the baggie, weighed it, sealed it, then tossed it into Wolf's unzipped backpack. "Think he'd take a hundred bucks to beat the shit outta some guy?"

"Probably." He passed me another bag. "Who?"

"Some guy that fucks around with Monroe's mom."

"Sure, Dizzy would do it. Want me to call him?"

I gave him a nod as a cloud of smoke drifted across the table.

We bundled up a few more dime bags before Wolf broke the silence. "You like her."

I focused on the numbers flashing on the scale. Of course I liked Monroe, but something about admitting it seemed too personal. Even for Wolf.

"Dude, you kissed her in the parking lot."

"And?" I chucked the bag into his backpack. "I've had girls give me blowjobs in the bathroom."

"Zepp Hunt having anything to do with a girl outside of a bedroom is weird as hell." He pushed up from the chair and went to the fridge. "She's all right, though," he said. And that was Wolf's way of saying he wouldn't give me any more grief about it.

Gravel crunched beneath the tires of Dizzy's Cadillac when he backed out of Wolf's drive.

Wolf propped the ladder against the side of the trailer. He made it up the first few rungs before he froze and looked back at me. "Wait. Why aren't you just beating Jerry's ass?"

Because I had promised Monroe I wouldn't touch him. "It's complicated."

"Whatever, dude."

We fell into the ratty lawn chairs, and my gaze locked on the license plate of a brown Camaro that read: DABIGBOSS.

"Da Big Boss, 'bout to get his ass beat."

Wolf chuckled before he leaned over to grab a drink from the mini-fridge. He sighed. "Dude, we haven't had any parties since Monroe started hanging around."

"There's been a lot of shit going down."

The deep gurgle of an engine echoed over the trailer park before a Mustang came flying down the road, a cloud of dust kicking up in the glow of the taillights. It idled to a stop outside Monroe's trailer. The door swung open, and Monroe climbed out, then disappeared behind the trailer. Seconds later, she emerged from the shadows with a tarp.

Wolf coughed out a laugh. "Oh, I forgot to tell you. She beat the shit out of Dale Davison today."

I swung my gaze from Monroe to him. "Why the hell are you just now telling me this?"

Wolf shrugged, holding up the joint permanently attached to his fingers. "Forgot."

Jesus Christ. Blood pulsed through my temples, slowly building while the possibilities of why she would punch someone flipped like a Rolodex through my mind.

When Monroe started toward her door, I wet my lips and whistled. She froze, glancing down the street in our direction.

"Hey, Roe!" I shouted. "Why'd you beat Dale's ass?"

Her hands went to her hips. "Because he's a dick."

I had been the king of all dicks to her, and it took her a good few weeks to punch me. "Did he touch you?"

Her head dropped back on a groan, then she tossed something inside her trailer, and hurried across to Wolf's porch. The ladder creaked before her head popped over the gutters. Her gaze bounced between Wolf and me, a small grin pulling at her face. "Well, this looks cozy."

Wolf slumped in his chair. "This is guy's time, dude. She's interrupting man-hour."

"I'm sorry, I don't want to shout across the trailer park like a redneck. Don't worry. I'm not staying."

I snatched her wrist before she could descend. "Did he touch you?"

"No."

My hold on her tightened. "Then why did you punch him, Roe?"

"I told you, he's a dick. He pissed me off." She studied me for a moment, then huffed. "Will you stop?"

She told me the other night that she trusted me, and yet,

here we were dancing around the truth. Like Monroe always did.

"What did he do exactly?"

Wolf sighed, then pushed up and shuffled toward the ladder. "I'm hungry," he said on his way down.

Monroe's teeth raked over her bottom lip. "Apparently, I must have a golden pussy to lock you down. His words. Not mine."

Wolf laughed from the porch, mumbling golden pussy before the door below us opened and shut.

That was shit Monroe would usually roll her eyes at—shit *I* would usually deck someone for.

"Don't look at me like that. I was feeling temperamental this morning." She dropped onto the lawn chair, crossing one leg over the other.

Part of me wanted to put him in a chokehold, but then I figured, Dale getting a smackdown by a girl was humiliation enough. Monroe was the kind of girl who could fight her own battles.

"Do you have a golden pussy?"

She shot a sharp glare at me. "You're funny."

"So, I've been told." I glanced back at her trailer.

A massive guy circled the tarp-covered car. My jaw tensed while I played with the idea of going over there and throwing a punch at him. I jerked my chin toward the bastard.

"That why you wanted the Hurst back so bad?"

"Yeah. Thanks for that, by the way." A half-smile flashed over her face. "He was so pissed when you stole it right off the damn drive."

My jaw tightened, and I leaned over my knees, staring at the bastard as he peeked under the tarp. "It's not funny, Roe." Had I known, I would have just let her have it.

"It is what it is."

It is what it is... I knew her mom was there. I knew she was a crackhead. My mom may have let guys smack her around, she may have hidden it from anyone who tried to help, but high off her ass or sober, she would never let any of her piece-of-shit boyfriends touch us. The one that actually did whack Hendrix got stabbed in the gut. Monroe had told me the other night that her mom's boyfriends had tried to rape her—but that was something that happened behind closed doors in the silence of the night. The bruises Monroe had on her, no way that could go unnoticed—ignored but not unnoticed.

"And your mom just lets that shit happen?" Part of me wanted to go set fire to the trailer at this point. That was a question I already knew the answer to.

"She's too far gone to care about anything but her next hit." Monroe sucked in an uneven breath. "And he's giving it to her, so..."

Jesus Christ. I wanted to kill them both. "You don't have to stay there, you know." The words came out of my mouth before they had registered. And it wasn't that I didn't want her at my house, but more that I was afraid I would freak her out.

She hugged one leg to her chest, resting her temple on her knee. Monroe watched me like she was trying to work me out. "Where else am I going to go?"

"You can stay with me."

An uncomfortable expression knitted her brows, and I panicked. Too much, too fast. Too stupid. God, she made me stupid.

"Or Jade or something," I shrugged like it was no big deal. Just a suggestion.

"Pretty sure your parents wouldn't appreciate picking up a stray. Or Jade's."

I sank back a little in the chair, bouncing my leg as I swiped at my face. "I don't have any parents."

"What?"

"My mom's dead."

She sucked in a deep breath. "Sorry."

My chest tightened until I couldn't find a good breath. "It's fine." It wasn't. I missed her every day.

The sound of the cicadas seemed to grow louder by the second. I hated this shit. The entire "I feel bad, and I should act like it, but I don't know what to say" bullshit. It sucked. But it was life, and this was getting uncomfortable. "So, you wanna go somewhere?"

"Sure. Where?"

I studied her for a second, knowing damn well that there was a shitstorm brewing inside her. Max. Dale... I could tell her eight hundred times that those guys were assholes, but it wouldn't matter. She had probably punched Dale because she was angry. And she had every damn right to be, but beating that dipshit wasn't enough. Not for Max and Jerry and her sorry excuse for a mom.

Without answering her, I pushed up from the chair and climbed down the ladder. I went to Wolf's door and knocked. "Open up, shithead."

He cracked it half an inch, the security chain catching when he peeked out. "This better be good. I was watching PornHub."

"Can I get your bat?"

He shrugged and walked off, coming back a few seconds later with an aluminum Louisville Slugger.

Monroe jumped from the ladder, lifting a brow at the bat. "Do I want to know?"

"Probably not."

I parked behind Shit Shack; then, we headed across the street to the junkyard. I tucked the Slugger into the back of my jeans and scaled the fence.

"Is this where you kill me and hide my body in the trunk of some scrap metal?" Monroe asked, staring at me from the other side of the chain links.

"Maybe."

She quickly climbed up, slinging a leg over before she jumped, landing on her feet beside me.

"So, you think I'm gonna kill you, but you're still here, huh?"

"Yeah, well, I trust you."

And that...made me feel like I was worth something to her. And I liked it and hated it at the same time.

I headed through the piles of old washers and refrigerators, rounding mounds of dented fenders before we came to a stop. Staring at the heap of junk in front of me, I pulled the bat from my jeans and passed it over to her. "Windows and headlights are the most rewarding."

She looked from the bat in her hand to me. "You want me to hit things?"

"Hitting shit always makes me feel better." I pulled a cigarette from my pocket, lit it, then leaned against the bumper of a Chevy Silverado.

"Pretty sure hitting Dale did that," she said, lifting the bat before she swung at the front windshield. Glass shattered, and she moved onto the passenger side window.

"Don't lie to yourself, Monroe." It took a lot more than hitting one person to purge those emotions.

She made her way around the car, and with each

smashed pane of glass and dented panel, I knew the anger had to be bleeding through her.

"Feels good, huh?" I snatched a rusted muffler from the ground, then took a swing at a Toyota's hood. I thought about my mom and the guy who had never paid his dues when it came to her. And I swung again.

"Fine." She punched the end of the bat through a headlight. "I admit it. I'm angry." She put a few dents in the car, then stopped to look at me. "What are you mad about?" she asked through heavy pants.

And wasn't that a loaded question. "A lot of things," I said.

"Like what?"

I smashed the muffler through a windshield. Cubes of glass sprayed in every direction. Some vulnerabilities are better kept to oneself. Which is why it shocked the shit out of me when I said, "My mom."

"I..." Monroe stilled, tapping the bat against the ground. "How did she die?" she whispered, so quiet, I barely heard it. "You don't have to tell me," she said in a rush.

I took a few more swings, this time, at the door of the car. I beat the thing until my arms ached and sweat beaded my forehead. The one thing I didn't want to talk about was that —just like I figured, the one thing she didn't want to talk about was Jerry.

But she had.

"Some asshole beat her to death." And then I rammed the muffler through the hood. No one but Hendrix knew that.

Her chin met her chest. "Of course." The words were a mumbled affirmation. Pieces clicked together in her mind. "Did they find the guy?"

I closed my eyes. Counted to ten. And I told myself, Roe

was only asking because she cared, and I should appreciate that. "He was Barrington." I could hear my pulse in my ears.

I stared at the demolished car; the silence that stretched between us seemed like an eternity. Because she knew what that meant. That the guy got off because of his name. Because of his money. Because my mother was worthless compared to him—to everyone except Hendrix and me.

Her hand brushed my shoulder before her arms wrapped around my waist, her chin pressing to my shoulder. And goddamn, that broke me. I buried my face in her neck. Monroe was making herself a lifeline, and I was fucked.

"That's shit, Zepp."

"It's just life, Monroe."

22

MONROE

Warm breaths trickled over my neck before I slowly pulled away from him. Zepp was hard, the way only someone who was truly broken could be. Now I knew why, and it caused a twinge of pain to tug at my heart.

He leaned against the front grill of the Silverado, and I jumped up onto the hood beside him, resting my feet on the bumper.

"So, you and Hendrix live alone?" I asked.

"Since I was fifteen."

I swallowed around the sudden lump in my throat, picturing a young Zepp grieving for his mother, left to care for his brother. Zepp *had* to be hard. He didn't have a choice. The world had made Zepp an island of jagged, impenetrable rocks that no one could pass—unless he let them.

"No one came for you when your mom died?"

He traced a pattern over the dusty hood. "My uncle didn't tell the state he was fucking off to Florida. And I sure as hell wasn't going to say anything and get my ass put in foster care."

"I get it." I'd been in foster care twice when my mom had overdosed. No one wanted to be at the mercy of the system. "So, you take care of Hendrix?"

"We take care of each other."

His pain was visceral, lingering in the air like a toxic gas, and I wanted him not to feel so alone at that moment. I grabbed his hand, and he glanced down at our interlocked fingers. "Well, you're lucky. That you have him and the guys." Him, Hendrix, Wolf, Bellamy—they were a family of sorts. While I envied it, I was glad he had it.

He shifted, stepping between my legs, and placing his hands on my knees. "And what about you?"

"What *about* me?"

Those dark eyes searched mine. There was a desperation in them, a panic I'd never seen before. "Do I have you?"

My heart thumped, tripping in my chest like a lovesick little girl. His hands skimmed down my sides to my waist. I didn't need to think about it. I knew he had me, but saying the words felt monumental. It wasn't a simple "you have me," it was also an "I need you."

"Because I need this." His fingers swept my cheek.

Vulnerability equated to pain, and it felt like I was holding out my heart, ready to place it in Zepp's palm where he could easily crush it. Did I trust him not to? It was a simple question, but the truth equated to me jumping off a cliff and hoping he'd catch me. "You have me," I whispered.

His lips pressed to mine. He kissed me like I was oxygen and he was suffocating. It was so much more than a kiss; it felt like a promise, unbreakable and binding. His hands went to my hips, tugging me tight against him.

The sudden explosion of a shotgun rang out, sending dogs barking and howling. I tore away from Zepp, my heart almost exploding through my ribs.

"Hey! Git outta my yard." Another loud bang.

Zepp grabbed my hand, and we took off, sprinting through the rusted heaps to the fence. I climbed over the tall chain link, and Zepp followed, dragging me across the road to the Shit Shack.

"You couldn't have warned me about the crazy redneck who might pop up?"

He leaned against the rotting siding to catch his breath. "He's usually passed out drunk this time of night."

"Outta breath there?" I smirked at him. "You need to stop smoking so much."

"Why? Worried?"

I took the helmet from the handlebars of his bike before throwing a leg over it. "No."

"Liar."

FRIDAY MEANT SCHOOL spirit had been vomited all over the halls of Dayton High. Banners hung over doorways. Red and blue ribbons were taped onto the football players' lockers. The cheerleaders pranced around in their skirts, ponytails tied back with prissy bows. The entire thing was gag-worthy.

That morning, Zepp stood at my locker, smirking. "Ready to cage the panthers, Roe?" He chuckled, then slapped a palm over my chest, leaving behind a Cage the Panthers spirit sticker.

"I'm not going today. You can eat shit." I peeled the sticker off, putting it on him.

He pushed away from the wall of lockers and started along beside me. "You're always so angry."

"Tell me this shit doesn't put you in a bad mood." I

waved my hand around at the decorations, and Zepp ripped a wad of tinsel off one of the lockers.

"I find it entertaining."

Wolf rounded the corner. A string of ribbons hung around his neck as a makeshift necklace—the cardboard medallion hanging from it covered with glitter and his football number.

Zepp flicked it. "You're such a pussy."

Wolf shoved his shoulder. "Shut up, dude. The girl that made this has big titties and a big ass. I'll wear it if it gets me laid."

A group of deep laughs came from behind us, followed by Chase calling my name. On instinct, I turned around.

He shoved his hands into his pocket. "Can I talk to you?"

I had nothing to say to Chase. He'd pissed me off. Crossed a line. "No, fuck off."

"Ah, come on, Moe." He started toward me. "I just want to apologize."

"I don't want your apology."

Chase half-rolled his eyes. "Why are you always so stubborn?"

"Why are you such a prissy little bitch who listens to gossip?"

Zepp moved between us, shoulders squared and chin lifted. "Why the hell do you need to apologize to her?" He was like a massive, silverback gorilla beating his chest in the middle of Dayton's hallway.

"None of your business, Hunt."

Wolf leaped between Zepp and Chase, arms out like a starfish. "Dude, Zepp. He's the receiver. Can you wait to pummel him until Sunday?"

Chase grabbed Wolf and yanked him to the side. "I don't need your help, Brookes," he snapped. God, he was an idiot.

Wolf dropped his chin on a laugh, then clasped a hand on Chase's shoulder. "Trust me. You do."

"Zepp." My fingers threaded through his. "Come on." I tugged on his hand, trying to move him away from the middle of the hallway while Wolf pushed Chase around a corner.

"Have you fucked him?" Zepp yanked his hand from mine, his brow creased.

My temper spiked instantly. "Fuck you." I started toward class without a backward glance.

"Don't get pissed at me. It's a fair question." He was right back beside me. And I wasn't about to argue with him in the hall. I made a beeline to the girls' restroom. The door had barely had a chance to close behind me before it swung back open, and Zepp barreled inside.

The two girls at the mirror hurried out.

"No. I have not fucked him." I folded my arms over my chest, hating that I even dignified him with an answer; Chase was practically like a brother to me.

"He's got a fucking nickname for you."

"We're friends."

"Bullshit." Zepp glared at me. "Guys are not friends with girls."

"Well, we are." I leaned against the sink, glaring at him. "Got a problem with that?"

"Yeah, I do." He inched toward me, and I straightened. "Gotta problem with *that*."

"You don't own me, Zepp."

His eyes narrowed. "What's he apologizing for, Roe?"

"Nothing I can't handle on my own."

With every second that passed, the anger on Zepp's face deepened. "Well, he did something." He gave one curt nod, nostrils flaring like a psychotic bull. "That's all I need," he said, moving for the door.

"Wait. What?" I rushed after him. "What are you doing?"

He was already rounding the corner.

"Zepp, you fucking psycho."

His long legs ate up the ground, and I got lost in a sea of students who didn't part for me the way they did for him. By the time I found him, Chase was pinned against a locker, clutching a bloody lip while Zepp growled words in his face.

"I was a dick!" Chase said.

"Why?" Zepp banged Chase against the metal wall.

"I thought she had fucked Harford." Chase's eyes shifted to me. "I'm sorry, Moe. I didn't mean—"

Zepp punched him again before stepping back. Chase slumped to the floor.

"The receiver, man!" Wolf clutched at his head. "Dammit, Zepp."

Zepp grabbed my waist and dragged me down the hall.

I elbowed him in the ribs. "You're a psycho, you know it?"

"You make me one."

"Don't blame me—"

"You think a *friend* would get pissed off because they think you fucked somebody?"

"I..." I didn't have an answer for that.

A smug smirk shaped his lips. "Guys aren't just friends with girls, Roe. Accept that."

He kissed me before he walked off. He was wrong, though. Chase was just a friend.

―――

I SPENT the next two periods thinking about how much of a lunatic Zepp was. I shouldn't have liked it, and since part of me did, maybe that made me just as bad as him.

"Monroe James," my name crackled over the intercom, pulling me out of my thoughts. "You're needed in the office to check out."

I hadn't been checked out of school since I was in elementary school. I got up and slowly put away my books before heading to the office.

The secretary passed a check-out slip over the counter, a sympathetic frown on her face. "It'll be okay, sweetheart." She clasped her wrinkled hand over mine like someone had died. Maybe my mom had finally killed herself with that shit she put in her veins. "They said they'd pick you up out front."

"Uh. Thanks?"

She buzzed me through the front entrance, and I stared out over the parking lot, looking for Jerry's Camaro. Fear churned in my gut, because if she was dead, what would Jerry try to do?

Cigarette smoke wafted past. "My condolences," Zepp said, stepping out from the side of the school.

"Is this you?" I waved the piece of paper around.

"What?" Smoke billowed from his lips. "You wanted to go to the pep rally instead?"

I rolled my eyes. "A little warning would've been nice. I thought my mom was dead."

He said nothing.

"Wait, tell me you didn't kill someone."

"Actually, I paid a hooker five bucks to call in." He chucked his smoke to the ground. "Old Betty at the front office knows my voice."

It was quite sweet. For Zepp. His fingers swept over my

cheek, dark eyes studying me as he tipped back my face. Warm lips brushed mine before he tossed an arm around my shoulder, and we started walking toward his bike. "God rest your Grandpa Joe's soul." He snorted a laugh.

He pulled out of the school parking lot and sped down the highway that led into Dayton.

Two games into *Call of Duty*, and I had beat him both times. He tossed down the controller and huffed. "I never should have taught you how to play."

"The student has become the master."

"Does that mean anything I teach you, you're gonna be the master?" His teeth raked his lip, his gaze dropping to my mouth.

"Depends. What have you got?"

"One thing in particular." His hands went to my waist. "You're so fucking hot." He dragged me into his lap, then pressed his lips to mine. Hard and hungry, the kiss threatened to steal my breath. "You have no idea how bad I want you."

And I wanted him. But I was not ready to have sex with him. There was kissing. There was sex. Then there was that gray area in between that I didn't quite know how to tread. Especially with Zepp. He seemed to be all or nothing, and honestly, if we started something, I wasn't sure how easy it would be to stop. My fingers raked into his hair, pulling him closer. It felt like I couldn't get enough of him, and I wanted more—I just didn't know what exactly.

"You're thinking about it," he whispered against my lips.

"About what?"

"About fucking me." His fingers dug into my hips, each muscle tight with restraint.

Zepp felt like a ticking bomb just waiting to go off. Part of me wanted to push him over the edge, just to see what would happen, but nervous energy wound through my veins, making me hesitate.

He pushed me back on the couch, covering my body with his. "What it would be like for me to fuck you, face down on the hood of a car." His hands roamed along my sides.

Heat spiked over my skin, and my lungs suddenly felt too small.

"In my bed," he continued between kisses to my throat. "Against a wall..."

"Hard not to," I said on a ragged breath.

He pressed between my legs, and something else cut through the lust. "If this isn't an invitation, Monroe, you better tell me now."

Was it? I didn't know, but I didn't want him to stop. For the first time in my life, I craved a connection. I wanted things with Zepp I had never wanted with anyone else, but I was terrified what crossing that line with him might mean. "It's not an invitation to fuck me, but... It's something." I stumbled over words while his mouth worked down my throat, his fingers digging into my waist hard enough to bruise.

"We don't have to fuck."

I couldn't help but smile. From Zepp, it was almost chivalrous. It made me feel like I was important to him, and that was all any of us in this shitty life were really seeking: to mean something to someone.

"But, for the love of God, let me do something." His

hand wrapped around the back of my neck. Another brutal kiss to my lips. He was everywhere, all-consuming.

My mind lingered somewhere between nervousness and curiosity, while my body demanded more. "Okay," I said, trying to catch my breath.

He rubbed his hand along my thigh. "Good."

His fingers trailed beneath my skirt, slipping between my thighs. There was a moment, a pause where the only sound was my rattling breaths.

"You okay?" He was right there.

"Yeah." I grabbed the back of his neck and kissed him just as his hand slipped inside my panties, then his calloused finger pushed into me.

My breath hitched, and my body tensed before I gave into him.

"Does that feel good, Roe?"

I couldn't think past the feeling of him touching me and the primal need for more. The only response he received was the slight buck of my hips.

He worked his way deeper, groaning against my throat. "It's so hard not to fuck you right now." His touch was rough and dominating, and I imagined what it would be like to be fucked by him, to have his bare skin pressed to mine.

A moan slipped past my lips, and my back bowed away from the couch cushions.

"Fuck, Roe." His heavy breaths caressed my skin as he controlled every inch of my body while I cracked open beneath his skilled touch. It was like he knew every button to press, each stroke in exactly the right place that would get me off.

Tension built, my fingers clawed at his skin until I was desperate for the release I knew he would give me. And when he did, it crashed over me like a rogue wave, heavy and hard, stealing all sense of anything that wasn't him.

He kept going until I grabbed his wrist. "Don't want another one?" His fingers curled inside me again, and I flinched away.

"You're a dick."

When I looked at him, he pulled away, then slipped his fingers between his lips. I blushed, all the while needing more. I palmed him through his jeans, wanting him to lose control the same way I just had.

A bang sounded from the back door just as I reached for his fly. "Hey, cocksucker! Why'd you skip?" Hendrix shouted, rounding the doorway. "I knew you two were fucking!" A bookbag hurtled through the air, landing on the couch beside us.

"Get outta here, would you?" Zepp shouted.

"You're gross. Trying to wet the tip of your dick on the couch I sit on." He glared at me with a snarled lip. "Juices."

I rolled my eyes. "I've seen you get your dick sucked on this couch." That was a disgusting realization. "Gross," I shoved at Zepp. "We need to get off this thing."

"Hendrix!" Zepp shouted, shoving me back down. "Get the hell out before I kill you!"

He completely ignored his brother. "That's my juices. Not yours, Red." Hendrix ducked into the kitchen and came back out with a bag of chips.

His gaze bounced between Zepp and me. "This is weird. I don't like it." He flopped onto the sofa, cramming chips into his mouth. On a sigh, I sat up, and this time, Zepp let me.

"Oh my God. You're dating each other! That's gross. Like sick gross, man." He punched Zepp in the shoulder. "What's wrong with you?"

Zepp grabbed the remote from the table and chucked it at his brother, who then threw up his middle finger. "You've got a room. I wanna watch TV."

"It's fine. I should go, anyway." I pushed to my feet. "I have to work tonight."

"I'm still waiting on the part for your car."

"It's fine. I'll get Jade to give me a lift." I pulled my phone from my pocket to text Jade, and Zepp took it from my hands.

"I'll take you."

I paused. I did not want Zepp dropping me off at The White Rabbit. Shit. "Okay." I paused. "Thanks."

He snatched the remote from Hendrix. "What time you have to be at work?"

"Not until ten. Can you just take me home?"

One of his brows lowered. "Why?"

Because I didn't want him to know I stripped. "I have to shower and get ready."

"Is Jerry there?" His gaze narrowed. "Just get ready here. I'll take you."

He stared me down, and maybe it was just my guilty conscience, but I felt like he sensed I had something to hide. And I absolutely did. At that moment, I realized just how much I'd grown to like Zepp because I was terrified of him finding out that I stripped. No guy wanted to be with a girl who took her clothes off for other men, and I couldn't blame him. *I* was disgusted by it, and I was the one doing it. Zepp was no stranger to doing what he had to get by, but he had never sacrificed his dignity in the process.

"Okay," I said, even though all I wanted was for him to take me home and have Jade give me a lift to work.

WE WATCHED a movie and ordered pizza, Hendrix complaining the whole time. It felt normal just to hang out. And that scared me because this was not my life. I was used to being alone for the most part, okay with it even, but how could I miss something I had never had. Zepp was starting to become my normal, and this time, if I had to go back to being on my own, I'd know what I was missing. The movie went off, and Zepp grabbed my hand, leading me up to his room. The door shut behind him, the lock clicked.

The look he gave me made my stomach clench. I bit my lip, trying to hide a smile. "Do you need something?"

"To finish what we started earlier."

He closed the space between us and fisted my hair, sending a bite of pain over my scalp before his lips slammed over mine. Zepp got me so drunk on him that he made me want things I never had. Like wanting to watch Zepp snap and lose control the way he'd done to me.

His teeth sank into my bottom lip when I tugged at his belt. Swallowing my nerves, I shoved down his jeans and boxers, then dropped to my knees. A silver bar glinted under the light. Of course, Zepp would have a piercing in his dick. The skin over the bar looked so thin.

"Scared of it?" His gaze locked on me while his fingers played with my hair. "It's sensitive."

I wasn't exactly experienced with this. A two-week boyfriend my sophomore year hadn't prepared me in any way for a guy like Zepp, and I was worried I would be really bad compared to all the girls before me.

"You have no idea how many times I've imagined you on your knees." He fisted my hair.

I took a deep breath, swallowing down the knot of unease that lodged in my throat. When I grabbed him, that piercing was the first place my tongue trailed over. He hissed out a breath, his body going rigid.

"Shit." His hold on my hair tightened, and my confidence grew slightly, and I swallowed him back as far as I could.

Within a few minutes, Zepp was groaning, his fingers tangled in my hair before he pulled away, and I watched him lose control, fisting himself as a guttural sound tore from his lips. There was something unashamedly primal about it, and it made me want him even more than I already did. He glanced up, still holding himself in his hand.

"That look." He bit at his lip, pumping over himself. "I swear to God, Roe, if you don't want me to fuck you..."

He looked at me like he would ruin me and want quickly twisted into anxiety.

"I need to take a shower." I snatched his towel from the back of the door and went into the bathroom.

I got into the shower, with the door that wouldn't close because the frame was so warped. I had just lathered my hair with shampoo that smelled like pine needles when I heard footsteps, then the toilet seat creak. Someone whistled the seven dwarves theme song.

"That had better be you, Zepp," I said.

"Are you just moving in?" Hendrix groaned.

"No! You just come in for a shit when anyone else is in the shower?"

"When I have to shit, I have to shit." God, he was disgusting.

"Zepp!" I shouted.

The floorboards creaked. "What the hell are you doing?" Zepp's voice came from the doorway.

"I've got a dingleberry hanging out of my spider hole, man."

"Pinch it off and get out!"

The toilet flushed, followed by aerosol dispersing. "There. Pine Mountain Fresh and shit, for the princess." Hendrix huffed.

"Oh my God." I rinsed out the last of the shampoo and cut off the water, clutching the curtain to me as I reached for a towel. I wrapped it around myself and grabbed my clothes. When I stepped outside, I found Hendrix prancing around in the hall.

"All yours."

"I'm turtle heading," he said, running past me and not even bothering to shut the door.

"Wow." I walked into Zepp's room and closed the door. "I don't know how you do it."

All he did was sigh and shake his head. "Again. You're welcome I said you were off-limits two years ago."

Him pissing on me like a dog without having exchanged a word should have annoyed me. But in this instance, I was grateful. "Thanks."

I tugged on my jeans and shirt.

"Where do you work?" he asked.

"Uh, Cha Cha's." The lie fell from my lips far too easily. The bar right across from The White Rabbit was a reasonable cover, though. "I pick up glasses."

"You need to go home and get a uniform?"

A tiny thread of panic pulled at me. "Nope. It's at work." A locker of G-strings and lingerie.

I felt like shit lying to him. Zepp had done nothing but help me, but that was the very reason I needed to hide this from him. It was a problem I had no way out of. I was so far down the rabbit hole with him; I had no choice but to keep going and hope he didn't rip my heart out of my chest.

My stomach clenched when he pulled into Cha Cha's and parked beneath the flashing, neon light. I hopped off, handing him his helmet.

His gaze drifted behind me. "So, you pick up the glasses?"

"Yeah. I have a good fake ID." It wasn't a lie. I had to show a fake ID to get my job at The White Rabbit, but no way it was good enough that they didn't know I was underage. They just didn't care.

"I'll be back at what, one, to get you?"

Fuck me. "Two. One of the other girls can give me a ride, though. You don't have to come out here at two in the morning, Zepp."

His gaze swept back over to the front of Cha Cha's with its glowing sign. "Nah, I think I do."

"Okay." What else could I say? "Thanks."

Zepp kissed me before I headed toward the front of the bar, guilt eating away at me. The engine revved, the rumble of the engine fading before it disappeared. I spun around, quickly darting over to The White Rabbit. I didn't want to lie to Zepp, but for some reason, I was his exception, different from every other girl who threw themselves at him. I didn't want him to know that I was so much worse than any of them.

23

ZEPP

The past week had been a blur of blow jobs and heavy petting, and every time I thought Monroe might finally beg me to fuck her, she didn't.

She was making me wait. Monroe fucking James was making me wait.

Bellamy's Civic ran over a pothole, and I clamped onto Monroe's thigh to keep her head from hitting the ceiling. The friction of her on my lap when he hit another one, made my dick stand at attention.

Jade shifted beside me, fanning smoke from her face and coughing.

"What?" Wolf glanced over, eyes half-glazed. "Never done a little hotboxing before?"

"Yeah, but..." Jade shook her head and coughed again before she sank back against the seat.

Smoke filled the cabin, and by the time we turned off the highway, I wasn't sure how Bellamy could see to drive.

"Why are we going to this party again?" Monroe asked, scrubbing a hand through my hair.

"Free booze."

She leaned into my ear. "We could just go to your house, and I'll suck your dick."

My hold on her thigh tightened, and I pressed my dick up against her. "You can suck my dick at the party…"

"Do you ever think about like," Wolf said, drawing my attention away from Monroe. "What if we're all just amoebas in some giant's body. Just floating around and shit." He passed the joint to Jade with a slight smirk.

"You look like a deep thinker, weirdo."

The car stopped at a four-way, the streetlight outside letting in just enough light that I caught Jade glance at Monroe in a silent "help me" plea.

"Stop with your Play-Doh bullshit, Wolf." Hendrix nearly threw himself in the backseat to punch Wolf in the gut. "If Jade's giving anyone head, it's not you."

"Oh my God." Groaning, Monroe dragged a hand down her face. "It's Plato, you dick. And she is not touching your riddled cock."

Jade mumbled "shit" under her breath. The more Monroe told my brother to leave Jade alone, the more he would chase after her like a dog with his dick out.

"She has a mind of her own," Hendrix said.

"And unfortunately for you," Monroe flicked him in the forehead, "brain cells."

Wolf lowered his window, then shooed the smoke out. "Get high, neighborhood. Get high."

I dropped my head against the seat, drowning out Monroe and Hendrix's argument until Bellamy parked at the end of a cul-de-sac, and everyone piled out.

Music drifted from the house at the end of the dark street.

Monroe glanced from the house to me. "Seriously. Blow job." She held out her hands like weighing scales. "Party…"

I would have much rather had a blow job, but the guys were already giving me grief about not doing shit with them anymore. "You act like this is torture." I took her hand in mine and followed the guys across the street.

"It is."

Jade leaned in beside her. "You cannot leave me here."

"Fine." Monroe sighed. "Someone has to protect you from Hendrix."

Hendrix snorted when he shouldered past us. He stopped at the gate, then rubbed his palms together as he glanced over the party-goers crowding the back lawn. "I spy with my little eye something beginning with P. And it's pussy!" He whacked me on the back. "Don't worry, bro. I'll pipe one down in your memory."

I gave him a shove, then he and the other guys strutted off through the party while Monroe and I grabbed a beer from the keg. Full cups in hand, we went to the empty glider at the back of the yard and took a seat. I stared across the jam-packed yard, thinking about the fact that I used to come to parties for two things. Beer and girls. Now both seemed like a waste of time. I would have rather stayed at home with Monroe, but the guys would never have let me live that down.

"Friends in Low Places" blared through the busted speakers, the bass of the twangy country song humming. Everyone at the party sang along, except Monroe and me.

I nudged her in the ribs, scooting a little closer. "Don't wanna sing?"

"Do I look like the kind of girl who sings?" She lifted her cup to her lips, eyeing me over the top. "Don't *you* wanna sing?"

"Do I look like the kinda guy who sings?"

"No. And I'm so happy about that."

I stared across the yard. Hendrix threw his arm around some prissy-looking girl in a blue jean skirt.

"Your brother is such a dog." She looked at me, but I couldn't argue that. "Why do you never date girls?"

That was a simple answer. "Wasn't any worth dating." Every other girl had wanted to date me because I was the "bad boy" who didn't date. They wanted to be the one to change that. Monroe—at least I wanted to believe—was with me because I wasn't who she thought.

Jade came rushing through the yard and took Monroe's hand. "Save me from him." She glanced over at Wolf standing by the keg and shooting a stream of beer into his mouth. "He's talking about weird shit."

Monroe snorted as she pushed to her feet. "It's Wolf. He's always weird."

"Come to the bathroom with me."

I grabbed a refill from the keg, watching Monroe's ass shake until she and Jade disappeared into the house. Foam had just trickled over my hand when a hand slapped over my shoulder.

The stout scent of cologne washed over me. "Hey, Zepp. My man. My bro."

Dizzy skirted in front of me, draining the bottle of vodka in his hand before chucking the glass to the ground. "I'mma take care of your man Jerry real soon."

"Good."

"That motherfucker's bad. Why you got beef with him? You ain't into meth dealing, are you?"

I slapped his hand away from my shoulder. "Fuck, no."

"Then why you want ole' Jerry's ass whooped, homes?" Dizzy was sound, and one thing he hated was a guy who hit on women. Couldn't hurt to tell him.

I clenched my jaw. "He's fucking with my girl."

"Messing with your girl. Aw, hell nah, man." A deep scowl crept over his face. "Wait. *Your* girl? Shit, bitch. You gotta girl?" He jerked his chin back toward the now-empty glider Monroe and I had been sitting on. "That redhead?"

"Yeah."

"Shit, man." He whacked me on the back. "She's gotta pair of tits on her. My boys always be tryin' to get lap dances from her over at The Rabbit. And you're fucking that shit? Spreading those legs like peanut butter on toast." He laughed, and my fingers drew into fists. Part of me wanted to ask him if he was sure it was her, but then I knew.

She acted shady as fuck when I had dropped her off at Cha Chas because she worked at the strip club across the street, giving shitheads like Dizzy lap dances. It took everything in me not to nail Dizzy.

He kept running his mouth. "She gotta big ole' booty too. Really knows how to grind it. Bitch, you lucky."

The blood rushing through my ears sounded like a freight train. It took everything in me not to pop Dizzy in his mouth.

"Yeah, man," I said and started toward the house.

"Hey, Zepp!" Dizzy called from behind me. "Where you going?"

Ignoring him, I shouldered through the crowd of kids funneling beer and shoved into the kitchen. The underclassman shoveling dip into his mouth by the kitchen table froze when I stopped in the doorway.

"Where's the bathroom?" I asked.

Dip Guy slowly pointed toward a hallway with his chip, and I took off. I was pissed she had lied to me. Pissed that other guys put their hands on her. Pissed that I had no clue who she was when I thought I did.

Jade stepped into the narrow hall, her steps faltering when her gaze landed on me. "Um. Hi. Zepp."

I moved past her with a grunt, blocking the doorway just as Monroe made it to the threshold.

"What are you doing?" she asked.

I backed her into the room, then slammed the door behind me. A barrage of insults danced on the tip of my tongue, anger bleeding through my veins, but I forced it all back "You're my girl, right?" I gripped her waist, bringing my face inches from hers like I was going to kiss her.

"You know I am." A slight wrinkle set between her brows. "Zepp, what—"

"Which means no other guys can touch you."

"What?" She pushed at my chest, forcing space between us. "You think I'd cheat on you?"

The vision of her stripping, straddling men's laps flashed through my mind, and a surge of heat careened through my veins. "Not what I said." I stared down at her.

Confusion crumpled her face, and part of me thought maybe Dizzy didn't know what he was talking about. But deep down, I knew, and I hated that I had trusted her.

"Would you lie to me, Roe?"

The slight flush to her cheeks washed white. Her gaze dropped to the floor on a heavy swallow. "You know," she whispered.

I balled my fist against the wall, my jaw clenching. It pissed me off that she took her clothes off for men, that other men touched her, stroked her, but what made me angrier than anything else was that she had lied. Which meant she didn't trust me. Music from the party outside drifted underneath the bathroom door.

"Do you want to break up with me?"

"Jesus Christ, Monroe. I hate that you let men see you

naked." I grabbed her chin and lifted her face, but she tugged away from my hold. "But what I hate more is that you told me you trusted me when you don't."

"I do trust you."

"You don't, or you would have fucking told me."

"How was I supposed to tell you that? You look at Chase like you want to kill him, and he's never even touched me!"

"Because he looks at you like he can have you. It has nothing to do with you, and every goddamn thing to do with him." I thought about the way Chase looked at her, and how that probably paled in comparison to how those perverts at The White Rabbit looked at her while she was straddling their dicks.

"I couldn't tell you."

The anger humming through my blood finally boiled to the surface, and I slapped a palm over the wall beside her head. "The hell you couldn't. You lied to me."

"What was I supposed to say?"

I took a step back, swiping a hand over my face while I tried to collect myself.

"Tell me you wouldn't have walked away," she said.

"No."

I took a step back and dragged my hands through my hair. "I don't even care about that, Monroe. I care that you don't trust me."

She was the only person I had trusted outside of the guys. Outside of my mom, and I had desperately wanted that with her.

"I trust you. I just didn't want to lose you." That was a knife to my chest.

I wouldn't have left her over that.

Someone banged over the bathroom door, and Monroe slipped out from under my arm, unlocking the door. She shoved through the group of girls waiting outside the bathroom. By the time I made it to the back yard, she was over on the glider with Jade. She had looked ashamed as hell, so I decided just to leave her alone.

For the next hour, I watched her and Jade slam back drinks—right up until one of the private school girls sauntered over to me, batting her eyelashes. The girl had barely gotten the word "hi" out of her mouth before Monroe's drunk ass was right beside me, swaying and pointing at the girl's face.

"Move the fuck along." She shooed at the girl like a stray cat before tipping her drink back.

I took the now-empty cup away from her.

"Do you hate me?" She swayed before her hand landed on my chest. God, she was drunk.

"No." I looped an arm around her waist, plastering her against me before I claimed her mouth with a kiss. She pressed her tits against my chest.

"I want you, Zepp." She grabbed my dick through my jeans. "So bad."

And I wanted her. I could take her back into the bathroom, give us both what we wanted. "All right," I said, taking her hand and starting toward the house. "Bathroom it is."

Halfway across the yard, shouting broke out from the deck. Of course, Hendrix was in the middle of it, throwing punches.

"Jesus Christ," I mumbled. By the time I got to the porch, some guy was knocked out cold, and Wolf and Bellamy were holding Hendrix back by the arms.

Bellamy glanced over his shoulder when we walked up. "Ready to go?"

"Yeah." I didn't wait, just headed around the side of the house and climbed in the rear of Bellamy's car. The second the door closed, Monroe was in my lap, lips to mine, all tongue and teeth.

"Holy shit, Monroe." Jade smacked at us both. "I'm in here. Gross."

Monroe fumbled with my belt.

"I swear to God," Jade groaned just as the other doors opened and the guys climbed in.

Hendrix with a girl. How the hell my brother had managed to beat some guy's ass *and* pick up a girl on the way out...

"I want to fuck you," Monroe whispered in my ear, and my dick stood at attention.

"That a fact?"

I spent the next fifteen minutes trying to keep Monroe from pulling my dick out in the car, and by the time we got to my house, I was ready to strip her naked and fuck her on the lawn. The second the door to my bedroom had shut, her fingers went to my belt. "I want you."

"Yeah? You keep saying that." Before I could utter another word, she dropped to her knees and had my dick in her mouth. I bit back a groan.

Monroe had sucked me off countless times, but this... This was headed in the direction I had been trying to go for over a month. Every time I was around her, my dick felt like it was ready to explode from waiting. And every time we got anywhere close to both being naked, she would stop me. Tonight, though... Tonight I was fucking her until she would have no choice but to feel me for days when she sat down.

She teased her tongue over my piercing, and damn, that had my knees wanting to buckle.

My grip on her hair tightened, and my eyes closed while I imagined stripping off every piece of her clothing, settling between her thighs, and then destroying her. She got me right to the point of coming before I pulled away.

"Gonna come inside me instead?" She bit her lip on a smile.

"Holy fuck..."

The girl never talked dirty. She was downright awkward, but give her a little beer and... I grabbed her by the waist, kicking off my jeans then my boxers as I backed her to the bed.

"What do you want?" I shoved up her shirt and pulled her bra to the side, then sucked a nipple into my mouth while grinding against her. "Huh?"

"Everything." She clawed at my shirt, dragging it up my body.

I worked my way over her stomach, pulling her thong down her legs before I bunched her skirt around her waist. "You want me to tease you or make it quick?" I shoved her thighs apart, placing my face inches from her while circling my thumb in just the right spot to make her back bow from the bed.

"Zepp," she moaned, grabbing at my hair.

I gave one slow lick over her, nearly losing it. I was going to come on myself before I ever got the chance to screw her if this kept up.

"Like this?" I asked, giving her another swipe of my tongue.

She pitched up, moaning and swearing. Fisting the sheets, then my hair. I had her panting and grinding against my face, and when I felt like she was ready to come, I sat up, then flopped down on the bed beside her and fisted myself.

"Good?"

"No!" She tugged off her shirt, followed by her bra, but I stopped her when she went for the laces on her boots.

"No way. Leave those fuckers on."

Warm, bare tits pressed against my chest as she straddled me. And holy shit, nothing separated us. Not a damn thing. I flipped her onto her back, kissing her while I reached for a condom in my nightstand. "Are you sure?"

"Yeah." Her voice caught on a ragged breath.

I warred with myself while I kissed her. I shouldn't fuck her like this, but I wanted her. Just her. I needed that connection so damn much. And it wasn't like we hadn't done everything but. It wasn't like this hadn't been some fine line we had been toeing for damn near a month. So I ripped the foil open and rolled down the condom. Monroe invited me in by spreading her legs a little more. Then I froze inches from her, fighting the thought that I should wait until she was sober. We were dating. We had almost fucked ten times before. I groaned because the dilemma was real.

"You're sure? You want me to fuck you. Now. Here?" My dick was pulling toward her like a magnet, wanting to take the plunge before I changed my mind.

"Yes." She kissed me. "I just want you. No one else."

I shifted on my arms, tip in when she shoved me back a little.

"Wait. Will it hurt a lot?"

My stomach bottomed out. That wasn't a "be gentle." That was an "I don't have a clue what's going on. Is this going to hurt."

"What?" I moved back enough to study her face. There was a hint of something—something I didn't like. "Roe...?"

"Just do it." She grabbed my ass, wrapping her legs around me and trying to pull me close. "It's fine. I trust you."

No way in hell, she was a virgin. "Fuck." I rolled onto my side, grabbing my dick in my hand while I stared at the ceiling, panting for breath.

"What are you doing?"

I had no idea what I was doing. I turned on the pillow to face her. "You're drunk."

"So?"

My gaze dropped to her tits, to her pussy, and I had to close my eyes to keep myself from jumping right back on her. "And a virgin?"

"Oh, so now you don't want me just because I don't know what I'm doing?" Her words slurred together.

I swiped a hand down my face. That was where her mind had just gone. Not that, maybe, for the first time in my life, I was trying to be a decent human being. As horny as I was, it wouldn't take anything more than feeling her squeeze me one good time and I would be as good as done. I didn't need her to know what she was doing, and to be honest, the idea that I would be the only guy ever to have her was enough to make me come.

"Is that it?" She huffed, and I glanced back at her face.

"No. It's because I don't want to take your virginity when you're shitfaced."

Seconds passed, the bang of Hendrix's headboard next door, almost making my eye twitch.

Monroe eventually rolled onto her side hard enough that the mattress bounced. "Why does it matter, Zepp?"

"Because I don't want you to hate me tomorrow."

She trailed a finger down my stomach. "I could never hate you."

As much as I wanted to believe that, I knew better. Given the right circumstances, anyone could hate anybody. I still had my dick in a vice grip in my hand, trying to strangle the need out of it while I stared at the ceiling, my thoughts tangled together.

"You could," I said.

When I glanced beside me, Monroe had closed her eyes. Her bare tits rose and fell on steady swells. She had passed out in nothing but her boots, leaving me with nothing but my hard dick and my thoughts.

Then it hit me like an eighteen-wheeler barreling down a road: She was a stripper and a virgin. How messed up was that, that we lived the kind of life where she was rubbing her tits in men's faces and straddling their laps when she hadn't even had sex. Something about that was downright tragic. Monroe James wasn't at all what I had thought she was—what anyone thought she was. And she was so much better than I deserved.

24

MONROE

Groaning, I rolled my face into Zepp's pillow and inhaled the scent of him that clung to it. It was only when I shifted to my back and felt cold air touch my chest that I opened my eyes. I was naked. Well, except for my boots.

My head pounded like a marching band, and my stomach threatened to rebel when I sat up. Zepp sat at his desk, sweeping a pencil over a page. A little concentration line sunk between his brows, cutting into the perfect planes of his face. It wasn't Zepp himself, though, that had my heart racing in my chest. It was the sight of the used condom on the nightstand. I remembered kissing him, sucking his dick, and then, nothing. How was I so drunk that I wouldn't remember that? I took stock of my body because surely, I would know. I'd feel it.

"Uh, did we..." I pulled the sheet up over my body.

"Have sex?" Seconds of silence ticked by while he continued drawing. "No."

"Okay. Good." I didn't mean to sound so relieved.

He shook his head, his pencil sweeping faster over the page. "Good, huh?"

"No. Just, good because I don't remember that happening." And I didn't want to forget something like that. I fell back against the pillow.

He turned around in his chair, one arm still braced on his desk and a smug grin on his face. "It wasn't for your lack of trying, though. *A* for effort."

The way he said it had embarrassment creeping over me, and my cheeks grew hot. "I'm sorry."

Contemplation played out on his face. "You wanna know what stopped me?" He pushed up from the chair and started across the room.

I busied myself by kicking off my boots, trying not to look at him when he sat on the edge of the bed. "That I was shit faced drunk and probably really unappealing?"

"Oh, you were very appealing." He squeezed my thigh. "So it wasn't that."

My mind raced as I cringed. I knew Zepp wanted to screw me. Badly. I could only imagine what I had possibly done to put him off. I groaned. "What happened?"

"So. No memory of me eating your pussy?" His teeth raked his bottom lip. "That's a fucking shame."

The thread of memory flickered through my mind. Me grabbing his hair, thrusting into his face. Oh, God. "Maybe a little."

"What about you asking me if it would hurt?"

I literally felt the color drain from my face.

"Not if *I* would hurt you. But if *it* would hurt. Like you had no idea what to expect." His hand left my thigh, and his hard gaze set on me. No, I did not tell him that. Screw beer and all its consequences. Why? *Why*? I fixed my gaze on the ceiling. "What else did I say?"

"You're a virgin."

I slowly focused on him, wrestling with my embarrassment. "Is that an issue?" I could hear the accusation in my voice.

"No."

"Great. Well then, can we not talk about it?" I moved to the edge of the mattress.

"Why are you getting defensive?"

I snatched up my bra from the floor and slipped it on, then pushed to my feet while I tugged on my skirt. "I'm not. I just..." I found my panties on the other side of the bed and dragged them up my legs. "Don't feel like discussing this."

He rounded the bed and grabbed my chin, forcing me to look at him. "The only reason I didn't fuck the absolute shit out of you last night was that, as selfish as I wanted to be, I couldn't do that to you."

The tension trickled away from me. This boy had me dangerously on the ropes. My heart was ready to hop out of my chest and lay itself at his feet. And that was terrifying.

I gripped the front of his shirt and pressed my lips to his. "Thank you."

———

I HAD PROMISED Jade I would study with her, even though I felt like complete ass. Jade answered her door with an oversized hoodie pulled over her head. Jade looked like she hadn't slept in a week, thanks to the ring of mascara smeared below her eyes.

"You look how I feel," I said, slipping inside the entranceway.

"I have the worst hangover of all time."

We cut through her living room toward her room,

passing her dad laid out on the sofa, watching a football game.

Sunlight streamed in through the window, bouncing off Jade's bubblegum-pink walls. The brightness was unbearable to look at with my headache. I squinted before taking off my boots and collapsing onto her bed, the open books beside me bouncing from the sudden weight.

"You're actually studying?" I asked, thumbing through some of the pages. God, I didn't think my brain could process anything right now.

"Yeah, hangover or not, I have a math test next week." And like me, Jade was hoping for straight As and a scholarship into a college.

"I don't remember half of last night." I traced my finger over the stitching on Jade's comforter.

"Well, you were all over Zepp. I can tell you that much."

I groaned.

"Oh my God." Jade grabbed one of the fuzzy bears on her bed and whacked me with it. "Tell me you did not lose your virginity while shit faced."

"No! Luckily, Zepp was chivalrous." And I still didn't know quite what to make of that.

"Wait." She dropped the stuffed animal. "I thought he didn't know—"

I let out a sigh and flopped back onto the bed, hanging my head over the edge. "Yeah, well, apparently I told him."

"It's kind of ironic, though, right? Zepp Hunt is the hottest guy in school. And you're the only girl he's ever dated." She nudged me with her foot. "A virgin who won't sleep with him." She cackled at that last statement.

"Zepp screws a lot of girls." I focused on her pink lampshade, trying to push down the sick feeling that crawled up my stomach anytime I thought about him with any of those girls. "What if I sleep with him and that's it?" I closed my eyes, voicing the one fear that held me back with Zepp. "What if the only reason he even wants me is that he can't have me?"

"You're kidding, right?" She snorted. "God, Monroe. He looks at you like… I can't even explain it." She shook her head.

"Anyway, enough about me. We need to study."

I found it hard to focus, though.

My mind kept veering back to Zepp. And that was the way of things more and more these days. Sometimes it felt like I was only happy when I was with him. And that was where the dilemma was. Being dependent on another person for happiness couldn't be a good thing. Life had taught me that much, but he was like a drug I couldn't deny myself. And though I had planned to go home, the second I left Jade's, I was texting him.

```
Me: What are you up to?
Asshole: Heading back from the northside.
What R U doing?
```

I should probably change his name in my phone, even if it did make me smile.

```
Me: Just leaving Jade's. Want to do
something?
Asshole: Eat Ur pussy…
```

A little ball of heat settled low in my stomach at the thought of Zepp's face between my legs.

```
Me: Maybe… I'll come to your house.
```

No Prince

I did go to Zepp's, but I didn't go in, instead taking him to the outskirts of Dayton.

I turned onto the narrow service road that branched off the highway, allowing my car to roll to a stop in the small clearing at the base of the billboard. I shouldered my backpack as we headed toward the metal ladder attached to the post, then started to climb it.

I hauled myself up onto the platform. It always felt so much higher than it looked from the ground. The setting sun painted the horizon in tones of orange and gold that made the mishmash of small project houses and neon signs from fast-food restaurants almost seem pretty. I dangled my legs over the edge of the platform and grabbed a can of Grapico from my bag, handing it to Zepp when he sank down beside me.

He frowned at the drink like it offended him. "You're shitting me, right?"

I cracked the tab on mine, then tipped it back. "Hey, it's my favorite."

He opened his, staring down into the can. "You know this is pretty much hummingbird food?"

"Let me have my sugar fix. It's definitely not worse than beer and cigarettes."

"Bullshit." He took a sip, then made a face like I had just fed him pure shit.

"Shush. It's good."

He kissed me, then licked over my lips. "Tastes better on you."

"Eww, Zepp." I swiped the back of my sleeve over my mouth, and he laughed.

"You wouldn't be saying that if it were between your

legs." His hand went to my thigh, creeping higher and higher.

Despite the breeze up here, my cheeks started burning, and when his fingers crept beneath my skirt, my legs instinctively parted a little. And he immediately took the invitation.

"Now I know why you're so tight."

"Don't act like you haven't been stealing virginities since you were fourteen." My voice came out on a hitched breath as he crooked his fingers.

"I wouldn't know. Never bothered to ask." He pressed his lips to mine before moving to my neck.

"But you wouldn't take mine?"

"You're different." His touch deepened, and something about being above the highway with the cars zooming by underneath us, none the wiser to what was going on, gave me a little thrill.

"If I hadn't been drunk..." My hands gripped the railing hard as that first perfect wave washed over me.

"I would have fucked you until you begged me to stop." Harder. Deeper. "Then, I would have kept going."

His words only stoked the flames until I was burning and shaking, unaware of a single thing that wasn't him. Like coming up from deep waters, I sucked in my first full breath, then looked at Zepp. He licked one finger, then the other, and I knew that look.

"I'm not screwing you on a billboard," I said, half laughing.

"So, it's fine when you're shitfaced but not on a billboard?" He adjusted his dick through his jeans, lifting one brow. "It would be memorable as shit."

"And here I was, thinking you had your heart set on a stolen car."

"I do. A stolen car. And now a billboard…"

"What if I have *my* heart set on a stolen car?" I bit my lip, teasing him.

"So, what you're saying is, I can't fuck you until I steal another car?"

"You make me sound so demanding."

He stood and made his way toward the ladder, placing one leg on the first rung before glancing up at me. "Give me half an hour."

I laughed and grabbed his hand, pulling him back to me.

He dropped to the platform, placed his spine to the billboard, then pulled me into his lap.

"Back to the billboard idea, huh?" I said.

His lips met mine, fingers digging into my thighs as he pressed up against me. For a moment, I thought about it, but rationality quickly set in. We were on a billboard, with cars passing by, and truthfully, the thought of losing my virginity right here and now made me nervous. I wasn't mentally prepared.

I pulled my mouth from his. "I didn't bring you up here for that."

He looked at me, a small line sinking between his brows. "Well, then why the hell did you bring me up here?"

To show him somewhere I came when I needed to get away from shit. But now that I thought about it, I felt stupid. I shrugged a shoulder. "It's fine. We can go back to your house."

He adjusted his dick again, on a barely audible huff. "Why did you bring me up here?"

"It's just a place I like."

He stared out at the horizon, the hum of cars on the

interstate below mixing with the buzz of the cicadas in the treetops beside us. "It's important to you?"

"Kind of. Not like there's a whole ton of places to escape in Dayton."

"Why?" Another adjustment. He was trying, but God, he really did have a one-track mind.

"I just come up here to remind myself that there is more than this shit." I climbed out of his lap and sat beside him, glancing over the horizon washed in warm amber from the setting sun. "You can see the state line from here," I said.

He grabbed the can of Grapico from the ledge and took a swig. "You can see the state line...and?"

"And I imagine what it'll be like when I can finally cross it and not look back."

"You think crossing a state line changes shit?"

"Maybe. I don't know." I shrugged. "I like to hope."

He pulled a cigarette from his pocket, lighting it. "It's the same shit over there as it is here, Monroe."

"Don't you hate it here, though? In Dayton."

"Nothing I can do about it."

"So you just accept it? This?" I nodded toward the housing project that was probably better than my mom's trailer.

I was genuinely curious. I felt like I'd spent weeks trying to figure out what made Zepp tick, and I still didn't know. He took care of Hendrix, had the house, dealt weed to pay his way. His situation was hard, but I assumed he would want something more at some point.

There was a long pause. One where Zepp stared out at the horizon, a thin stream of smoke slipped through his lips. "This. That." He nodded in the direction of Barrington. "You think those assholes are happy?"

"I think they go to sleep at night without wondering

where their next rent check is coming from, or if the police will come knocking." Or if their mom was going to have overdosed in the night.

He sidled over on the platform until his legs brushed mine. I looked at him, and for a moment, I pictured what our life could be. If we escaped Dayton. For the first time, I dared to see a future for Zepp and me away from this place, but then it was gone. Snuffed out by our reality. I'd never asked him whether or not he wanted to stay in this town. I guess I had just assumed everyone wanted out. Then again, some people wanted out; they just didn't believe they could do it.

"You could do better than Dayton, Zepp."

He took another drag from his cigarette, then chucked it over the edge, sparks skittering the platform. Then he glanced at me, his eyes soft. "Put hope in whatever you need to. But don't put hope like that in me."

"What if I want to?" I whispered, my words barely carrying above the distant hum of traffic.

"Don't."

"You once said I was broken. But you're only really broken when you lose hope." Which made him the damaged one of the two of us, but didn't I already know that?

He was the guy I told myself I didn't want to save. Yet here I was, suddenly wishing I could save him. And I didn't know what that meant.

His fingers trailed my jaw while a deep frown set on his face. "The way I see it, only broken people need hope."

"So what does that make us?" Seconds ticked by.

"Fucked up?" Zepp finally said.

No, it made us both broken. And in that moment, I didn't

care if I was. I wanted Zepp to fix me as much as I needed to fix him.

"If you could go anywhere, where would you go?" I asked, staring down at the littered ground feet below.

He took a handful of leaves from the platform, tossing them over the edge. "Don't know."

I wasn't sure if he genuinely hadn't thought about it, or he simply wouldn't voice it.

"What about you?" he asked.

"I just want to go to a beach. Have you ever been?"

He laughed, grabbing a twig from the metal ledge and flinging it into the trees. "Yeah, right. You?"

"No." As if my mom would ever spend her drug money on vacation. I took a sip of my drink. "I imagine it feels like the end of the earth."

"Kinda is."

"It's pretty pathetic that I've never left this shithole town."

He stared at me for several moments before grabbing my hand and pulling us both to our feet. I followed him down the ladder, and when I reached the bottom and turned around, Zepp was standing at the driver's side door of my Pinto, palm out.

"Toss me the keys."

"Why?" I gave them to him. "Where are we going?"

"For a drive."

We climbed in, and Zepp pulled onto the highway, heading the opposite direction from Dayton. A little ball of excitement settled in my chest. I had no idea where we were going, but it felt like I'd been waiting my whole life to just drive in the opposite direction of that damn town.

We drove for hours through country back roads, only stopping once for Zepp to run into a Wal-E-Mart. At some point, I fell asleep, and when I woke up, the first thing I noticed was the headlights shining over dunes of sand.

The dim glow from the dashboard played over Zepp's features. My heart thumped awkwardly in my chest like it had forgotten how to work for a second. "You brought me to the beach?"

"Pretty sure that's what this is," he said with a smart-ass smirk

He brought me to the beach. On a whim. Because I'd never been. No one had ever done anything for me the way Zepp had. And he'd done a lot, expecting nothing in return. He may have been a bad boy, but he was the best person I had ever known.

Grabbing his face, I slammed my lips over his. "I don't deserve you," I breathed against his mouth.

His fingers swept my cheek. "You deserve better."

"There is no one better."

He kissed me again, then turned off the ignition, plunging us into darkness for a moment before he opened his door. "You coming?" He rounded the back and popped the trunk, grabbing a Wal-E-Mart bag before slamming it.

We made our way to the wooden boardwalk. The gentle wash of waves against the shore made me smile. It sounded so much better in person than in the movies. A warm breeze touched my face, whipping through my hair and bringing with it a scent I had never before smelled. Something thick and fresh and inviting that soothed me instantly—salt air.

The worn planks gave way to sand, and I kicked off my boots, sinking my feet into the soft surface, relishing the way it seeped between my toes.

Zepp nearly disappeared in the darkness as he headed toward the water and dropped the bags onto the sand. He pulled out a blanket, fighting against the wind as he spread it out. Before he'd even finished, I pulled my shirt over my head, stepped out of my skirt, and took off to the water.

Warm water rushed around my legs. I waded out thigh-deep before Zepp snatched me around the waist.

His lips brushed my ear. "Does it feel like the end of the world?"

"No." I turned and wrapped my arms around his neck. "Far from it."

"Good." He covered my mouth with his in a kiss, soft and slow. Waves crashed around us, and the kiss grew deeper. "Does it make you happy?" he asked.

I touched his cheek. "You make me happy." The words felt like a confession, though they were simple fact.

"And you used to say you hated me." His hands dropped to my ass. "You also said the last thing you would ever do was fuck me."

"I haven't fucked you yet," I whispered. But I wanted to. Whatever had been holding me back with him had vanished.

"There's some bullshit line about good things coming to fuckers that wait." His fingers dug into my waist. "I'll wait as long as I have to."

I wrapped my legs around his waist, kissing him again. "Well... You don't have to," I said against his lips. The hard length of him pressed against me. "Unless you know, you want to wait a little longer." I fought a smile.

He didn't need much more than that. He carried me out of the surf, his lips never leaving mine when he dropped me onto the blanket. Within seconds, I was naked, his fingers buried deep inside of me while he sucked one of my nipples into his mouth.

"You're sure?" His hands roamed along my side as he reached for the bag.

"I'm sure." A wild tornado of emotions pummeled through me, foreign and overwhelming. I had never felt any kind of attachment to anyone, and of all the people in the world, it was him. Maybe I was stupid, but in that moment, I didn't care. I threaded my fingers through his hair, pulling him close, craving everything he had to give.

His fingers moved in a steady motion inside of me when he brought a foil wrapper to his mouth, tearing it open with his teeth. A nervous flutter took root in my chest when he sat up and put on the condom, and the second his weight settled over me again, my muscles tensed.

He moved between my legs, and for a second, I stopped breathing. He kissed me again, hesitating. "Tell me if it hurts, okay?"

"Okay." My nails dug into his shoulders because he was right there.

He studied me for a moment, his brow creasing before his tongue wet his lips. "Roe. I..."

I could see the words playing out on his face, the same ones I almost wanted to say to him, but I wasn't ready. To hear them or say them.

"It's okay, I trust you," I said in a rush.

And then he pushed into me. Slow. Steady. Each second stealing my breath.

He paused to kiss my neck. "You okay?"

"Yeah."

He went deeper, then stilled on a low groan. "Fuck..."

I just needed to get it over with. Like a Band-Aid. I grabbed his ass and yanked him fully into me. Pain spiked through my core, and breath hissed through my teeth.

"Jesus Christ." His forehead dropped to mine with a hard grunt. "Give me a second."

Every muscle in his body was rigid, and I could practically feel the chains of his restraint tightening around him.

He rocked into me gently. "You feel so fucking good."

The waves washed against the beach, the stars twinkling above us. I'd never felt more connected to another person in my life than I was to him in that moment.

Zepp was everything I never asked for and didn't want, but needed. In a short space of time, he'd become vital to me, the only hope in a bleak world.

"Roe, I can't..." He stilled, pushing into me so hard that it shot a twinge of pain through my stomach.

I slid my palm over his face, and he turned his head, brushing his lips over the inside of my wrist. "It's okay."

His movements grew more stilted. Then his lips slammed over mine on a deep groan.

"One minute." Panting, he collapsed to the blanket beside me. "Just give me one minute. I'll get you off. That was just..." His hand brushed my cheek, and he rolled onto his side. "I couldn't help it."

"I'm fine, Zepp."

A few seconds passed before he moved on top of me, kissing along my throat, then down my body. He nipped at my stomach, flashing me a cocky grin. "I'm gonna make this memorable."

"You brought me to the beach. It couldn't be much more —" My breath hitched when his tongue swiped over me.

"Oh, it can."

25

ZEPP

I sat across from Monroe, the early morning sun spilling over the patio table. I couldn't stop staring at her. Never in my life had I wanted to be with a girl the way I had her. I couldn't get enough of her; I couldn't kiss her enough. She had made me a certified pussy, and I didn't even care. And last night—that was a hell of a lot more than chasing a moment of bliss. I was pretty sure what I had with her was what most people spent an entire damn lifetime searching for. And in the back of my mind was the thought that, in a few months, this could all be over. Because she wanted to go to college, and I had no idea where.

The waitress came by and dropped a stack of pancakes onto the table before walking off with a grumble. "She seems like a bitch," I said.

"Must suck, though. Working so close to the beach but being stuck in here."

"Yeah." I stabbed one of the pancakes with my fork and crammed half of it in my mouth. "So, where do you want to go to college?"

"Depends who offers me a scholarship. If any."

That didn't make me feel any better. She was smart. I would think she would have a few offers. I dumped a load of syrup onto my plate before shoveling back more food.

"I've never asked you what you want to do."

"Don't know." I had no idea what I wanted to do, ever since my mom had died, Hendrix and I had been hustling, which left little time to contemplate shit that seemed as frivolous and farfetched as college. "Work on cars or some shit like that."

And she wanted to be an accountant. God, she was out of my league. She had to know that.

She smiled at me like it was the best thing she'd ever heard. "Well, you managed to fix the shit box, so... You must have magic hands." She lifted her coffee mug to her lips, but it didn't hide the slight pink tinge in her cheeks.

"*Must* have." I shook my head, wanting to divert the subject from anything to do with my shitty life goals and me, and the only way I knew to do that was make it sexual. "If I'm not getting a definite 'your hands are epic, Zepp,' I must not be doing my job."

She blushed even harder. "I have never once said those words."

"Then, I'm sorry. I'll try harder." I glanced at my crotch. "Maybe you'll have a better shot since you're in on the action now."

"Oh my God." She grabbed a hash brown and tossed it at me. "I can't with you."

"Oh, but you have with me." I picked up the potato round and threw it down the hatch.

She put down her coffee. "You think we have time to go to the beach before we leave?"

"We can skip school tomorrow for all I care."

She shifted in her seat, looking anywhere but at me. "I have to work tonight."

My jaw set, and I tried to force it to relax. I hated what she did, but I didn't want to make her feel bad for it. It was evident enough she was ashamed. But in Dayton, we all made money the way we could. And there weren't many good options.

It was midnight when I dropped off Monroe—at The White Rabbit, not Cha Cha's. She had on more makeup than I had ever seen her wear. The heavy eyeshadow and lipstick made her look at least twenty-three, and I absolutely hated it. "Want me to pick you up?"

"Crystal's working tonight." Monroe scuffed her boot over the ground. "She lives right by me. She'll take me."

I leaned over the bike and kissed her. "See you tomorrow?"

"Yeah." A small smile touched her lips. "Thanks. For taking me to the beach." Then she turned away.

She headed underneath the neon lights toward the entrance. Two bikers by the door catcalled her, and it took everything in me not to get off my bike and punch the bastards in the head. She was my girl, and regardless of what they thought of her, she deserved respect.

I cranked my bike but couldn't make myself leave. I worried about her, worried that some asshole in there would try to cop a feel, and I wondered if she just had to take that. I guessed most people would say a girl who chose to strip should deal with that crap, but I knew Monroe, and I knew she didn't choose this. A group of men in collared shirts lined up at the door, and if I had to guess from the way they dressed, they were from Barrington. Soon enough, I found myself behind one of them in line, handing my fake ID to the steroid-pumped bouncer along with the ten-dollar cover before slipping into the club.

Heavy bass vibrated through my chest, strobe lights flickered over the black walls, and I shifted to the side of the room, positioning myself behind one of the curtains that covered the hallway to the men's room.

Girls gave lap dances by the stage, older men sliding their filthy hands over their thighs. The song changed from rap to heavy metal. Men whistled and cheered when Monroe walked onto the stage. Her legs looked a mile long in those stilettos, and the black-lace lingerie she was wearing left nothing to the imagination. She hooked her thigh around the pole. She leaned away, back arched and her red hair spilling to the floor. Men stood up, shoving money toward her. And the moment she straightened and started over to them to take their dollar bills, anger ripped through me like an F-5 tornado. This was a fucking mistake, and I needed to leave because watching the girl I was falling in love with undress in front of men who would disrespect her in a heartbeat was something I knew I couldn't manage.

I'd pushed myself out the door of The White Rabbit faster than I'd gone in, and thoughts swirled through my head like an angry vortex on the drive to my house. Hendrix had passed out on the couch, the TV on, and I was glad. I couldn't deal with his bullshit right now.

The moment I got into my room, I threw a fist through the wall behind my door. My knuckles split, but even that didn't make me feel better. I paced for a moment before the adrenaline slowly subsided, then I sat at my desk and flipped to a clean page in my sketchbook.

The lead made a soft scratch as I traced an outline of

Monroe's figure. Then drew the straight lines of the pole. With each stroke of the pencil, I allowed myself to go down a rabbit hole I wished I hadn't. I worked on the drawing until sunlight streamed through the window and cast shadows over the red hue of her hair, the dark navy hue of the stage and the men leering at her from below.

I had never given a shit about a girl before, and somehow, this girl had managed to break me apart without even trying. Because I was pretty damn sure I was in love with her.

26

MONROE

Crystal dropped me off in the early hours of the morning. The security light from the neighbor's trailer flashed on, reflecting over the shit-brown paint of Jerry's car. Great. Just what I needed. I expected him to be passed out on the couch. What I didn't expect was the cardboard boxes stacked around the tiny living room. A horrible feeling crawled up my throat. I had seen this time and time again—my mom was moving him in. And that was always where the problems started, when they thought they were my new step-daddy.

I refused to let Jerry ruin the little glow of happiness Zepp had planted in me, though, so I ignored it and went to my room. I pulled the wad of money from my bra and knelt next to the chest of drawers, stuffing the cash through a little hole on the backboard. Then I undressed and got into the shower, washing away the heavy makeup and the scent of cologne that clung to me.

When I got into bed, I wished I was at Zepp's house, in his bed. For the first time, I understood my mom's string of shitty men. Maybe this sense of belonging was what she had been chasing—someone to give a shit about her. But she always picked the wrong guys, time and time again.

The next morning, I went to grab a Pop-Tart from the cabinet and was greeted by Jerry in his ratty, old man boxers. I wanted to tell him to get the hell out, but I knew better than to make enemies with someone I now lived with. My life was already hard enough. So I grabbed the pastry and my bookbag, and I left.

I zoned out during first period, doodling in my notebook while I tried to ignore the anxiety Jerry created permanently being at the trailer.

"Assignments will be set today," Mrs. Johnson said, slamming a book down on her desk with a thud. "Take your seats. I will be calling your name, along with your partner's. You will have three weeks to complete a ten-thousand-word essay on the effect of social media on social and political reasoning."

She picked up a piece of paper from her desk. "Laura Smith and Bobby Jones..." I scribbled more shapes along the edge of my paper until I heard my name. "Monroe James and Chase Matthews." Oh, great. Just great.

My gaze swung across the room to Chase. He glanced over his shoulder at me, a miserable expression on his face. We hadn't spoken since he had attempted to apologize and Zepp had punched him.

"Pair up and start discussing your project."

I didn't move. After a few minutes, Chase shoved to his feet, dropping into the seat beside me.

"Maybe she'll swap us if you ask..." he started.

"What? Don't want to work with me?"

His palm slapped down on his desk. "I tried to apologize to you, Monroe. And you sicced your boyfriend on me."

"Oh my God." I glared at him. "I did not sic Zepp on you.

He asked me why you were apologizing because he thought I'd screwed you." I tapped my pencil over my notebook. "Trust me, the truth was a far better option."

"You realize he's a psycho, right?"

"I'm aware."

"And yet, you're dating him. Never took you for that kind of girl." The judgmental look he gave me set me on edge.

I tossed my pencil at him, and it bounced off his chest. "My dating life is none of your business. I still haven't forgiven you for being a prick."

"I'm sorry, okay?" He threw up his hands. "I shouldn't have said what I did about Harford."

"But you did."

"And you wouldn't let me apologize. How long have we been friends?" He stared at me like he wanted an answer. "You can't give me one mistake? So freaking stubborn." We had been friends for a long time. In some ways, Chase had been the most consistent thing in my life.

"Fine, I accept your apology. You're still a prick. Better?"

A small smile touched his lips, and he pushed a book in front of me. "We gonna do this project now, or what?"

"Fine."

By the time the bell rang, we barely had an outline together. Chase glanced up while gathering his books. "Guess we'll need to work on this outta class, huh?"

"I guess."

On a smile, he left the classroom. I stood beside my desk, clutching my books to my chest before I finally filed into the hall. Chase was my friend, and there was nothing Zepp could say to change that, but I wasn't excited about the guaranteed level of psycho this would trigger.

Zepp leaned against the wall outside of the classroom. His arm immediately came around my waist, creeping lower until it was on my ass. "All I've thought about this morning was fucking you."

Heat spread over my skin. I had so little control over how my body reacted to him; it was embarrassing. "I'm not fucking you in the girls' bathroom, before you ask."

"What about the art supply closet?" We were still walking down the hall when his lips pressed against my throat. "I don't know if I can wait until after school."

"You waited for weeks," I said. "You can manage a few hours."

He pressed me against the nearby lockers, caging me against the metal. My pulse picked up at the memory of his body over mine, now branded into my mind.

"I really can't." His nose skirted along my throat, warm breath fanning over my skin while he pressed against me. "Come on. Give me five minutes." He nipped at my neck.

My fingers gripped his shirt as my pulse skittered. He was persuasive; I had to give him that. His touch trailed down my side, my thigh, then disappeared beneath my skirt. My breath caught when his fingertips brushed against me. "You're wet, Roe."

I was. In the middle of the hallway, with Zepp's hand between my legs, my heart ready to bang out of my chest at the idea of getting caught.

He pushed into me. "I could just fuck you right here..."

I clamped my thighs around his hand, but it did nothing to stop him. "You're awful."

"Not what you said the other night." Another thrust of his fingers. A door at the end of the hallway opened.

"Mr. Hunt!" Mrs. Smith shouted. On a smirk, he pulled away his hand, then spun on his heel to face the teacher, now storming down the hall. "What are you thinking?"

"That I wanna fuck my girlfriend."

I wanted the floor to swallow me. God, he really was awful.

She froze mid-stride, her weathered face reddening. "That's detention! Come by my class to pick up your slip."

"Whatever." He waved her off, then turned back to me and grabbed my hand. "You coming over after school since I can't fuck you in the school?"

I shook my head on a smirk. "After your detention?"

"I'm not picking up the slip." He gave me another kiss, his fingers digging into my waist. "God, you make me crazy."

My stupid heart tripped over itself. Then he pushed away, ducking into one of the classrooms.

27

ZEPP

The last three hours of school almost had me in the bathroom, jerking one out just so I would last more than five seconds when I finally got inside Monroe. I had sped through Dayton, weaving in and out of traffic until Monroe punched me.

My dick pressed against my zipper, begging to get out as I slid the chain lock on my front door into place. I could honestly say I had never wanted a girl so badly in my life. It wasn't ten seconds later that I had Monroe's clothes off and her naked body plastered to the couch, my face between her thighs. "You're evil, you know it?" I said before swiping my tongue over her. My dick felt like it was ready to split.

"There's that saying about good things..." She yanked at my hair, grinding against my mouth.

"Come to fuckers who wait." I slipped my finger inside of her, feeling her tighten around me. She was so close. "Right, Roe?"

"I...God."

I licked and bit at her, bringing her right to that edge

before I stopped. Then I sat back on my heels and swiped the back of my hand over my lips.

"Zepp!" she said on a frustrated groan.

"Like waiting?" I shot a smart-ass grin at her before pulling my shirt over my head and tossing it to the floor.

She yanked at my belt, shoved my boxers down, then fisted me. "You're a dick, you know it?"

"No. That's a dick." I glanced down at my cock in her tiny hand, looking swollen and angry as fuck. I shoved my fingers back inside her, crooking and bending. "Gonna let me fuck you now?" Then I kissed her, pushing her back against the sofa while I picked up my jeans from the floor to fish in the pocket for the condom. I tore open the foil, then shoved the rubber over my dick. "Or you gonna make me wait again?"

"You just have those on you?" she asked.

"I was trying to bang you at school. Remember? I'm a responsible boyfriend."

"Whatever." She grabbed at my hips, pulling me between her open legs. But I stopped before I got inside her.

"So, was that a no to the waiting? I said."

"Oh my God, Zepp. Just fuck me!"

I fought the smirk. "Now, we're getting somewhere." I bit at her nipple. "Beg me again." Her grip tightened when she tried to force me toward her. "Tell me how bad you want it."

"Zepp!" She tossed her head back. "Just fuck me already."

God, she was so bad at this. I brushed against her, the heat nearly drawing me in like a magnet. "Tell me you want my cock in your pussy."

She glared at me. "I want your cock in my pussy." Anger

bled through her tone. *Almost* ruining it for me. "Happy?" she said.

"Yep." Then I pushed into her. Slow. Hard. Deep. Until my jaw clenched and my fingers balled into a fist because I was already about to lose it. I stilled, and she tried to pull me farther inside. "Wait a second."

I refocused, then took my time, making sure each movement made her grip on my shoulders tighten or forced an uneven breath from her lungs. I may have been with girls before Monroe, but none of them mattered. As far as I was concerned, she may as well have been my first.

I brought her to the point of getting off a few times, only to keep her right there and drag it out before I finally let her fall over that edge. Her back arched off the couch, she buried her fingertips into my skin and moaned. That breathy sound sent me over the edge. Balls tightening and heat spreading over me like an inferno before I released and collapsed on top of her.

I pressed a breathless kiss to the side of her neck. "I can't get enough of you."

"Good."

Someone tried to open the door, but the chain caught. "What the...Zepp!" Hendrix shouted from the front, slamming the door shut then trying to open it again. I handed Monroe her clothes while taking my jeans from the floor. "It's locked, dumbass."

"No shit." He closed it then tried to open it. Again. "You're in there with your dick and balls out, aren't you?"

Monroe rolled her eyes before she tugged her shirt over her head, then started through the doorway to the stairs.

"Yeah," I said. "I had my balls all over your favorite spot on the couch." I waited for Monroe to make it to the top of the steps before I snatched the chain from the lock.

Hendrix barreled through, bumping his shoulder against me. "You're sick. And your balls are sick." He bumped me again. "Balls are for the bedroom."

That nasty asshole had more sex on the couch and the kitchen counter than he ever did in his bedroom. "I've seen your taint more times than I need to." I shoved him, knocking him into the wall before I headed to my room.

Monroe looked up from her phone when I closed my bedroom door, then tossed it to the bedside table.

"Hendrix is..." One of her brows lifted in thought. "Did he get dropped on his head as a child?"

"Probably. Also, I beat him with a whiffle ball bat a lot when we were kids." I flopped onto my back, grabbed her, and pulled her against my chest. I wasn't sure when this had become normal, but it was, and the thought that it could all end in a second, made my stomach knot.

Before Monroe, all that had mattered were those moments of bliss, a quick high, a quick fuck, but now all that mattered was her. That was all that mattered, which meant I was screwed because I was undeniably in love with her. I combed my fingers through her hair, the soft scent of coconut settling around me like an invisible shield of comfort. The words crept to the tip of my tongue. Three words that would make me more vulnerable than I wanted to be. Words where there was no protection if she didn't feel the same. And for every reason I thought I should tell her, I could think of fifty reasons why I shouldn't.

Monroe shifted on the bed, drawing tiny circles on my chest with her fingers. And instead of telling her, I kissed her. Long and hard, pretending that she'd know how I felt without me saying. And then I couldn't feel guilty when it bit us both in the ass.

"You gonna stay here tonight?" I asked.

"Yes. Please." On a sharp exhale, her fingers splayed across my chest. "My mom moved Jerry in."

Every muscle in my body tensed. That piece of shit. I didn't want Monroe over there. "You know you don't have to go back there."

"You want me hanging around your house all the time?"

"You already do."

She swatted at my stomach. "It's fine. I can handle Jerry for a few months."

I tightened my jaw. Her need to pretend she could manage something she couldn't irritated the shit out of me. Then what she had said dawned on me. "A few months?"

"If I get into a college, yeah."

And then she would leave.

"Hey." She moved, the mattress springs creaking when she dug her chin into my chest, then looked up at me. "It won't change anything, Zepp."

"I didn't say it would."

"You didn't have to." She cocked a brow.

Seconds ticked by, thoughts weighing heavy on my mind while I stared at the ceiling. "If you could get an offer anywhere, where would you want to go?"

"Dixon is my first choice. It's at the beach." A kink formed in my stomach. It was a good thing I had swallowed those words down earlier.

"Yeah..."

"Zepp..." She touched my cheek, turning my face toward hers. "I probably won't even get an offer. Let's just cross that bridge if we get there."

Cross it and fall straight off the edge. But whatever. I kissed her forehead. "Yeah. Sure."

Her eyes narrowed for a moment. Her teeth bit into her lower lip. "You're still thinking about it."

I squeezed her tighter. Somehow, in the matter of a month, she had become everything to me, and I had no idea how I was supposed to let that go. "I'm thinking about pizza."

She smirked. "You're a horrible liar."

I focused on the ceiling again, sweeping my fingers over her back for a few minutes. There were two colleges a hell of a lot closer than Dixon… "Why Dixon?"

"I don't know. Go to the beach. Run away."

That gave us eight months, maybe. I bit at my lip, thinking it was easier when I didn't give a shit.

"I've always been living for the day I could get out." Her finger tapped my chest. "Until I jacked a car off this asshole, and now he's kind of become a problem."

"A problem, huh?"

"All kinds of trouble," she said.

"I have the same kind of problem with this redhead. She's turned me into a pussy." I shifted on the bed, turning to face her.

Monroe had made me the kind of guy I used to despise, the kind who would do anything for a girl, regardless of what it meant for him.

28

MONROE

Mine and Zepp's conversation had played through my mind on repeat.

It didn't take a genius to see it bothered him. I was going to college; he wasn't planning to. If I was honest with myself, I didn't want to leave him, either. There was no doubt anymore that I loved him, and love had made me weak. But more than that, it made everything else seem unimportant. I'd dreamed of getting out of Dayton my whole life, but suddenly, it wasn't this awful place I'd always seen it as. Because *he* was here. But he didn't have to be. Zepp didn't want to go to college, but he also didn't know what he wanted to do with his life. He'd never had any opportunity, and he had no idea how talented he was.

Zepp had gone outside to work on one of the cars, and I sat on his couch, reading over the webpage for the Elizabeth Roux School of Art in Florida. Before I could think it through too much, I clicked on the contact tab and typed out an email, attaching a picture I'd taken of his sketchbook a couple of days ago. It was a picture he'd drawn of me, not the best one, but the least invasive to his privacy, I thought. I hesitated before clicking send. Would he be annoyed that I'd showed one of his drawings to someone else? He didn't show them to anyone. Then again, what if they offered him a place in their school? That had to be worth it. I clicked send, holding my breath until I heard the little ding that signaled it had gone, no taking it back. The worst they could say was no, in which case I'd never tell him.

The front door banged closed, and Hendrix rounded the living room doorway. "Where's Zepp?"

"Out back."

He nodded. "Wanna come to Taco Casa for lunch?"

For the past three nights, all we had eaten was pizza, so I was game. "Sure."

Wolf and Bellamy already had a table by the time we walked into the brightly lit Mexican restaurant. I slid into the booth between Hendrix and Zepp while Wolf mumbled something about Barrington, his fist balled on the table.

"Pussy dicksuckers." Hendrix grabbed the menu, popping it open. "Don't worry, man. I got you."

I elbowed Zepp. "Did I miss something?"

"Barrington emptied a garbage bag onto Wolf's truck."

Wolf crumpled his straw paper up and tossed it to the floor. "Diapers and tampons and shit."

"Gross." And of course, any move that ballsy from Barrington would warrant retaliation. I opened my menu and glanced over the options.

"You ever eaten here before, Roe?" Zepp glanced over the top of his plastic menu.

"No."

"Whatever you do. Do not get the inferno fiesta bowl."

"Okay."

I sat there and ate a taco while watching Hendrix wolf down food like the plate was about to grow legs and run away. He ate not one, not two, but three of those inferno fiesta bowls, and the smirk on Zepp's face told me he was going to regret it. After we paid, Hendrix strutted up to Wolf's pickup, clutching his stomach.

"You gonna come?" he asked Zepp before hauling himself into the back.

Zepp glanced at me, fighting a smile. "Hell yeah." He chuckled. "I'm not missing this shit." Zepp waved me into the back, and I wedged myself between him and Hendrix.

The engine cranked, and Hendrix's stomach rumbled. He grabbed Wolf's headrest and shook it. "Go, man. Go! Floor this bitch."

Wolf threw the truck into reverse and peeled out of the parking lot, cackling.

We stopped at one of the four-way intersections, and Hendrix's stomach gurgled again. The aroma of dead animals filled the car.

"Oh my God." I gagged, burying my face in Zepp's jacket.

"Run the light, Wolf!" Hendrix swiped the sweat from his brow. "I'm not gonna make it."

I practically climbed in Zepp's lap, trying to get away from Hendrix, who wriggled around in the seat like he was about to shit himself.

"Can you hold it?" Bellamy said through laughter.

Hendrix crossed himself. "Lettuce pray."

We were about five minutes away from Barrington when the smell worsened. Zepp cracked his window. Bellamy hung his head out of the passenger side window like a dog on a joyride, and I buried my face deeper into Zepp's shirt.

"Did you shit, Hendrix?" I asked.

"A little shart never killed anyone," he grunted.

The Barrington High sign with its stuffy, coat of arms emblem whizzed past. Wolf whipped it into the parking lot, flooring it around behind the stadium where the football player's shiny SUVs were parked.

I looked from Zepp to Hendrix just as he threw himself out of the truck. "What is he... *Nooo!*" There wasn't much I would put past Hendrix, but whatever he was about to do involved shit and Barrington.

The guys all cackled, struggling for breath when Hendrix yanked down his jeans.

I looked away before I saw far more of him than I ever wanted to. "I absolutely do not need to see your brother's dick. Or his asshole fall out."

Wolf lowered his window and cupped a hand to his mouth. "Squeeze it out, dude."

"There's no squeezing." Hendrix grunted. "It's more like." Another grunt. "Power washing and plastering."

Minutes ticked by. The guys were laughing so hard they were gasping for air. I looked up just as an army of red and white jerseys jogged off the field. One of the guys stopped at the gate and pointed in our direction.

"Uh, guys. He needs to hurry up," I said. "They're coming!"

"Shit." Bellamy lowered his window, shouting for Hendrix to pinch it off.

"I can't." There was an edge of panic to Hendrix's voice. "It's a water hose, man!"

"I swear to God." Zepp grabbed the door handle. "Had to have three intestinal bowls."

I reached over him, holding onto the door. "You cannot get in a fight just so Hendrix can have a shit!" I leaned over to the open door, shielding my eyes. "Hendrix, get in here!"

I looked up just as half the Barrington football team started toward the Range Rover—the white one with a fresh pile on the once pristine hood, a piece of shitty toilet paper strung over the antenna. Hendrix sprinted across the parking lot, yanking up his jeans before he hurled himself into the backseat, and Wolf took off with a screech of tires and a backfire of the engine.

Hendrix slouched down in the seat on a sigh. "Man, I feel so much better."

I just shook my head because I had no words for him. None.

I pulled up outside my mom's trailer, right next to Jerry's car. I could have stayed at Zepp's, the same way I had for the last three nights, but I wasn't about to start living at his house. It felt like I practically did anyway, and I didn't want to be the full-time girlfriend he never signed up for. So I had decided I was staying at home that night. No matter how much Zepp sulked about it.

The hinges to the trailer door creaked when I pulled it open, and I froze. Jerry was lying on the couch, wheezing, his face bloodied, lip swollen. Mom buzzed around him with a bag of frozen peas in her hands that trembled on a come down.

"What the hell?" The words fell from my lips.

"Oh, baby." My mom came at me with wild eyes, her greasy hair in disarray. "Ya stepdaddy got beat." Stepdaddy? She was on that again? Every time, she thought we were going to be one big happy family with a crack whore, a meth dealer, and a stripper daughter. Fun. How Dayton.

On a grunt, Jerry managed to sit up. And holy shit, Jerry

did some sketchy shit, but I had never seen him hurt. And this was beyond hurt. His right eye was swollen shut, and a few extra teeth were missing. The uncomfortable feeling tearing down my spine quickly replaced my temptation to smile.

Jerry stared me down like he thought this was something to do with me. "When I find out who would have the balls to try to come at me..." Rage filled his one good eye. "I'm gonna bury the little shit. Don't think I won't find out, Monroe." The accusation was right there, written all over his face. Why the hell would he think I had anything to do with this?

A thread of fear pulled at my gut. Call it intuition.

I had no doubt that Jerry had enough dirty cops, desperate hookers, and shady drug dealers in his pocket to find out almost anything in Dayton, and I knew—I just knew this was Zepp. And that terrified me.

29

ZEPP

"Hand me that wrench."

When Hendrix scooted out from underneath the car, I tossed the tool to him, then went back to the engine. Working on cars brought me some sort of peace, a way to lose my thoughts in hand motions, the way drawing did.

"Shit. Hey, Zepp. Incoming!" Wolf shouted from the back porch just before the door banged shut.

I glanced around the hood at Monroe barreling off the porch, face red and fists clenched at her side. Holy shit. She was pissed. What the hell could I have done to piss her off within the hour since she had left? Swiping the sweat from my brow, I stepped around the front of the car.

"Was it you?" she shouted when she passed the birdbath.

"Was it me what?"

"Did you go after Jerry?"

I hoped Dizzy had beat the shit out of him. "Jerry?" I grabbed a screwdriver from the grass and went back to the car.

"One request." She paced beside the car, shaking her head and rambling to herself. "Don't go after him."

"Roe!" I glanced over the hood. "You've been with me the past three days..." And what a fucking alibi.

She stopped mid-step to look at me, her teeth working over her lip. "Well, someone beat his ass, and he's pissed."

He was a drug dealer. A roughneck. Like he hadn't had a beating or two in his life.

I almost snorted while I tightened a lug nut. "Ass beatings are part of the business."

"Not for Jerry," she mumbled.

I tucked the socket wrench into the back of my jeans, then slammed the hood. I couldn't figure out why she was pissed; the shithead beat on her; she should be gloating that someone handed his ass to him. "Why do you even give a shit, Monroe?"

"Because he's practically digging a hole in the damn woods for whoever did it already."

Good luck killing Dizzy. Jerry didn't stand a chance against him. "Again, why do you care?"

She punched me in the chest. "Why do you think, asshole? I swear if you had anything to do with this, Zepp..."

I fought a smile. She was worried about me. "Like I said, Roe. I've been with you for the past three days."

"Doesn't mean shit. You're a shady fuck, you know it?"

I grabbed her by the hips and yanked her against me. "Good to know." Then I kissed her.

Something whacked me on the side of the head. "Sick-ass fuckers," Hendrix mumbled, pushing up from the ground and dusting his hands on his jeans. "I thought you were going home, Red? I need a break."

"Changed my mind." Monroe flipped him the bird. "I'm staying."

"So I gotta listen to you two bumping uglies? Again." Hendrix groaned. "I can't deal with it. You sound like a hyena when you get off."

She glared at him. "Like you aren't trying to take out your bedroom wall with some random skank most nights."

I grabbed the glove Hendrix had hit me with and whacked him in the face. "Shut up." Then I snagged Monroe by the waist and led her toward the house. Those two would keep going at each other until they were separated. "Come on, my little hyena. I'mma make you howl."

Laughing, she elbowed me in the ribs. "God, your brother is a dick."

THE NEXT DAY I got sent to the principal's office at the end of last period for breaking some dickhead's nose for calling Monroe a slut. Two days of detention. Brown was going soft as shit.

I skirted down the hallway just as Monroe slammed her locker closed. She glanced over her shoulder at me, and I proudly held up the pink piece of paper. "Got detention defending your honor."

"That would be sweet if you weren't in detention most days anyway."

"Don't try to downplay my chivalry, Roe." I wrapped an arm around her shoulder, and we started toward the exit. Sun heated my skin as we crossed the parking lot teeming with students. "Wanna order Chinese tonight?"

"Sure." She placed a hand on my stomach before slamming a kiss to my mouth. The kind of kiss that usually meant she was about to drop to her knees for me. Her tongue swiped my lips; she pressed her tits against my stomach. Roe didn't do stuff like this in the school parking lot... I pulled away from her, brow cocked with suspicion.

"But I have to go study first. With Chase." That last bit came out fast and quick, like she was spitting out fire.

I hated that shithead. They may have been friends back when she didn't have tits, but there was no way that guy didn't grab a bottle of Jergen's lotion and rub one out to the thought of her.

"Yeah?" I asked, tempering the flame of jealousy begging to combust in my chest.

"Remember? The social studies project..."

How could I forget? "Yeah. So, you going to the library?" We stopped beside my bike, and I tossed her the helmet.

"Uh, not exactly. The computers keep crashing, but Chase's dad has one."

His house. Of course the little shit would invite her to his house. I bet he'd even have some refreshments and fucking candles for her too. I gave a curt nod before swinging my leg over the seat. "I'll take you."

"Really? This is very...rational." She climbed on behind me and pressed her lips to my neck.

Then I cranked the engine and pulled out of the parking lot.

It was very rational of me.

I stopped in front of the mailbox with Matthews painted in sloppy, white letters along the side. An Alabama football flag flew from the front porch, right below the American flag, and the lawn was actually cut, flowers in the bed by the front steps. The house looked completely out of place nestled amongst the dilapidated houses that covered the rest of the block. No wonder he felt entitled. Prick.

Monroe hopped off the back of my bike and handed me the helmet. It looked like she was about to lean in for a kiss when I cut the engine and climbed off myself. Her eyes narrowed. "What are you doing?"

On a smile, I started up the sidewalk to the front porch. By the time she caught up, I had already rung the doorbell.

"Zepp..." She gave me a stern look right before Chase opened the door.

His gaze pinged between Monroe and me. "Hey, Moe." A crease formed between his brows. Damn right, dickhead, I'm here.

"Hey. Zepp was just dropping me off." She gave me a quick kiss before crossing the threshold. When dickwad went to close the door, I grabbed it and shouldered my way inside.

"What the hell, Hunt?" Chase stood at the open entrance like he expected me to leave.

I shot him a smile, then pushed the door closed for him. Annoyance radiated from him like a hydrogen bomb when I placed a hand on Monroe's waist. "Don't mind me, Matthews."

"Whatever." He led Monroe and me to the eat-in kitchen, pausing by the mail-covered table. "I just have to go get my books," he said on his way to the stairs at the far side of the room.

Monroe fell into a chair at the end of the table, glaring at me. Before she could open her mouth, I was looming over her.

"His books were in his fucking room." I pointed toward the steps. "Guys take girls into their room for one thing and one thing only." Heat bled over my face. I debated ramming Chase's face into the stainless-steel fridge.

"I was here all the time when we were kids." She swatted

a few envelopes across the tabletop and huffed. "I've been in his room, and before you say it, we were playing Candyland, and we were twelve."

I pulled out a chair, flipped it around, and straddled the seat while staring at her. How in the hell was my girl this damn naïve with guys? "And doctor?" I asked. "You play that too?"

"No." She rolled her eyes. "We were best friends. That's it."

"The girl I used to play board games with was the girl I lost my v-card to when I was fourteen, so don't act like being childhood friends makes a guy immune to a pair of titties."

She swiped a hand down her face on a groan. "Not all guys are as perverted as you, Zepp."

"Really?" I folded my forearms over the chair back. "It's not perverted, Roe; it's called having a dick and using it."

Her lips pressed together. I could just imagine she was trying to figure out something else to try to prove her point, but Chase came back into the room. He dropped books and a laptop onto the junked-up table and sat next to Monroe, scooting his chair closer to her.

I drummed my fingers over the table while he booted up the laptop. "Planning to study in your room?" I asked.

Chase's hostel gaze met mine. "Moe's been in my room plenty of times."

I grabbed the roll of paper towels sitting in front of me and squeezed. Snarky son of a bitch. "And yet, you still haven't gotten what you want." I shrugged a shoulder. "Not all of us can, I guess." I really, really wanted to slam his head against that freezer now.

"Ooookay." Monroe pointed at me. "Stop." Then shoved the laptop in front of Chase. "Focus. Type."

I threw up both hands in surrender. "I'm just trying to have a conversation."

She ignored me, snatching one of the books from the stack and flipping to a page. "We only have two more topics we have to put in. One is, what are the pros and cons of social media in a modern society versus thirty years ago?"

What kind of bullshit was this? I tossed the paper towels back to the table.

Chase cleared his throat like he had some grand revelation he was about to vomit out. "Well, I think one of the biggest downfalls of social media is the way it places value on people or the opinions of people who really don't matter. Instead of placing that value on real, long-standing friendships that are far more important." He looked at me like a proud little dipshit. "It promotes false relationships with no real foundation."

Oh, I supposed that was meant to be some dig. "You realize society has always placed value on the opinions of people who don't really matter?" I said. "That's not some new phenomena that happened due to social media, you dumbass."

Chase glared at me.

"Thanks for your input, babe." Monroe gave me a stern look before turning her attention to Chase. "He does have a point, though."

Of course I did. Dipshit typed something for a few minutes while Monroe looked through her notes. Every time he tried to make some comment that he thought made him sound smart, I debunked it. After half an hour, steam was swirling from the top of his head. He grabbed his backpack from the floor and hauled it into his lap, rummaging through it and pulling out a joint.

Monroe tapped her pen over the open book in front of her. "Your mom's gonna kill you if you smoke that in here."

"She's working night shift tonight." Chase lit the joint and took a puff. "So is Dad."

That dickhead had every intention of trying to screw her. I knew he had. On a smirk, he blew a cloud of smoke into the air before offering it to Monroe. She shook her head.

"Hey, Moe, remember that time we went up on the billboard and got so stoned we slept up there?"

He stared me down like he wanted me to think something had happened between them.

"Yeah, your dad said I was a bad influence. Now look at you, smoking in the house." She flashed a condescending smile.

That little asshole wanted to try and show me how special he was to Monroe? Fuck him. "Hey, Roe. Remember that time I fingered you so good and got you off on top of the billboard?" My jaw clenched, my stare aimed at Chase.

"Okay." Monroe choked on a nervous cough. "You know, I think you can just write this section, Chase. I'll write the next. It'll be fine." She pushed to her feet so fast the chair teetered on its back legs for a second. "Zepp," she said through gritted teeth, spinning on her heels, then leaving the room.

I slowly rose, looming over him. "She may think this is all innocent. But I know it's fucking bullshit." I jabbed a finger at his forehead. "Don't make me kill you, Matthews." I shoved his head back before storming out of the room.

Monroe ignored me until we got home, where I begged her to forgive me by face planting between her thighs.

30

MONROE

I could think of a million better things to do on a Friday night than following Zepp through the crowded entrance of Dayton High's football stadium. Hendrix and Bellamy flanked Jade, Hendrix walking way closer than necessary. Half of the people in the stadium wore school colors. If there was one thing the people of this town had in common, it was their love of football. I was the odd one out, apparently.

"I swear," Zepp mumbled. "I'm gonna kill Wolf for making us come to this shit."

"You know, I would not have taken Wolf for a football player."

Zepp tossed his cigarette to the ground, maneuvering around a screaming child. "His dad played NFL."

"Huh." And now he lived in a trailer a couple down from my crack whore mom. That was what you called unjust.

"He got injured or some shit... Wolf only does it for his dad."

"That's actually kinda sweet."

We headed toward the stands, passing by the Barrington

cheerleaders on the sidelines, all prettied up in their red-and-white uniforms. Several of them glared at me through the chain-link fence that separated the field from the track around the stadium. And, of course, smack dab in the middle stood Leah with her blond hair tied up in a bow.

"Hey, Zepp," she sang, giving a pageant queen wave.

Zepp didn't so much as glance in her direction.

But I smiled when I noticed the bump in her once-perfect nose. "You should probably get that broken nose fixed, Leah."

She glared at me with pure venom. Zepp snorted a laugh, and his arm came around me, squeezing me to his side as we continued through the cluster of people.

Hendrix and Bellamy stopped in front of one of the sections of bleachers. One glare from those two and the poor guys sitting on the stands grabbed their popcorn and shot up, hightailing it out of there.

The discordant rhythms from the marching band carried over the rumble of the crowd. Dayton's band sucked. God, how long was this shit going to last?

By the third quarter, Dayton was up by fifteen points, and I was bored shitless. Something must have happened because whistles blew, and Dayton's side of the stands went wild. The game paused, the refs were talking, and then Barrington's number twenty-seven sacked Wolf, laying him out on the ground. More whistles sounded and the refs moved across the field.

Hendrix jumped up, spilling popcorn all over the place. "That's bullshit! That's a penalty!" He grabbed his crotch. "Suck my dick, Barrington."

I breathed a small sigh of relief when Wolf climbed to his feet, grabbed the guy by his face mask, and threw him to the ground. Within seconds, most of the players had rushed the field, leading to an all-out brawl on the fifty-yard line. Hendrix let out something akin to a war cry, banging his chest before he leaped out of the bleachers, jumped the chain-link fence, and threw himself right in the middle of the fight.

"Shit," Zepp mumbled, swiping a hand over his face.

Shouting erupted a few rows back. A group of Dayton and Barrington guys started exchanging punches. Soon enough, little wildfires of fights between the two rival schools were popping up everywhere in the stands.

Zepp took my hand and pulled me to my feet, leading me down the steps, Jade and Bellamy right behind us. The farther away we got from the field, the quieter it was, the roar and rumble of the huge fight drifting away.

"What about Hendrix?" Jade asked.

"Why do you care?" I pointed at her. "You had better not even be considering his nasty dick, Jade."

She stopped and put her hands on her hips. "Uh, you're screwing Zepp."

"Hey!" Zepp swept a hand over his body. "I'm right here."

I glared at my friend again. "I'm not taking you to the clinic when you get crabs."

"Forget the crabs, man. Check this shit out!" Bellamy rounded the side of a gold '82 Challenger. The stadium lights reflected from the metallic paint. It was something a porn star would drive, but it was a nice car all the same. A classic. Bellamy caressed the lines of the hood with his palm "How much do you think we could get for this?"

Zepp went to the driver's side window and ducked his head to peer through the tinted glass. "The insides all ripped up." He circled the vehicle, dragging a finger along the side. "Got some dents. Scratches. But I bet we could get about eight grand." He glanced over the roof. "If we didn't get caught." The sarcasm in his last statement was thick enough to choke on.

I laughed when Jade shot a nervous glance at me. "Calm down. They aren't going to jack a car from a football game." I stroked a finger over the paint, before glancing back toward the stadium. "It is nice, though." The owner would probably be here any second, and a little chat couldn't do any harm. "Give me fifteen minutes."

Bellamy and Jade started toward his car, but Zepp stayed right there, glaring at me. "No," he said. "And don't roll your eyes at me. You're not taking that car."

"I'm not going to steal it right now. It's called groundwork, Zepp." I put my hand on my hip.

"Let's go." He started toward Bellamy's car, but I stayed back, my gaze darting between his retreating form and the Challenger. "Roe?" He stopped beside Bellamy's Civic, one hand on the open back door. I swore I could see his anger ticking up with each passing second.

My indignation bubbled to the surface. I flipped Zepp off and diverted my attention to the guy walking past Bellamy's car, heading straight for the Challenger.

"I swear to God, woman," Zepp practically growled.

Asshole.

The kid was only a few feet away. He had one of those preppy Barrington haircuts, but instead of the standard collared shirts, he had on a Yoda T-shirt. He definitely had to be one of Barrington's geeks.

He froze when he noticed me in the shadows, then slowly put his key into the door.

"Nice car," I said. When I stepped into the light from the streetlamp overhead, he dropped his keys.

"Uh." He cleared his throat, fumbling to pick them up and adjusting his glasses when he straightened. "Thanks."

"Maybe we could hang out sometime." I placed my back against the car parked beside his, keeping an eye on Zepp.

Psycho Sally stood halfway between Bellamy's car and me, a glare fixed on his face that might have worried me at one time.

"You could take me for a ride?" I said, flicking my attention back to Yoda.

His eyes went wide, mouth gaping. "S-sure."

"Great. I'll give you my number."

He fumbled with the phone before I typed in a name and number, then walked off with a little wave.

Straight toward Zepp, his arms crossed, jaw tense.

"You are stubborn as fuck," he said, falling in step beside me as we approached the Civic.

"Don't act like you don't like it."

We hadn't made it to Bellamy's car before my phone beeped.

Unknown: Hey. This is my number. I'd really like to hang out with you.

Zepp stopped and snatched my phone from my hands. The jealousy rippled across his face like a rogue wave. "You did not give him your phone number."

I snatched it back. "Not like I'm gonna fuck him, Zepp."

"I don't give a shit." He pointed an angry finger behind us. "He *thinks* you're going to."

"But, I'm not." I slid my hand over his chest, brushing my lips over his jaw. "Haven't we been over this? I'm never going to fuck anyone but you."

That seemed to appease the beast. The tension on his face softened—enough, and we climbed into the back seat of the car. "Never, huh?"

I stumbled for a second. I'd said that. Never. "As long as you behave," I said, skirting around the subject.

His gaze drifted to my lips before his mouth met mine. "I can sure as shit try." Zepp deepened the kiss, then suddenly pulled away. "What the hell, Bell? Don't throw shit at me!"

"Don't be trying to fuck in my backseat then! It took a steamer to get that jizz stain out your dumbass brother left in here."

I eyed the front seat. "Eww! Now I feel like I might get pregnant from the upholstery."

Jade looked over at me. "Really? *This* is going on"—she placed a palm up and circled it at us—"and you think the seat is gonna get you knocked up."

Bellamy cranked the engine and shifted into drive, pointing through the windshield. "Where the hell is he coming from?"

Hendrix sprinted across the parking lot. And not from the direction of the football field but from the woods at the back of the stadiums—wearing Barrington's number twenty-seven jersey. He yanked open the front door and threw himself in, just as the red and blue flash of police sirens appeared at the end of the road. They whizzed past us before taking a screeching turn into the school parking lot.

"Drive, dipshit!" Hendrix yelled, banging his fist over the back of the seat in front of him. "Drive."

"Jesus," Bellamy said, pulling away

Hendrix tugged at the jersey. "This smells like shit. You'd think with all that money they could buy better cologne."

"I'm curious," I said. "Did you just knock him out and start stripping him in the middle of the field?" The imagery was entertaining.

"I got so excited," he panted. "I think I blacked out." Hendrix was possibly a little insane.

By the time we pulled into Zepp's drive, the entire car reeked of body odor and feet from that damn jersey, which Hendrix refused to toss out the window. He claimed it was a trophy. How he managed to get into a fight full of football players and come out without a scratch, I'd never know.

Jade glanced over at me for a second before looking at Zepp. "Is Wolf coming back here?"

Hendrix spun around in the front seat. "Why do you give a shit about that dumpy fuck?" He snaked a hand down his body, rubbing over his crotch. "I got what you need right here, baby." He tossed his head back on a cackle before opening the car door.

I looked at Jade. "Just so you know, I approve of neither. They probably have enough STDs to stock a lab…"

She frowned at me. "Again. You're screwing Zepp."

Zepp climbed out, ducking his head to glare at Jade. "I'm clean as a fucking whistle. I get tested on the regular."

I groaned on my way out of the car. "Reassuring, babe."

"I mean. Not now… Just, you know." He shrugged a shoulder. "Before."

"Not the point," I said, waving at Jade as Bellamy backed over the overgrown lawn and pulled out of the drive.

Zepp's hand landed on my ass. "Never, right?

"You're hung up on that, huh?"

"Hell, yes, I am." His grip tightened. "Let's go fuck."

And just like that, my whole body lit up like Santa's grotto. We went straight through the front door and up the stairs. Zepp's shirt was off before we reached his room. The sight of all that tattooed muscle never failed to garner my absolute attention.

The bedroom door slammed shut, and within seconds, my shirt was on the floor and my back was against his mattress. Every touch of his hands sent heat tearing over my skin. I could never get enough of him, and it always felt like a dangerous rush. Like no one should want something this badly.

My phone beeped. Then beeped again and again. And again. I reached inside my bra for my phone, and Zepp groaned, adjusting his dick.

"Who the hell is texting you?"

I skim read the series of texts from the unknown number and couldn't help but smile. This would get a rise out of Zepp. "My new boyfriend."

On a smirk, Zepp placed his hands beside my head, caging me in. "That so?"

"Yep. Rich boy. Nice car. Bit geeky." My fingers trailed over each hard bump of his stomach. "Between you and me, I'm going to rob him blind."

His mouth worked over my throat to my collar bone. He yanked down my bra and traced a path over my skin with his tongue. "Too bad for him, huh?" He bit down on my nipple, the sudden sensation sending my back bowing away from the bed. "Maybe you should send him pictures of what I'm about to do to you."

"Poor kid would come in his batman boxers."

Zepp chuckled, his hands roaming over my body while my mind raced with thoughts about that car. About what stealing it could do for me. I'd never actually taken anything for myself, and I knew the money from cars could give me enough to leave The White Rabbit.

Zepp's fingers went inside my panties.

"I have a proposition for you," I said.

His thumb circled me in just the right spot, and I struggled to think clearly. "I bet you do."

"I'll get that car. You sell it. We split the money." The words were a rush.

He groaned when his fingers crooked inside me. "Didn't learn your lesson the last time you made a deal with me, Roe?"

"Didn't end so badly," I gasped, sinking my nails into his arms.

His movements grew more deliberate and determined until he pushed me to a point where words were no longer an option because my lungs were straining for air. I broke apart for him, the same way I always did, almost shamefully fast.

I waited until I could catch a breath. "So?"

"So what?" His hungry gaze locked with mine.

"Do we have a deal? Again."

"What?" He shoved his boxers down. "I'm not trying to talk about that shit right now; I'm trying to get my dick wet." He moved on top of me, and I placed my palms on his chest to keep some distance. I needed an out. From The White Rabbit. From Jerry...

"Yeah, well, I'm trying not to strip for rich guys who think twenty bucks is worth a grope."

His chin dropped on a hard breath. Then he moved off of me, flipping onto his back and staring at the ceiling. "Way to kill the mood."

"Fine." I rolled my eyes. "You don't want in? I'll take it and sell it myself."

"I want my dick sucked is what I want..."

"Well, you might have got it if you had just said yes."

He turned on the pillow to face me, one brow twitching. "I might would have said yes had you not brought up shoving your tits in guys' faces."

"Oh my God, Zepp." Sitting up, I glared at him. "I brought up getting out of it, you prick."

He moved, bringing his face inches from mine. "When I had my fingers inside you."

"You were done by then."

He pointed at his crotch. "Does that look done to you? Fuck my life."

"I'm sorry my problems are getting in the way of you blowing your load."

A look of disbelief crossed his face before his eyes narrowed on a groan. "You are fucking impossible sometimes, you know it!" He flopped back onto the bed, then fisted his dick. "Go ahead." He gave himself a few pumps. "Tell me about your problems, Roe."

"Fuck you, Zepp." I wanted to flick him in the dick. "Go spank one out like a twelve-year-old."

"This bother you?" He glanced down at his crotch, pumping harder.

"No." Truthfully, even though I was mad at him, there was something ridiculously hot about watching him stroke himself. Tattooed fingers wrapped around his dick, that little piercing making an appearance. Screw him for being so...*him*.

"Good." He closed his eyes, biting at his lip while he worked over himself, like he couldn't care less that I was right there. God, he was an asshole. I pitched up, tore off my bra, and straddled him.

"You about to dry hump my pillow like a twelve-year-old or what?" His brow lifted, his lips twitching like he was fighting a smirk.

"Fuck you." I grabbed a condom and slapped his hand away, rolling it over him a little harder than necessary.

A guttural grunt bubbled from his throat when I slammed down on him. "So angry," he said.

"I'm selling that car."

"Yeah." His fingers gripped my hips, guiding me over him. "I bet you are."

I raked my nails over his chest, leaving behind angry red lines while he thrust up against me. "You don't think I can?"

"Don't know. After all, you are *just* a girl, Roe."

My blood pressure spiked, and I wrapped my fingers around his throat. "I can do all kinds of things for a set of keys, baby."

Too far. His jaw set, and in one swift move, he had me underneath him, pinned to the bed while he drove into me like an animal. "You're not doing a damn thing for those keys."

I should have stopped, but I liked it—craved it even. "You think?" The two words fell from my tongue like a match to a pool of gasoline.

He shoved my knees back by my head until my muscles burned. "It would be stupid of you to." The headboard banged against the wall. It was raw and angry like he was halfway between wanting to kill me and fuck me. "You close?" he asked.

"God, yes."

"You wanna come, Roe?"

I grabbed at his ass, attempting to hold him in place. "Don't you dare."

He flipped onto his back, then placed both hands behind his head. "Work for it," he said.

I rolled over him, working him deeper. I could see the tight lines of restraint, the need to grab me and fuck me written all over his face.

Within seconds, warm heat flooded my skin. The rush of endorphins made my head light. I hadn't even started to come down before Zepp's hands clutched at my thighs, and he pushed up against me, a deep groan tearing from his throat.

We looked at each other for a moment before I climbed off him.

I was taking that damn car.

31

ZEPP

The next afternoon, I sat on the couch playing *Call of Duty* with my brother.

I shot his avatar in the head. Blood splattered the screen before his player crumpled to the pixelated sand. "You suck at this."

"Yeah. Well. You suck at life," Hendrix shifted to the edge of the couch beside me, his focus on the screen. "So are you and Monroe into that BDSM shit now or something? Last night sounded ruff."

I cut my eyes away from the TV. "Mind your own business, would you?"

"We're brothers. You're supposed to confide all your kinky shit to me." He moved his character across the screen, ducking and weaving like a complete cracked-out feen.

Sometimes I worried my brother was a complete mental case and that it was my fault for whacking him in the head with a whiffle ball bat repeatedly when he was five. The rumble of an engine pulled into the drive, then around the back of the house. Hendrix sat up like a prairie dog at the sound, then chucked his controller down, and rushed to the back door. "Aw, hell no!" he grumbled before the screen banged shut.

I pushed off the couch and slipped outside, skirting around my seething brother. "I don't like this."

That damn Challenger sat parked in our backyard. Monroe in the driver's seat, window down.

"She better not be stealing cars for us now," Hendrix grumbled as I approached the idling car, taking note of the *Star Wars* sticker on the back bumper.

I stopped beside the car and folded my forearms over the sunbaked roof, looking down at Monroe. "If the guy hadn't thought he was going to get his dick sucked by my girlfriend, I would almost feel bad for the fucker."

"Why? He's from Barrington."

I stepped back when she opened the door and climbed out, pressing a kiss to my lips. "He has a Yoda bumper sticker on the back fender." I thumbed behind me. "He's not real Barrington."

She frowned. "Now, I feel a bit bad."

Hendrix stomped down the steps, a deep scowl on his face and his arms crossed. Like an angry toddler that had shit his pants. He pointed at the car. "Did she steal that?"

"Are you..." She looked at me, brows creased in disbelief. "Is he judging me?"

"I'm judging my pussy-whipped brother!" Hendrix stepped up to the passenger side of the car and kicked the wheel. "This is bullshit, man. Practically move her in. Fine! Fuck her in the kitchen where I have to eat my food. Great! Get your balls on my couch. Whatever." He tossed his hands into the air, glancing from the car to her to me, then back. "But letting her steal cars. That's over the line."

"Hendrix..." I dragged both hands down my face, annoyed as hell with him. "Shut up."

"Zepp doesn't *let* me do anything." Monroe rounded the front of the Challenger and squared up to him before poking him in the chest. "I already stole cars, you asshole."

"Yeah? Well..." His brow wrinkled, and for a split-second, he looked like he was at a loss for words. "Who's gonna get rid of it for you?" His gaze swung from her to me.

"Oh, like he's doing me a favor." She thumbed back at me. "He's taking a cut."

Damn her and her mouth. I hadn't really thought she was going to steal the damn thing. At least not this soon. "Hey!" I held up both hands. "She was talking about it when I was fucking her. It's basically like agreeing to something when you're drunk. And I didn't think she was actually going to do it."

"Fine. You want out?" She made her way back to the driver's side. "I have my own guy. I can take it there right now."

"Roe..." I started, but Hendrix was already taking a step and swinging at me. I caught his wrist and bent his arm back, slamming him against the hood of the car. "I'll split my half of the money with you, dickwad. Shut up." I gave him another shove before letting him go.

"Stealing cars is our shit, man," he whined, then sniffed. "Nothing's sacred anymore. Not our couch. Not our cars. Nothing." He pushed away from the hood and pretended to wipe at tears.

"Do you want it, or not?" Monroe asked, hands on her hips.

That was a few grand. She had already stolen the damn thing. "Yeah. We'll take it over to Billy Bob and the guys at the chop shop."

"Unbelievable." Hendrix sank to the leaf-covered ground on a huff. My seventeen-year-old brother was sulking.

Monroe rolled her eyes at him. "Your maturity never fails to astound me, Hen."

His wide-eyed gaze met mine. "She just called me a chicken!"

Ignoring Hendrix, I grabbed the toolbox from the back porch and dropped it in the grass beside Monroe's feet. She rummaged through the tools while Hendrix stayed all criss-cross applesauce in the middle of the yard.

"You want a cut," I said. "Go file down the VIN, dipshit."

An hour and a half later, we'd dropped the car at the chop shop. I sat in the passenger side of Monroe's Pinto, counting through the stack of hundreds. "Poor fucking kid," I said, grinning. Honestly, I didn't feel bad for the guy. At all.

He had a nice car. He had a cushy Barrington life. *And* he thought he was going to bang my girl. He could suck my nuts. Besides, Dayton was the mange-riddled lions, and Barrington were the sleek gazelle, ripe for feasting. It was just the circle of life.

Monroe's phone vibrated in the cupholder. She gave it a brief glance before tossing it to me. "Can you check that?"

```
Challenger Geek: Sorry I didn't text you
back. Someone stole my car.
Challenger Geek: It was my granddad's car.
Challenger Geek: Please tell me I can see
you. I need some for real cheering up
right now.
```

I stared at the phone, half wanting to laugh, half wanting to punch the kid. God, we were assholes.

"Who is it?" she asked.

"Your boyfriend."

"Just block the number."

"Seriously?" I shook my head, typing out a response. "You can't steal a guy's car, then block his number."

Monroe took a hard turn off the highway, slamming me against the window. God, she was a shit driver. "Why not?" she asked.

"Because it makes you look guilty as fuck." I added a heart to the end of the text.

Monroe: That's so awful. Maybe I can see you later. I have to go to communion and promise my virginity to the church today.

Challenger Geek: I didn't take you for a church girl ;)

I snorted and typed another response.

Monroe: What's that supposed to mean?

Hell no, Monroe wasn't a church girl. She'd give half those senior citizens cardiac arrest the seconds she stepped in with those tits and those bare legs.

Challenger Geek: I don't know. You're hot.

That was it. The kid had to be a virgin. No game whatsoever.

Monroe: Aw. Thanks. Pulling up to the church. GTG. TTYL.
Challenger Geek: Tell Jesus I said hi.

Monroe fishtailed around the corner of my street. Cars were parked along the road and in the yard. People were sprawled over the sagging porch, drinks in hand. And my brother was leaned against the open door, sweet-talking a girl.

"What the hell?" There was no space on the driveway, so Monroe cut around the lawn, blocking in a couple of cars. "I'm not moving." She opened the door, and rap music from the house poured in. "They can walk home."

"Got a few people over," Hendrix said, like the people on the porch and the haze of smoke drifting through the open door wasn't a dead giveaway.

"No shit." Monroe glared at a girl nearby.

I flicked my brother on the forehead on my way across the threshold. Wolf and Bellamy sat on the couch, both of them with their hands up the same girl's skirt while the bass pumping through the speakers rattled the walls.

"Didn't take them for the crossing swords type," she whispered in my ear.

That was a mental image I could have gone without. "I'm grabbing a beer." I pushed through a group of girls crowding the kitchen and went to the fridge, bending over to dig through the shit beer Bellamy had stocked the shelves with.

"You like the view?" Monroe growled. "I'm gonna count to three. One."

I slammed the fridge and turned around to only Monroe in the kitchen. I cracked open the can. "I like it when you go all Harley Quinn on people."

"Girls, Zepp. Not people. Looking at you like you're an all you can eat buffet."

"All *you* can eat." I wrapped an arm around her waist,

lifting her and placing her on the counter. "Want me to go down on you right here? Show them they don't stand a chance?" I placed the beer down and grabbed her thighs, spreading them just enough.

"So romantic." She gave me a slight shove. "But no, because Hendrix will probably film it."

"Oh, the hell no!" Hendrix barreled into the kitchen, a sadistic grin in place as he hopped on his heels and thumbed toward the front of the house. "The Barrington cocksuckers just pulled up. They want a beat down." He ran through the kitchen and grabbed the nine iron.

"What?" I snatched the back of his shirt when he rushed past.

"They're shitting on our territory, man, which means we are gonna fuck them up." He broke free of my hold and darted into the living room.

"Stay in here," I said to Monroe on my way through the doorway.

Wolf stood at the window, peeking through the mangled plastic blinds. "Shit, dude. They got bats."

Hot anger tore through me. Those assholes came to *my* house to start shit. I snagged my Slugger from the coat closet, Wolf and Bellamy in tow.

Hendrix was already on the porch, shirt off, chest puffed out. Guys piled out of the shiny Range Rover parked beside Monroe's Pinto, bats in hands. Their shoulders were back, chins lifted like they were on their high horse. But what pissed me off more than anything was that Max fucking Harford was sitting in the passenger seat with a shit-eating grin on his face.

The Barrington crew stopped when the guys and I stepped onto the first step. "I suggest you leave," I said.

The prick at the front of the pack laughed. "Don't think so. You cost us the championship. Fucked up our quarterback and a few of our wide receivers." He hitched a thumb over his shoulder. "And shit on my ride."

"I diarrhea-ed on your hood, man!" Hendrix shouted before cackling.

The guy's jaw clenched, his gaze shifting to my brother before coming back to me. "We're gonna dish out some justice, Hunt. I'm gonna beat you in front of your little Dayton minions there."

"You just gonna stand there and talk all day, or what?" I gripped the bat in my hand, adrenaline firing through me like radioactive material. I wanted to take a swing so damn bad, but I wasn't making the first move. I knew better than that. "Or you starting to rethink getting your rich-boy ass beat?"

His nostrils flared, before he charged at me, swung, and missed. Then all hell broke loose.

It was only a matter of minutes before most of the Barrington guys were rolling on the ground, groaning and clutching at their limbs, and Max was still in the Range Rover, like a coward, with a phone to his ear. Wiping sweat from my brow, I crossed the yard, stopping at his window. I took the end of the bat and smashed the window. "Didn't learn your lesson last time, shithead?"

Max's mouth moved up and down like a fish out of water for a second.

"Yes, ma'am. Victory Lane," he muttered into the phone.

"Calling the cops, Harford? Or an ambulance? Because you're on my property. With bats," I rested an arm over the window ledge, shards of glass tearing into my skin. "Self-defense is a bitch, isn't it?"

He swallowed hard enough that I noticed. "Um. I'm sorry. No, ma'am. I don't need assistance. It was a, umm. It was a prank." Then he dropped the phone.

The image of him on top of Monroe surfaced, and I wanted to take the bat to his face again, but I knew killing a guy still on crutches wouldn't look like self-defense. "You're a piece of shit," I said, pushing away from the car when I spit in his face. On my way to the porch, I snagged Hendrix by the back of a shirt and dragged him off one of the Barrington guys.

"I wasn't done, dickwad." Hendrix swatted at my arm.

"He's knocked out."

"And?"

I slapped Hendrix on the back of the head, then shoved him toward the door. Everyone filed back inside the house except Monroe. She lingered on the porch, eyes set on the Range Rover.

"You didn't kill Max." She patted my chest. "Proud of you."

Someone turned up the music. "I'm going to get this shit off of me," I said, heading upstairs to wash the blood off my arms. I took the washcloth on the ledge of the sink and glanced up in the mirror to wash my face, and Monroe's reflection caught my attention.

"Can I help you?" I smirked into the mirror, scrubbing at the speck of blood on my cheek.

The look in her eye made my dick hard. It was the look that said she was down to fuck. I turned from the sink, and her shirt hit the floor, followed by her bra. I cupped her tits in my hands, biting at her lip. "Like a bit of violence, huh?"

She grabbed my wrist and shoved it under her skirt. "You tell me." Holy shit, she was wet.

Biting back a groan, I slipped my hand inside her panties. "I'd say that's a definite fucking yes." I lifted her onto the edge of the sink, spreading her legs. "I bet I can get you off at least three times."

"Ambitious."

"No, Roe. I'm determined."

32

MONROE

The party had thinned out, except for the girls who still lingered nearby, waiting for their friend to get finished with Hendrix. Pretty sure Wolf had another in the spare room. I didn't get it. They were assholes. These girls had no shame.

I took a drag off the joint Zepp offered me, feeling the weed trickle over me like a warm blanket. Some of the other Barrington guys had come by earlier to scrape the football players off of Zepp's lawn. I smiled at the thought of Max sitting there, like a spoiled little brat, waiting for someone to come to rescue him because his legs were still too messed up to drive. The fact that he came for round two had me questioning whether Zepp might have given him mild brain damage the first time.

The thud of Hendrix's headboard silenced just before someone pounded on the door. None of the guys made any effort to move. They were all probably too high. On a sigh, I pushed out of Zepp's lap and answered it, nearly shitting myself when I saw that asshole police officer, Jacobs, standing on the porch. He stood with his fingers through his belt loops and a smug grin on his face. My pulse ticked up with a thread of panic. Jacobs could probably smell the weed on my breath. Hell, there was probably a cloud of smoke pouring through the cracked front door. I glanced over his shoulder at the now empty lawn, the only evidence I could see were the tire tracks in the overgrown grass.

"You sure are hangin' out with those Hunt boys a lot." He hitched up his pants, then glared over my shoulder inside the house.

"Is having a boyfriend illegal now?" I half laughed.

"Didn't your momma teach you to make better decisions?" My momma was a hooker. His gaze veered back to me. "They're gonna get you in trouble."

"Thanks for the advice." I offered him a fake smile. "Is there something I can help you with?"

"Seems there was a confrontation here earlier. Which means, I need to talk to Mr. Hunt."

"Sure. Let me get him." I shut the door on him and hurried down the hall.

Zepp and Bellamy were sitting on the couch, passing another joint back and forth. I snatched the joint from Bellamy's hand.

"That cop is at the door," I whisper-shouted, panic lancing through me as I ran to the kitchen and chucked the weed into the garbage disposal.

I walked back into the hallway just as Zepp opened the door, crossing his arms over his chest. "Yeah?"

"Heard you had a little disagreement over here earlier today?" Jacobs said.

"I think we all came to an understanding."

"That a fact?" He paused. "That blood on your porch?"

"Probably." Zepp huffed, leaning against the open door, and I shifted a little closer.

"Assault has a hefty jail time, son."

"Yeah? So those Barrington fucks gonna spend some time behind bars? They showed up. On my lawn. With bats."

A few seconds ticked by. "Now why on earth would they do that? Wouldn't have nothing to do with that quarterback of theirs who got beat, would it?"

"Do you have a warrant or what? Because I'm not trying to shoot the shit with you."

"That girlfriend of yours..." Jacobs clucked his tongue. "Shame if she got tangled up in a mess due to you." God, he was a bastard. The porch creaked before his footfalls disappeared down the steps and Zepp slammed the door.

"Asshole!" He placed his arm around my shoulder on his way back to the living room. "Tell me you didn't throw away my weed, Roe?"

"I panicked!"

He pressed a condescending kiss to my forehead. "You're so fucking cute."

"All right, Al Capone."

———

Days had passed since the encounter with Jacobs—days since I'd stolen the Challenger. The kid had finally stopped texting me after a few clipped responses, and I'd told my boss at The White Rabbit to shove it. The morning sun crept in through the window, and I rolled over, glancing at Zepp's sleeping form. He was almost cute in sleep, innocent, though I knew that was far from the truth. I didn't want to wake him, so I grabbed my phone and started scrolling. After a few minutes, I checked my email, my pulse beating a little faster when I saw the message from two days ago.

It was from The Elizabeth Roux School of Art. My stomach knotted when I opened it, skimming over the body of the email:

This level of talent is always welcome at our school. We encourage and invite you to complete an application for one of our scholarships. We hope to see your exceptional work on our campus next fall.

Hope blossomed in my chest. This meant we wouldn't have to do a long-distance relationship. Zepp could go to Elizabeth Roux while I attended Dixon. We could *both* get out of Dayton.

I waited until the sun's rays inched across the bed before sliding my hand over Zepp's stomach. Anywhere within a foot of his dick was usually enough to wake him.

He rolled over, his lips seeking out my neck on autopilot. "Hey," he mumbled, then grabbed my hand and placed it on his hard dick. He was so predictable.

I pulled away and touched his cheek. "Wait, I have something to tell you."

"Okay..." He caught my wrist again, putting my hand down his boxers, this time with a smile. "You can still talk with your hand on my dick."

"Fine," I sighed. "So, I sent an email to an art school in Florida." I gave him a pump. "And they want you to apply for a scholarship."

His expression went blank for a second before the dark storm clouds rolled in. "You did what?"

I stilled, suddenly unsure of myself. "This is a good thing... Right?"

A deep line sank between his brows, and he grabbed my

hand, yanking it away from him before he sat up in bed. He had never taken my hand off his dick before. *Shit*.

"You sent them one of my pictures? Why the hell would you do that?"

I was so confused. "I mean, a picture of a picture. It's not—"

"I don't give a shit. Those are personal, Monroe!" He threw the covers off, getting out of bed and dragging an agitated hand through his unruly hair.

"And if you get a scholarship?"

"If I wanted a scholarship, don't you think I would have applied for one myself." He glared at me, anger mixed with hurt. "I'm not stupid. I know I'm good enough."

"Then why don't you want it?" My anger and frustration spilled out. He was so unbelievably talented. And his aspirations amounted to this. To Dayton.

"Why the hell would I want to go to college?" He paced for a second.

"Why wouldn't you, if someone offered you a full ride?"

His nostrils flared, fists clenched. "Because I don't want to fucking go. If I did, I would take care of it myself."

A sinking feeling settled in my gut. Zepp was going to stay in Dayton. The very place I was so desperate to get away from. More than that, though, he had an opportunity to do something he loved, and to be with me, to get out of here. And he didn't want any of it.

"I can't believe you did that." He shook his head.

"Really?" I got out of bed, turning my back on him while I got dressed.

He had pissed me off, but more than that, I was disappointed, and I didn't want him to see it. I went to the bathroom and brushed my teeth. Seconds later, and he was standing at the toilet, pissing.

"I can't believe you would just take the liberty to. Damn, Roe."

I spat into the sink and glared at him in the mirror. "Take the liberty to what? Give a shit?"

"That's not giving a shit, Monroe. That's wanting me to be someone I'm not." He shook his dick before flushing the toilet and storming out.

Is that what I was doing? Did I want to change him? I didn't think so, but evidently, he did. How did this go so wrong? I really thought he'd be happy.

His bedroom door slammed shut, loud music cut on, and I made my way downstairs. Zepp and I always went to school together. But instead of waiting on him, I grabbed my backpack and my keys, and I left alone.

Zepp skipped the class we had together, which did nothing but add to the unsettled feeling churning in my gut. By the change of class at lunchtime, that painful twinge had only grown worse. I shoved my books into my locker, bending the pages. It had been a long time since I'd been truly scared of anything, but now a reality and its infinite possibilities terrified me. Zepp had become necessary to me, like air. And yet this niggling feeling told me that he didn't need me the same way. It wasn't even about college. It was about the opportunity to be with me in Florida, and his rejection of it hurt more than it should have. I slammed my locker and met Jade's concerned gaze.

"I'm going to go to the library. Chase and I need to put our project together and write a summary."

She lifted a brow. "You've been weird all day, and Zepp

isn't hanging around like your personal guard dog. What's going on?"

"Nothing. It's fine. I'll see you later." I walked off before she could ask any more questions, texting Chase on my way to the library. I told myself it was because I didn't want to have to stay after school. But truthfully, I was avoiding Zepp. My emotions were raw right now, and I didn't want him to see them written all over my face.

I ducked into the library, trailing my fingers along the spines of books as I inhaled the dusty scent of old paper. A couple sat at one of the tables in the study area, making out. They didn't bother to draw a breath as I passed. The computer table in the back corner by the window was empty, and I dropped into the seat. The machine had just booted up when several books and a king-sized bag of chips landed on the desk beside me.

"Do we have to work over lunch?" Chase slumped into the plastic chair.

"Well, this way, we won't have to work later."

"Right. Don't want to piss off Zepp." The annoyance in his tone did not go unmissed.

"This—" I gestured between us—"Has nothing to do with Zepp and everything to do with you becoming a football prick." I shoved his shoulder when his expression hardened, but he didn't crack a smile.

"I never changed, Moe." And this was something I was absolutely not in the mood to discuss.

"Whatever. Doesn't matter." I pulled up our assignment on the computer. "So, the summary..."

After fifteen minutes, I was typing in the concluding sentence. That was when I felt Chase's eyes on me. "What?" I stared straight ahead at the computer and jabbed at the period key. "Do I have something on my face?"

"What's wrong with you?"

"Nothing," I said, my eyes fixed on the screen.

"You act like I don't know you, Moe."

For a second, I found myself wanting to talk to him, to tell him everything. I guess I was just so lost and out of my depth with Zepp, and I wanted someone to tell me what to do. Chase knew me in ways even Jade couldn't. He'd known me before life became really hard. When I was just a little girl with simple dreams, untainted by the adult understanding of Dayton and what my mom did. What was the saying? Innocence, once lost, can never be regained. Ain't that the truth.

"I made a mistake," I said. "And now, I don't know how to fix it."

"Well, did you apologize?"

"No," I mumbled.

He looked at me like I stupid. "Well, maybe start there."

I really was stupid. "Thanks, Chase." I fought a smile and pushed to my feet. "I think we'll get a good grade on this." I left him at the table, gathering his things as I headed through the bookshelves to the door. There were still a few minutes of lunch left, which meant I could talk to Zepp.

But I didn't have to go to the cafeteria to find him. I stepped through the library doors, greeted by Zepp leaned against the wall right across from me, thick arms folded over his chest. Dark, brooding, and dangerous as always, but that air of danger seemed far more intense right now.

Like an idiot, I stood there, fiddling with a strand of hair, unsure what to say or do. "Hey." I took a small step forward when the door creaked open behind me, and Chase walked out.

Zepp gave him a fleeting glance, then shook his head and pushed off the wall.

"Zepp!" I jogged after him, grabbing his arm, though I didn't actually know what to say.

"What, Monroe?" He glared down at me not so differently than he had that night I'd stolen that Hurst. Like he hated the idea of me.

He was still mad. Zepp made me vulnerable, and while part of me needed to fix this, the other part told me to let go, that it would be best if we just ended this now before I was any more attached. Everything in life had taught me that Zepp would leave, that it was inevitable. And as the silence stretched between us, that fear dug beneath my skin.

"Do you want to break up with me?" My heart let out an accusatory thump like I was a traitor for saying the words.

His back hit the wall of lockers. "That easy, huh?"

"No, it's not easy. I'm asking you."

Seconds ticked by. Seconds where I felt like an exposed nerve.

"You need to calm the hell down. I don't want to break up with you." He stepped forward, wrapping his arms around me and tugging me against him. "I'm just pissed."

My forehead rested against his throat. I inhaled the scent of leather and smoke that was all Zepp.

My fingers twisted in his shirt. "I don't want you to be someone you aren't."

"Okay." His chest rose on a hard sigh.

I hated that he sounded so unsure of himself. His lips brushed my forehead, and the little knot in my chest eased. He felt like home when I'd never truly had one, and I wasn't sure that was a good thing.

33

ZEPP

They say it takes twenty-one days for something to become a habit. It had been well over twenty-one days of Monroe staying at my house, and I found myself more than happy with the routine of waking up next to her. Screwing around in the kitchen with her. Going to school and coming home with her. For the first time since my mom had passed away, I was happy.

Hendrix sat beside me, playing PlayStation—losing. And bitching about losing.

A charred scent wafted in from the kitchen. "What the hell is that?" Hendrix said, jabbing his fingers over the controller.

"Roe!" I shouted, focusing on shooting Hendrix's avatar. "Something's burning."

When she didn't answer, I tossed the controller down and went to the kitchen. Whatever was in the oven was smoking. I turned the temperature off and opened the window over the sink. Monroe was at the plastic patio table on the back porch, hunched over papers.

"Whatever's in the oven is burned," I said when I stepped outside.

She looked up on a groan. "Pizza?"

I laughed, rounding the table and stopping behind her chair, glancing at the half-completed form in front of her. "What's that?"

"Scholarship application."

Alabama State University was at the top of the page in bold type. "Yeah? I thought you said Dixon?" Not that I was upset. Alabama State was a thirty-minute drive, and Dixon was all the way in Florida.

"I thought so too." She finished a line, then dropped her pen to the table. "But Alabama has its merits."

I draped my arms around her, leaning down to kiss the side of her throat. "Yeah? Like?"

"Well, it has a good business program…"

I gave her another kiss, slipping my hand down the front of her shirt. "And it's close." I squeezed her tit.

"And there's this guy here…" She tilted her head to the side and grabbed my hair, pulling me closer. "The sex is definitely a selling point."

"Definitely." I smirked against her neck, grabbing the back of her chair and spinning it around. "Want a quick reminder of just how good it is?" I slid my hand along her thigh, getting so close to where I wanted to be before the back door slammed open.

"Yippy-ki-yay, motherfuckers," Hendrix shouted before popping me on the ass with a dishtowel, then darting back into the house.

I took off after him, catching him by the front door and tackling him to the ground. "I'm gonna beat the shit out of you, Hendrix, if you don't stop being a cockblock." I punched him in the shoulder a few times.

"Man, you're sitting on my junk."

When I stood up, Wolf's truck pulled into the drive. "Unlock the door, dipshit," I called over my shoulder before I went back to the couch to play a game.

Wolf strolled in a couple of minutes later and plopped down beside me, snagging the controller. His brow wrinkled, and he took a sniff. "What the hell did you set on fire?"

"Monroe burned something."

A few minutes into the game, he exhaled a hard breath. "Dude, I forgot to tell you. Dizzy's dead."

"What?" I looked away from the screen, but Wolf zoned into the TV. Stoned as hell. "Dizzy's dead?"

"Yeah, I think Jerry killed him. Sucks ass."

I dropped my controller and punched him in the shoulder, my pulse ticking up because he'd mentioned Jerry's stupid name. "Shut up, man."

"What the hell, dude?" Wolf scowled, rubbing at his arm. "That hurt."

"Are you serious?" Monroe stepped into the living room doorway. Jaw tensed, face red. "You lied to me."

Great. Here we went. "I did not *lie* to you."

"Don't give me that shit." Taking a step forward, she jabbed a finger at me. "I asked you if you had anything to do with Jerry getting beat."

Wolf shifted beside me, then stood up, and skirted around Monroe into the kitchen. The backdoor closed, and I swept a hand through my hair before setting my gaze back on an angry Monroe. "And I said I had been with you for the past three days. That wasn't a lie."

"Well, it was an omission! What's the difference?"

That set my skin on fire. I pushed up from the couch and closed the space between us. "A lie of omission, huh? Like you not telling me you got your tits out for old men?"

Oh, that got her. Her nostrils flared, eyes narrowed. "You're gonna bring that up now?"

"Damn right, I am." I backed her across the room. "Because, now that I think about it, that wasn't even a lie by omission. That was a straight-up lie. You said you worked at Cha Chas. So get off your high fucking horse, Monroe."

"Screw you, Zepp. You know damn well why I didn't want to tell you that."

Because she was worried she might lose me. And that's why I wanted Jerry's ass beat. Because I was worried I might lose her, just like I did my mother if he took it too far. That girl was literally everything to me. Every-fucking-thing, and I couldn't imagine my life without her.

"Why did you have to go mess around with Jerry?" There was an edge of hysteria to her tone. "If he finds out you had anything to do with it, you'll be dead, and—"

"Because I fucking love you. Okay?" I scrubbed a hand over my jaw, panic winding through me at the abrupt confession. "I love you, and I'm terrified of losing you. I hoped Dizzy would kill his ass because you wouldn't let me do it, and I can't lose you."

She stilled. "I love you too," she whispered, her teary gaze meeting mine. "I'm scared he's going to get to you. And...I can't."

I pulled her into my arms, resting my chin on the top of her head. "He won't. I promise."

Her arms came around me, clinging to me like I was a lifeline. Just like she was mine.

THE NEXT NIGHT, Monroe talked me into going to the shitty little carnival set up in the parking lot of the Wal-E-Mart.

Hendrix invited himself. I paid for the tickets, eyeing the cracked-out-looking jack-off behind the booth.

"These people put together stuff that spins you around in the air." I nodded toward one of the lit-up rides, twirling and flipping a few stories up. "And you feel like getting on it is a good idea?" I hated carnivals. I hated the smell and the Dayton yokels that came out of the woodworks to get a little rush.

"I mean, they must be safe," Monroe said, her eyes glowing at the sight of all the rides. "Right?"

"They're fine." Hendrix stopped mid-stride, his gaze fixed on the cotton-candy stand—or rather, the blonde dipping the paper cones into the machine. He patted me on the back. "Have fun on your death traps. I've got a cooter to catch." And then he was gone.

"What do you want to ride?" I asked.

"That one." She pointed, and I glanced behind me at some metal shitshow called "The Roundup." Music blasted from it, and the motor made a screeching sound as the thing took off, spinning fast enough to give me vertigo just watching it. On a small sigh, I took her hand and maneuvered through the families with screaming kids. "You aren't going to throw up, are you?"

"I don't know. I've never been on a ride."

I had. Once. My mother had brought Hendrix and me to one of these traveling carnivals when I was seven. We had three tickets, which meant we could ride three rides. All I wanted to ride was the Ferris wheel, but Hendrix cried and made us go on the merry-go-round. Then my mom picked something fast, and Hendrix threw up on me. So no Ferris wheel. I stepped up to the carney and handed him our tickets.

"Well, if you throw up," I said. "Turn your head." I

followed her around the metal grate until she found one of the booths she wanted and tucked herself in. I pressed my back against the stall beside her.

Other people filed in, then the worker staggered by, hooking a rinky-dink chain across my hips, then Monroe's. Her brow wrinkled as she watched him go.

"Zepp, why is there just a chain?"

"Still feel safe?" I snorted.

"I'm gonna throw up and direct it at you."

The buzzer sounded, and the machine slowly spun in a circle. By the time it was going fast enough to plaster us to the walls, it lifted into the air, and my stomach churned. My grip on the bars tightened while I fought back the urge to toss the hotdogs I had eaten earlier. Monroe screamed beside me. At least she wasn't going to puke.

We rode just about every ride in that damn park before I managed to drag her to the Ferris wheel. We were next in line when she pulled back on my hand, staring up at the top of it. A breeze picked up, and the metal frame creaked and groaned. "Okay, that one doesn't look safe."

"It doesn't even go fast."

She narrowed her eyes at me and stepped forward. "Fine. But if we die, it's your fault." She had ridden things that had some of the safety straps duct-taped together and she thought this was going to be the one to kill us.

"Whatever, Roe." We took a seat in one of the baskets, and the bar came down over our laps. I tapped the metal with my finger. "Look. Totally safe. No chain," I laughed.

She wobbled the bar. "That's not gonna save us if the whole thing collapses."

Something dropped onto my head, and I looked up.

"Cocksucker!" Hendrix was in the basket above us with a

girl, feet dangling. He cackled before tossing another piece of popcorn onto my head.

Monroe looked over her shoulder. "He totally got the cotton candy girl to suck his dick up there."

He probably did. Bastard. "No way a girl could suck a dick that fast."

She bit at her bottom lip, her gaze dropping suggestively to my crotch. "That feels like a challenge." The ride made its way around as people filled up the seats. As soon as we were halfway to the top, Monroe yanked at my belt.

I had always wanted to ride a Ferris wheel, and now I was going to get a blowjob while doing it. I fought a smirk when she pulled me out. "You only got about two minutes," I said.

And down her warm throat I went. I didn't know if it was the music blaring from the speakers, the flash of lights, the open air, or the fact that if anyone looked up, they would absolutely see her head bobbing up and down, but by the time we reached the very top, my hand was on the back of her head, and my head was thrown against the seat.

"Shit," I groaned, my toes curling in my shoes when she took me over the edge.

Monroe sat up, wiped the back of her hand over her mouth, then smiled. "That wasn't even two minutes." She cocked a brow on a laugh.

"No, it wasn't." I slid my hand over her thigh, dipping underneath her skirt. "Give me thirty seconds."

34

MONROE

After the carnival, I left Zepp's to run home and grab some clothes. The trailer park was dark, aside from the red and white lights flashing over the trailers. For a second, I hoped the cops were coming to arrest Jerry for killing that guy, but the farther into the park I drove, I realized the lights coming from in front of my trailer weren't from a police car, but from an ambulance.

I parked in front of the neighbor's driveway, gripping the steering wheel on a hard breath before I cut the engine and hopped out. She had overdosed again, and I wasn't sure what was more concerning: that this was so routine or that I had become numb to the idea of her dying. I rounded the back of the ambulance while the paramedics carted a stretcher through the trailer door, then down the steps.

"She OD'd?" I asked.

One of the medics glanced over at me. "This your mom?"

I nodded, and I didn't miss the flash of pity in his eyes. Another poor trash kid with a junkie mom. They probably saw ten a day. "We're taking her to hospital. You're welcome to ride in the back of the ambulance."

My gaze strayed to my mother in the middle of the stretcher, eyes rolled back in her head, foam on her purple lips. "No, I'm good." The confused look the medic gave me sent a twinge of guilt through me. "I'll just follow you there."

I trailed behind the ambulance to Dayton hospital, gave my name to the triage nurse, and took a seat in the waiting room with the rest of the gangbangers and addicts. This was her third overdose this year, so I knew the drill. Within the hour, the doctor would come and tell me whether he'd managed to save her this time or not.

An hour passed, then two. My leg bounced while a tightness wound through my chest. I told myself that I didn't care. That the feeling in my chest was because I needed her not to die so I wasn't homeless. I needed a distraction. I took my phone from my pocket to text Zepp. My battery was on one percent. Of course.

Me: I can't come over tonight.

As soon as I sent it, the screen went black.

"Miss James?"

I looked up at the middle-aged man lingering in the emergency room doorway, his gaze scanning over the people waiting.

I pushed to my feet, and he offered me a polite smile before guiding me to a corner of the room.

"Your mother had a cardiac arrest. She's stable for now. You can go and see her if you wish."

I gave him a nod, and he walked me through the automatic doors, asking one of the nurses to take me to the ICU.

The lady didn't say a word, just showed me through several sets of doors until I came to the room with my mom's last name written in Expo marker over the board.

The door clicked shut behind me, the nurse glancing through the glass wall before she walked off.

I stared at the floor, listening to the beep and hum of machines before I looked over at the hospital bed. An oxygen mask covered most of her face, and a myriad of tubes connected to the IV in her arm.

She looked bad, pale and lifeless. There was a time when my mom wasn't awful, when her smiles made me feel safe and warm. When she would braid my hair and buy me candy on the way home from her job at the Bunny Lounge. She had never been the best person, but there was a time when she wasn't the worst. A small bit of pain sprung to life, but it quickly morphed into anger, hot and wild. She chose this—over me. She'd rather kill herself shooting that shit into her veins than be my mother. It was something I knew all too well, and I thought I had come to terms with a long time ago. People always left. It was a fact of life. But it didn't have to be.

Zepp wouldn't leave me. I pulled my phone out to see if he'd texted back, but the battery was dead. Great. At least he knew I wasn't coming so he wouldn't worry.

I could have gone home, but for whatever messed up reason, I thought I owed it to her to at least be here if she died. Nurses came in and out throughout the night, and at some point, I fell asleep.

The next morning the doctor said he was moving her out of ICU, and I left. I wasn't hanging around if she wasn't dying.

My mind wandered while I drove down the back road that led into Dayton. I wanted out of this shithole town so bad. Away from her. Away from the reminders. But I didn't want away from Zepp.

A few miles down the road, the engine coughed. Then rattled. "No, no, no. Don't you dare!" Steam belched from the hood, streaming over the windshield before it cut out. "Piece of shit!" I slammed my hand over the steering wheel, then fought with the locked-up steering to force the car onto the shoulder.

I tried to give it a minute to cool down, then attempted to crank it. But nothing happened. Not even the tick of the engine trying to turn over. My car was dead. My phone was out of battery. I was tired. And I was miles from Dayton. I sat behind the wheel and sulked for a few minutes before I climbed out and did the only thing I could—started walking.

I must have walked close to a mile before I heard the hum of an engine in the distance. My thumb wanted to hitch up, a lift would be welcomed, but Zepp's voice was in the back of my mind. Getting picked up by a murderer would be just my luck today.

The engine downshifted, and I glanced over my shoulder, relieved when I saw Chase's blue Nissan. His window lowered as the vehicle chugged to a stop beside me. "Car broke down again?"

"Yeah."

He reached across his console to unlock the passenger door. The overbearing smell of his piña colada air freshener nearly made me sick as I sank into the upholstered seat.

The Nissan started down the highway, and I leaned back against the headrest, sighing.

"You okay, Moe?"

"Yeah. Mom OD'd again."

"I'm sorry."

"Don't be." I watched the dried grass and busy billboards pass by the window. "You know how she is."

"You'll be out of here soon, though, right? Just like you always wanted." He sounded so peppy, and I couldn't help but snort.

"Happy to get rid of me, huh?" I turned to look at him.

His arms seemed tense, his gaze fixed on the road. "Well, actually..." He cleared his throat. "I got scouted. Looks like we'll be going to college together." He took a quick glance at me, no doubt seeing the confusion on my face. "Dixon wants me for football."

"Oh. Congrats!" I probably wasn't going to Dixon now, but he seemed so excited, and I didn't want to shit on his parade.

He slowed as he approached the road for the trailer park. "Congrats? I thought you'd be excited," he said.

"I uh." I swallowed when he turned onto the dirt road. "I'm not sure I'm gonna go to Dixon now."

"Well, yeah. They haven't made you an offer yet, but you know they will."

"No, I mean, I applied to Alabama State." I fidgeted with the ratty seatbelt. "And if they make me an offer, I think I'll take it."

"What?" We rolled to a stop outside my trailer, the early morning sun just creeping over the top of it. "But you've always wanted to go to Dixon."

Chase knew me, maybe better than anyone. He knew how badly I wanted out of here. How badly I wanted to go to Dixon—until Zepp.

"Yeah, well... Things change." I threw open the door and smiled back at him. "Thanks for the lift."

I was almost to the trailer when I heard his car door slam. "Monroe." That stopped me, for one, because Chase never called me anything other than Moe, and for two, he sounded pissed. "You're doing this for him, aren't you?"

"Chase, I don't want to talk about this right now." I knew how it looked. Like I was a stupid girl making rash decisions. I knew, because any other time, I would be the person judging that girl, but Zepp was different. But I couldn't explain that to Chase.

"Thanks again for the lift," I said, unlocking the door and stepping inside.

The trailer was a mess as always, but right now, it felt like a haven of sorts. I got some water, then collapsed onto the couch, ready to shut my eyes when someone banged over the door. My temper spiked. Why couldn't Chase leave it alone?

"I told you, I don't want to talk about it," I snapped, answering the door.

Instead of Chase, it was Zepp standing on my front step, a world of chaos swirling in his eyes. He shouldered his way inside, his broad frame filling the doorway. "What. The fuck. Was that?" He pointed toward the yard. "Did you stay with him last night? I tried to call you and text you, and what the hell, Monroe!"

That was where his mind went? That I'd stayed with Chase. "What? No." I groaned. I didn't have the patience for his jealousy. "Zepp, I really can't do this now."

He grabbed my elbow when I turned around. "Oh, you're gonna have to do it right now, or we are fucking done."

A cold thread of panic pulled at me, followed by a spike of anger. That easy? He would break up with me that easy? "You think I stayed with Chase?"

His gaze dragged over me, a ripple of disgust snarling his lip when he tugged at the sleeve of my shirt. "You're in the same clothes you left my house in, Roe. What am I supposed to think?"

"That I wouldn't cheat on you!" Emotionally drained, I had lost the ability to reason. I could have just told him the truth outright, but the fact that he thought I would be unfaithful had me so pissed. I had told him two days ago that I loved him, and here he thought I would jump straight from that to Chase's bed. Suddenly everything I thought I knew about him, about us, seemed in jeopardy.

"You know what." I stormed to the door and threw it open, pointing to the porch. "Get out!"

His nostrils flared. Jaw ticced. He stared right through me, cold and hard, then gave a curt nod before shoving through the doorway. Minutes later, the distant rumble of his bike in Wolf's drive broke through the silence in the trailer, the engine screaming when he, no doubt, shot off down the road.

Pain dug into my chest, and a lump settled in my throat. I went to my room and plugged my phone in before falling onto my bed. That tugging sense of need consumed me, and I hated that I missed him because he was an asshole. I fell asleep, telling myself that the tears in my eyes had nothing to do with my dickhead boyfriend and everything to do with my mom's not caring if she died. Again.

I slept for a few hours before Jade's string of text messages asking why I hadn't been at school woke me up. She came by and grabbed me after school, taking me to Waffle Hut to get some food, and when I told her about the fight with Zepp, she gasped. "He said that?"

I picked up my soda just as the waitress walked by in a cloud of cheap perfume. "Yep."

"So, he thinks you fucked Chase?" She shook her head when I nodded. "What a dick."

With a bit of sleep, I'd realized I probably could have saved myself a lot of hassle and just told Zepp the truth, but it was the principle of it. He didn't ask where I'd been, only if I stayed with Chase. It should have been the last thought that crossed his mind. Not the first. And it hurt. Far more than I ever thought it would. I glanced at my phone, something that had become a habit in the last twenty-four hours. Still no texts or calls. His words rang through my mind on repeat: *you're gonna have to do it right now, or we are fucking done*. So were we done? Was this it? That reality hadn't really settled in—like my mind chose to hope and my heart refused to accept it.

I fiddled with my straw. "I told him I love him." Silence. I lifted my gaze to Jade.

"Wow. That's..." Her eyes went wide, and she took a hefty swig of her drink.

"Stupid?" I felt stupid right now.

"No, but for you, that's like, huge."

The waitress placed plates of wimpy hamburgers in front of us. The thought of food had my stomach turning.

"Did he say it back?" Jade asked, lifting the greasy bun to pick off her pickles.

"Actually, he said it first."

Her brows tugged together on a frown. "And you didn't think to just tell him your mom OD'd?"

"That's not the point, Jade!"

Grease dripped to the table when she took a bite of her burger. "Yeah, you're right. You're totally right. He's an asshole."

We changed the subject and finished our meal. Then Jade drove me to get my car. I always half-expected it to be gone every time I left it on the side of the road. But no, there it sat, in all its shitiness, no longer billowing steam. Where was Zepp when I needed him? By the time I got home, my mom was back from the hospital. She laid sprawled on the couch, and for the first time in a long time, I actually pitied her. She looked so thin, so battered by the world, worse than normal. Her skin was waxy, and she was shaking from head to foot. Withdrawals. Where the hell was Jerry? He had just let her overdose, and now he was letting her go cold turkey.

"Baby, I need... I need..."

"Yeah, I know, Mom." I took my phone out and dialed a number. This wasn't the first time I'd had to buy drugs for her so she wouldn't die, and it probably wouldn't be the last.

35

ZEPP

Hendrix sat beside me on the couch and handed me a drink. "This is why us Hunts don't do mahogany, man."

"It's monogamy, dipshit."

"Whatever. One girl." He waved a hand through the air. "Why the hell would you do that?" He motioned toward my crotch. "Why the hell would you do that? The sword of valor is meant to be wielded, not sheathed in one punani."

Hendrix would never get it. Hell, I wouldn't have gotten it a few months ago because I would never have believed I could have cared so much for one person. And it sucked because it hurt. I had trusted Monroe. I had allowed myself to be vulnerable, and she stabbed me in the damn heart with a piece of shrapnel. What was worse was that, even though it was plain as day, I was still struggling to believe she would screw around on me. I guessed that was what happened when you loved someone; you wanted to see the best in them.

I took a sip of my drink and slouched back against the couch cushion. "Maybe she didn't fuck him."

"You said she was in the same clothes." Hendrix popped me on the head. "That's as tell-tale as you get. Man, she rode his cock like a mechanical bull."

The image had my stomach churning.

He grabbed the controllers, tossing one to me. "It sucks. But... come on. You had to be getting bored of that shit." The game started. To my brother, this probably seemed easy.

I stared at the screen for a moment before taking my drink and heading to my room. I felt like an idiot, and when I collapsed on my bed, tears blurring my vision, I felt like a pussy. All I wanted to do was text her. Call her. Ask her why, but the answer didn't matter.

Pretty certain this was long overdue karma coming in for the kill.

THE NEXT DAY AT SCHOOL, I stood with the guys at the end of the hall. Girls in a semicircle around us. My dumbass brother had made a show this morning, standing up on the hood of Wolf's truck and shouting that I was single across the entire parking lot before I managed to yank his ass down.

Hendrix glanced around at the girls and grinned. "The blonde said she'd give you some head in the bathroom." He whacked me on the back, and I shoved him away. "That should get you over her."

"I'm gonna kill you."

Holding up his hands, he took a step back. "Just trying to help you get some of that aggression out. A back up of jizz never did anyone any good."

"Man, fuck off." I made it halfway down the hall before Wolf caught up with me.

"You look like shit."

I yanked open my locker door, rummaging through the shitshow of books and loose-leaf paper crammed inside before I dug out my chemistry book. When I shut the door, Wolf was still there. "What the hell do you want, man?"

"Dude…" He leaned back against the metal wall of lockers, then took a heavy breath. "I can't believe I'm saying this. Because I liked the way shit was before her, but…"

I frowned and shook my head on my way through the crowded hall. "Save it, Wolf."

But he was right there, by my side, running his mouth. "I don't think she would mess around on you."

I snorted, shouldering through a group of girls fawning over my brother, then I hooked it around the corner, and Wolf was still behind me.

"She like…" He paused, then coughed like he was choking on something. "Loves you or some shit. I mean. Come on."

What the hell did Wolf know about relationships or Monroe. "Go to class, Wolf."

I went into the lab and flipped open my notes about some bullshit convalescence bonds and tried to ignore the empty feeling taking root in my chest, but that feeling only grew worse over the course of the day. By the time our English class came around, I wanted to skip. But I refused to be that pathetic dick.

I took a seat at the back of the room—where I sat before Monroe, and with every student that filed in, my chest grew tighter. The bell rang, and Mrs. Smith went to the head of the class. While she scribbled *American Writers* over the board, Monroe slipped inside and sank into her chair. She took one glance at the empty seat beside her, then opened her book.

My face warmed, anger brewing beneath my skin when I thought of the smile she had given Chase when she had hopped out of his car. The teacher passed around folded slips of paper, and I didn't even bother to look at mine. I couldn't focus on anything but how screwed up this was that a single person could take everything inside of me and rip it out with one single action. On how shit this was that I loved her and had thought she loved me. I looked away from the back of her head, spinning my pencil on the desk to try to clear my mind.

Mrs. Smith started around the class. Each student read the line from their piece of paper while the rest of the class guessed who the author was. When the teacher called on Monroe, she sighed, mumbling over her line: "The best way to find out if you can trust somebody is to trust them."

"Hemingway," the girl beside me shouted. The irony of that quote did not go unmissed. I had trusted her when I shouldn't have. My grip on the pencil tightened until the wood made a soft crack. Mrs. Smith called my name, and I unfolded the piece of paper, wishing I had looked at it before.

"It's fucking bullshit," I mumbled. Trying to keep my emotions in check. Yeah, karma was a dick.

"Mr. Hunt! Read the line."

My jaw set. Heat ate me up from the inside out. "I love her and that's the beginning and end of everything."

"Fitzgerald," Monroe said quietly, gathering her books, then pushing to her feet. "May I be excused?" She opened the door before Mrs. Smith had responded.

I crumpled the piece of paper in my palm, tapping the toe of my shoe over the floor for a moment before I got up. Mrs. Smith shouted for me to sit back down before the door slammed closed behind me. I started after Monroe, fuming and hurt. She reached the end of the hall, stopping by the fire exit.

"You realize this is your fault, right?" I yelled, my voice echoing from the lockers and down the empty hallway.

She spared a cold glance over her shoulder. "I hear you're single now." Then she opened the exit and stepped outside. The door banged shut behind her.

Two days ago, I had told her I loved her. I had every intention of spending the rest of my life with her, and now it felt like none of that ever mattered.

———

THE PAST THREE days had felt like a fucking year. I had never been so glad for a Friday to roll around because I couldn't take one more day in class with Monroe. Not that hanging out on Wolf's roof was much better, seeing as how I was staring at her trailer. None of her lights were on. Jerry's car wasn't there, and neither was hers. I wondered if she was with Chase now, the bastard hadn't been at school all week, probably because he knew he would get his ass handed to him.

Wolf passed me a beer before folding himself back into the lawn chair. "Sucks, dude."

"Man, I don't care." I tipped my drink up.

Wolf knew it was a lie. I knew it was a lie, but it made me feel better to pretend I wasn't torn up over it.

"I'm eighteen. What do I need a girl for?" Saying that caused a little ball of guilt to settle in my gut. Because I did need her.

"Yeah." He huffed, then slouched lower in his chair before chugging his drink. "Why would we need a girl." He fiddled with the ratty hemp bracelet on his arm, then sighed. "Fuck girls, dude. Just..." Another hard sigh.

"What's wrong with you?"

He shrugged a shoulder. "Nothing. What's wrong with you?"

The hum of the highway rolled in the distance, mixing with the loud classic rock blaring from the neighbor's backyard. We sat in silence for a while, until Wolf's phone dinged with a text. He chucked his beer over the edge of the roof, then grabbed his phone. A short snort left his lips while he stared at his screen. "Davison just sent me a text. Kreuger's got a party going on. Wanna go?"

Kreuger was a dick, and his parties always sucked. Plus, I didn't feel like being around anyone right now. "No."

His foot tapped the shingles for a moment. "Monroe's there."

"And?"

"And Matthews." He turned his phone around, and on the screen was a picture of Monroe and Jade between Chase and a few of the other football players. "Davison sent it to me."

I finished off my beer, my blood pressure spiking before I crushed the can in my fist. "Can I borrow your bat?"

I left the bat in the back of Wolf's truck and followed him up the drive that led to Kreuger's bright-blue house. A handful of girls leaned against the siding, laughing and waving at us while they held up one of their friends who was taking a piss.

"I hate Kreuger's parties," I mumbled as we stepped through the open gate into the backyard.

Kreuger had graduated two years ago; then his parents

had died in a car accident. He took his inheritance and tried his damnedest to turn the house into something worthy of an under-budget porn film.

"He's a dick," Wolf said, snagging a cup on our way to the keg. He nodded toward the heart-shaped hot tub filled with topless girls. Wolf chuckled before lifting the plastic cup to his lips. "But at least there's titties. Dude, Hendrix is gonna kill us for not bringing him."

I filled my cup and followed Wolf through the yard to the hot tub. He crouched by the edge, flirting with one of the girls. The only reason I had come was to... I felt my brow crease. I wasn't even sure why I had come. To beat Chase's ass? To rub salt in an already raw wound by seeing my ex-girlfriend with another guy?

"Hey, Zepp." One of the girls edged to the side of the tub, pressing her shoulders back to lift the bottom of her massive tits above the steaming water. "Like that shirt."

"I don't give a shit."

She gasped before sinking back onto the seat amongst her equally horrified friends. I looked across the yard, through the swirling steam, and my stomach sank just before the lava-hot adrenaline surged through me. Monroe was by the hammock, next to Chase, and laughing like she was completely fine.

God, I must look like an idiot. Right under my nose. And now she was out with him. At a damn party. I glanced across at Wolf. His gaze pinged between Monroe and me.

"Hey, hey, hey!" Wolf skirted over, grabbing my elbow and tugging me out of earshot. "Look. The bat's in the car, but wait until it thins out. Or until everyone else is shitfaced. 'Cause it's just you and me." He did a quick take over his shoulder. "But meanwhile, dude. Just fuck with her head.

You got about ten topless chicks back there willing to suck your dick. Don't forget who you are."

Yeah. Right. Don't forget who I am. A guy who used to be a player and was taken to his knees by a girl who stole his heart.

36

MONROE

Even through the crowd of people, I noticed Zepp the second he walked into the party. I hated that he'd come because all I had been trying to do was escape him.

"You okay, Moe?" Chase bumped his shoulder to mine, his gaze shooting between me and Zepp, who was standing by a hot tub full of topless girls. No, I was not okay.

Jade persuaded me to come to this stupid party, and now all I wanted to do was leave, but I wasn't about to let Zepp chase me away. Especially when this entire thing was his fault, and I had done nothing wrong. If he didn't trust me, we didn't need to be together. I knew that, and yet the sight of him surrounded by girls was like a knife in the chest.

"I'm fine." I directed my attention back to Chase.

"She's tough enough to deal with that asshole." Jade punched him.

"Don't let her fool you, Jade." Chase flashed a wide smile. "She's soft as shit. One time, she got a ladybug in her ponytail." He flicked my hair. "Freaked out. Screaming." I couldn't help but laugh at the memory. I knew what Chase was trying to do, though: distract me.

I downed my beer, hoping that if I got blind drunk, I would feel numb to all this. When I lowered my empty cup, I noticed Jade staring at Wolf—and the girl in his lap.

"They don't change, Jade. Don't waste your time chasing guys like that. One minute you think they give a shit. The next..." I waved a hand toward Zepp and his flock. "They're all the same."

"Hey," Chase pointed at himself. "I'm right here."

"You don't count." I gave him a playful shove, and he nearly toppled into the hammock.

"So, I'm what, the token dick?"

"Pretty much." Jade laughed. "You might as well be gay."

"Gee, thanks." He took our cups, and we followed him to the keg where other members of the football team and a few cheerleaders hung around in a group. Chase fell into easy conversation with them, but I instantly felt out of place.

This wasn't me. When I chanced a glance at Zepp, his gaze fixed on me, while some girl pawed at him. God, I couldn't do this.

Kreuger came by, dancing with bottles of liquor held above his dreadlocked head. He stopped to exchange a fist bump with Chase, then handed him a bottle of tequila, which I promptly snatched. I broke the seal, swallowing a few burning gulps before I nearly gagged.

"Hey." Chase touched a hand to my back. "Go easy, Moe."

I took another look at Zepp and those slutty girls. "Fuck that." I tipped the liquor back again.

"Chug! Chug! Chug!" The football players chanted, then Jade grabbed the bottle off me.

She took a small swig, sticking out her tongue while she choked. "That's awful. You're so gonna throw up."

Some time and a lot of tequila later, a warm tingle trickled through my veins. Suddenly, it felt like nothing mattered. Everything around me swirled in a blur of color while I danced with Jade.

The song ended, and when I stopped to catch my breath, a scrawny guy shoved a shirt at me. "Wanna do the wet T-shirt contest?" He grinned like the perverted guys I used to give lap dances to.

My gaze veered behind him to the group of girls surrounding Zepp and Wolf. Rebellion bled through my soul.

"No, she does not." Chase went to shove him away, and I snatched the shirt from the guy's hand as he stumbled backward.

"What do I win?" I asked.

"Ten bucks."

"Sure." God, I was cheap these days. "I'm not getting them out, though. That'll cost at least fifty."

Jade leaned in by my ear. "Zepp is giving you a death glare."

"Fuck him!" I shouted, grabbing the tequila bottle from Chase and taking another swig.

Jade facepalmed before snatching the bottle from me. "You're absolutely gonna puke."

"Whatever." I stumbled toward the house to find a bathroom. I made it past the double-doored fridge before someone grabbed my wrist.

"You are not doing this." Chase moved in front of me, shaking his head. "Absolutely not." It took me a moment to figure out how I felt about that, but when I did, I was pissed.

"Excuse me?"

"You're not flashing your tits to everyone."

"Let me make this clear." I held my finger up, swaying when I tried to focus on it. "You have *zero* say in what I do."

His brows creased before he took a step back, a fissure of disgust tearing across his face. "Is this because of him? Are you trying to make him jealous?"

Was I? I didn't really know. The music of the party hummed through the walls. "No."

"Because he's not worth it. He doesn't get you, Moe. You're better than some street thug."

My face heated. Chase didn't know a thing about Zepp. "He's not a street thug."

"No?" He shook his head. "He's a drug dealer, Moe, that's it."

"You don't know him!"

"I know you!" He grabbed my arm, yanking me close to him. "You're the best person I know, Monroe." But he didn't know me. Not now.

"I'm not, Chase."

"You deserve someone who loves you. Really loves you."

"I'm…" I didn't know what to say to that. I'd never been loved—until Zepp. And he had broken me.

Chase's lips suddenly pressed over mine, and my mind blinked out for a second. Like it couldn't even comprehend what was happening. I slammed my palms against his chest and pushed him away.

I swiped my hand over the back of my mouth. "What the hell, Chase?" That unwelcomed kiss left me feeling violated, and that was a catalyst to a form of rage that burned me up. "You think you can just kiss me?"

"Shit. No, I just—"

"Just what, Chase? Just take what you want?"

"No." He rubbed a hand over the back of his neck. "I'm sorry. I didn't mean—"

"I will never want you like that."

His face fell, pain crossing his features. Chase backed away like a kicked puppy before shouldering through the back door. For a second, I felt bad because I knew what that kind of rejection was like.

Guilt quickly jumped back to anger. Zepp had been right. And that just made everything worse, because I couldn't see it. Just like I hadn't seen it with Max. Chase was supposed to have been my friend. And Zepp was supposed to trust me and love me. Guess I was wrong on both accounts. Screw them both.

I glanced down at the shirt clutched in my hand, feeling the urge to do something reckless.

On my way through the house, I found some more tequila in the liquor cabinet, and it was the good shit. I downed a few gulps before I staggered into the bathroom and changed into the oversized shirt. I even tied it up, exposing my stomach before I made my way back outside.

Jade stood at the bottom of the stairs, eyes wide before she took a drink. "I can already see your nipples, Monroe."

I didn't care. Right now, I was in the impenetrable tequila bubble. "Is it turning you on?" I asked, and she just shook her head.

A small crowd had gathered around the hot tub, girls in white T-shirts lined up at its edge. The guys cheered when I hopped up beside them and lifted my arms over my head, nearly losing my balance. The applause grew louder, and I just knew Zepp would hate it.

A guy moved next to me with a megaphone and a bucket in hand. "First, in our lineup of lovely ladies. She's a redhead with some double *D*s." A small gap appeared in the middle of the party-goers. "She likes long walks on the beach, and her favorite position is doggy style."

Zepp steamrolled through people, fists clenched at his side. Jaw ticcing as he made a beeline toward me.

"You know what they say, guys. Red in the head, fire in the..."

Zepp was nearly to me. Oh, fuck him. Fuck him hard. I snatched the bucket from the guy commentating and dumped it over my chest, the cold water stealing my breath.

The party went wild, and Zepp hit me like a linebacker, wrapping his arm around my waist and hauling me over his shoulder. A loud boo echoed across the yard as he carted me away from the crowd.

"Fuck off, Zepp. I could have won ten bucks." I thumped a hand over his back.

He rounded the side of the house. Gate hinges creaked, and the music and cheers from the backyard faded to a low hum.

"Put me down, you dickhead."

My ass hit the warm hood of a car. Then he leaned over me, practically pinning me against the metal. My entire body lit up like Times Square because it was him. God, I hated him. And I loved him.

"This is bullshit, Monroe." The dim glow of the streetlight highlighted his cheekbones and the angry expression on his face. "Fucking bullshit." The stout smell of whiskey carried on his breath.

"*You're* bullshit." My stomach rolled like a cement mixer. "Leave me alone." I tried to shove him away, but it did nothing.

He balled my soaked shirt in his hand, twisting it. "I'm not okay with this shit." He inched closer. "Any of it, Monroe."

"I don't care." The heat of his body soaked through my wet shirt, but it only made my nipples stiffen further. "You don't get a say. You don't own me, Zepp." The words sounded pathetic, even to my ears.

"Oh, you made that apparently clear."

"It's a wet T-shirt competition. You're single, remember, which makes me single."

He moved closer. Each hard breath of his fanning across my lips. "Still want me, Roe?"

With each passing second that he pressed against me, I was finding it harder and harder to deny that I did. "I can still smell the cheap perfume on you, Zepp. So no."

His warm hand glided over my leg. "And I can still smell him on you."

My heart stumbled for a second as I wondered if he knew Chase had kissed me. No, he'd still be beating Chase's unconscious body if he did.

My breath caught when Zepp's fingers brushed my thigh. I should have stopped him, but my brain was swimming in tequila, and I craved it every bit as much as I hated it. His hand slipped under my panties, fingers easily finding their way inside me. My head fell back against the windshield while I struggled to catch an even breath.

"I hate you." His fingers moved, angry and hard, and so damn good.

I grabbed the back of his neck, pulling him closer. "I hate you more."

Lips slammed against mine. Tongue and teeth. I tugged at his belt, and within seconds, I was face down on the hood, and he was inside of me, fucking me the way he always said he would.

"The way I see it." His teeth sank into my neck. "You owe me this."

I was high on him, my head swimming, my body burning up. I pushed up onto my hands, shoving back against his hard thrusts. "I don't owe you shit," I moaned.

He went deeper, then stilled. "Tell me to stop." I couldn't. Seconds ticked by. "Exactly what I thought," he said before he resumed his pace.

We were right there, screwing on the hood of a parked car right outside a house full of people. And I didn't care. I let him take me, going harder and deeper until my body tensed, heat tore over my skin, and every muscle went lax. Until I broke apart for him.

Zepp fisted my hair, yanking back my head while he drove into me. Hard. Heavy. Desperate. "Fuck you, Monroe," he said before he groaned and stilled behind me. "Just…" I heard his fly zip. "Fuck you."

He was halfway across the road when I pulled my skirt down and turned around.

"You're an asshole, you know it?"

He stormed back toward me, the anger rippling across his face, catching in the streetlight. "I'm an asshole?" He jabbed a finger at my chest. "No. You slept with another guy! And I loved you." His expression crumpled like a piece of paper. "I told you I loved you. And I meant it." His pain and my anger cut through my drunken haze, making me feel sober in an instant.

"And I told you I loved you! And it didn't mean shit."

"You. Fucked. Another. Guy."

"I didn't screw him!" I punched him in the chest. "You idiot."

"Whatever, Monroe." He swiped a hand through his hair. "I fucked plenty of girls before you, so…" A slight frown set on his face.

That really hurt. "Stupid me for thinking you were different, right?"

"No. Stupid me for thinking *you* were different." He turned to walk away. "You're just like the rest of them."

"My Mom OD'd. And the first thing you did was accuse me of screwing Chase." I started back toward the house. "There's your fucking trust for you." I was halfway down Kreuger's drive before he caught my elbow.

"Why wouldn't you have just told me that? Jesus Christ, Roe. I'm on Wolf's roof, thinking I did something to piss you off, then you turn up in Chase's car. In the same clothes from the night before. Just..." He dropped my arm and dragged both hands through his hair on an angry groan.

"You didn't ask." It stung that he thought I'd slept with Chase so easily. "I got out of his car, Zepp. And you assumed that quickly."

"Are you serious?" Both of his hands went in the air. "You're serious right now?" He stepped forward, pointing a finger at me. "You tell me, Monroe. Situation reversed. What the actual hell would you have thought? I don't answer your calls. Then you see Leah's whore ass drop me off in the same clothes I left your house in. The next morning. What the hell would you think? Huh?"

"You've fucked, Leah!" I put my hands on my hips, dropping my chin to my chest. My pulse was hammering through my veins so hard, I could barely breathe.

"And how the hell would you know?"

"Oh, like you haven't. You were a whore."

He paced the drive for a second, then grabbed a cigarette from his pocket and lit it. "Doesn't mean I stuck my dick in her."

"Oh my God." I raked my fingers through my hair. "Why are we talking about Leah?"

"I don't fucking know!" A large cloud of smoke left his lips before he tossed the cigarette to the ground and charged at me, pinning me against the side of the house. His mouth covered mine, the kiss hard and desperate, and everything I needed in that moment. "All I know is that I love you. And I hate this."

My heart skipped, and warmth trickled through my body. "You really thought I cheated on you?"

His teeth raked his bottom lip; his chin dropped to his chest. "Monroe. You are the only person I've let get close enough to hurt me..." His gaze met mine, his fingers gripping my chin. "I'm sorry."

"I would never do that to you." I touched his cheek. "I love you."

He kissed me again. "Can we go home?"

"Yeah."

The next morning my phone beeped nonstop. I laid on Zepp's chest, the heat of his skin seeping into me. The last three days without him had made me realize just how much I needed him. His fingers played over my back, tangling in my hair. Another text came through. Then another.

"You gonna get that?"

Groaning, I reached over to the nightstand. "It's probably my mom." Then I laid back and opened the messages, fully expecting to see a plea from my mom, wanting a hit. But it was Chase. On a sigh, I tossed the phone to the mattress, my pulse ticking up. I thought I had made myself pretty clear.

"Roe?" There was a hint of something in Zepp's voice.

I sat up, swiping hair out of my face as I met Zepp's gaze. "So, you might have been right..." Crossing my legs, I pulled at a loose thread on the comforter. God, he was going to lose it.

"About?"

"About Chase."

He grabbed the phone from the end of the bed, and I nearly shit myself when he tapped the screen. I hadn't even read the messages, but I could guess what they said. It was likely another apology for the kiss. I watched his jaw tic. His cheeks slowly grew red before he handed me the device. I could feel the rage radiating from him like he was ready to explode.

"Like I said. Guys aren't friends with girls."

The message on the screen forced a sigh from my lips.

```
Chase: I'm sorry I kissed you.
Chase: I've been in love with you since we were ten years old.
Chase: Please talk to me.
```

I closed my eyes, my heart letting out a guilty squeeze. I was horrible to him last night. And he was in love with me. This was all so messed up.

"Tell me *you* didn't kiss him."

My eyes snapped open. "No! I shoved him off."

Zepp bristled beside me, his gaze aimed at the wall, most likely plotting where to bury Chase.

"Pretty sure he wouldn't have done it if we weren't broken up," I said.

Chase took what he saw as an opportunity. It wasn't a personal affront to Zepp, but Zepp probably wouldn't see it that way.

"You know, if it's any consolation."

One of his brows lifted. He thumbed over his nose ring.

"You're mine, Monroe. Any guy should know that. Regardless."

I wasn't even going to address that right now. Because I had bigger problems. Like my childhood friend declaring his love. On a long groan, I fell back against the pillows. God, was there something wrong with me? How did I not see this shit coming? First Max... "Is it something I do?" I asked.

The anger on Zepp's face faded. He took the phone from my hand, then tossed it across the room. "It's nothing you do." He settled over me, kissing my throat. "It's just because you're you, Monroe. I can't blame the fucker for being in love with you." His lips met my jaw. "Even if I want to kill him."

"Don't kill him," I said, grabbing his face.

"Fine." His lips pressed to mine with a little swipe of his tongue. "I'll just break his arm."

"No broken bones." I kissed him. "If you loved someone else, it would break my heart. I feel kind of bad. For him."

"I could never love anyone else, Roe. You're it for me."

And he was it for me. Because no one had ever loved me like he did. And I wasn't sure I could live without it.

37

ZEPP

I had spent the last day, out in the cold, under the hood of Monroe's car, tuning the engine and tinkering with the alternator. Nothing worked. The car was as good as scrap metal.

I slammed the hood and started across the yard. "You need a new engine, and that orange piece of shit isn't worth the money."

Monroe sat on the back steps, one of my sweatshirts nearly swallowing her. She frowned when I dropped to the stair beside her, then kissed her forehead.

"We can find you a new car for the cost of an engine."

On a groan, she dropped her head to my shoulder. "Thanks for trying."

"And whatever you get, it's not gonna be orange."

She snorted a laugh. We sat there for a minute, both staring at her car until her phone beeped beside her on the step. She glanced at the screen and sighed. "I need to go somewhere before I go to Jade's. You should probably come with me." She shifted on the step, shoving her hands in the front pocket of the sweatshirt before she pushed to her feet. "Jade might shit the bed on this one."

I squinted against the bright sun spilling through the trees. If she was *asking* me to go with her, I knew it had to be bad. "Where do you need to go?"

"Northside."

People didn't go to Northside unless they were selling or buying. Or looking to get killed. "Why?"

"To buy some crack." She grabbed her phone from the stair and tapped the screen. "My mom's withdrawing, and Jerry's disappeared."

I leaned back on the step. This was Dayton. Through and through. Most of us wouldn't bat an eye at someone overdosing anymore, because we grew up seeing it. As much as I didn't want to go, I knew she didn't have a choice. And that was shit.

"All right."

By the time I had scored some crack for her mom, the sun was setting. The cold wind bit through my jacket when I sped back to the trailer park, and when we pulled up in her drive, it was completely dark outside.

I climbed off my bike, heading up the stairs after Monroe.

She paused with her hand on the door. "You don't have to come in, Zepp."

But still, I followed her inside.

A heap of blankets sat bundled on the couch, and when the door closed behind me, the pile moved. A woman sat up, bleach-blond hair in disarray, cheeks hollowed. My stomach kinked and knotted because she reminded me of my mother, of the moments I had tried my damnedest to push into the dark recesses of my mind and forget.

Monroe chucked the bag at her.

Within seconds, her mom had tied off her arm and was thumping at the syringe. Her furrowed brow relaxed, and she sank back against the couch on a relieved sigh, her gaze drifting from Monroe to me.

"This your boyfriend, baby? He's a looker."

Monroe crossed her arms over her chest. "Mom, where's Jerry?"

"Dead." Her mom's eyes lolled closed. "Got shot over on Northside."

Monroe glanced at me, a line sinking between her brows. The bastard deserved to die. For what he did to Monroe and Dizzy, for the long string of women he had most likely left behind beaten and bruised.

Monroe cleared her throat. "You need to find a new dealer, Mom. I'm not getting that shit again."

"Yeah. Yeah." She exhaled, a grin settling on her face. She was high off her ass. From the looks of it, that euphoria impenetrable.

I couldn't manage it because it reminded me of my mother. My chest felt like it was in a vice grip, so I took Monroe by the elbow, gently pulling her toward the door. "Come on, Roe. Let's go."

The toxic tension seemed to lift the moment we stepped off Monroe's porch, the crickets in the long grass silencing.

"It's not...:" She ducked her chin. "She wasn't always like that."

I wrapped an arm around her shoulder. "I know. Neither was my mom.".

I dropped Monroe at Jade's and went home to play PlayStation with Hendrix.

"You suck!" He tossed the controller down, jumping up

from the couch and thrusting his crotch while pointing at me. "I beat your ass. Because you suck!"

Ignoring him, I started another game, shooting his avatar in the back of the head before he had picked up the controller again.

Bellamy shuffled into the living room from the back of the house, dropping his backpack to the floor. "Got half a kilo from Owens today." He kicked at the overstuffed book bag. "That's gotta be worth a few grand."

I pushed up from the couch, snagging the strap and hauling the bag over to the kitchen table. I took a seat and slid the scale across the tabletop, glancing at Bellamy when he sank to the chair beside me.

He grabbed a Ziploc bag and stuffed it with bright green buds before tossing it on the scale.

"Man..." He sighed. "I saw Monroe at the drugstore when I was getting some rubbers."

I weighed a gram out before I looked up at him. "And?"

"She was getting a pregnancy test."

A sinking feeling bled from my head to my stomach. Numbers flashed on the scale. "Shit."

"Yeah. Man. Shit." Bellamy shook his head before passing me another bag. "What the hell are you gonna do if she's knocked up?"

I slouched in my seat, scrubbing a hand over my face. I had no idea. None. I mean, I would marry her. Raise a kid with her. But... Hendrix passed behind me, opened the fridge, then flopped into the chair across from me with a slice of cold pizza.

"That's what you get for raw dawging it. Supposed to bag that shit up." He snatched up one of the baggies and shook it in front of my face. "Not just squirt baby juice all over the place."

I glared across the table while Hendrix crammed his face with food. "Shut up."

"Think it'll have red hair like Monroe?" He cackled. "You're gonna have a kid. You suck."

I stared across the kitchen at the broken clock on the wall. Nine months. School would be finished by then, but... I dragged a hand down my face again, swallowing around the lump in my throat.

"Hey. Doesn't mean she is." Bellamy tossed another sack of weed onto the scale. "That private school girl I screwed around with for a little while last year, she took a test every month. And I never screwed her without a rubber—that I remember." He shrugged a shoulder then filled another bag with buds.

I nodded. Monroe would have said something if she thought she was pregnant. That would be the rational thing to do—I exhaled. Which meant Monroe would do the exact fucking opposite. We finished bagging the weed; then the guys went to the living room to play *Call of Duty*.

"Not gonna play?" Hendrix called when I passed in front of the sofa. "Gonna go upstairs and look up baby names?"

"Shut up, Hendrix." I jogged up the stairs, slammed the door to my room, then fell onto the bed. If I had gotten her pregnant. Jesus...

I grabbed the cigar box from my nightstand, rummaging through the contents and pulling out the faded Polaroid of me when I was a few months old in the arms of the man I had no memory of—other than the things my mother had told Hendrix and me about him while we were growing up.

My mother had, at one time, had her shit together. She made straight As in high school. She'd enrolled in college to study nursing, and then she had met Paul. Any time she would mention him, her entire face would light up before the tears came, at least. All I knew about my father was that he was the lead singer to some shit Led Zeppelin cover band and a druggie who left my mom with two kids and a bad habit. I tossed the picture back into the box, telling myself this was different. I loved Monroe. I wouldn't leave her. And if she were pregnant, we would find a way for her to get her degree. But why hadn't she said something to me? I typed up a text and sent it off.

```
Me: I love U
Roe: I love you too
Roe: I'm going to stay at Jade's tonight
```

My pulse ticked up a little. The plan had been for Jade to bring her back.

```
Me: You OK?
Roe: Yeah. Fine. I'll see you at school tomorrow. <3
```

Shit. She was being short. And putting heart emojis in her texts. She was pregnant. God, I had knocked her up. And she wouldn't even tell me.

```
Me: You know. No matter what. I won't leave you.
Roe: I know. Are you okay?
```

Aside from the crippling anxiety coursing through me.

```
Me: Yeah
Me: Just miss you
Roe: Miss you too.
```

I tossed the phone onto the bed, then turned out the light. The noise of the TV downstairs crept underneath my bedroom door. Every once and a while, Hendrix shouted, "cocksucker" while I tried to find sleep, but I couldn't. I wanted her to tell me shit, not hide stuff from me. Monroe was the most stubborn person I had ever known. Wouldn't ask for help, would hitchhike before she would call for a lift. I didn't know why I took it personally; it was just how she handled things. But something like this—the potential fuck up to all her future plans... A kid... Just shit.

38

MONROE

I sat in the hallway of Jade's parent's house, my back pressed to the bathroom door. I glanced at the timer on my phone screen.

"Two minutes is up, Jade." Silence greeted me, and I pushed to my feet. "We're gonna be late for school. Just look at the damn thing already."

She tugged the door open, and her tear-filled gaze met mine.

"Are you...?"

She shook her head, then shouldered past me and down the stairs. I didn't know what to do, so I just followed her out to her car.

We listened to the radio the entire drive to school, and Jade never said a word. I was admittedly shit with situations like this. I wasn't sure if the tears meant she was knocked up, or if the head shake meant she wasn't. But if she wasn't, why would she be crying? She definitely was, and I felt horrible for her, but in Dayton, it was pretty common.

"Look, if you are, it's fine," I said. "You have options."

We turned into the school, speeding through the

parking lot and right past Wolf's truck, the guys on the tailgate, smoking weed. She pulled into a spot a few spaces down.

"I mean, do you know whose it is?" Shit. That made her sound like I thought she was a whore. "Not like that—"

Jade was out of her car and halfway across the lot before I had closed the door. She didn't even lock her car.

Jesus, I was bad at this. I jogged after her. "Jade?"

"I've gotta talk to Mr. Weaver about a *C* he gave me." She hurried up the steps and through the doors, leaving me in the middle of the lot.

On a groan, I started toward Wolf's truck. Zepp's gaze met mine, a steady stream of smoke drifting through his lips. The second I stopped beside the lowered tailgate, Wolf and Bellamy got up and walked off without a word.

"Uh, do I smell bad or something?"

Zepp tossed the roach to the ground, his lips pressing into a hard line before he hopped off the truck and took me into his arms. "You okay?" The heavy thud of his heartbeat was audible through his shirt.

Aside from Jade... "Yeah. Why wouldn't I be?"

"So." He stepped back, ducking his chin to look at me. "Are you?"

"Am I what?"

A few seconds passed. A group of students passed behind us laughing, and Zepp eyed them until they disappeared across the lot. He exhaled a hard breath, his uncertain stare meeting mine. "Pregnant?"

My eyes popped wide. "No! Why would you—Oh, shit."

"You're not?" Relief washed across his face.

"No." Though now I thought about it, we probably weren't as careful as we should have been. I grabbed his arm, glancing over my shoulder before I moved closer. "How did you know, though?"

"So, you thought you were, but you didn't tell me. Roe, why would you—"

"It wasn't mine," I said, raising a brow and waiting for him to put two and two together. "Does Wolf know?"

The lightbulb went off over his head. "Fuck." He swiped a hand through his hair. "*Fuuuck.*"

"Don't say anything."

"I'm not saying shit." He snagged me by my waist and headed toward the school. "Wolf would shit himself."

"So that's why you look so tired. You spent all of last night thinking I was knocked up?"

"Yeah."

I actually felt bad for him, but I was curious. "Did you have a plan?" I fought a smile. "Change your identity and move out of state?"

"So far from the plan." He hopped over the curb, then grabbed the door and held it open for me. "I had just asked Wolf if he'd be my best man when you two pulled up."

I laughed and threaded my fingers through his as we maneuvered through the crowded halls. "You're crazy. No shotgun, teenage weddings."

"Crazy about you, maybe." He bit his lip on a smile before stopping at my locker.

"God, you used to have so much game."

"No. I used to be the game, Roe."

A group of girls sidestepped us, every one of them looking at Zepp like he was the only water in a scorching desert.

"And then I met you," he said. "And you fucked me up. So good." He traced his finger over my cheek, completely oblivious to the girls beside us.

"Good."

Zepp had fucked me up; I just didn't like admitting it.

THE HUM of conversation and laughter bounced around the busy cafeteria while Jade sat beside me, poking at her food.

"You okay?" I asked quietly.

"Yeah, I'm fine." She speared a carrot and took a nibble before setting her fork back onto her plate. I had no idea what to say to her. She visibly stiffened, right before the clatter of trays hit the table. Zepp's hand landed on my thigh as he took a seat next to me, the other guys falling into the seats around us. I was acutely aware of Wolf sitting right next to Jade. Zepp kissed my head before he stabbed a green bean.

"How big do you think your tits are gonna get, Red?" Hendrix grabbed at his chest, pretending to grope a pair of breasts.

Zepp tossed a bean at his brother's face. "Don't talk about her tits, dickwad. I'll punch you in the throat."

"I've been thinking about it." Hendrix opened his chocolate milk and chugged it. "I wanna be called Unky Nook Nook."

I finally clicked what he was talking about.

"Shut up, Hendrix." Zepp glared across the table at him, his grip on my leg growing tighter.

I leaned into Zepp. "You told Hendrix?" Of all people. I glanced at Jade. Her face was pale, and she looked like she wanted to crawl under the table.

"No. The little shit overheard Bellamy." So they all knew, except Wolf—shit. Correction, they all thought it was me.

"Well, Unky Nook Nook, go adopt a stray cat or something," I said. "You aren't getting a baby."

Hendrix scowled. "That's bullshit. I had plans for the kid." He pointed a fry at Zepp. "Knock her up."

"You're an idiot," Zepp mumbled.

"Look." Hendrix crammed his face full of food, pieces of chewed potatoes dropping to the table as he spoke. "I thought it was hilarious last night. Thinking about Zepp with a kid. But then." He shoved more fries in his mouth, his expression far too serious. "I thought about it. And I need a protege."

Zepp facepalmed and shook his head, mumbling whiffle ball bat under his breath.

Bellamy frowned at Hendrix. "The last person who needs a protegee is you, man."

"You go fuck yourself with that negativity." He chucked a fry at Bellamy's forehead. "I could teach a kid a shit ton of things. Like, how to piss in a Cheerio. Not to mention, kids are hilarious on social media."

Wolf elbowed him. "You know they shit and scream, right? It'll ruin your life."

I glanced at Jade, and she looked like she was about to freak out.

"Okay! No babies, let's change the subject."

"No." Hendrix pounded a fist over the table. "Did my brother's swimmers permenate your egg or what? And don't you bullshit me, Red. My next life decision is based on this."

I slapped a hand over the table so over Hendrix's dumbass comments. "It's penetrate!"

"Penetrate with a dick!" he snorted.

Wolf and Bellamy doubled over, cackling like a pack of Hyenas. When I looked at Zepp, he was trying his best not to laugh.

"Firstly," I said. "I'm blaming you for not sending him to school enough. Secondly," I looked at Hendrix again. "Taking a test does not mean you're knocked up." I had to take one for the team here because if any of them figured out it was Jade... She at least needed time to deal with this.

Bellamy raised a hand. "Told you, Zepp."

"Fine." Hendrix scowled before narrowing his gaze and searching the cafeteria. "I'll just make my own protege."

"You are not knocking up some girl." Zepp shook his head. "I swear to God, Hendrix. I will kill you."

Hendrix screwed anything with a pulse. "He's probably already got a few strays out there," I said.

He frowned at me. "I do not go into the flood without a raincoat, Red." His gaze strayed to Zepp. "Unlike you, evidently. Just sowing seed left and fucking right." He pretended to toss out feed for hens.

Sowing seed? Like he was banging half the town. "No, there is no sowing anywhere but here." I pointed at my chest.

Zepp slammed his palms on the table. "Jesus Christ, Hendrix. Shut the fuck up."

Jade grabbed her tray and pushed to her feet. "I'll see you in class, Monroe."

Wolf watched her go, a line sinking between his brows. "Hey, is she okay? She's really quiet."

I could have said yes, that would have been the reasonable thing to do, but instead, I panicked and blurted, "Her cat died!"

Jade didn't even have a cat.

"I'm gonna go check on her." I dropped my fork onto my plate, then hurried across the cafeteria. I caught up to her just as the bell rang and people started pouring into the hallway. "I'm sorry. They're idiots," I said when I reached Jade's locker.

"Thanks for covering for me."

"It's fine. But... Your cat died."

She frowned. "I don't have a cat."

"I panicked."

A tiny smile touched her lips before she turned to her locker and twisted the combination. "Okay."

"And, you know, I'm here for you. Whatever you need."

"Thanks. I'm not pregnant. I just...freaked out. Like how stupid can I be? Wolf of all people." She shook her head, and her gaze shifted over my shoulder. "Uh, Chase is staring at you like a dog begging for scraps."

I groaned, refusing to turn around. "He kissed me on Friday night."

Her brows hiked up. "Does he have a death wish?"

"It's really awkward."

"Well, it looks like he's going to come over, so good luck with that."

Jade smirked before she slammed her locker and walked away. God, I wanted to climb inside her locker.

"Good luck with what?" Zepp snuck up behind me, pressing a kiss to the side of my neck.

I was grateful for his presence because I wasn't ready to address the whole thing with Chase. If there was one thing that would undoubtedly keep him away, it was my mildly homicidal boyfriend.

"I promised I wouldn't break his arms, but..." He grabbed my shoulders and spun me around, pinning me to the lockers and covering my mouth with his. "Fuck his heart," Zepp mumbled against my lips before deepening the kiss.

Zepp had a way of making me forget about anything that wasn't him.

A loud clap sounded by my ear. "Mr. Hunt. Miss James!" Mrs. Smith huffed. "That's enough!"

Zepp swiped his tongue over mine once more before slowly moving away, then taking my hand in his and walking me to my next class.

39

ZEPP

Hendrix grinned like an idiot at the half-dead Christmas tree he had propped in the corner.

"What the hell are you doing?" I asked.

"What's it look like, ball bag? I'm putting up a tree." He shook his head before crossing the room and plopping down on the couch beside me. "It's festive and shit."

"Where did you get it?"

"Stole it from the boy scouts." He swiped the game controller from the side table.

I stared at my delinquent brother. Never mind the fact that I had no idea how he had brought the thing home but stealing from the Boy Scouts? That was low. Even for us. "You're fucked up. You know that, right?"

"Jesus wouldn't like you calling the spirit of Christmas the F-word, fuckface."

For the past two weeks, Hendrix had been messing around with some preacher's daughter. That had to be where the Jesus comment came from.

He started a game, and halfway through, paused it. "I'm

hungry. Get Monroe to grab some Burger King on the way over or something, would you?"

"She's over at Jade's studying."

"That's bullshit. I want Burger King."

My stomach grumbled at the mention of food. I pushed to my feet and swiped my keys from the table.

Hendrix scooted to the edge of the couch. "Where are you going?"

"Burger King."

"Fuck you!" He tossed the controller down and hopped up, following me to the door.

I glared over my shoulder at him. "What are you doing?"

"Coming to Burger King."

"You don't have a car."

"And whose fault is that?" he asked.

I cocked a brow as I opened the door. Hendrix had totaled three cars in the past year, which meant the police had revoked his license. "Yours."

Grumbling, he shouldered past me and down the steps. When I got to the drive, Hendrix was straddling my bike. "Get off," I said, shoving him.

"No. I want Burger King!"

I stood beside my bike, picturing how ridiculous we would look riding through the slums of Dayton with his bitch ass holding onto me. He may have been my brother. But, hell no. "You are not riding bitch behind me." I slammed a fist into his shoulder. "Get off."

He crossed his arms over his chest. "I won't even hold onto you. Just suck it up and be a man."

I snatched my helmet up and pulled it over my head. "Get up."

"Fine." He huffed. "I'll buy."

It was concerning what I would do to save five bucks.

No Prince

After Burger King, we walked over to the Wal-E-Mart. Hendrix ducked off to the bathroom to take a shit, and I went to the jewelry counter. I had pushed an extra five hundred bucks' worth of weed to save up for Monroe's present. She was absolutely not the jewelry type, but I kept coming back to the diamond rings. Eighteen. Twenty-five. What did age matter? I loved her. More than anything in this world, and I just wanted to know that no matter what, she would always be mine.

The lady behind the counter shuffled over to me. "Y'ant to see something, dumplin'?"

Sweat beaded on my brow, and for some reason, I felt a little choked. "Uh..." I dragged a finger over the smudged glass. The diamonds were expensive as hell, and the ones I could afford were barely visible. My finger stopped over a gold ring with a round, green stone, tiny diamonds on each side. "That one?"

"The emerald one, sugar pie?"

"Yeah. Sure." I didn't know what the hell it was. I just thought Monroe would like it.

She pulled it out of the little velvet slot, handed it to me, then shoved her glasses up her nose while she peeked at the price tag. "That one's five hundred twenty, sweetie. Want me to put it back?"

"No." I snatched it from her hand. I knew it was supposed to be a diamond, but that seemed kind of mindless. Plus, diamonds were plain. And nothing about Monroe was plain. I handed it back to the lady. "Can you put it in a box?" I asked, already digging in my back pocket for the cash.

"I surely can." She tucked the ring inside a box, then

dropped it inside a bag. After I had paid, I turned around to head toward the bathroom to find Hendrix.

A few guys in Dayton letterman jackets passed by, Matthews in the middle. The son of a bitch actually paused for a second, his gaze aimed at me.

I cocked a brow, daring him to say something to me, but he followed the rest of the football players toward the entertainment section.

I was halfway through home goods when I heard my last name echo down the aisle. God, that shithead was brave. My muscles coiled when I turned around.

"This is bullshit," Chase said, barreling toward me. "Monroe won't talk to me. I know you're keeping her away."

He had to be kidding. I thought about him kissing her, and every part of my being wanted to punch him right in the mouth. I pushed my shoulders back a little, preparing to knock him the fuck out.

"God, you're stupid, aren't you?" Come a little closer, asshole.

"I don't know how the hell you've managed to get a girl like her, but we both know she can do better."

And that, unfortunately, was the truth. But she was with me. And this dick wasn't worth it. She would kill me if I hurt him, so instead, I shook my head, and I turned the other way.

"That girl has wanted to go to Dixon since she was eight years old," he said. "Then she shacks up with you. She's giving up on everything, applying to some shit Alabama college..."

Closing my eyes, I stopped mid-stride. My fingers pulled into my palms, and I told myself I couldn't hit him, telling myself he had no clue what he was talking about.

"Matthews," I turned to face him, anger tearing through me at Mach speed. "You should shut the fuck up. Now."

"She loves you. And she's never had that. She'll give up everything for you, and you know it."

That hit hard. Too close to home. In a matter of milliseconds, I was comparing myself to my father, comparing Monroe to my mom.

"What can you offer her? Dayton? Drug dealing? Stealing cars? What about when you go to jail?"

The thing that sucked, he was right. And the fact that she deserved so much better was something I had tried to ignore for so damn long; something I had told myself wasn't true because I loved her. Love had to count for something, right?

"Let me guess, Matthews," I spun around and took a step. "That's when you'll swoop in and save her? Fuck off with your bullshit." But it wasn't bullshit. It was the awful truth.

"You know, I can handle her not loving me. I just can't watch her destroy herself to be with you." He eyed me up and down while backing away. "Are you really gonna make her stay in this shit hole, just so she can be with you? So much for love, huh?"

I stood in the middle of that aisle, the bag with Monroe's ring clutched in my sweating palm and my stomach in absolute knots while he stormed around the corner. That dickface had no idea what he was talking about. I did love her. I loved her more than anything else. And the idea of letting her go nearly killed me.

Because I was a piece of shit.

Hendrix booked it down the main aisle, ornaments falling out of his hoodie. "Come on, cocksucker. We gotta go." He nearly busted his ass when he hooked it through the bath section.

Shaking my head, I followed the trail of shattered reindeers and Santas to the exit, taking the box from the bag and tucking it in my front pocket before climbing on my bike to head home.

"Dammit!" Hendrix shook his shirt out in the living room, kicking a toe over his haul of stolen ornaments. "I lost Frosty the Snowman."

"That's what you get for stealing shit," I said.

"Like you don't!" He snatched up one of the ornaments and hung it on the tree. There was no arguing with him, and even if there were, Chase's words kept playing on a loop in my head. I did love Monroe. More than I had ever loved myself. And what the hell was I supposed to do with that?

I watched him hang a few more decorations before I went to my room and grabbed my sketchbook. I didn't think. Just let the pencils form lines and shapes over the paper. Purples and blacks. Bright reds and greens. My fingers cramped by the time my bedroom door creaked open.

"Just so you know," Monroe's arms came around me, her lips pressing to my neck, "that is the worst Christmas tree I've ever seen."

My chest ached; she deserved so much better than this. Screw Chase for making me see that. "Yeah." I inhaled a breath, trying to push away the notion that we weren't meant to be with each other. "Hendrix stole it. And the ornaments."

"Of course he did." Her lips touched my neck again. "What are you drawing?"

"Don't know." I stared down at the mess of shapes and colors, then moved the chair back from the desk.

A few weeks ago, I thought she was pregnant. Because

she could have been. I had been that stupid and careless, screwing her without a rubber. Out of all the girls, Monroe was the only girl I had done that with. Because I trusted her, loved her, and wasn't that fucked up? The one girl I loved, that had a future—I could have totally ruined because I couldn't be bothered with a condom. Because it felt too good and I trusted her. Worst of all, though, she had trusted me.

I grabbed her hips, staring at the stained carpet under my feet. "What would you have done? If you'd been pregnant?"

"Uh, there was never a moment where I thought I was."

"Roe." My grip on her tightened. "We both know you could have been. What would you have done?"

"I don't know. Figured it out, I guess."

"What about school?"

"I haven't thought about it. Because it didn't happen." She touched my cheek, her eyes searching mine when my gaze lifted to hers. "But, *we* would have figured it out."

And screwed up her life. Just like my mom had.

Monroe made her way to my bed, stripping out of her skirt before she laid down and snagged the half-smoked joint from the ashtray on the nightstand. "Wanna smoke?"

Had I messed her up there too? I pushed up from the chair, crossed the room, and took the joint from her, dropping it into a soda can. "You always smoked weed?" I caged her in my arms, kissing her while gliding my hand along the curve of her waist.

"Occasionally."

"Occasionally..." I pushed her shirt up, biting the top of her tit.

Her breath caught, her thighs parting before she pulled me between them. "It's only a habit if you pay for it."

But that was so far from the truth. God, I was screwing

her up, and I knew it, but I fought through that knowledge and pressed my lips to hers. Hard. Desperate. Because I had never had anything like Monroe before, and I knew I never would again.

"I love you," I whispered, unhooking her bra. "So damn much." Enough that I couldn't let her fuck everything up just for me.

My hands roamed over her thigh to her hip. I took the side of her thong, and she helped me pull them off by wiggling her legs. After they hit the floor, I grabbed her face. "You know that, right?" Then I planted another hard kiss to her lips. "I love you more than anything."

"I know." She touched her forehead to mine. "I love you too, Zepp."

The next morning, the noise of the shower echoed down the hall. I opened my drawer to take out the little blue box. The ring sat in the middle of the velvet, sparkling against the Wal-E-Mart logo in the background. I could get down on a knee and give this to her, and I knew she would say yes. She'd put that damn ring on her finger and smile and think her life was grand when all I was doing was taking a huge shit on every aspiration she ever had.

That's what love did.

It made people blind. It made people do stupid things. Like stay in Dayton...

40

MONROE

The last week had felt like nothing but a battle between Zepp and me. The love hazed bliss of only weeks before felt like a distant memory, and I couldn't pinpoint the moment when it changed or why. There were moments when he looked at me like I was his entire world, and others where he felt so far away that it was as though he wasn't even in the same room.

I got to his house, and Hendrix answered the door, a headset on his head, and a bag of chips in his hand.

"Zepp isn't here." He rammed a chip into his mouth, crumbs falling to his shirt.

I stepped inside, and he wandered back into the living room, electronic gunfire rang out before Hendrix shouted at whoever was playing online with him. I typed out a text to Zepp on my way up to his room.

Me: Where are you?

Without him here, it seemed so empty. My phone dinged.

Asshole: Out

A weird sensation settled in my chest. It was somewhere between panic and anger, and honestly, I was getting fed up with whatever this shit was.

His closed sketchbook sat on his desk, tempting me to look, even though it was off-limits. I trailed my fingers over the matte-black surface, debating it. It was an invasion of privacy, but at a time when I couldn't read Zepp, that book had told me more than words ever could.

I picked it up, thumbing through the pages until I came to the last picture. A car? His most recent drawings were random objects, some just blurs of color. His sketches were usually emotive, but these were just...nothing. And that almost worried me more.

It was past midnight when Zepp slipped into bed beside me, whiskey strong on his breath. "You're still here," he asked.

"Did you ride home drunk?"

"No." His arm came around me, tugging me close. "You shouldn't care, though."

Of course I should care. I loved him. And that comment annoyed me. "Why wouldn't I care?"

"I didn't say you wouldn't." His hand pressed between my thighs, and I clamped my legs shut. "I said you *shouldn't*."

"Well, great. That really clears shit up, Zepp."

"Don't." He slurred against my throat. "Don't do that. I want you, Roe."

My temper bubbled to the surface, driven by hurt. He hadn't touched me in days, and it felt an awful lot like he was avoiding me. I just couldn't work out what I'd done. "Do you? Or is it just because you're drunk?"

"I always want you, Roe." His mouth covered mine, and as hard as I fought it, I caved for him. Until hot, angry tears stung my eyes. Then I shoved away from him and sat up, pushing the comforter away.

"Where are you going?" he asked.

"Home."

"This *is* your home." It shouldn't have felt like a blade in the ribs, but it did. I grabbed my shirt and tugged it over my head. "I didn't stay here, just to be a hole for you to stick your drunk dick in."

"Then *why* did you wait?" He got out of bed, stumbling to the side before regaining his balance.

"You know what. I don't know." I threw my hands into the air, hating that I suddenly felt so unimportant to him. Like I could be any girl in his bed.

He wrapped his arms around my waist, and I tried to pull away, but he wouldn't let me. "I need you, Roe." His lips pressed to my neck. Warm and soft. "I love you. Please..." The sad thing was, I craved his touch, his love, and I hated myself for it. "I'm sorry I've been a dick. I just..." He kissed my throat again.

"You what, Zepp?"

"Don't deserve you." His hand crept over my chest. "But fuck, I'm selfish."

"You're only selfish when you're a dick."

A soft laugh rumbled over my skin. "If only that were the truth. We'd be good."

Which meant we weren't good. Or at least he didn't think so. I was losing him, and it felt like I was clinging on by my fingernails. "I love you, Zepp." It was a confession, a plea.

"And I fucking love you."

Then why did this suddenly feel so complicated? Within

seconds, he had me undressed and pinned to the mattress, his heavy body on top of mine. His mouth covered mine.

"I would marry you if I could."

And I'd give him forever if he'd let me, but I knew he wouldn't. He moved slow and steady, so unlike him. I grabbed his face and kissed him, the taste of whiskey transferring from his tongue to mine.

He shifted me until I was straddling his lap. "You fucked me up, Roe."

"You fucked me up, too." My hips rolled over him. My body sought him out as naturally as it drew breath. Then he buried himself so deep my lungs caught.

"I'm sorry."

I gripped his hair and touched my forehead to his. "You screwed me up in the best way, though."

"I really didn't." He guided my hips over his for a minute, closing his eyes. "But, I promise, no one will ever mean as much as you."

And those words chased away every trace of pleasure in my body because he'd just told me we had no future. That someone else would come after me. Tears stung my eyes, and I forced them back.

He groaned into my throat, his body stiffening beneath me, fingers digging into my hips like he'd never let me go before he collapsed to the bed.

His ragged breaths broke the silence while I laid, staring at the dark ceiling. I could feel his eyes on me, but I couldn't bring myself to look at him. *No one will ever mean as much as you*. The words went round and round my mind, until I'd twisted them every way, trying to convince myself they meant anything other than the only thing they possibly could.

"I'd do anything to make you happy," he said.

"Then why are you trying to leave me?"

He exhaled, then shifted on the bed. "I'm not."

We were right beside one another, yet there was a void of space between us, a thousand unspoken words hanging in the air. "You will, though." People always left.

"No." A hard exhale left his lips. "I'm too selfish to leave you."

Anger flared up inside me, frustration and pain bubbling over. I pitched up on my elbow, glaring down at him. Too selfish to leave me? The past week, I had barely seen him, and when we were together, it felt like we were miles apart. Was he trying to push me away so *I* would leave *him*?

Moments passed. "Why are you doing this?" I whispered.

His fingers skimmed my waist. "I love you, Roe."

I was so confused. But this wasn't supposed to be complicated. I loved him. He loved me, and none of this was fair. He was playing with my heart, and I was just along for the ride. I needed off before he messed me up beyond recognition, but I didn't know how.

Fighting my emotions, I got out of bed and dressed. Hating that I wanted to stay while having to go. I was just a girl who was hopeless for a boy. Even though I knew he would break me.

"You leaving?" Hurt laced his voice.

"Yeah." My voice hitched. I took a step toward the door, then stopped, turning to look at him. The mattress springs groaned as he flipped onto his front, ignoring me completely.

It wasn't until I hit the street corner and texted Jade, asking for a ride, that I broke down. Pain lanced through my chest. Ugly sobs clawed at me until I couldn't breathe. He said he loved me, but he didn't try to stop me from leaving. He had just let me go.

He let me go...

JADE SPENT most of the drive looking at me every two seconds like she expected me to have a mental breakdown at any moment. When she dropped me off, I could tell she was reluctant to leave, but I didn't want to be around anyone right now.

I made my way up the rickety steps as her Jeep chugged away. I stopped at the door, staring at the piece of paper fluttering in the breeze. An eviction notice. I ripped it off, balling it my fist as I shoved inside, the stress and tension mounting. It felt like the whole world was against me right now.

No surprise, my mom was cracked out on the sofa, eyes half shut, and a syringe on the floor. I wished I had a mom who would be here for me, but I didn't have time for self-pity. The tears started again. We would lose our home if I didn't pay the damn rent, and I had enough saved up to cover a few months. I went to my room and dropped to my knees beside the chest of drawers. My palm slid down to the hole in the pressboard, and my heart rate ticked up when my fingers met nothing but wood. In a panic, I yanked out the bottom drawer, frantically searching for the money I had spent a year of my life stripping to save up, and now...

Rage tore through me as I stormed into the living room. I was so tired of the world taking a shit on me, and the only thing—the only person that made anything seem worthwhile, had turned out to be a letdown as well. Because people always left, whether physically or mentally, like my mom—they left.

I kicked my mother's leg. "Did you take my money?"

Her head lolled to the side, and an incoherent groan slipped from her lips.

"God, I fucking hate you!" I screamed, wanting some sort of acknowledgment, but she didn't even respond to my hate. There was nothing that could make her do a damn thing besides a bit of crack. It didn't matter now. Either she took the money or Jerry did, but it was long gone.

It felt like the weight of the world pressed down on my shoulders. A continuous stream of tears tracked down my face. Whatever it was in me that had somehow remained intact through all the awful shit I had endured, Zepp had managed to break. Loving him had made me weak.

For the last two days, I had tried to pretend my life was normal. I tried to forget that I had left Zepp's house in the middle of the night. That he hadn't bothered to call me or text. That he ignored me in the hallways at school.

I thought my life was hard before, but this was a new breed of agony. His rejection wasn't obvious; it was more of a low burn, eating away at me minute by minute, hour by hour. A soul-deep ache.

My mom bumbled around in the kitchen. We were out of money, waiting on money from the government, and I was having to ration her crack, which meant she was almost lucid. The crash of pots and pans made my head hurt.

"Mom," I said, stepping to the doorway. "Did you get those checks from the state yet?"

She fiddled with the gas. "Not yet, baby." We were going to get evicted in four days. I was running out of time. She looked at me, the wildness in her eyes still for once. A line sunk between her brows as she stared at me. "You okay, baby?" The softness in her voice tore open old wounds.

It had been years since I had heard her sound like she gave a shit. Her arms came around me, and though she smelled like death, I fell into her embrace, fighting back the tears.

After a few minutes, she pulled back, grabbing my face and swiping her thumbs below my eyes. "Whoever he is, he's not worth your tears."

For the briefest moment, I was eight years old again, and my mom was cleaning a cut knee, caring about me. But it was just a pretty lie. As soon as the drugs came, she would no longer care.

"I have to go." I fought back a sob on my way through the door. I had to do something.

My frayed nerves were on edge as I made my way down the deserted alley. The smell of urine from homeless people was staggering, and I held my breath. I had been driving around in the cold for over an hour, trying to find something I could steal, a car tucked away from the main roads and that would bring in at least a grand, and in Dayton, that was a tall order.

This Nissan at the end of the cramped throughway would have to do. I breathed a sigh of relief when I tried the handle and the car was unlocked. I checked the alleyway before I slipped behind the wheel and fiddled with the steering column. It took longer than usual to pop the thing loose, and every few minutes, I was checking the rearview to make sure I was still alone. The tangled mess of wires fell free, and I started stripping them. I twisted the ends, waiting for the engine to crank, but nothing happened.

"Shit." I tried again, nervous sweat forming on my brow. But again, nothing. And then a tap came from the window. I froze, swearing under my breath when I glanced up at Officer Jacob's smug face on the other side of the glass.

He opened the door. "Well, well, well. Looks like you're having a problem getting it started."

I groaned. Of all the cars I'd stolen, it was this one, the one *I* actually needed that I got caught for. And of all the cops in Dayton, it had to be him.

He motioned me out with a jerk of his chin, then circled his finger in the air. The moment I spun around, he cuffed my wrists, then led me to his patrol car.

"Watch your head, now," he said, placing a hand on me when I ducked into the cramped back seat. Jacobs stood by the door, one hand on the roof, the other on his belt loop. "Shame. You know? Smart girl getting messed up with the wrong guy. Fucking your whole future up for some worthless boy."

For once, though, this had nothing to do with Zepp. The door slammed, and he rounded the hood, whistling when he climbed into the front and pulled away. I was eighteen, and this—grand theft auto—would ruin any hope I had for a scholarship; for a future outside of Dayton. Tears stung my eyes as I watched the shit hole town I called home pass by the window. Turned out, Zepp was right; there was no getting out of Dayton.

The cuffs bit into my wrists when I tried to lean back against the seat, so I rested my forehead against the plexiglass divider and closed my eyes. I tried to drown out the muffled sound of the scanner calling in cases of overdoses and assaults until the police car finally rolled to a stop.

Jacobs' door opened, then closed, and I lifted my head, a fog of confusion clouding my brain when I looked through the window at the sagging front porch of Zepp's house. Jacobs twirled his keys around his finger, a little pep in his step as he jogged up the front steps.

Why the hell was he at Zepp's house?

Zepp's frame filled the doorway as the light from inside cut across the lawn. My heart let out a pathetic little hiccup, and I sucked in a painful breath when his gaze strayed to the street. He dragged a hand through his hair on a nod, then stepped outside. Jacobs smiled when he placed a pair of cuffs on Zepp's wrist. Taking him by the shoulders, he forced him toward the stairs. What was he doing? Why was Zepp being arrested?

Zepp's gaze dropped to the ground when Jacobs stopped him at the curb, then opened my door. "Seems there was a misunderstanding." He motioned me out before unfastening my restraints. "You're free to go, Miss James."

"What?" I glanced between the two of them. "Zepp, what are you doing?" Tears filled my eyes as realization crept over me. Jacobs had been after Zepp for so long, and now Zepp was taking the fall. "No, you caught me red-handed. Arrest me," I said to Jacobs.

"The suspect is in custody, Miss James. I suggest you move along now."

"Zepp?" My voice broke. He had priors, and he was eighteen. They'd lock him up for sure. "Don't do this." But Jacobs shoved him into the back of the cruiser.

"Told you I was gonna go to jail for something, Roe. Might as well be you." Then the door slammed closed, and Jacobs climbed behind the wheel, flashing the lights before he peeled off.

"What the fuck?" Hendrix shouted from the porch. Footfalls jogged down the steps and across the drive before he skidded to a stop beside me, staring down the street. "Did Jacobs arrest Zepp? What the hell for?"

For me. "Grand theft auto," I whispered.

"There's no way the guys at the chop shop would rat him out. No fucking way!" He clasped his hands behind his head, elbows out as he mumbled, "We haven't even lifted a car in weeks."

No, but I had, and I couldn't bring myself to tell Hendrix that his brother had just traded himself for me.

His narrowed gaze aimed at me. "Why are you here?"

I sucked in a breath. "I got arrested."

Hendrix's jaw set. "Fuck you, Monroe." Then he turned his back to me and headed toward his house.

"I didn't ask him to do this!" I shouted after him, my voice breaking.

He flipped me off before the door slammed.

Screw him, and screw Zepp for being so self-deprecating that he would take the fall for this. A sob caught in my throat at the thought of him in jail. Because of me. He didn't deserve it.

THE PAST MONTH had been shit. I'd heard nothing from Zepp since the night I watched Jacobs take him away. It was like he had died, and I was grieving his absence that was so absolute. I struggled to sleep. I struggled to adjust to my life without him in it. The hateful glares Hendrix shot at me every time he passed me in the hallway at school didn't help. I hadn't asked Zepp to do it, but it didn't make me feel any less guilty. It didn't hurt any less. And yesterday, when Wolf sent a text saying I was on Zepp's visitor list, I broke all over again.

I took a trembling breath as I looked up the razor wire fencing surrounding Hucksfield Penitentiary.

I stepped inside the cold, gray building. A sense of depression lingered heavily in the air. It should have been me locked away like an animal.

The guard took all of my possessions, and I signed a form before he escorted me into the bleak waiting room. By the time I got through, my nerves were so fraught, my hands trembled. A line of tables filled the room, each with a prisoner in an orange jumpsuit. Zepp sat at the table against the far wall, his gaze fixed out the barred window. A lump formed in my throat when I noticed the bruises on his face, and the fresh split in his bottom lip. Taking a breath, I crossed the room and pulled out the chair across from him.

I was standing on one side of a very messy, blurred line, and he was on the other. I didn't know what to say to him.

"Why?" It was the one question that had been burning through my mind since his arrest. Why did he push me away? Why did he take the fall? Why didn't he call me for the last month? Why, why, why...

He turned away from the window, his eyes unreadable. "Because I love you." He placed his cuffed hands on the table, clasping them together. "And you deserve better than Dayton, Roe."

"You didn't do it, though! This is bullshit, and you know it." My voice hitched.

"Doesn't matter if I did or not. I'm here." He nodded toward me. "You're there. And that's the way it belongs."

And I knew he believed that. "No, it's not. You're not..." This. He wasn't a guy who belonged behind bars. He wasn't a good guy, but he was to me.

"Jacobs wanted my ass in here. He offered me a deal. You for me." He tapped his hands on the table, the cuffs clinking. "You and me both know I was gonna end up right here at some point. I didn't have plans. You did. You wanted to get out of Dayton, and had you been booked, you wouldn't have."

I had stolen my fair share of cars. I had earned a spot in here just as much as him. But he wasn't supposed to care. He let me go days before the arrest. Never called. Never texted. I didn't understand. "It wasn't your problem."

His feet tapped the floor under the table, knuckles washing white as he stared at his hands. "You'll always be my problem, Roe."

I choked back a sob because I hated this thing that lingered between us. I wanted to run to him, but he constantly held me at arm's length. I placed my elbows on the table, raking both hands through my hair as I stared at the steel surface.

"Then why did you push me away?" I whispered.

Seconds ticked by before he sighed. "You know how you said your mom hadn't always been like she is now, Monroe? Neither had mine." He slumped back in his chair, eyes set on me. "Mine was in nursing school. She had plans. Then she met my piece of shit father and became another Dayton statistic. Knocked up. On drugs. Dreams down the toilet."

And that was shit, but it wasn't us. "You're not him. And I'm not her. You'd never let me not go to college, but Dixon isn't the only college. And you didn't have to break my heart to do it."

"So, you'd go to college. Then what? Marry me?" He shook his head. "I'm not gonna have shit to offer you."

"You don't have to offer me anything. And you don't get to tell me what I do or don't want."

"It wasn't about what you wanted, Roe. It's what I wanted for you."

I could feel the chasm between us, and I knew the clock was ticking. In just minutes, I'd have to walk out of here, and I didn't know when I'd see him again. Something in me broke. "All I wanted was your love, Zepp!"

"And that's something you'll always have." The resignation in his words killed me because it wasn't what I wanted to hear. It was "I love you, but I'm letting you go," and I didn't want to let him go. Ever.

"So, what now?" I said. "You expect me to go to Florida and just forget about you?"

"I expect you to get the fuck out of Dayton."

"Move on...meet someone else..."

His jaw ticced. His gaze dropped to the table.

The crack in my heart tore wide. I had to get out of here. I hated that he saw himself as so worthless because, to me, he was my entire world.

"I don't..." His brows pinched together, nostrils flaring. "I don't want you to come back."

"You—"

"I'm taking you off the visitor's list." He might as well have thrust his hand into my chest and pulled out my heart because this felt so final, and I knew it was.

I fought tears as I pushed to my feet, knowing there was nothing I could say.

He looked out the window, his jaw slowly ticcing. "I'll never love anybody the way I love you, Roe. That I promise."

"I love you." And then I walked away, my heart shattering into little pieces that I left on the floor of that visiting room. Zeppelin Hunt would always be the boy who had shown me what love was, even when he couldn't love himself.

41

MONROE
TEN MONTHS LATER

I tossed the pen onto my lilac bedspread, tired of studying for my world history exam next week. "Why the hell do I need to take history when I'm going into accounting?" I asked, glancing at Jade.

She laid, sprawled on her bed on the other side of our dorm room, the oversized Alabama State hoodie drowning her. The sound of heavy metal music from her headphones reached me even from here. She yanked one bud out and glanced at me. "Did you say something?"

I rolled my eyes. "Don't worry about it."

"You should stay this weekend and come to Brandon's party." She lifted a brow, and I dropped my gaze to the book in my lap. "Dayton sucks."

It did suck. Truthfully, I'd never go back there again if I didn't have to. It was full of memories, and it wasn't the bad ones I was hiding from. It was the good.

"And you know Brandon wants to see you." She smirked. "You should totally date him. He's hot."

Part of me wanted to stay and go to the party—even though I hated parties. Maybe even date Brandon. I knew I needed to move on with my life, but I couldn't. The thought had a sick feeling settling in my gut. I'd tried to forget about Zepp, but it wasn't easy. It was like there were parts of me that were missing, and he was holding them hostage. The constant ache had faded over time, but still, it would flare up and catch me off guard when I least expected it.

A brief knock sounded on the door before it flew open, and Jonathan burst in, dragging a Louis Vuitton suitcase behind him. "I am so ready for some redneck luvin'."

My gaze swept over him in his designer jeans and crisp, white, button-down shirt. The first day of my English class, I would have never pegged him as someone I would become friends with. He was from Upper Manhattan, and his family had more money than anyone at Barrington could have dreamed of. But, he grew on me. And I was pretty certain if I took him to Dayton, he might get himself killed. One catty remark to some redneck in Velma's would be all it would take.

"Jonathan," I said, giving him a once over. "Tell me again why you'd want to come to Dayton."

"Girl." He propped a hand on his hip before making some zig-zag snapping motion with his hands. "Having some real country boy to have a tumble in the hay bales with has always been my fantasy. I want me one of those down and dirty whorebags."

"Trust me, you don't," Jade mumbled.

He was about to get the shock of his life.

"Oh, trust me. I do." He waved a sassy finger in the air. "I waxed for this."

"I...don't even know what to say." I pushed to my feet and tugged my shirt over my head. "You know this is going to be a bitter disappointment."

He scowled, then took my bra strap and popped it. "No

more of a disappointment than that brazier of yours. What kind of statement is this, anyway? It's cotton for Christ's sake."

Jade snorted. "That she isn't getting any action."

Jonathan turned to Jade. "I got her one of those King Dong dildos for her birthday. She's getting plenty of action." He patted my back. "Isn't that right, Moe Bear?"

I ignored him and pulled on a shirt. Then I shoved some clothes in a bag and my toothbrush. "Right. I'm ready."

Jonathan touched a hand to his chest, pointing at my bag. "What's that?" With a shake of his head, he opened my closet and rummaged through my belongings, criticizing everything I owned."

I sank to the bed on a sigh. Once he started, there was no stopping him.

Jonathan repacked my bag three times before he let us leave. Forty minutes later, Jonathan turned his brand-new Mercedes into the trailer park. Most people would be ashamed of being seen in a shit car, but in Dayton, a shiny Mercedes just screamed Barrington, and that was never good. I wanted to crawl into the back seat.

Jonathan emerged from the car with a flare, swatting at the gnats buzzing around. He pulled his sunglasses down the bridge of his nose to look around. "This is way more redneck than you let on, honey. I feel like a man with a banjo is going to come out any minute."

"This is as redneck as it gets."

The second I breathed in the filthy Dayton air, I remembered why I avoided coming back here. I couldn't help but glance at Wolf's roof, like I expected to see Zepp up there, just hanging out on one of the ratty deck chairs. Of course, he wasn't. I told myself I had come back here to check up on my mom, but if I was honest with myself, I chose this weekend because I knew Zepp got out last week.

I knocked on the trailer door before tugging it open. Inside was clean, though the furniture was still ratty.

"That you, baby?" My mom poked her head out from the kitchen doorway. She looked good or as good as she could. She had a job at the local Waffle Hut and a spot at the methadone clinic. From what I could remember, it was the longest she had ever kept her shit together.

"Yeah."

Jonathan sashayed past the beat-up sofa to my mom. "Hey there, Miss James." He took her hand and kissed it. "It's so lovely to meet you. I love the way you've gone with the quaint, floral decor. It really brings out the Alabama in the place."

I snorted. "Mom, this is Jonathan."

Her eyes lit up. "This your boyfriend, baby?"

Jonathan wrinkled his nose. "Oh, no, honey. No, no, no."

"He's gay, mom," I laughed.

She looked disappointed. "Knew he was too pretty."

Jonathan preened under that comment. God, why did I bring him here?

THE ONLY PLACE I could take Jonathan that night was Velma's —it was the only bar aside from The White Rabbit that didn't ID, and I was not taking Jonathan to a strip club where I used to work. The twang of country music poured through the front doors of the shithole bar, the beat moving in time with blinking Christmas lights that stayed up year-round. Jonathan stopped at the bottom of the steps and touched a hand to his chest. "Oh, my God. It's a honky-tonk!"

The door hadn't had time to close behind us before he made a beeline for the bar, dragging me behind him. Velma stood behind the counter, a cigarette dangling from her lips and her bleach-blonde hair piled high on her head in a messy beehive. "What you want, sugar?"

He glanced at me with a smile, mouthing "sugar" on a laugh. "I'll have an appletini, and..." he motioned to me.

"Just a beer."

Velma's gaze shifted from me to Jonathan. "We don't serve no fancy drinks."

Jonathan's lip curled in offense. "Fine. Martini?"

She half rolled her eyes before waddled off. I knew, for a fact, she was just gonna dump vodka in a glass and call it a Martini.

She popped open a beer and slid a plastic cup of vodka in front of Jonathan, dropping an olive in it with a splash.

"This is how you grew up?" He stared down into the drink. "This is messed up, Monroe. It's like I'm in *Deliverance.* I mean, not that I'd mind if some hot guy in a wifebeater told me to squeal like a pig, but..." He took a sip, and his face immediately puckered up. "Velma! Honey." He placed the cup on the bar. "It's been a while since my gag reflex has been tested and that..." He pointed at the offending cup. "Just tested it."

Velma chucked another olive into his cup, then ashed her cigarette on the floor before shuffling off.

I nearly choked on my beer at the look of horror on his face.

"Right," he said. "Get me some good country music. If I'm drinking neat vodka, we're dancing."

I scooped up my beer and went to the jukebox, picking "Tennessee Whisky."

An hour later, Jonathan had ordered three more of

Velma's "martinis." He passed the cup to me. "It's so nasty," he choked. "Drink some."

And yet he kept ordering them—and making me drink them with him. Now we were both drunk. I hung off his arm as I tipped the drink back, wincing at the burn.

He grabbed the empty cup and threw his arm in the air. "Another!" Then he plucked the olive from the bottom of the cup and shoved it in his mouth.

"Hey!" I swatted at his arm. "I want the olive. You had the last one."

He grabbed my face, pressed his lips to mine, and rammed the olive between my lips. "There." Then he waltzed off to the bar for more drinks.

My gaze swept over the people crammed in the tiny room, pausing on Wolf's familiar form. My stomach clenched, tightening further when I saw Hendrix, then Bellamy—both ignoring me—and I knew he was there. I could feel his gaze on me long before I met the dark eyes that had run rampant in my dreams for nearly a year, torturing me. My heart squeezed, long dormant, and trying to wake while my lungs seized in my chest like they'd forgotten how to draw air. He lifted a drink to his lips, his gaze never straying from me. Until Jonathan came back and wrapped an arm around my waist, blocking my view.

"I see you, girl, eyeing up that tall drink of manly water." Jonathan looked over his shoulder at Zepp. "Tattoos, muscle. Mmm. Bet he's been to prison a few times. You know, prison always turns them."

"He's not gay."

Jonathan slicked a hand through his hair. "Because I—"

"That's Zepp," I said, the buzz from the alcohol dissipating almost immediately.

Jonathan's eyes went wide. "Oh. My. God."

The walls felt like they were suddenly pressing in on me. Zepp was here, in the same room, and I couldn't breathe properly. "I uh, I need to go."

Jonathan chugged his drink before grabbing my hand and leading me through the maze of people, stopping in front of two girls blocking the doorway. "Excuse me. We've got an emergency situation here, and you need to move your unfortunate-looking asses out the way."

He shoved through them, speed walking me to the middle of the parking lot before he stopped and pulled out his phone. "Oh, look. They do have Uber in the middle of Bumblefuck Nowhere." The colored lights flashed off his face when he glanced up at me. "You okay?"

"Yeah." No. I knew I would see him at some point. I just didn't expect to feel like that. I'd pushed Zepp from my mind, fought my feelings for him every day, but it was so pointless. Because they were all right there, almost as fresh as the day he had broken my heart. That wound hadn't healed at all. It was still festering away.

THE NEXT MORNING, I woke with the hangover from hell. Jonathan laid passed out, his leopard-print eye mask in place.

"Jonathan," I mumbled, nudging him.

He groaned and nudged me back, then whispered, "Don't speak."

"We need to get your car." Although, the chances someone stole his A-Class were pretty high. It would have stuck out in Velma's gravel lot like a beacon.

"I can't, muffin. I think I've had a stroke."

"Oh my God." I smacked him with a pillow. "You have not."

"I think Velma gave me some janky Moonshine."

"Well, we still need your car."

"Please go get it. Be my hero." He took a hard breath. "The wind beneath my wings."

I hit him again with the pillow, then crawled over his corpse, my head pounding. I brushed my teeth, yanked on my Alabama State sweatshirt and a pair of sunglasses, and braved the bus I had to take to Velma's.

On the way back, I drove Jonathan's car well below the speed limit, terrified I would somehow damage it. I was so focused on making sure the gravel on the dirt road didn't fling up and ping the hood, that I didn't notice Zepp's bike in my mom's drive until I had parked. I groaned, my stomach rolling even more than it already was. Zepp leaned against the wooden railing. All muscle and tattoos, looking better than he had any right to. My heart let out pitiful, pained beats.

I stepped out of the Mercedes and leaned against the sleek side, a good few feet away from Zepp. I needed that distance right now; I really did. My gaze hit the gravel, and awkwardness wound tight around me.

"Nice car," he said.

"It's not mine."

"Figured."

I let out a sigh. "You got out then." I knew he had.

Jade had told me, but he certainly hadn't. Not so much as a text. But then, why would he? He made it very clear in that visiting room. What I wanted didn't matter.

His gaze veered back to Jonathan's car. "You moved on then."

I glanced at the car. The trailer door flew open. Jonathan stood in the doorway, nursing a mug of coffee, my mom's pink robe on, and his eye mask on his forehead. "Moe Bear, what you doing hanging around in the street like a two-dollar hooker in all her—Oh my...!" His words trailed off when Zepp shifted on his feet. Jonathan clutched the mug to his chest, gaze glued to Zepp. "Tell me you have a brother. Please, for the love of Ru Paul. Tell me there is some more of that genetic pool to go around."

"Zepp. Jonathan." I waved a hand between the two of them, then eyed Jonathan.

"Oh, yeah. I'll just..." He backed inside the trailer pulling the door shut slowly. "Thanks for getting my car, Moe Bear. You're the wind beneath my wings," he sang through the closing gap before it shut.

One of Zepp's brows was raised, the other angled down. "What. The fuck." His eyes were still on the trailer; Jonathan could have that effect on people.

"He's not from around here," I tried to offer as some kind of explanation. Truthfully, I couldn't think of a place on the planet where Jonathan would be considered normal.

A silence fell between us, and his gaze dropped to my State hoodie. "Why didn't you go to Dixon?"

"I don't know." I'd asked myself that before. I had the offer, full-ride scholarship, just like I had always wanted. But something kept me here. "I guess Alabama grew on me."

"I'm glad you're doing good, Roe." He gave me a nod, turned his back to me, and headed for his bike. Just like that.

There was no reason for him even to show up if all he was going to do was leave. He had no idea how hard it had been for me to find some kind of normal in my life, and just when I was starting to be okay, he shows up. I hated him.

Anger heated my skin. I wanted to shout at him. Tell him how much he had screwed me up. I took a small step toward him.

"Good? Sure." I paused, fighting the tightness in my throat. "You know, why are you even here, Zepp? Why do you care? Do you just need to feel validated that you played the hero?" My fists clenched so hard that my nails cut into my palms. Over the past year, I had pined for him and hated him, but I could never stop loving him, and that was the worst part of all this.

"The fucking hero? Really?" A sarcastic laugh fell from his lips before he faced me, jaw tight. He grabbed his helmet and threw a leg over his bike. "I'm not a knight in shining armor. I'm an asshole. Don't know if you remember that or not."

He was right, but I'd never cared. "But you were mine!" My voice broke. "And *you* left me when you said you never would."

His chin dropped to his chest, one hand rubbing over the back of his neck. I couldn't do this. Not again. I hurried past his bike to the trailer, then slammed the door.

The engine to his motorcycle rumbled to life a few seconds later, the noise vibrating through the aluminum windows before it faded.

Jonathan stood in the kitchen with my mother, a frown on his face. "Moe Bear..."

"I uh, I need to get back to school. I forgot I have a paper to turn in."

He nodded. "I'll go pack my things."

42

ZEPP

She thought I had left her when all I was trying to do was save her. Going to Monroe's house had been the worst thing I could have done. I hadn't even tried to fool myself into thinking that I was over her, but I never expected it to hurt that much. I underestimated how shitty it would feel to be that close to her and not be able to hold her.

I sat in the living room crowded with people, but I couldn't focus on anything but Monroe. Hendrix popped me on the back of the head before he yanked his shirt off, screaming, "It's my birthday!"

One of the strippers Wolf had hired for the party pranced over, shoving her tits in his face while he motorboated them. And there came another thought of Monroe, of how men used to do that shit with her. Ten months later and my blood still boiled from that thought.

Wolf leaned in beside me, laughing. "Dude. Those chicks are all over each other."

I didn't even bother to look. I finished off my beer, then went to push up from the couch, but one of the topless girls latched onto my shoulders, pushing me right back down. "Wanna dance?"

"No." I went to stand up again, but she shoved me into the seat and straddled my lap.

"You look so angry." She leaned in by my ear. "I'm sure I could loosen you up."

I pressed back against the sofa, closing my eyes when her bare tits rubbed against my shirt. The last time I had fucked was the last time I had fucked Monroe, and that had almost been a year. I should have enjoyed this, but I hated every second of it. All it did was remind me that I didn't have her—of how much I wanted her.

The girl pressed her lips to my neck, and I pushed her off, then got up.

"Dude," Wolf cackled, grabbing the girl by the waist and yanking her into his lap. "She would have fucked you." He glanced at her. "Right? You would have fucked him?"

She wrapped her arms around Wolf's neck, eyeing me up and down. "Totally."

Scrubbing a hand over my face, I walked off to the kitchen and grabbed a drink. Ten months in that shitshow of a jail had given me ample time to think about shit. Time had never passed more slowly than it had in there. Sleep. Eat. Go to the yard. Study. That was it. None of Hendrix's stupid metaphors or Wolf's rooftop. No Monroe.

Out of all the things I had missed the most. It had been that girl. I thought I had done what was best—loved her enough to let her go, given her a chance to get out of Dayton, but the look on her face last week when I went to her mom's trailer... I couldn't help but wonder if I had hurt her more than I had saved her. I had never wanted to leave her; I had only wanted her to leave me.

Because she deserved so much better than me.

Thoughts went around and around in my head, guilt eating me up at the idea that I had hurt her. I couldn't take it anymore. I typed out a text, sending it to the number I had in my phone, not even sure if it still worked.

Me: I never meant to hurt you
Monroe: I hate you

I paced the kitchen because that was not the answer I wanted. At one time, she had loved me, and if she hated me, that meant I had hurt her. A person can only hate something they wanted to love.

Me: We need to talk

But the message didn't go through. Not delivered. I tried again and again. And when I attempted to call her, it didn't connect. Shit, had she blocked me?

I tossed my drink into the trash and snatched my keys from the counter before heading through the living room. "Hey, Wolf."

He had the stripper's nipple in his mouth, one hand palming her other tit.

I kicked at his shin, and he glanced up with a scowl. "Where does Monroe live?" I asked.

"Dude, I don't know."

"You said she lives with Jade. I know you know." He and Jade had this weird on-again, off-again fuck buddy thing going on.

He tossed his head back on the couch, patting the girl's ass to get her out of his lap. "That was the best dry humping I've had since I was twelve, and you just ruined it." He dug in his pocket for his phone.

"Aw, hell to the fuck no!" Hendrix shouted from across the room. He pushed the now-naked girl out of his lap, adjusting his dick before storming toward me and snatching Wolf's phone from my hand. "She can fuck off. She left your ass. After you went to jail for her."

My brother didn't get it. But I didn't expect him to. "Give me the phone, Hendrix."

"No." He fiddled with his crotch again. "She's a bitch, Zepp."

Before I realized what I was doing, I had nailed my brother in the face. He clutched at his nose, blood trickling down his chin.

His brows pulled together. "You fucking punched me!"

"You called her a bitch."

His eyes narrowed. "She is."

I nailed him in the gut, then Wolf pulled me off. "Hey. Dude. Hey. Calm down." Wolf held out his hand, and Hendrix slammed the phone down in his palm. "They live in Sassnett dorm. Room 311."

Hendrix grabbed the remote from the coffee table and chucked it at Wolf. "Oh, fuck you, you hairy sack of balls. You suck!"

Half an hour later, I parked in front of a tall, red-brick building. I had no idea what the hell I was doing, but to be honest, when had I ever known what I was doing when it came to Monroe?

I went to push open the glass door, but it wouldn't budge. Through the window, I could see a girl behind a desk. I banged over the door, and a buzzer sounded, my muscles tensing because it reminded me too much of jail.

"Can I help you?" She grinned, shimmying up in her

chair before her gaze skirted over me, head to toe. "Like the tattoos."

"I need to see Monroe James. Room 311." I swiped a hand through my hair, the nervous energy getting to me. "I think."

"No can do. It's past midnight." She tapped a pen over a laminated piece of paper that read: *No male visitors from 12:00 a.m. - 9:00 a.m.*

I laughed. "You've gotta be kidding me."

"Wish I was." She grabbed the book she had shoved to the side, opening it back up. *The Notebook*. Fine, she wanted to try and stick to her rules...

"Look." I folded my arms over her desk and leaned toward her. "I just drove like eighty miles. And I really need to see her. I haven't seen this girl in almost a year. I went to jail for her—"

Her eyes went wide. "You went to jail for her?"

"Yeah. I just got out, and I saw her in our hometown last week with another guy." I let a frown settle over my face. The girl didn't need to know the guy wasn't a threat. "And I can't lose her. I just really need to tell her I'm still in love with her."

"Oh my God." Her hand went to her chest, eyes softening. "That is so romantic."

"Can you just..." I poked a finger at the sign. "Can you just let this go. For once. For love."

She glanced up, then down the corridor. "I'm gonna take a bathroom break. The stairs are down the hall to the right." She winked when she stood, then whispered, "Go get her," before she walked off.

I booked it around the corner, shoving open the door to the stairwell and taking the three flights. The hallway light flickered on when I stepped into the corridor, passing several rooms before I came to the one with Monroe and

Jade's name in bubble letters on the front. No way in hell she did that. I bet it was Jonathan.

Sweat slicked my palms, nervous energy wound through my body. I loved her, but I had hurt her. And what if this was the last thing she wanted. I had to know, though. I raised my hand, pausing before I knocked.

The hinges creaked, and Jade's face appeared in the crack doorway. She squinted. "Holy. Shit." The door shut, and I raised my hand to knock again but heard her say: "Monroe. Fucking Zepp's here."

There was a mumbled exchange before Jade stepped out in an oversized robe. "I'm not staying in there for this shit." Then she shuffled down the hall in her slippers. "And I don't even wanna know how you got past the front desk."

The dimly lit room reminded me of an oversized jail cell. Painted cinder block walls. Two small beds. A mini-fridge. A lamp clicked on, and Monroe sat up on the edge of the bed, all bare legs. And wearing the T-shirt I had given her the first night she stayed with me.

"What are you doing here, Zepp?"

"You told me you hated me. Then you blocked my number."

"Yeah." She folded her arms over her chest. "Because I don't want to talk to you."

That hurt to hear, but the part of me that couldn't get her telling me she loved me out of my head, refused to believe it. "I didn't mean to hurt you," I said.

Her chin dropped to her chest. She traced small circles on her knee. "I would have done anything for you. And you just..." She shook her head. "You know what, it doesn't matter."

"Everything I did was because I loved you."

"Then, I don't want your love because it hurts." When

she looked up at me, tears welled in her eyes. "It still hurts! I can't move past you. And now you're back."

I felt like an asshole. I had never been in love with someone before her, so I had no idea that love wasn't something a person got over. It was like a piece of shrapnel buried underneath the skin. Something not visible, but something painful that would always be felt.

"And I can't move past you, so what the hell are we supposed to do, Roe? Huh?" I took a few steps across the room, wanting so bad to kiss her. Feeling every bit of me rip wide open for her. "I meant it when I told you I would never love anyone the way I loved you. Because I won't love anyone but you." My throat tightened. My chest caught. I crossed the small space, dropping to my knees and taking her face in my hands before pressing my mouth to hers.

She tensed in my hold for a second, her hands going to my shoulders before her lips parted. Having her lips against mine like this again, it took everything in me not to break down. I pressed my forehead to hers, fighting the raw emotion clawing up my throat. "Please, don't hate me. I can't take that."

"I can't stop loving you." Her voice broke on a soft sob while her fingers wrapped around my wrists. "I tried. So hard."

I kissed her again. Harder. Longer. "If you'll give me another chance, I swear to God, I won't leave you."

"Can we start with three months?"

I fought a smile, then kissed her again. Fuck three months; I was getting that girl for the rest of my life.

EPILOGUE

MONROE

Zepp's navy work coveralls crumpled around his waist, exposing his white wife-beater covered in oil. I raked my eyes over him. Biting at my lip, I reached inside his coveralls. He was the hottest mechanic I'd ever seen, that was for sure.

He pressed a kiss to my forehead. "After dinner. I made reservations."

"You made...reservations?" I lifted a brow.

"Yeah." He finished stripping down. "Gotta be there in an hour."

"I think we should stay in," I said, trailing my fingers over his chest. "Order pizza later..."

He grabbed a towel from his dresser. "I don't want pizza."

"You always want pizza, Zepp!" I folded my arms over my chest.

"If you want pizza, you can get it at Olive Garden." He shot a smile like he was proud of that before he went into the hallway.

"Olive Garden?" What the hell? Olive Garden was

Jonathan's favorite restaurant back at school. And he'd put me off it for life. It was so very not Zepp. "To eat expensive pizza?"

The water in the shower cut on. I waited a second before following him into the bathroom. I had to wonder why the hell he wanted to go so badly. I stripped out of my clothes and pulled the curtain back before getting into the tub. He ran his hand through his soaked hair, a slight smirk working over his lip when he fisted his dick. My skin flushed instantly.

I trailed my fingers down his hard stomach. "If I suck your dick, can we stay here?"

"No." He gave himself another tug while his gaze swept over my body.

"No?"

Zepp had never turned me down in my life. And he wasn't about to start now. I stepped into the warm water, pressing my body to his before I slapped his hand away, replacing it with my own.

"I mean, you can suck it, but we're still going to dinner." He gave a little thrust in my slick hand. "Your call, Roe."

"You know I don't need fancy restaurants. I just want you." I bit his bottom lip, and his fingers dug into my hip.

"Why do you have to be so damn stubborn?"

"How am I being stubborn?" I squeezed his dick, and a breath hissed through his teeth. "I want to fuck and eat pizza, like normal."

"And I just want to go to Olive Garden. Damn." He sure was getting agitated over some Italian food.

I dropped to my knees on the shower floor and licked him. He slammed a palm over the tile.

"Suck it all you want, Roe." He groaned. "We're still going."

We weren't going. I swallowed him back until his muscles were rigid tense. "What about Nero's?" I asked.

I licked him again, his fingers knotting in my hair. "Or Frank's Famous Chicken? You love it."

He groaned when I took him all the way back. "Why the hell can't you just go to Olive Garden?"

"Why do you want to go to that fancy shit?" God, he was pissing me off.

"Jesus Christ, woman. Why does it matter? Are you against spaghetti?" He thrust into my mouth, and I took it until I knew he was about to come, and then I stopped.

"Final answer?" I asked, his dick still in my hand, my lips so close to the head.

"Don't you fucking dare..."

I pushed to my feet with a smug grin when I grabbed a towel because I knew I was going to win. This wasn't about a damn restaurant anymore. It was the principle.

The moment I stepped into his room, I dropped the towel and hopped onto his bed, sprawling out, naked.

It was all of thirty seconds before Zepp came in. His gaze landed on me, and he looked like he was ready to blow.

"You really wanna do this?" he said. His towel hit the floor, and he crawled onto the bed, pinning me to the mattress. "You know who will win this, Roe." He nipped at my neck, then slammed into me so hard my breath caught.

I loved him angry. I pulled at his hair before I brought my lips to his ear. "This feels a lot like winning," I said on a ragged breath.

"Does it?" He went deeper. Harder. Bringing me right to the edge, right to the moment where my entire body started to heat with that warm buzz, and then he pulled out and flipped onto his back. "Good to know."

"No. No!" I slapped his chest before straddling his body.

When I tried to move, he gripped my hips and pinned me in place.

"Still feel like you're winning, Roe?"

I grabbed his throat, digging my nails into his skin. "Fuck you, Zepp." I tried to move again, but his hands were like shackles, imprisoning me. I leaned forward until my lips brushed his. "You know I can get myself off." And then I said the one thing that I knew pissed him off every time. "I don't need you."

That did it. He guided me over him, far rougher than I would have ever been able to manage on my own while he thrust up from below, burying himself as far as he could go.

My back hit the mattress, and he drove into me while his warm, hard body slipped over mine. "I don't for one second believe you come as hard on your own," he said.

I didn't. I couldn't. It was more than just a rough touch, though, it was him. It was us.

I fell apart beneath him, my nails clawing at his skin, my lungs straining for breath while his powerful body turned to stone beneath my hands. Then he collapsed onto the bed.

After he caught his breath, he rolled over and checked the clock, groaning before he fell back on his pillow. "Don't bitch at me about how I'm about to do this. It's your fault." He pushed up from the bed and took something from his drawer. "You know our three months is up today?"

"It is?"

Still naked, he dropped down to one knee and held out an opened box. In the middle of the blue velvet sat an emerald ring with diamonds on each side. My pulse raced. My heart spluttered in my chest.

"All I wanted to do was take you to Olive Garden." On a sigh, he shook his head. "I never thought three months would turn into the rest of my life, but..."

"Oh my God, Zepp." I stared at the box, completely shocked.

"You gonna marry me, Roe?"

"Yes, Zepp. I'll marry you." I kissed him, knowing there would never be anyone else for me but him. No one could come close. Our happily ever after wasn't shiny or pretty, but it was ours.

He was no prince, but Zepp Hunt was mine. Always.

THE END

If you're in the mood for a another angsty high school romance, Click here to read The Sun by Stevie J Cole free in Kindle Unlimited.

If you're looking for a sexy read with an another sassy female, check out Tiger Shark by LP Lovell, Free in Kindle Unlimited

If you're ready for a gritty love story between two head strong characters, try Wrong by Stevie J Cole and LP Lovell.

Do you want a little MFM action, one with a twist? Check out The Game by LP Lovell and Stevie J Cole.

Printed in Great Britain
by Amazon